COLD JUSTICE

Lee Weeks was born in Devon. She left school at seventeen and, armed with a notebook and very little cash, spent seven years working her way around Europe and South East Asia. She returned to settle in London, marry and raise two children. She has worked as an English teacher and personal fitness trainer. Her books have been *Sunday Times* bestsellers. She now lives in Devon.

ALSO BY LEE WEEKS

Dead of Winter
Cold as Ice
Frozen Grave

COLD JUSTICE

LEE WEEKS

SIMON &
SCHUSTER

London · New York · Sydney · Toronto · New Delhi

A CBS COMPANY

First published in Great Britain by Simon & Schuster UK Ltd, 2015
A CBS company

1 3 5 7 9 10 8 6 4 2

Simon & Schuster UK Ltd
1st Floor
222 Gray's Inn Road
London WC1X 8HB

www.simonandschuster.co.uk

Simon & Schuster Australia, Sydney
Simon & Schuster India, New Delhi

A CIP catalogue record for this book is available from the British Library

Paperback ISBN: 978-1-47113-363-3
eBook ISBN: 978-1-47113-362-6

Typeset in the UK by Hewer Text UK Ltd, Edinburgh
Printed and bound in Great Britain by CPI Group (UK) Ltd, Croydon, CR0 4YY

For Darley Anderson. He knows what my dreams
are, and he believes in them too.

Prologue

As the bath was running, Jeremy Forbes-Wright laid out his toiletries on the bathroom shelf. The room was in the art deco style that he loved, the tiles on the floor were black and white and the wall lights above the shelves were mounted with elaborate chrome fittings: sleek, shiny and with a touch of the ostentatious.

He had chosen to come back to this hotel because it was one of his favourites. It had an old-fashioned class and service about it that made him feel at home and there was a comforting solidness about its dark curtains, dark wood, its quiet corridors and the fact that it didn't object to him bringing his dog – there was no way he was leaving him home tonight.

He caught a glimpse of himself but didn't linger on his reflection. Instead, he went across to the bath and poured in some orange-blossom bath oil and breathed it in deeply – a little smell of heaven as it turned the water an apricot colour. He turned off the water and left it to steam gently while he went back into the bedroom. The television was on. The 24-hour news channel had moved on to world affairs, wars and massacres, and typhoons; but along the bottom of the screen ran the words:

Former senior politician drops out of race for top Tory seat.

He went back into the bathroom and sat on the side of the bath, dangling his hand in the water, checking that it wasn't too hot. As he did so, he looked back into the lounge. He had placed the dog basket where he could see it from the bathroom, and now Russell, the Jack Russell terrier, rested his head on the side of his basket and looked at his master with worried eyes as he gave a tentative whine.

'Hush now, Russell, you'll be all right.' Jeremy looked at his reflection in the misting mirror and could see only half of his face. 'I'm dammed if I'm going to just fade away, Russell, that's for sure.'

The dog seemed to contemplate a reply as it opened its mouth but then closed it again with a sigh.

'Exactly, Russell, no one to blame but myself. That's the trouble – all I ever had was myself and I turned out to be so bloody unreliable.' He laughed and his laughter echoed in the bathroom.

He smiled at the dog as he stood and pushed the bathroom door to. Then he hung the thick white cotton dressing gown neatly on the back of the door. He stepped into the bath and lay back with a sigh into the warm scented water; closing his eyes he breathed deeply, felt the sting of a tear as the scented steam filled the bathroom, misting the black and white tiles on the wall, steaming up the cold mirror completely.

He reached for the razor blade and positioned it on the inside of his wrist where he could see his pulse beneath the skin. He pushed and dragged into the vein and pressed his hand beneath the water as a ribbon of blood snaked from the wound and turned the bathwater the colour of blood oranges.

Chapter 1

'Are you okay, baby?'

Lauren Forbes-Wright came up behind her husband Toby and slipped her hands around his waist to hug him; she looked over his shoulder out of the French windows down towards the Thames. He'd taken off his jacket but was still wearing the crisp white shirt they'd had to buy him especially for the funeral.

'Yes.'

She felt his body resist her touch as she tightened her arms around him, her chin resting on his shoulder. He stayed where he was, hands in his trouser pockets, gazing out of the window. Visibility was down to twenty feet. It was all a mass of grey with the rain sleeting against the window. She knew he wasn't really looking at the view. She knew he was thinking of a million things, none of which brought him peace. They had been married three years but she felt she knew less about him than ever. Now, when he had something monumental like the death of his father to cope with, was the time she realized how distant they truly were.

'Sure?' she asked.

'Of course – why shouldn't I be?' He sighed again, shook his head. 'Sorry, Lauren, that came out wrong.' He placed a hand on her arms wrapped around him and gave them a dismissive squeeze. She didn't let go.

Lauren closed her eyes. 'You don't have to say sorry,' she whispered into his ear. 'It's a big thing.'

She felt Toby shift his weight. She felt his body prepare to move, long to move, but she fought to hold on to it a moment longer. She wouldn't let him run from her and find his cave.

But Toby managed to unhook himself from her arms and Lauren accepted defeat as she watched him walk away from her and into the kitchen, passing their son Samuel on the way.

She watched her husband's back disappear out of sight and picked up Samuel, who had started grizzling; then she followed Toby.

'Shhhh.' She kissed her son's blond curls as she stood rocking him on her hip.

From inside a metal cage in the corner of the kitchen, Russell observed the world with the fixed, worried expression he'd had ever since they'd brought him home from the hotel.

'Shall we go down to your dad's apartment tomorrow – we need to go through his things?' she asked.

Toby picked up his wine and walked past her as he

went back into the lounge and sat, elbows on knees, on the sofa. 'Maybe.'

She followed him. 'It has to be done.' He didn't answer. Lauren put Samuel back down on the floor with his toys and walked towards the window as the sun came out. The glare bounced around the room, ricocheted off the glass table, the mirror, the stark white walls. The day outside transformed itself in seconds. She sighed as she stood looking out across the Thames. In the distance, the sun hit the sides of the Shard.

'Shall we go to Cornwall instead?' She softened her American tones. 'Now that the sun has come out? What do you think, baby?' She had loved calling him 'baby' when they first fell in love. He was ten years younger than her. He had been fresh-faced and innocent and so nerdy and earnest. So absolutely shy that it amazed Lauren that he had ever lost his virginity. He worked in the Royal Observatory and was a genius when it came to understanding the universe. But he didn't understand other people. He definitely didn't understand women or what made a relationship work. He was twenty-nine, she was forty-one. She was fast realizing that Toby *really* was a baby.

'Thought you had work to finish?' He was irritated, anxious to the point that she thought he looked ready to cry or scream or down the bottle of wine he'd already had two large glasses from since they'd got back from the funeral.

'Yes, I have. But I'll take it with me.' Lauren worked for an American drugs company. She was writing up her research project on dementia drugs. 'We could all do with a change of scenery – even the dog,' she said. 'It's funny how he left instructions about the dog, about the funeral, about what he wanted doing with his bloody ashes, but not about his estate.'

She looked at Toby's face – so pale in the low winter sun that was making him squint. He looked like a lost boy. She hated to see him in such misery.

'You'll never get it done there,' he said, more to himself than Lauren.

Lauren watched Samuel playing with his toys on the floor. He was a quiet boy, sensitive, anxious and very bright; a lot like his father. He was so bright but he rarely smiled.

'We should let the dog out; it can't do any harm,' said Lauren.

'We're not allowed dogs in the flat. Anyway, we don't know if it will turn on Samuel,' he replied.

'It's a tiny dog – not exactly a Rottweiler.' Lauren smiled. 'I feel sorry for it.'

'It's a terrier – they can be really snappy when they're old,' Toby retorted.

'But it's only four. We have all its papers from the hotel. Anyway, it's been with us a month and it still barely comes out of its cage. There we go – the dog needs a holiday. It's more stressed than the rest of us ... Settled! Samuel? Shall we go on vacation?' Samuel looked up at his mother and nodded. She got a tissue from a box on the coffee table and wiped his runny nose. 'Shall we build sandcastles? See some little fishes in the sea? Throw a ball for Russell? Have some fun?'

He nodded as he watched her facial expressions and

tried to mimic them. She kissed him and reached behind her head to unpin her hair. She rubbed her scalp as her hair unwound itself into a bob, short fringe. She didn't wear make-up as a rule. She had one colour lipstick and it was the one she'd worn on their wedding day. It was pink. She was wearing it today. Toby didn't look at her; he had a frown on his face. Lauren watched his face contort as he grew more anxious. He was chewing the inside of his cheek.

'Toby, shall we just go to Cornwall now? I mean, why wait till tomorrow? What do you think? We only need to pack a few things. We'll wash stuff down there.'

'Can we think about it tomorrow, please?' There was an exasperated, persecuted edge to his voice.

'Yes . . . of course.' Lauren accepted the setback, walked across to her desk and opened her laptop, but changed her mind as Toby walked back into the kitchen. She followed him and stood watching as he poured another glass of wine. 'It's a bit early, isn't it?'

'Is it?' Toby finished pouring himself the large glass of red and took a swig.

She smiled but her eyes remained watchful. 'Did you know many people at the service?' Toby answered with a shake of the head. 'I recognized one of the names at the end when people came past and paid their respects. I saw that man, Stokes, who's been bothering us about your father's house. You'd think he'd leave us alone at a time like this.'

She went to find the letter from her desk in the corner of the lounge. 'Yeah, here it is – Martin Stokes. He wants to know whether we've changed our mind about letting it out. He has to return a lot of deposits, he says. He implies that we'll have to meet the cost if we do that. I don't see why, unless your dad kept the deposits. I suppose that's possible.' She sighed. 'Christ . . .' She looked to Toby for a reaction but he didn't speak. 'He also says that a private purchaser from the village would like to make us an offer for the house of five hundred thousand – contents not included.' Lauren shook her head incredulously. 'They must be joking; we know it's worth a million? What do they want with it?'

'I have no idea.'

'Let's tell Stokes we want it left empty,' she said. 'We need to go and have a proper look at it. The quicker we sort out your dad's estate the better. I have no worries about getting rid of the house in Cornwall but we may not be able to afford to keep it, if we have to pay death duties.'

Toby looked her way briefly then turned away as he said, 'We will have to; it doesn't look like he had any money at all.' He gazed out of the kitchen window down the three storeys towards the street and the parking spaces below them. A woman was struggling past with a buggy. The wind whipped through the new tower blocks and the ones under construction. There were tastefully designed walkways and children's playgrounds, even a new Waitrose store at the entrance to the complex. It was all very new.

'What do you mean?'

'It doesn't look good; I mean, it doesn't look like he had any money. I went to his flat . . . he doesn't have much antique-wise. I saw nothing we can hope to sell.'

Lauren knew her husband didn't want to make eye contact with her. He busied himself setting his iPad up.

'We said we'd go together.'

'I didn't want to bother you.' He glanced up as she heard the familiar jingle of the iPad starting. 'You were at work.'

'I think I should be involved. Two heads better than one and all that?' Her mouth formed a half-smile. Her eyes stayed cold.

He shrugged dismissively. 'The solicitor has all the papers now, he's handling it, not me, so we needn't be concerned. Whatever has to be done, he will do it.'

'What did you find there? What's his place like?'

Toby stopped tapping on the keyboard and looked at her, irritated. 'It's a plush flat with a hot tub and a sauna. It's the same sort of place as this, a riverside apartment with a view, but a hell of a lot more rent than this and a lot more view.'

'What about all of his things?'

'I don't want anything.'

'What? You are kidding me? Those are things that Samuel can inherit. Even if they aren't worth anything – they have sentimental value.'

'I wasn't thinking about Samuel at the time. I certainly wasn't feeling sentimental.'

'I understand. Of course; but we are a family and one day Samuel might want to know about his granddad.' She took a step towards Toby, almost reached out a hand to touch him, but stopped when she saw the look of hostility in his eyes.

'Can you just leave it, for fuck's sake. I told you I *would* handle it all. My problem, my fucking father. I'll deal with it, all right? This is not about you or Samuel.'

Lauren looked stunned. She nodded meekly and retreated to the lounge.

Toby's phone rang; he looked at the screen and went into the bedroom to answer it. Lauren heard him moving about the bedroom and talking on the phone. After ten minutes he came back into the lounge with his coat on. Lauren was back at her desk, Samuel was playing with some Duplo pieces.

'Where are you going? Who was that on the phone?'

'It was work. They wanted to tell me my new exhibits are up and running. I thought I'd go and have a look. I'll take Samuel out and give you some peace. We'll have a wander and come back in time for his tea. Samuel will like it up there in the Observatory.'

'Really? Okay, if you feel like it, that would be great. You better take him a biscuit. He usually needs feeding after a nap. He'll probably fall asleep for an hour in the buggy.'

'Don't worry, I'll get him something. There's plenty in the café to eat and plenty of people to make a fuss of him.'

'Okay, but he's getting a cold, I think. His face looks flushed,' said Lauren.

'The fresh air will do him good. He could do with hardening up.'

'Fresh? In the middle of London?' As soon as she

said it, she wished she hadn't. Toby turned away. Lauren swivelled back round. 'I've just emailed the man, Stokes, about the house in Cornwall, confirming that we need it left empty for now. Let's go down tomorrow, like I said. I need to finish this piece today then maybe we can have a stress-free evening. Are you sure you're happy to go out? I must admit it would help me concentrate enough to get this work done.'

'Yes, of course. It's only two thirty. We won't be long.'

'All right, baby, if you're sure. Take the dog.'

'I can't. He'll be a nuisance and he won't be allowed into work. I'll take him out when I get back.'

Lauren knelt before Samuel and pulled up the zipper on his all-in-one suit. Samuel stared down at his front as he pressed one of the appliquéd snow-flakes on the front of the suit.

'Grandma give it to me.'

'Yes. You lucky boy.' She kissed him.

'And Grandma give me this . . .' He frowned and tugged at his snowflake mittens threaded on a string through the arms of his suit. 'From A-merr-icka.'

'Yes. That's right.' She pulled on his hat and then his mittens. 'Be a good boy for Daddy.'

He nodded enthusiastically.

Lauren attacked her work with full concentration for an hour. Then she became distracted. The wind got up outside and the day turned stormy and prematurely dark. She reached for her phone. She'd just give Toby a call and see that Samuel wasn't too cold out there. There was no answer.

She stood and went to the window. The view of the Thames was lost in the downpour. She glanced down at the street below.

She looked at the phone in her hand. He must have gone inside, she reassured herself. Samuel would be warm in the Observatory. Maybe Toby was right – she babied him too much. But, after all, there would never be a brother or sister for Samuel.

Her eyes looked back down to the road below. A woman had stopped and was staring up at her – her face was partly covered with a black scarf. She had a hood pulled up over her head and was standing with her hands in the pockets of her long dark coat. She looked immovable against the gusts of wind. One of the plants on the balcony blew over and crashed against the windowpane and Lauren jumped. When she looked back the woman had gone.

Lauren went back to her desk, but deep in her stomach she had the feeling of anxiousness, and it was growing. It was Samuel's dinnertime now and after that she would run his bath. He'd have so many toys in there that there would be barely room for him. He'd play for ages filling up cups with water, making the waterwheels turn. Then she'd get him into his pyjamas, give him some warm milk and she'd read him stories and lie down beside him and drift off with him. That was her guilty pleasure, falling asleep next to him just for ten minutes or so, and then she'd creep out and Toby would have made her some dinner, poured her glass of wine and their adult time would begin.

The phone rang.

'Toby? Where are you? It's a quarter past five.'

'Sorry we're late. I'm coming up the street right now. It's been hell trying to get through the crowds. There's something wrong with the buggy's steering.'

She laughed, relieved. 'You'll get used to it. I'll meet you downstairs at the door.'

'No need. I can manage.'

'I want to.'

Lauren came out of their flat and took the lift down to the foyer. She nodded hello to the security guard and saw Toby, using his weight to pull the pram inside backwards. He managed to pull it so easily, she thought. It was always a struggle for her.

Lauren wanted to run over to Samuel. She wanted to take hold of him in her arms and kiss and cuddle him. She hated being apart from him but she knew she should be happy that Toby took him out on his own. She should be glad that he was showing an interest in his son at long last. She didn't run, she walked across the foyer, past the pebbles and fountain and the reception desk. Toby was inside now. He turned the buggy forwards to push it towards her and he kept his eyes on hers. His shoulders were stiff. His gait awkward. She looked at his face and wanted to ask, 'What's the matter?' Her eyes travelled down to his hands, down to the buggy and the loose strap on the seat. She felt her knees begin to give way. She felt her breath stop and her heart try to hammer blood round but it didn't move. All time stopped. A heartbeat freeze-framed.

'Where's Samuel?'

Chapter 2

Detective Inspector Dan Carter watched and waited for the group of officers to form a circle around him. It was seven thirty p.m. and the sky was black. The open doors of the police van offered a partial wind-break from the deep cold that skimmed icy breaths across the River Thames and gusted around the police officers searching the park. Carter was standing in the glare of the Maritime Museum at the base of Greenwich Park, waiting to address the newest search team. He looked across to where his partner, Detective Constable Ebony Willis, was standing, wearing her trademark black quilted jacket, but today she also had a black beanie hat pulled down over her ears. Her ponytail ballooned from beneath it, lifting in the gusts of wind and floating around her shoulders like a black shawl. She stood with a map in her hands. He knew she was working out the logistics of the search parties. He saw her taking in the layout of the park that rose above them in the darkness, covering nearly two hundred acres. The Royal Observatory was on the brow of the hill, above them. He wondered if she'd ever been up to the Observatory. He knew he

hadn't. It was on his list but one of those things tourists did rather than Londoners. He watched the
torchlight of officers as they fanned out along the
paths that crisscrossed the park. The noise from the
busy streets nearby rolled constant in the background. Access to the park was closed to the public.
In daylight they would start a fingertip search, for
now they were just looking for a two-year-old boy
who had managed to give his father the slip.

Carter stood tapping his right foot, without realizing, as the feeling of anxiety, the pressing need to
act, made every second he was waiting feel like an
hour wasted.

He pressed his hands deep into the pockets of his
dark-grey overcoat as he focused on each one of the
officers. Willis came across to join him, laying the
map out on the floor of the van.

'The last sighting of Samuel was in his buggy at ten
minutes past four when he was seen leaving the Royal
Observatory with his father Toby.' Carter addressed
the hundred officers who stood around him.

Willis picked up the photo pack prepared for the
officers and handed it out among them. 'It is crucial
that we find him fast,' Carter said as he waited until
all the officers had the pack. 'You now have a photo
of Samuel. He was wearing a navy all-in-one suit,
which has two large snowflakes appliquéd on the
front. This is distinctive and unusual; the maker's
label is Ski-Doo from the States. There are matching
mittens, label just inside the cuff. He's also wearing a
cream-coloured knitted bobble hat and red snow
boots from GAP. He has blond hair, blue eyes.' Carter

looked around and made sure each officer made eye contact. 'We know how fast a kid's hair can be dyed, how much a change of clothes and buggy can throw us off, but check every small child you see. Be polite but be insistent. Samuel's only differentiating feature is a small raised birthmark the size of a five pence piece beside his left eyebrow. Make-up would have to be quite thick to cover it. We need to find this little boy. If he's been dumped he won't last the night in these temperatures.'

Carter pointed to the map layout on the floor in the back of the van.

'We have divided the route into sections. You will be searching the section just west of the Cutty Sark DLR station – the officer in charge of your unit will divide you into teams and I'll hand you over to them in a minute to explain in more detail. But before I do I just want to make sure each one of you understands – no stone left unturned. No bin unchecked, every space where a child could be hidden has to be examined. Remember, Samuel is smaller than your average two-year-old. He could have been squeezed into a very small space. I want you climbing walls and getting under cars. I want every inch checked. Any problems getting access to an area of interest, alert your commander straight away and we'll get officers there to assist you. Good luck . . .'

Carter picked up his case and he and Willis walked across to his car, the black BMW parked on the approach to the park. Carter started the engine and reversed at speed.

'We need to throw everything at this, Eb.' She

nodded. She was deep in thought. Carter was used to being the one who chatted. 'The father's story is too vague,' he continued. 'Sensitive type, isn't he? Doesn't say a lot. He's really vague when it comes to pinpointing his movements; there's a missing period of almost forty minutes after he leaves the Observatory. Have you ever been there?'

'Once.'

'I'm impressed. Was it with that boyfriend who liked train sets?'

She didn't rise to it; she'd heard it before. Instead, she reached into her backpack and pulled out her phone. Carter continued, 'First he attends his famous dad's funeral, then his son gets abducted. Been one hell of a day.' In his head Carter was running through the checklist: ports, trains, motorway cameras. Service station, lorry drivers ... 'Robbo's checking for any history on the father,' said Carter, as he looked about him for a way out of the traffic jam they were in and decided to take a different route. Being the son of a London cabbie, and spending a lot of his spare time sitting next to his dad, meant that Carter's knowledge of the streets of London was extensive. He also knew where to stop for the best bacon sarnies.

Willis had several things on her lap at once. The police radio was the best for receiving a signal no matter where but it wasn't good at downloading data quickly. The smartphone was best at that. But for a bigger screen she needed her iPad and then she always had her notebook.

Carter glanced across at her lap. 'Sort yourself out, Willis, for Christ's sake.'

They'd worked together for the last four years. They knew one another's strengths and weaknesses. Carter knew that Willis would have recorded all the facts in her analytical brain. But if he asked her what it was like to lose a child, she would look at him blankly and she'd struggle to put herself in those shoes. Whereas Carter came from a big part-Italian family. Family was everything to them. Willis had grown up with a mother whose cold heart and deranged mind led her to murder easily. Luckily, Ebony had been taken into care for a good part of her childhood.

'He had a famous father but I doubt if anyone's heard of Toby Forbes-Wright until today,' said Willis.

'Have we got Family Liaison in place? asked Carter. Willis made a grab for her lap as Carter did a U-turn and headed back the way they'd come, then scooted up a back street.

'Yes, Jeanie Vincent has gone over already.'

'Great, she's the best. Any similar incidences, any attempted abductions in this area?' asked Carter.

'No, not so far as we know. We may get someone come forward after the public appeal; it's just gone out on the radio,' said Willis.

'We're going to need the public on this one,' Carter said. 'If the father left the belt undone on the buggy, and Samuel wandered off, he could have fallen into a gap somewhere. Jesus . . .' Carter banged his hand on the steering wheel. 'My Archie's just a year older. He wouldn't last two minutes in this cold. We have to find him fast.'

'Would Archie ever have got out of his own buggy and run off?'

'You're kidding me? First chance he got! You have to have eyes in the back of your head with kids. Tell Robbo we'll be back in twenty. I'm not waiting in this traffic any more.' Carter put on his emergency lights and swerved into the bus lane.

The Murder Squad was part of the Major Investigation Team in London. They were based in three locations around the capital and served different areas. From its Archway location, tucked behind the tube station and connected to the local police station, Fletcher House housed three MIT teams and served north London.

It was an inconspicuous concrete box of a building joined by a door linking the buildings at the first floor. The officers in Archway police station said the door marked the entrance to the Dark Side. Carter and Willis worked on the third floor of the Dark Side in MIT 17.

When they got back, they went straight into the Major Incident Room to see if there had been any calls from the public. It was where all the information came in first before being filtered and then farmed out to the other departments. Inside the MIR there were four civilians working behind the desks, manning the phones, and two detectives sifting the information as it came in. A category-A incident – a missing child – drew a full team of both civilian staff and police officers. All leave was cancelled.

Carter approached a desk straight ahead.

'Anything?' he asked as he waited for the operator to come off the phone. Willis was checking the screens to see what information had been fed into HOLMES, the central program designed to coordinate major investigations. She gave Carter a sign that she was heading out. He nodded he understood.

'One sighting of a kid with a snowflake on his jacket, sir,' the operator answered. 'But turned out to be a picture the child was holding on his lap. Several new sightings of Toby Forbes-Wright – all confirm the first half of his route.' The officer from the desk on the left looked through the pages of notes beside him and said, 'A woman in a café saw him. A man walking his dog on the park. All of them confirm seeing Toby pushing a buggy but no one looked inside it or noticed Samuel after four fifteen.'

'No one saw him on the walk back from the Observatory to his home?'

'Not so far.'

Carter followed Willis down to the Enquiry Team office. Long desks housed detectives working diagonally across from one another, their monitors back-to-back. He negotiated his way across the busy office. The commotion of a full team working flat out made the room squawk and yell like a stock market on a 'boom or bust' day. All officers who had been working on other cases were now focused on Samuel Forbes-Wright's disappearance. Everything else could wait. Carter stopped at the second of six desks from the left and looked over Willis's shoulder at her screen. She was looking at CCTV footage from the camera outside the *Cutty Sark*.

'Anything?'

'It was very busy, that's one thing.' She tapped her

pen on the list of names next to her: 'Looking at the sex offenders' register.' Each name was accompanied by a duo of mug shots and a brief resumé. 'All the addresses were around the Greenwich area. Number four on the list looks interesting – Malcolm Camber. He's only just come out of prison and he went inside for child abduction – he kidnapped and assaulted a four-year-old boy, released him after four hours.'

'Where did he let him go?'

'Parkland near his home.'

'Does he work alone?' asked Carter.

'He did then. We have no idea what friends he might have made in prison.'

'Have you been in touch with his parole office?'

'Yes, his parole officer said he called in sick the last few days.'

'Did she go round to see him?'

'She went round this afternoon but he wasn't there.'

'Put a warrant out – pick him up urgently. Anyone else?'

Ebony pulled out three files.

'There are seven more living in the same area who are high priority.'

'Get someone round to their houses with a search warrant now. I'll head down to talk to Robbo.'

'Yes, guv.'

Across from Willis was an empty chair, that of Jeanie Vincent, the Family Liaison Officer.

'Jeanie been in touch yet?'

'Not with me, maybe with Robbo?' answered Willis.

*   *   *

Robbo looked up from his desk as Carter walked in. Robbo had worked in the force for over twenty years and sat next to his 'work-wife' Pam. He'd had a life-long affair with Haribo sweets and great coffee but he was really addicted to work and had to be reminded that the purpose of work was to enjoy a better life and not the other way round.

'How's the father's background looking?' Carter asked Pam.

Pam looked over her leopard-print reading glasses as she answered: 'Private education, the best. He went on to study Physics and Astronomy at Oxford. He's been working in the Observatory, full time, sourcing and making the interactive exhibits for the last seven years. He's extremely bright. The Observatory job is almost a volunteer post. He gets paid less than twenty thousand a year.'

'It's a hobby then,' said Carter.

'He's capable of a lot, on paper.' Pam scrolled down her screen and made notes as she went. 'I mean, I'm not being funny, but if my kid had gone to Eton I would have wanted him to aim a bit higher, at least earn a good salary. That's a hell of a lot of invest-ment.' She glanced up and over her glasses. 'Not keen on living in the real world, maybe?'

'And what about her?' asked Carter.

'Lauren Forbes-Wright works for an American drugs company with a research department over here in east London,' answered Pam. 'We are guessing that's how they can afford to live in the middle of Greenwich; it's the usual thing for Glastons to pick up the tab on their overseas workers. Toby and her married in 2011 and they produced Samuel bang-on nine months later.'

'There's a twelve-year age difference,' added Robbo.

'So she could have been looking at a ticking baby clock when she married him. And what about him? What was he looking for, do we think?' Carter asked.

'The mum he never had, maybe?' answered Robbo. 'She ran away to live in Argentina with a boyfriend when Toby was seven. His dad packed him off to boarding school soon after. Seems like Jeremy Forbes-Wright concentrated on his career, for all the good it did him.'

'That's the trouble when you set yourself up as Mr Traditional Values and spotless,' said Pam, 'and then caught with an underage escort.'

'That was denied, and a long time ago,' said Carter.

'Maybe he just couldn't pay his way out this time,' said Robbo. 'But is that enough to kill yourself over? Politicians have survived worse.'

'I think he was banking on getting back into the Cabinet. He must have known he had no chance,' Pam said.

'The missing forty minutes, Robbo?' asked Carter. 'Any nearer to solving it?'

Robbo stood and used a marker to draw a balloon shape on the whiteboard behind his desk. 'This is his verified route.' Robbo drew in the *Cutty Sark* and the Royal Observatory. 'Here's his house. We know that Samuel and his dad Toby left the Riverview apartments on Thames Street at two thirty.' He wrote the times on the map as he talked. 'They were seen by a neighbour as they left. He was seen passing by the *Cutty Sark* and then he headed up to the Royal Observatory. We know Samuel was still inside the buggy at this point because work colleagues saw him in there. After Toby leaves the Royal Observatory at approximately ten past four and makes his way home we lose any sightings of the buggy until we pick him up again at just before five in the middle of Greenwich, *here*, and then again *here*. But we do not know whether he still had Samuel in the buggy then. At twenty past five he arrives home without Samuel.'

'What about the internet?' Carter continued. 'If he's with a paedophile there will be footage being circulated on the net, I'm sure.'

'All being monitored, sir, so far as we can,' answered Hector, a detective who had been seconded in from the Exhibits Room. He'd helped out in Robbo's department before and was needed again now. 'We've distributed Samuel's photo to every officer looking at tapes.'

'There's an alert out to all Special Branch officers within a three-hundred-mile radius of here.' Robbo went back behind his desk. 'You could get far in that missing forty minutes. And, what if it wasn't a random abduction? What if it was planned?'

'Then there are a few areas we are looking at,' Carter said. 'The father is socially inept. He seems to have a touch of Asperger's to me. He's shy and awkward and he didn't have the kind of childhood that involved any parenting. He was abandoned soon after his mum left. I doubt very much if he wanted Samuel.'

'So we step up the search for a body in the park.'

'Yes, and all around the Royal Observatory. He could have killed and hidden his son's body there. He knows the place back to front.'

'Then the Royal Observatory stays shut until we also know it back to front,' said Robbo. 'What else do you have?'

'There's always the possibility it has something to do with Jeremy Forbes-Wright,' said Carter.

'Best to talk it through with Toby,' Pam said. 'See what paperwork he's got on his dad's finances, everything. Get his permission to contact the solicitor holding all the probate papers.'

'Has Lauren's family got money?' asked Carter. 'Have they got any dubious connections that might stretch this far over the sea?'

Hector answered: 'I'm talking with Interpol but so far there are no skeletons in Lauren's closet.'

'If it's a ransom, there's still time for them to come forward,' Carter said.

'There's no doubt that without her wage they could not enjoy their current lifestyle. But they don't own a property,' said Pam. 'We know her company pays for the flat they live in. No one could have thought they were worth a ransom.'

'We don't know what other secrets JFW might have been concealing?' Pam added, already amassing intimate details of the former politician's life.

'We need permission to search his father's flat,' said Carter.

'Where was it?'

'Canary Wharf,' replied Carter. 'It's a rented flat.

We're not going to have long before it has to be vacated.'

'Revenge then?' Robbo said, as he rocked on his chair and laid out his Haribo in a line. 'After all, politicians piss people off, especially ones who specialize in having underage sex and getting away with it. He must have committed suicide for a reason.'

A missing child and a dead politician – the press will think all their Christmases had come at once.

The door opened.

'Sir? A man's been detained at Folkestone trying to board a ferry with a young boy answering the description of Samuel Forbes-Wright.'

Chapter 3

Folkestone

The reversing vehicle backed noisily, spreading its flashing orange glow across the wet tarmac. Carter pulled over and parked.

'Jesus Christ!' The wind almost took the door from Carter's hand as he fought to hold on to it. He slammed the door shut and started walking.

To their right, the black water was a bitter-cold backdrop to the bright lights of the ferry as it was being cleaned ready for the next passage to France.

'We could be in luck here,' he said to Willis as she marched across the tarmac, slightly ahead of him, head down. Willis's eyes were watering. She wiped her nose with the heel of her hand and dried it on her trousers as they walked together towards the terminal building. Carter's metal-tipped shoes scraped as he walked smartly across to the harbour master's office.

'I sent a photo to the parents,' she said, taking out her phone to check for a reply.

'And?'

'It's come back as a "Negative".'

'Shit. Well, we need to check it out anyway. Kids can be made to look very different very fast.'

A dark-haired man of about fifty looked up at them as they entered the office, a small blond boy asleep on his lap. A police officer was sitting between the man and the door. He stood as Carter and Willis entered the room. Carter took out his badge; Willis did the same.

'PC Littlemore, sir. This is Mr Mancey and his son Drew.'

'Sorry to put you through this, Mr Mancey.' Carter came to perch on the corner of the desk next to them.

The man blinked red-eyed at them as he held tightly on to the sleeping child, who looked a lot like the pictures of the Forbes-Wright child. Carter reached forward as he studied the boy.

'Do you mind?' He went to sweep the child's hair away from his eyes so that he could see his eyebrow. Mancey raised a hand to stop him and then withdrew it with a disgruntled nod.

Carter lifted the lad's hair and moved in to look at the left side of his face. Willis stepped in close beside him. Carter looked at her; she confirmed what he was thinking with a small shake of the head.

'I hear you didn't have the right documentation to take Drew on board the ferry?' Carter said as he withdrew.

'I didn't know he needed a passport to cross the Channel. Since when?'

'You wouldn't be able to get back into the UK without a passport for the boy. He's your son?'

'Yes.'

'Do you have any form of ID for him?'

'No – like I said to the idiot who stopped me – if I'd realized things had changed I would have brought it. We've missed our ferry. What are we supposed to do now?'

'Apologies, Mr Mancey, we have to be very cautious these days. We can let you go now, if you wish to continue your journey. Sorry to have troubled you.'

On the way out Carter called Robbo. 'Any luck with the searches?'

'We have hundreds of people out there, dogs and helicopters. The public have really rallied for this. If he'd got out of the buggy by himself, I think we would have found him by now. We are definitely looking at abduction. Chief Inspector Bowie says he'll head up a press conference tomorrow.'

'Okay. Makes sense; they're going to want to see some brass. I'll have the release ready for him to deliver in the morning. What about Jeanie, has she phoned?'

'Yes. She says she'll see you back here. I guess we'll all be working through the night?'

'I don't think you even have a home, Robbo.'

'Yeah, yeah, don't let my wife hear you say that.' He laughed.

Jeanie was waiting for Carter and Willis when they got back at eleven. Willis had made Carter stop and pick up supplies for the night. The smell of kebab filled the inspector's room. Carter shared an office with two other inspectors but they were both out coordinating the search for Samuel.

'Any muffins?' asked Jeanie as she joined them in

the office. 'No wonder you're hiding in here, you two. They're a hungry pack of wolves out there.'

'I've ordered pizza for the office. It's on its way, just Willis wanted extra,' Carter said.

'Here, Jeanie.' Willis handed her a bag. 'Carter said you'd go for a blueberry with a lemon-curd centre.'

Jeanie stood and blinked at Carter and then chuckled, embarrassed.

'Perfect, thanks.' She looked genuinely touched.

Carter grinned smugly. He could have added that you don't have a long relationship with someone and not know what kind of muffin they like but he didn't. They were both with different partners now, both had kids. The fact that they still worked together was difficult, but not impossible.

'What are your thoughts on them, Jeanie?' he said, opening the takeaway containers on his desk and trying to fend Willis off as he ate his chicken. 'What kind of things are they saying to one another?'

'There's definitely more than a hint of blame creeping in now. Only Toby has the answers and he's out with the fairies most of the time.'

'Are we completely discounting her as a possible suspect?' Willis said with a mouth full of food as she attacked her large doner kebab in pitta, extra chilli sauce and mayo.

Jeanie nodded thoughtfully as she picked at her muffin. 'Yes, almost definitely, she had neither the motive nor the opportunity. She has nothing to gain and everything to lose. We know how hard this is for her.' Jeanie looked to Carter for confirmation. He nodded.

'It's the worst possible thing you can imagine.'

'Right then.' Carter opened one of six files on the desk. 'Here are the photos taken of Toby's walk. I want us to look for people passing by who appear more than once. We need to double-check all this footage. There is no such thing as plain careless, lots of people are not the most watchful parents and they don't have their child snatched out of their buggy. Someone must have been following, must have hovered, must have looked like they were ready to snatch.'

Chapter 4

Detective Chief Inspector Bowie stood on the stage at ten the next morning. Behind him was the bold blue backdrop flag of the Metropolitan Police.

'Yesterday afternoon, between the time of four ten and five fifteen, two-year-old Samuel Forbes-Wright went missing from his buggy while out with his father Toby. Before I bring in Samuel's parents I will give you an update on the investigation so far.'

Carter studied the audience from his seat on the stage behind the long desk. Willis stood at the back of the room. DCI Bowie looked a little more groomed than usual. Someone had bothered to tell him that just wetting his hair and plastering it back wasn't the same as washing it. His uniform had replaced the cheap work suit: starched and pristine with shiny buttons. His watery blue eyes seemed fixed on a horizon above the press.

'As soon as we received a phone call from Lauren Forbes-Wright telling us that her son was missing we immediately began a detailed search of the area.

Hundreds of officers have been deployed. We have brought in every resource at our disposal, no expense has been spared. This includes helicopter and river-boat searches and analysing CCTV footage as we piece together the last hour of Toby Forbes-Wright's movements with Samuel. Yes?'

'How large is the area being searched?'

'We are searching a substantial area of Greenwich Park and the town itself.'

'Do you have any idea how long the Royal Observatory will remain closed? Is it considered one of the most important sites?'

'I can't tell you how long it will remain closed. It is of interest to us, that's all.'

'Have you any suspects in custody?'

'No.'

'Any recent incidents that are similar?'

'No one has come forward with any information as yet, no.'

'Any paedophiles operating in the area?'

'A thorough investigation is taking place into anyone known to the police. We are committing huge resources to enable us to put as many feet on the ground as necessary.'

'What about Jeremy Forbes-Wright? Could it be connected to his suicide?'

Carter watched Bowie preparing for the question. That was the only reason Bowie was up there now. He wasn't the Senior Investigating Officer on the abduction case – Carter was – but he was giving the press what they expected when such a high-profile family hit the news. Bowie's job was as a spokesman.

'We do not know what the motive was for taking Samuel. We are urging whoever has him to release him safely now. We need the public's help to find him. Look in your garden sheds, look in any outbuildings, get outside today and search for us. I will bring in Mr and Mrs Forbes-Wright to make a personal appeal now, thank you.'

Jeanie led Toby and Lauren into the room. She showed them to their seats centre stage and sat down on the far side of Lauren. The room filled with camera flashes and the sound of digital shutters clicking furiously.

Jeanie leaned across to adjust Lauren's microphone. Before turning it on, she whispered: 'I will draw back from you and Toby when they start asking questions. It's going to be a mass of flashes and noise, don't let it get to you. Remember – when you read your statement, make sure you look at the cameras.'

Lauren nodded. Toby Forbes-Wright sat, head bowed.

Willis stayed at the back of the room and watched them. Lauren didn't seem to want to offer any comfort to her husband, thought Willis. She wasn't leaning towards him, or including him. She looked like she was dealing with it on her own. Lauren turned back towards Jeanie.

'Are you ready, Lauren?' asked Carter.

She nodded.

'Lauren Forbes-Wright will read a statement,' Carter said. The room went quiet.

Lauren took a deep breath. She had her statement

on a sheet of paper in front of her but she didn't read from it. She looked around the room helplessly.

'When did you first notice that Samuel was missing, Mrs Forbes-Wright?' asked one of the broadsheet journalists.

Jeanie looked at Carter and he nodded that they should run with it.

'I was finishing off some work . . .' She stopped and fought back the tears. 'I was waiting for them to come back. Toby had taken him for a walk.' She looked across at Jeanie. Willis wondered why she didn't look at her husband. She was alienating him. He sat with his head bowed. They did not look like a united couple. The press had already picked up on it. The cameras clicked continually in his direction. 'I met them downstairs. I was going to open the door for him, to help with the buggy. Then I saw that Samuel was gone.' Lauren turned to Jeanie.

Jeanie gave her a smile that said: *Let's go back to the script.*

'Toby.' A journalist at the front addressed him directly: 'Was your father, Jeremy Forbes-Wright, close to Samuel?'

Toby looked around the room as if seeking help from anyone who might give it. He opened his mouth but nothing came out.

Jeanie intervened. She picked up the statement in front of Lauren. 'Lauren and Toby are finding it difficult to cope with the events that happened yesterday. They are living through a nightmare. They have no idea who would want to do this to their son, to themselves or to anyone connected with their family.

Lauren and Toby want to appeal to everyone out there to look for Toby.' Jeanie turned to Lauren.

Lauren nodded in response. She lifted her head up and fought back tears. 'Please don't hurt him. Please tell us what you want and give me my little boy back. Samuel ... Mommy and Daddy love you very, very much.'

Chapter 5

Carter came to find Willis at her desk after the press conference. She looked up from studying the CCTV footage of Toby walking past the *Cutty Sark*. 'Jeanie's still here, she says the Forbes-Wrights want to be on their own for a while,' she said.

'I bet they do. They were pretty convincing, I thought.'

Willis nodded warily. 'They looked numb.'

'I thought Lauren would manage better than that,' Carter said as he pulled up a chair beside Willis. 'She seemed to crumble, didn't she? You never know how you're going to react, I suppose. Must be a living hell.'

'She blames him. That's why she can't bear to look at him,' said Willis. 'The press picked up on it.'

'Samuel is the same age as Archie. I can imagine that Cabrina would be the first to blame me if it happened to us,' replied Carter.

'It wouldn't.'

'It can happen to anyone.'

'No, guv, it wouldn't happen to you. You constantly check on Archie. You would have noticed anyone coming too near him. I feel sorry for Toby – he's not a natural dad. I don't think they are a united couple in any way. They should be clinging to one another right now, not pushing one another away. This isn't just to do with Samuel's disappearance. I don't think they have a strong marriage,' said Willis.

'Maybe ... something in that press conference definitely wasn't right. Something's not being said between them. I want his phone checked and I want their flat bugged if Samuel isn't found tonight.'

'We could move them out to a hotel – tell them it's to give them some privacy. Hotel rooms are easier to bug,' suggested Willis.

'No, I'd rather leave them where they are. How did the searches on sex offenders' homes work out?' Carter asked. 'Anything promising?'

Willis stood, her chair grating as it pushed backwards on the wooden floor. She picked up the half-eaten doughnut she'd bought from the canteen much earlier that morning.

'Nothing so far – three down, two to go.'

'Don't get that on my coat,' Carter said as Willis came too close to him with the doughnut. Jeanie walked in just as they were about to leave. Willis smirked.

'How are the Forbes-Wrights after the press conference?' Carter asked as Jeanie sat down at her desk.

'My hunch? There will be a few angry words being exchanged, I think. This is when the major cracks in their relationship start to appear.'

'What's the deal with them?' asked Carter. 'She's much older.'

'She seems to have put her career first,' replied Jeanie. 'She left it late to find a partner and then they met and married within six months. He's difficult to fathom. I can see what he'd find to like in her – if he's into older women, that is, but I'm sure she could have bagged a fifty-year-old divorcee to give her a child and some security. He must have hidden depths – he's not my type. He seems so young, even younger than his twenty-nine years.'

'He's sensitive, arty,' said Willis. 'Lauren obviously likes mothering him. If it works, it works, I suppose.'

'Until it stops working,' Carter said. 'Until he wakes up and decides it's not what he wants and he's not enough of a grown-up to say "I want out".'

Jeanie looked deep in thought as Willis said, 'We're sending officers round to interview the staff at the Observatory this morning. We should know more about him then.' Willis shoved the last of the doughnut into her mouth, screwed up the bag and lobbed it at the bin. 'We have a call logged on Toby's phone at two sixteen yesterday. That was from one of his co-workers, Gareth Turnbill. He phoned him before his walk with Samuel,' Willis continued, looking at her notes. 'He lives in Blackheath. He's a lad of nineteen. We'll talk to him first.'

'What have the couple said to you about Jeremy Forbes-Wright?' Carter asked Jeanie.

'Very little. Lauren never met him. He didn't attend their wedding. Toby said he hadn't seen him in ages.'

'Where was the funeral?' Carter asked Willis.

'Ladywell and Brockley Cemetery.' Carter looked

at it over her shoulder as she brought up a link on screen: Friends of Ladywell and Brockley Cemetery homepage.

'I know it,' he said. 'I have a relative on my dad's side buried there. It's a beautiful old cemetery. What did they say went on after the funeral, Jeanie?'

'They came back to the flat, they had a discussion about who was there, well, more just agreeing that they didn't know anyone, and then they talked briefly about his father's affairs. I think there was some tension over Toby having gone to look at his father's flat without Lauren. They were considering leaving this morning to go to Cornwall. Jeremy Forbes-Wright had a house there but it's let most of the time. That was one thing Lauren did say – that the man who was responsible for letting that house was at the funeral.'

'We had to send a few officers to the cemetery to keep the press at arm's length,' said Willis. 'But it's useful for us to see who actually went inside. There were several news companies filming. Some say Jeremy Forbes-Wright had a chance of being Prime Minister one day,' Willis added as she watched some footage of the funeral on her screen.

'He was expected to run for one of the vacant seats in Kent, prime Tory country, but he was reported as having dropped out of the race at Christmas,' said Jeanie. 'There's been speculation about it but no real reason given.'

Carter was watching the screen with Willis. He turned back to Jeanie. 'What about Lauren, what's in her past?'

'She's super-bright ... very academic. Only child. Parents are professors. She has a great job; earns about eighty grand at the moment but she's still working her way up the ladder.'

'I think we're right to count her out. That leaves Toby and his dad, which doesn't seem a hell of a lot of good. The public will want to know how a kid can be snatched from his father's buggy in broad daylight and then disappear.'

Jeanie nodded. 'Okay, give me an hour to write up my notes and I'll head back over to see them.'

'We'll join you there at their flat. We need to put some pressure on Toby now to start remembering things.'

Chapter 6

Willis stood in front of the French windows, looking out at the Thames. Pots of herbs battled against the odds on the small balcony. One was upturned, rolling around in its own dirt. There was a small dog turd getting turned over in the wind. Today the Thames was the colour of slate. She could see the river police – she knew they were still looking for Samuel's body. It was twelve noon but already the day was getting dark. Storms were on the way.

She and Carter were alone in the lounge – a large through space with white walls and pictures of Manhattan. Jeanie was talking to the couple in the kitchen. Carter took the opportunity to look at the photos on the walls, the knick-knacks on the shelves. There weren't many in the minimalist rented apartment. There was a desk in the corner, which had a laptop on it. Carter could guess which pieces of furniture each half of the couple had conceded to the other. The desk had to be Lauren's: neat, bundles of papers. A lot of things carefully managed. Compartmentalized. A white-framed portrait of the three of them was on the wall above her desk. The sofa looked like it had come out of Toby's bedsit. It was ropy and had been covered loosely with a green and white Lauren-type throw. One wall was given over to gadgets and systems: 3D TV, docking stations, CDs and films, mainly sci-fi, in alphabetical order. This was Toby's wall. In the corner of the room was a white box full of Samuel's toys. Carter sympathized; Lauren was working very hard to keep their identity in the baby takeover bid. It was a tricky balancing act for any couple.

From the kitchen behind them they could hear Jeanie running through the events of the day before once again with Lauren. The door to the kitchen opened and Toby came into the lounge. He sat on the sofa and held his head in his hands.

First Jeanie, then Lauren followed him in. Lauren remained standing.

Willis was still standing at the French windows but had turned, her back to the Thames. She could hear the dog whimpering in the kitchen. She looked at the couple. The one thing that working in MIT 17 had taught her in the last two years was that when something like this happened most marriages fell apart. It would take a miracle to save theirs now. Her phone buzzed in her pocket. She took it out and read the message then replied and replaced it in her jacket. Carter whispered: 'Any news?'

She shook her head. 'Negative on the ports and trains.'

'Toby,' Jeanie continued calmly in her professional, caring, no-blame voice, 'when was the last time you looked into the buggy and checked on Samuel? The last time you actually saw him?'

Lauren walked forward so slowly, hardly making a sound. She stood at the end of the sofa staring at her husband, side-on.

Carter knew what she'd be thinking, what they were all thinking. *Yes, for Christ's sake – when was the last bloody time you even checked on your son to see that he was alive?*

'I think it was when we went into the café at the Royal Observatory. I thought he might want a biscuit. I wiped his nose.'

'Did he?'

'Sorry?'

'Want a biscuit?'

'No. I don't think so. I gave him a drink.' Toby glanced at his wife as he spoke. Every word that came out of his mouth was filled with agonizing self-recrimination. Carter could see that he longed for her to say something to make him feel better; he expected it; but it wasn't coming this time.

Lauren stared at Toby's profile, her eyes full of the pain of a moment lost to her.

'Do you remember anyone who was there at the time?' Jeanie continued. 'Someone who might have seen you?'

He was trying hard to recall. 'There were the usual café staff.'

'Did you speak to them?'

'Just hello, how's things?'

'Was there anyone else there?'

'It was getting busy as I left. There was a man reading a book near the entrance. There were a couple of people as well – I didn't get a look at them. There were people arriving as I went out. Someone held the door open for me.'

'Can you remember what they looked like?'

'No. I was concentrating – it's not always easy to get the buggy out of places. I was trying not to catch the wheel on the door frame.'

'Where did you go then?'

'I went to see if my new exhibition pieces were working okay then I went into the shop as well – it's in the same building.'

'You are an expert on black holes, aren't you?' said Willis from her place by the French windows.

'Yes.' Toby turned and smiled at her. 'It's my passion.' She thought it was the first time she'd seen anything but panic on his face. That was his world, not pushing babies around in buggies.

'Where did you go then?' Carter asked as Toby turned to look at his wife. She stared coldly back.

'I just kept on walking.'

'Where?'

'I walked home,' he said, exasperated. He was squirming on the sofa, obviously feeling persecuted.

'How long would it normally take you to walk to work from your house?' asked Carter.

'Twenty-five minutes.'

Willis was going through the statements in her notebook.

'Gareth said it was ten past four when you left,' she read out.

'So tell me what you do remember about leaving the Observatory,' Carter asked.

'I just pushed Samuel towards home.'

'Which took you over an hour to do. We've been walking that a few times in this last twenty-four hours. I would say – even on a leisurely walk – we managed to make it from the Royal Observatory to your home in less than thirty minutes.' Toby shrugged and shook his head. Carter continued: 'So you left the Observatory and you started back towards home. Was it dark?'

'Yes.'

'Must have been cold?'

'Yes, the temperature had dropped considerably.'

'Maybe you checked that Samuel had his hat and gloves on, did you? My kid Archie is around Samuel's age. He won't keep things on for two minutes.'

Toby gave a small, hopeless shake of the head: 'I presumed he was still asleep. I never thought about it . . .' His voice trailed off as he looked up and around the room at the waiting faces – only Jeanie smiled encouragement. 'It had been a long day. My mind was elsewhere. I should have checked him.'

'Did you see anyone you knew after you left the Observatory and said goodbye to Gareth?' Carter asked.

'No.'

'After you left there where did you go exactly?'

'I walked along the top, looked at the view of London, I did a roundabout route back down.

'Again, did you talk to anyone, Toby?'

'No. I don't think so.'

'No casual word? No interaction of any kind?'

Toby shook his head.

'After you left the park, where did you go?' asked Carter.

'I decided I'd head home via the music shop near the market.' Toby said it so casually it was as if he were testing it out to see how it sounded. He shook his head. 'I thought I'd have time to browse while he was quiet.' Lauren turned her head from him. 'I wanted to look in the window – there was a saxophone I'd been keeping an eye on – just wanted to see if it was still there. I used to play, years ago.'

'Did you go inside the shop? Maybe you left Samuel outside?'

Toby hesitated. 'No, I didn't,' he said, and then shook his head vigorously.

'You didn't park the buggy somewhere for a few minutes so that you could browse?'

Toby shook his head in denial but his expression said the opposite. Somewhere in his memory banks he remembered having left the buggy just for a few seconds, a minute at the most. Maybe it was more than once, Carter thought to himself.

'Think carefully,' he said to Toby. 'Did you feel his weight shift, hear him move? Maybe he chatters, does he?'

Lauren fought back the tears. Jeanie reached out to place a hand on her arm.

Carter called Willis to follow him out into the hallway where the buggy was. He held it by the handles and bounced it gently.

'I admit, this is a heavy buggy. With Archie's you'd know if he wasn't in it but it's possible you could push this along with a lighter kid and have no idea. What d'you think?'

Willis repeated the action and nodded. 'And, he's

not used to pushing it – he's not thinking like everyone else.'

'Let's go outside.'

They walked towards the river and the Thames path. Carter pulled up the collar of his coat. It wasn't enough. The icy wind cut between the apartment blocks. He pulled his yellow cashmere scarf up around his mouth, tried to make it reach up to his ears but it wasn't happening.

'He's saying what we want to hear now – or what his wife wants to hear. He's too scared to admit he left the buggy – certainly not in front of his wife. We need to split them up,' Carter said as he slipped into a doorway to shelter from the blasting wind. He unwrapped a piece of gum. 'So, what else is Toby lying about?' Carter stamped his expensive shoes against the cold. Willis didn't seem to feel it. 'We'll double the searches up around the Observatory. What would he have done with his own kid on a cold afternoon in January? It was dark when he came back, he could have walked along the path and jumped down onto the river bank, weighted the child down and thrown him into the river.'

'Shall we order the divers in?'

'No, if Samuel is down there he's not going any-where. I'd rather concentrate everything on finding him alive. Has Pam had any luck looking into the grandfather? What about his connection to Cornwall?'

'Just the holiday home down there.'

'That's it? No relatives or ex-wives?'

'That's it, so far.'

'Where is the house?'

'It's a village called Penhal. It's popular with people from London. Most people have heard of it or its posh neighbour Rockyhead.'

'We never came to Cornwall when I was a kid,' said Carter. 'The furthest we went was Margate. Well, let's scan the footage of the funeral again. We're running out of options. Plus, Jeremy Forbes-Wright didn't just die, he committed suicide – is there something in that? He books into a hotel and then calmly slices through his own wrist. Christ almighty – I'm flippin' freezing. Let's go back in there and I suggest you take the wife somewhere and get her to open up.'

'Guv? I'm not sure.'

'Yes. She's your type – straightforward, no frills.'

'I'm not the best in these circumstances. I'm not trained as an FLO.'

'Just do it for me, Eb. Trust me. I know what you're good at and what needs work.'

When they got back to the flat, Lauren looked perplexed but relieved to be getting out of the house. She went to get her coat without hesitation at Ebony's request to talk privately. Toby watched her put it on with a pleading look in his eyes; as if she was leaving him to be thrown to the lions. He was looking for a small sign that she didn't blame him. He didn't get it. She would blame him for ever.

'I think we should take Russell,' Lauren said, and Willis went to get him.

Jeanie handed her a small backpack like the one Willis used when she was running. 'It's got the poo bags and some treats in it. I took him out yesterday – it's best to keep him on a lead because he tries to run away.' Jeanie put Russell on the lead and handed him to Ebony. She followed Lauren outside.

'Do you mind if we walk towards the park?' Lauren asked. 'I feel somehow nearer to Samuel there.'

'We can walk around the outside,' answered Willis, as she noted the search parties had sectioned off the far and central sections of the park.

Lauren pulled on her mittens and hat and buttoned her sheepskin jacket up to the top. 'I'll take him,' she said, referring to Russell, and Willis happily relinquished the lead and the backpack. They walked in silence for a few minutes and Willis watched the officers searching further up the hill and to the left of them. She looked at the buildings that lined the park. Some were residential and she could see people inside, looking out wondering whether Samuel would be found.

Lauren walked slowly to allow Russell time to explore.

'If this is an opportunist thing then my son will be long gone from here, won't he?'

'It's too early for us to draw conclusions.'

'Really? I always thought the first few hours were crucial.'

'Lauren, I know it feels like you're in a nightmare at the moment but please take a few good breaths and try and stay calm.'

Lauren stopped walking and looked at Willis. At the same time a photographer came within a few feet of them and started taking photos. Willis stepped in front of him and an officer appeared to escort him away. 'Do you think he's dead?'

Willis was wishing that Carter hadn't sent her out with Lauren. She knew her job was to allow her to talk in the hope that she might reveal some important facts, but it wasn't her forte.

'We are doing everything possible to find Samuel. Tell me about yesterday. There might be some tiny, minute piece of information that starts a chain reaction.'

'How can this get Samuel back? Why don't you just get in your car and drive around the streets? Someone might have left him somewhere. That happens, doesn't it? People abandon the child?' She looked at Willis, pleading with her eyes, 'When they're finished?'

'We have patrol cars out looking, Lauren. We have officers swarming these streets to find him. We've put out a public appeal. The best thing you can do for me is talk.'

Lauren sighed, frustrated. 'What do you want to know? My husband went for a walk with our son and he came home with an empty buggy. I don't know how the hell it happened.' She turned away as she fought back the tears.

'Tell me about the funeral.'

She took a deep breath. 'Where do you want me to start?'

'How was Toby in the morning?'

'Toby was the same as ever: quiet, introspective, didn't want to talk about it. We left home at ten. We arrived early. Toby stayed in the car. I got out and walked around with Samuel, looking at the graves. It all seemed so farcical and yet so sad. I'd never even met Jeremy Forbes-Wright, for Christ's sake. Never seen him, so far as I knew. He'd never asked to meet me or to see his own grandson.' Her voice rose in the damp dead of the park. She took a deep breath and shook her head, calming herself. 'A police cordon had been set up around the small chapel.' They walked and Lauren talked. 'We'd been told there would be press, there would be politicians wanting to pay their last respects. It seemed like it was such a lot of fuss to me, but we didn't really have a choice. He left exact instructions – we just had to follow them – it felt weird.' They walked on around the park.

'Six pallbearers carried the coffin in. Toby didn't want to do it.

'The coffin came out with flowers on it but nothing personal. I guess that was no surprise. I don't know whether you know or not but for most of Toby's life he didn't see his father.' Lauren sighed heavily. They had been walking for half an hour now. Willis wiped her frozen nose with a paper tissue from her pocket.

'How was Toby coping?' she asked.

'I looked across at him – he was chewing the inside of his cheek as they carried the coffin inside. Does that when he's stressed. I knew what was worrying him most – the speech. For Toby, that's far more difficult than you can imagine. He is so shy, so cripplingly shy.' She paused as she collected her thoughts. 'I tried to help him. I knew it was the worst day of his life – the final humiliation by his father. Toby hates to attend any gatherings of more than two other people. He sneaks away early if we ever have a dinner party. But yesterday he had to read a poem and talk about a father he hated; and who, for some reason, hated him. Jeremy Forbes-Wright was a lot of things to a lot of people – but to Toby he was a controlling bully. Toby didn't find much to say that was good about his father. The Home Secretary got up and told a few funny stories about Jeremy. Then someone read a psalm.'

'How did Toby cope with it all?'

'After the service, Toby didn't answer anyone, whatever they said. He just stuck out his hand and let people shake it. I said, "Thanks for coming," but it felt stupid. I had no idea who they were, except for the guy who'd written me about the house in Cornwall – Stokes, who introduced himself to me. Toby seemed to be in meltdown. We'd opted for a private burial so luckily we could get away from the crowd. The coffin was put back inside the hearse and driven further into the cemetery. The vicar said a few words. Toby said nothing as we stood around the grave and then Samuel started to really whinge.'

'Do you remember seeing anyone else there then?'

'There were people tending graves, laying flowers, and groundsmen. There seemed to be a few joggers. It all seemed quite a buzzing place. People were walking their dogs. The burial was over quickly and we headed home. We stopped on the way to get something for Samuel to eat. That's it really.' She looked across at Willis and shrugged. 'We got back to our flat but we just were so deflated. I suggested we should head down to take a look at Jeremy's house in Cornwall. I wanted to see it.'

Willis didn't interrupt as Lauren talked and they walked on.

'Toby and Samuel don't have a great relationship. I mean, they do, but he doesn't usually care if Toby is there or not. I have had to make big compromises where Samuel is concerned. You must have noticed the age difference. For me, I wanted a child whatever. But Toby didn't. I must be honest, I think he married me thinking that I was past it.'

Lauren stopped and grabbed Willis's hand. 'Please, please, just tell me it will be all right. Tell me that he will be found safe and alive. Please tell me they won't make him suffer – he's my world.' Lauren looked about to collapse.

Willis was thinking of an honest but hopeful response and wishing Carter hadn't made her do this. Lauren watched her closely.

'I can promise you that we're doing everything to find him.'

'What? What are you doing, tell me.'

'We have to cover all bases until we have more of an idea why he was taken. So, we have posted extra officers on every exit out of London and out of the UK. We are looking into every known paedophile who is on the sex register and who lives in this area. We are searching houses. We are also looking into the possibility that there will still be a ransom demand. The person who took Samuel may know that Toby has just inherited from his father. We are looking at all the CCTV footage of Toby and the route he said he took when Samuel went missing.'

'What do you mean, "said"? Don't you believe him?'

'I don't mean to imply anything by that – it's

standard procedure that we look into every possibility. The truth is that Toby was with Samuel when he was abducted. He is the last contact we have with Samuel. Whether I believe him or not, we still have to do that in order to try and pinpoint the exact spot Samuel was taken. Tell me what you were doing.'

'I was working for a while. I tried Toby's number but he didn't answer and then the weather outside seemed to be getting really bad so I stood and went to see if I could spot them. A woman had stopped outside. She was staring up at me. Then something distracted me and when I looked back she was gone. Toby phoned and I went down to the foyer.'

'What was she like, the woman you saw?'

'She was dressed in dark clothes. She had a scarf around her face and her hood was up.'

'Did you recognize her from the funeral? Do you think you could have seen her before?'

'I didn't see her face but I would have remembered what she was wearing probably. She wasn't smart enough to have been one of the mourners. Her coat was a shiny oilskin type, too big for her. It was dark green.'

'How old would you say she was?'

'I have no idea. I didn't see her face at all. Only her eyes and she was too far from me to tell anything.'

'Her body language? Was she slight, short? Tall?'

'As I looked down at her I remember thinking she was able to stand the gusts of wind and hold her own.'

'So stocky?'

'Not stocky but steady on her feet. I don't know – that doesn't make sense, does it?'

'Keep thinking for me and we'll get her drawn up when we get back to the apartment. Jeanie will help. So, when you took the call from Toby, how did he seem?'

'He was distracted. I guessed he was battling the wind, he wasn't used to the buggy. I should never have said they should go out. I knew Toby wasn't in the right state of mind and Samuel was just getting a cold – grizzling.' She looked across at Willis.

Willis thought to herself: *If he's still alive that'll be the least of his worries*. She stopped and turned her head away from the icy wind. Below them the Maritime Museum was lit up. Willis noted the officers around the entrance.

'Lauren – I think it's time we got back.' Willis was a few steps ahead before she realized Lauren wasn't following. 'Is there something else you wanted to tell me about yesterday?'

Willis looked at Lauren's expression. She seemed to be struggling with something.

'Not about yesterday.'

'Then what?' Willis was distracted by the commotion going on. There was a flurry of activity around one of the bins by the entrance to the museum. She wanted to get Lauren away just in case they'd found Samuel's body.

Lauren caught her up. Willis sped up as they walked towards home.

'Toby and I haven't really been getting on for a while. We don't share a bed any more. I sleep in with Samuel.'

'Has that been going on for long?'

'Two years.'

'I'm sorry, Lauren. I suppose the pressure of having Samuel changed your life?'

'Toby's not interested any more. I knew he was bisexual when I married him. I thought we'd be fine. I thought we were well matched in our own way. I don't need a macho-man. But I think he's become interested in someone else. I don't know whether that's a man or a woman. Could it have anything to do with Samuel going missing?'

Chapter 7

When Willis got back Carter was still there, waiting for her. They went into the kitchen to talk privately.

'They've found something.'

'What?'

'Just been verified now. It's Samuel's suit,' answered Carter.

Willis and Carter went to join the others in the lounge and share the news. Jeanie sat next to Toby on the sofa as Lauren stood, shell-shocked, in the middle of the room.

'It means he's dead,' Toby said as he stared dumbstruck at his wife.

'No, it doesn't.' Carter was stern. 'They changed his clothes for a reason. They wanted to disguise his identity. That means there is still hope he's alive.'

'Lauren,' said Willis. 'Can we sit down and draw the woman you saw on the street below?'

'What woman?' Toby asked. 'You never said about a woman before.'

'There was a woman staring up at me, that's all. I'm trying to remember every small detail, anything that will help.'

'Was she at the funeral?' asked Carter.

'I didn't see her there.'

Lauren went to her desk to get some paper. She sat with Willis and Jeanie at the kitchen table.

Lauren shook her head as she looked at the finished drawing. 'It isn't much to go on, is it?'

Jeanie picked up the drawing and went to show Toby and then Carter. 'Toby, did you see a woman like this, while you were out?'

He shook his head. 'I honestly never looked at anyone. I pushed Samuel around in the buggy. I looked at the view across London but most of the time I had a lot to think about. My father had just died. A father who hated me and then left me a dog and a load of debt. Sorry I can't be more helpful.'

'Toby, we need to look into your father's affairs, his personal correspondence. We would like to search his flat and look into his phone records. We need to look at every possible lead now. Do you have a set of keys?'

'The solicitor is dealing with all that,' Toby answered, looking from one person to the other.

'Yes, I understand that, but can we have your permission?' Carter pushed. 'It saves getting a search warrant – saves time.'

'Of course you can, for Christ's sake,' Lauren spat out angrily as she came in from the kitchen. 'You can do anything you want if it will help find our son.'

Carter watched as Lauren took several paces towards Toby and looked like she was about to hit him. Toby recoiled from her. 'Just fucking do it, Toby. Just do it without thinking about yourself for one fucking moment,' she screamed in his face. 'You lost our son. You lost our son . . .'

Jeanie stepped towards her and led her away. Toby got up and left the room, and when he came back he handed a set of keys to Carter.

'The solicitor gave me a set.'

Carter felt his phone vibrate and excused himself. 'Willis, can you cover for me a min? I need to make a call.'

Carter left the door on the latch as he stepped outside onto the landing and stood looking over the view of the building site around them; the lift shaft was at his back.

'Cabrina?'

'Dan, I've been trying to get you for hours.'

'I'm sorry, love – we're in the middle of that missing-child case in Greenwich.'

'Oh yes, I know. I heard about it on the radio.'

'What is it? What's wrong?'

'We've had a break-in. I'm not sure what they've taken. It looks a mess here.'

'Shit. Are you and Archie okay?'

'Yes, we're okay, it happened when I was at work and he was at nursery. Sorry to bother you – I know how big this case is but I don't know whether to get the locks changed?'

'How did they get in?'

'Through the flat downstairs. They busted her window and then climbed up and through our landing window.'

'Bastards.'

'Yeah . . . horrible. I feel so angry.'

'Look, I'm going to be late again tonight. I might just catch a bit of sleep here.'

'Please, Dan, come home. You didn't come home last night.'

'I'm sorry, love – this is a crucial time. We're all working flat out. Are you taking Archie to your mum's?'

'Yes.'

'I'll get Robbo on to it and send a couple of Archway officers round to see what needs to be done.'

'There's nothing they can do.'

'We have to add our name to the statistics, love, otherwise we can't claim on the insurance. I'll get them to dust for fingerprints.' There was a silence at the other end of the phone. He heard Cabrina sigh. 'Can you manage?'

'Of course I can manage, but that's not the point, is it?'

'Sorry, honey, I really am but . . .'

'Yes, I'm sorry too. I'm just so upset and I need you. I know you can't spare anyone to help. It's nothing. I'll sort it. I'll get some help in to run the shop while I clear it up.'

'That's why I love you, Cabrina. Come hell or high water, I'm going to be sneaking into your bed tonight so you'd better warn your mum to put her earplugs in.'

Cabrina laughed.

'The key will be under the mat and I'll make sure Archie sleeps in with Mum and Dad. Love you, babe.'

'I'll see you later, honey.'

Jeanie appeared at the door to the flat and mouthed, 'Can I have a word?' Carter nodded. He watched Jeanie walk across towards him. She smiled and looked away. The awkwardness between them always caught her off guard. He knew it. Sometimes she was able to forget it, ignore it. Other times she looked like it was going to affect their working relationship but it hadn't, because, in the end, she went home to Pete and he went home to Cabrina. He looked away. He didn't want her to think he was still smarting.

'Okay?' he asked, as she got within hearing distance. She stood by the landing window and gave a small shake of the head. 'What's bothering you?'

'He can't sit still for a minute. He's forever jumping up and going off into the next room. He makes calls that he'd prefer I didn't hear.'

'Shall we bug his phone?'

'Yes, we have to. Willis told me that Lauren confessed her and Toby's relationship is not the best. He definitely didn't marry her to carry on his name.'

'Why did he, do you think?'

'Maybe he was trying his hardest to fit into a certain-shaped mould. Maybe he knows he can't but he's too frightened to face it.'

'Gay, you mean?'

'Gay, bisexual, apparently. Lauren suspects there could be someone else. He's had relationships with men in the past.'

'Most likely to be someone at work, if he doesn't meet people online, that is. What are your thoughts about the missing suit found in the bin?' asked Carter.

'I've been thinking about what kind of person would risk changing the child rather than bundle him into a car and get away fast?'

'They obviously didn't have a car within a few feet,' answered Jeanie.

'But, they threw the suit in a bin nearby the scene. Didn't they realize we would find it?' Carter said.

'I don't think they could have,' Jeanie answered.

'Which means this is an amateur or a first-timer, do you think?' asked Carter. 'The established paedophile network is too slick to make a mistake like that.'

'But if it was opportune?' asked Jeanie.

'Can't have been, can it? Because they had a change of clothes ready and they had an exit planned.'

Back inside the flat, Willis was waiting for Carter. 'Robbo's come up with some interesting stuff to show you on film.'

'Okay, good. I think we'll grab ourselves a respite and regroup.'

They said goodbye to Toby, Lauren and Jeanie and drove towards the centre of Greenwich. They parked outside the *Cutty Sark* museum. When they walked past it, it was winding down for the day and a young male assistant was cashing up at the desk.

Carter cocked his head towards the entrance.

'Let's just go and chat; see how his day has been.'

Willis smiled to herself as she followed. She knew Carter would have many 'off-piste' episodes, as he called them, on the way through an investigation.

They walked across and Carter knocked at the window and showed his badge. The young man looked nervously around but Carter's broad smile had opened many doors and the lad nodded and came forward to unlock.

They stepped inside. 'Getting brass monkeys out here.' Carter gave an exaggerated shiver. He showed his warrant card. Willis showed hers.

'Okay if we take up five minutes of your time?' Carter asked. The youth nodded cautiously. Carter wandered around the displays of London souvenirs and the plastic rats, the miniature glass bottles with tiny *Cutty Sark* models inside.

'Do people still buy all this stuff?'

The lad nodded.

'What's your name, mate?'

'Rex.'

'Well, Rex, you're obviously doing a grand job here. We're not here to cause you any trouble. I just need your help with something. Yesterday, about this time in the afternoon, a man walked past here pushing a buggy. He was probably walking quite slowly. Look, let me show you a photo.' Willis took out a folded sheet of paper, which had been given to the search officers, and opened it. It was a still from the CCTV cameras around the museum.

Rex studied it. 'He's the man whose kid was snatched?'

'Yes, that's him.'

'I was already asked if I saw him and I didn't.'

'Good – good that my officers are doing their job, but I just want to ask you about the other people you had in that afternoon. Was it busy?'

'It was. We seemed to have large groups of foreign tourists in. I think it must be cheap to come to London in February. We had a big party of Japanese, some schoolchildren from France. There was a Dutch tour.'

'What about UK accents? Did you hear any of those?'

'Yes, I did. Some people up from Cornwall.'

'Cornwall? You're sure, not Bristol, not Exeter?'

'I'm a hundred per cent sure. I go down there all the time. My mum's from there.'

They thanked Rex and walked towards the Cutty Sark pub on the corner. Willis ordered a Coke.

'A large white wine, please,' Carter ordered. 'Something decent.'

They picked up their drinks and went to a table. Willis placed a black, mock-crocodile, zip-up file on the table. Carter picked it up between finger and thumb, swinging it gingerly in the air.

'What's this?'

'I found it in the Incident Room. Just by my desk, no one claimed it.'

'Yeah – you know why, Eb? There's a bin at the end of your desk, isn't there? Have you sprayed it – sanitized it?'

She rolled her eyes and ignored Carter's scathing looks.

'It's fine. Must have been Jeanie's, I think.'

Carter was taking a drink and nearly choked. 'Don't, for Christ's sake, let Jeanie hear you say that. Jeanie has some taste – she would not be seen dead with a skanky file. Believe me. You ought to take a look at your habits. Good detectives are methodical types, not messy.' Carter reached for his hand sanitizer and squirted some in his hand, then left it on the table with a push in her direction. Willis looked at him incredulously. He held his hands up. 'I'm just saying, that's all. Don't pick things out of bins. You don't know where they've been.' He pushed the hand gel further towards her. She rolled her eyes but did it anyway.

'Can I get on with showing you what's been found?' she asked.

'Go for it.'

Willis opened her iPad.

'Here's the footage,' she said as she turned the screen towards him so he could see it run. Carter watched the last of the funeral-goers leaving the chapel. 'We've looked into nearly everyone on the list of people at the funeral,' Willis said as Carter watched the screen. 'We concentrated on the Cornwall lot because the politicians seemed unlikely. We found a few with records: kerb-crawling, GBH, a bit of robbery. But basically the village keeps itself very clean. One of the Cornish mourners was a retired police officer who used to run the station at Penhal until it closed. He still lives in the area. His name is Michael Raymonds. This is Raymonds again, here.' She pointed to the slick-haired man standing at the church entrance talking to Toby. Willis pulled out a service photo of Raymonds from the early 1990s.

'He hasn't changed his style much,' Carter remarked as he looked at it. 'Just that now he has to dye his hair black. That'll be me one day; probably not, think I'll go for the silver fox look instead.'

'If I rewind that, guv,' Willis did it as she said it,

'have a look at Toby's face when he first catches sight of Raymonds.'

'I see,' said Carter, looking at the screen. 'He can't take his eyes off him, and Raymonds is all smiles by the look of it. He even takes hold of Toby's hand.'

'Yeah, and really keeps hold of it,' said Willis. 'Almost looks to me like Toby's scared,' she added.

'What's Raymonds saying, can we make it out?' asked Carter.

'I got someone to lip-read. It starts with sympathies about Toby's loss but then he leans in and says something else; as he pulls back he says: "*Something something*, you need to start answering my calls."'

'Look at Toby's face – he is definitely trying to sort out something in his head,' said Carter.

'He doesn't answer but then Raymonds says: "*Something . . . something . . .* things need clarifying. A great offer . . ." That's where we lose it. It can't be lip-read when he's covering his mouth with his hand,' concluded Willis.

'Toby looks really flustered by it.' Carter sat back and took a drink.

'Yeah – I'm not sure if he hears it properly, or understands what it means – he doesn't make a verbal response. Lauren comes into shot. Raymonds has to pull away from Toby. Notice – Raymonds didn't talk to her.'

'It looks like she's busy placating Samuel, who's obviously had enough. Anyone else get close?'

'No, not that I can see.'

'Toby was scared, felt threatened. Let's get hold of Raymonds and talk to him.'

'Do you want me to ring him?' asked Willis.

'No, we'll drive down. We need a better view of what Jeremy Forbes-Wright was to the community anyway.' Carter studied the film again. He peered closely at the screen and paused it mid-frame, looking at the striking man. 'Do we know his connection to Jeremy Forbes-Wright?'

'No. We don't know that any of the people who came up from Cornwall are directly connected. Only the man who acts as the holiday letting agent. That's about as near as we can get. He's called Stokes.'

'And we need to re-examine all the CCTV footage of Toby on his walk; see if we can spot any of these mourners. The man at the museum said he heard Cornish accents yesterday. Any sign of our mysterious woman?'

'Not yet.'

'Any news about the snowflake suit?'

'No signs of blood. The bag it was found in is a Tesco carrier bag – there's a small Tesco Metro here on the other side of the park. Robbo's looking at the CCTV now.'

'So someone got him out of his outfit as fast as possible and into new clothes. Is there a public toilet in the park?' asked Carter.

'There are a few. We'll get the CCTV.'

'I suppose if they had a buggy waiting they could have changed him anywhere on the park, there's a lot of tree cover. We need officers asking questions of anyone who crosses the park and see if there is any mobile phone footage that could be useful.

What were the impressions from the statements taken from the staff at the Observatory?'

'That Toby is a loner. He is well thought of, quiet. Very keen on his work.'

'Does he socialize at all?'

'Yes, with his workmate Gareth Turnbill, who phoned him before the walk.'

Carter looked at his phone as it vibrated on silent on the table top. He raised his eyes to Willis as he answered the call.

'Yes, sir?'

'Can you talk?' Bowie asked.

'Go ahead.'

'I've had a call from the Home Secretary regarding Jeremy Forbes-Wright. I started asking questions about his reasons for deciding not to run for the Kent constituency and was warned off. The Home Secretary said that Jeremy had debts and liked a lavish lifestyle. He wasn't keen to relocate to Kent. He would have had to sell his house in Cornwall to do it. So he decided that wasn't an option and withdrew his candidacy a week before he killed himself.'

'Is this something to concern us?'

'The phone call came pretty quickly from the Home Secretary. Even so, it may have nothing to do with Samuel's disappearance. But he was a high-profile man, he had debts and people would assume he had money. Maybe someone's been a bit hasty in taking Samuel before the house in Cornwall is sold.'

'What do you want to do about it? Willis and I were thinking we should talk to the people who came up from Cornwall for the funeral. We could take a look at his house down there?'

'Absolutely. Get it searched, low-key. I don't want my arse roasted and I don't want a feeding-frenzy from the press.'

'Are you going to request more information from the Home Secretary?' asked Carter.

'Is the Pope a Catholic? We'll discuss later. What time can you get to me?'

'We have a couple of jobs to attend to, then I'll be over.'

'I'll be at the bar.' Bowie rang off.

Chapter 8

'Okay.' Carter drank up the last of his wine. 'We ready to pay a visit to Toby's workmate? We have a lot to get through this evening and the boss wants to see me.'

'Ready.' Willis did up her jacket, packed up her case and followed Carter outside onto the cobbled street.

'Christ . . .' Carter pulled up his collar and tucked his chin into his scarf as the bitter wind hit him. 'You need to get a proper coat for this weather, Eb. That thing you're wearing's seen better days.'

'It's fine, guv. Honestly.' She rolled her eyes.

They reached the black BMW. Willis got into the passenger seat and Carter started the engine. Before pulling out he picked out a tissue from the compartment between the seats. He handed it across to Willis, who hadn't managed to stop sniffing since they'd met. Carter knew there was no point in telling her she needed to wrap up warmer. She was a hardy animal. She might not think she felt the cold but her nose dripped like a tap.

'Thanks.' She took it and gave one wipe of the

nose, then stuffed the tissue into her pocket and sniffed loudly again. The gap in Ebony's social etiquette was too big to fill and yet it didn't amount to anything in real terms. She ate off her knife. She ate with her fingers. She piled ketchup on everything.

'There it is, guv.'

They pulled up across the street from the house and walked towards the neat front garden, split by a path running down the centre.

'This area costs a fortune to live in,' said Willis. 'You can see the new money along here.'

'Whereas this place looks like it's been a while since it saw a paintbrush. Looks like it has probably been in the family a long time. The front garden has that look of someone older's planting,' mused Carter.

'How do you know one plant from another?'

'My mum loves her garden. She's always working on colour schemes,' answered Carter. 'We took her to Chelsea Flower Show last year – she loved it. This wouldn't be risky enough for her. There's a lot of variegated shrubs, bark; this is a low-maintenance garden.'

Carter knocked on the door. A woman in her late sixties answered.

Carter showed his badge. 'Mrs Turnbill?' She nodded, looking from one officer to the other. 'I'm Detective Inspector Dan Carter, this is Detective Constable Willis. Is Gareth in? Could we have a word with him, please?'

'Gareth?'

'Yes, nothing to worry about, it's just about where he works.'

'It's closed today.'

'Yes, we know, we are part of the investigation surrounding it.' Carter smiled again. 'Gareth?' Willis took a step closer to the door to give Mrs Turnbill a hint.

'Yes, please, come in.' She stood out of the way for them to pass.

'Thank you.' Carter wiped his feet on the mat. 'Would you like us to take our shoes off?'

'God, no! We've got stone floors – your feet'll freeze. Follow me.'

Willis was almost disappointed – it must have been one of the rare times she'd ever managed to find matching socks. She lived in a shared house where they didn't have luxuries like a dishwasher or a washing machine. She took her laundry to the laundrette to be service-washed if she didn't have time to do it herself – she gave it to the woman who smiled a lot but didn't speak any English. She never seemed to get it all back. Somewhere out there were a lot of her socks.

Mrs Turnbill led them down towards a kitchen at the back of the house. The place hadn't been redecorated for at least fifty years. There were 1950s-style cabinets in the kitchen that were now very sought-after. But it hadn't been cleaned in a long time either. The only warmth was coming from an Aga.

'Mrs Turnbill – Gareth's your son, isn't he?'

'Yes. A late gift from God.' She was obviously used to being confused with his grandmother. She smiled. 'I'll just fetch him – he's outside. He spends nearly all his time in the shed.' She left them in the kitchen as she went out through an ancient conservatory, which was dark and cold; thin, pale spider plants hung down from overcrammed hanging baskets. She opened a door that was just out of sight. Willis took a look around the corner and came back to Carter.

'It's impossible to see outside,' she said. 'It's dark as a cow's guts out there. Funny time to go to the garden.'

'A man and his shed. One of those essential relationships.' Carter took a step nearer to the Aga. 'I'd love one of these.' He was just about to say something else when they heard voices and the sound of the conservatory door.

Gareth and his mother came back in. Gareth didn't make eye contact. He was a flush-faced young man, who looked more fifteen than nineteen. When he did look up it was with a nervous smile. He had a large flat section of hair down the centre of his head, sweeping down over his eyes. The sides of his head were shaven.

'Hello.' Carter smiled. 'You have a man shed out there, do you?'

Gareth looked embarrassed. 'I have my music collection.'

'Isn't it freezing out there?' Carter asked.

His mother laughed. 'Goodness me, not in the shed he's got. He's got one of those with a wood burner and goodness knows what else in it. It's warmer than this old house.' Carter could well believe it. Gareth smiled awkwardly.

'Gareth . . . we've been working out Toby Forbes-Wright's movements yesterday and, of course, you know what has happened to Toby and his son Samuel? We are pretty sure that you were the last person to see Samuel.'

'Oh.' He avoided looking at his mum. She was looking at him curiously. 'I gave a statement.'

'Yes, we appreciate it. We would like you to run through things again with us, if you don't mind?'

'Okay.'

Mrs Turnbill went to lean on the Aga facing her son, along with the detectives. Willis got out her notebook, checked and said, 'In your statement you said that Toby came to see you in the gift shop at . . .?'

'At four I looked at the clock to see how long it would be before I could shut up shop.'

'And did you see Samuel then?' asked Carter.

'Yes, I saw him; he was asleep.'

'He didn't wake up at all while you and Toby were talking?'

'No.' Gareth's hair flopped down over his eyes as he shook his head nonchalantly.

'And what did Toby and you talk about, do you remember?' asked Carter.

'We chatted about the new exhibit, about the photo gallery. Toby's amazing new photos. We talked about the new shop, the stuff on sale.'

'Toby and you worked together in the shop sometimes?'

'Yes, occasionally. Mainly, I work in the café or the shop. Toby maintains the exhibits. He does the technical things. He's the clever one,' Gareth giggled.

'What time did you finish yesterday?'

'At five thirty.'

'Dead on?'

'Yes. We close the Astronomy Centre at five. I just have to make sure it's all ready for the next day.'

'And when you left work where did you go?'

'I came straight home.'

Carter looked at Mrs Turnbill beside him. 'Mrs Turnbill, were you in then?'

'Yes, I must have been. I suffer from rheumatoid arthritis, I was here trying to keep warm upstairs.'

Carter turned to Gareth. 'I hear you and Toby get on very well? Is that right?'

'I suppose. Yes, we do.' Gareth blushed.

'You see each other outside work?'

'Sometimes.' He glanced towards his mother, who was staring and smiling.

'Have you met Toby, Mrs Turnbill?'

'Toby? Yes, I have. A lovely young man. I didn't know he had a child though.'

'And a wife,' added Carter.

'A wife?' Mrs Turnbill glanced at her son.

'Toby comes round here a lot, does he?' Carter asked.

'Once or twice a week.' Mrs Turnbill was starting to prickle. Carter could see her mind working, wondering what she should say and what she definitely shouldn't.

'When was the last time he came round?'

'Oh . . .' She shook her head as she thought. 'Not sure, really.' She turned to her son. 'When was it now?'

'A couple of days ago.'

'So, can you tell us, Gareth, when Toby was about

to leave yesterday, what were you doing? Where were you when he said goodbye?'

'I was standing behind the counter.'

'What did Toby say, do you remember?'

'He just said, "See you soon."'

'And then you saw him leave?'

'Yes.'

'Was it the first time you'd ever seen Samuel?'

'It may have been; I can't remember.'

'Did he say anything about the fact he was on his own with Samuel that day?'

'He said he'd been to his dad's funeral. He said he needed some fresh air. He wanted to get back to work but he was taking a few days off to sort out his father's things.'

'Did you ever meet Toby's father?' Gareth shook his head. 'Did Toby ever talk about him?' Gareth shrugged and left his shoulders in the air. 'What did he say?'

'Just that he didn't really know him. That he didn't feel right going through his father's things when he didn't know him.'

'Did you go with him to his father's flat?'

Gareth nodded. 'He asked me to.'

'Did you have to help Toby do anything there, look for anything while you were in the flat? What did you do in there?'

'I just waited for Toby. I looked through his dad's music collection. He had a lot of stuff I'd never heard of.'

'How long were you there with Toby?'

'About an hour or two.'

'And did Toby find what he was looking for?'

'I'm not sure he had anything in mind.'

'Did he leave with anything?'

'Just a backpack with a few things in it.'

'Okay, thanks, Gareth. You've been a lot of help. I don't expect we'll need to bother you again, but just in case you remember anything you think might help us . . .' He handed Gareth a card. 'And please don't leave the area for now.'

Carter and Willis walked across the street to the car. Willis opened her notebook on the way.

'Before you look at that,' Carter said, 'what do you think of young Gareth? Gay?' he suggested as he got into the driver's seat. Willis got in the car, closed the door and buckled up her belt. She didn't answer as she thought for a minute. He started up the engine and switched on the lights.

'I'm not sure if he is or just considering his options,' she said.

'What do you mean? You think he's bi?'

'I mean, I'm not sure if he's ever been in a physical relationship. He lives with a much older mum, looks like there's no dad. I think her son lives a sheltered life.'

'Toby took Gareth to help him deal with something intensely private, like his father's flat. He took him instead of his wife.'

'I think Toby has the same mental age as Gareth – a young nineteen,' said Willis.

'I could smell weed,' Carter said.

'Yeah, me too. But it could be the mum. She would be in a lot of pain with her illness.'

'Or it could be that's what's in his shed. Could be Gareth has a sideline going. I want to take a look at that shed. Let's get some officers up searching this street. No sign of a weed patch, we would have heard about it from the helicopters.'

'What's the plan for going down to Cornwall?'

Carter looked at his watch. 'It's already six. We'll head down early in the morning. Get down there by lunchtime.'

At six that evening, the wind was picking up at the Gordano services on the M5 on the outskirts of Bristol. It had been busy all day with a steady stream of lorries and cars. Viktor, one of the team of cleaners who were responsible for keeping the services in good shape, was finishing up in the men's toilets. He checked his watch. He still had two hours to go until the end of his shift. Next on his rota were the outside smoking areas, just in front of the entrance. He needed to check and empty the bins. Not many smokers had braved sitting out there with their coffees today. They had gone back to their cars instead.

As the sliding doors at the entrance opened he felt the gust of cold air almost bowl him backwards. It reminded him of his home in the Ukraine, except Viktor had never actually been there for more than a two-week holiday – he had been born in the UK. He stepped outside; litter was flying about. He went up onto the decked area – the chairs had been removed before they blew away. He checked the bin and bagged up the insides, left the bag to collect on his way back. First he needed to check the bin near the cashpoint just below him.

He walked back and down the steps towards the right-hand side of the car park and noticed how the ornamental hedges had become a magnet for every piece of flying litter.

As he neared the bin he saw something dangling from the conifer in a pot. He noticed it because it was shimmering as it turned in the wind. White snow-flakes on mittens on a string.

Chapter 9

By the time they got back to the Riverview apartment, Jeanie was just leaving for the evening. She stopped to talk with them on the stairs.

'How is it in there?' asked Carter.

'It's tense.' Jeanie kept her voice low. The stairwell was absolutely quiet, the lift silent. 'What are you going to do now?'

'We thought we'd ask Toby a few more questions.'

Jeanie didn't answer. She looked past Carter at Willis. 'Eb? What do you think?'

Willis turned back. 'I don't know. If we put too much pressure on Toby at this time he'll crack up. But . . .'

'Yes, I agree,' Carter interrupted. 'I just think – this is about his child, not him. This is not about what he should or shouldn't keep from his wife. I want to ask him about Gareth.'

'It's your shout,' said Jeanie. 'But I don't think it will serve any purpose to put them at each other's throats at this hellish time.'

'You're right, it's my shout.' Carter took a step forward and passed Jeanie. 'All I care about is finding

Samuel. The child is my priority. I don't care if they end up divorced so long as I get him back safe and sound.'

'I heard about your burglary. Really sorry, Dan, is Cabrina dealing with it okay?' Jeanie asked as she took a step closer to him and waited for his eyes to focus and stay on hers. 'Are *you* okay?'

He smiled and gave her a hug.

'You know me – I'll be fine and Cabrina, well, she's decided it's a good excuse to redecorate.'

Jeanie left as Lauren answered the door; she looked exhausted. 'Come in,' she said wearily.

She nodded towards the lounge. Toby was sitting on the sofa staring at his laptop, headphones on. Carter threw a glance towards Willis and she went back to talk to Lauren.

'Lauren, can I help you source a takeaway for your tea?'

Lauren took a few seconds to grasp what Willis meant. 'No, it's okay, thanks. I'm sure I can rustle up some pasta if we're hungry.'

'You have to eat, you know?'

Lauren snatched up some bedsheets to fold.

'I know, I know, it all seems so normal, the only thing missing here is my two-year-old son. I don't want it to be normal.'

'I understand, but there is nothing you can do except do your best to stay sane and healthy and keep positive.'

Lauren smiled at Ebony and nodded as the detective took the other end of the sheet to help fold it.

Carter walked across the room behind Toby and

glanced down to see what he was looking at on his laptop. He was on Facebook. Carter walked around to the front and waved in his face. 'Facebook?'

Toby snatched the headphones from his head.

He looked caught out. 'I thought that might have been one of Gareth's playlists you were listening to?' Toby shook his head. 'Was that Gareth on Facebook?' Carter persisted. Toby didn't answer. 'It's just that we went to see him earlier this evening. He seems very fond of you. You're good mates?'

Toby blinked at Carter. 'I suppose you could say that.'

'We met his mum,' said Carter. 'Seems she didn't know you were married or had a kid.'

'Why should she?'

'Just wondered why you hadn't mentioned it?'

'It's my private life. I like to keep it separate.'

'Separate or secret?'

He shrugged. 'I just don't choose to share my private life with work colleagues, that's all.'

'Except Gareth – you took Gareth to your father's flat.'

'Well, he's a friend. He had the afternoon off; he suggested it.'

'Gareth suggested you have a look around your late father's flat?'

'Yes. He was free that afternoon.'

'What did you do there then, you and Gareth?'

'We didn't *do* anything. We just went inside and took a quick look around. It didn't feel right so I didn't want to stay there.'

'What didn't feel right?'

'I just wanted support, so I took Gareth.'

'What did you find? What were you hoping to find?'

'Nothing. Anything. Anything about my father. I don't know. I was just really anxious.'

'When was the last time you saw your father?'

'Three years ago. I bumped into him in the street. He tried to ignore me but I wanted to tell him I'd just got married and Lauren was expecting, so I made sure he had to stop. He already knew about the marriage – Lauren sent him an invite, which he declined, saying that he was busy. I didn't want him to come anyway. The whole conversation lasted about three minutes. He couldn't wait to get away. He was charming but cold and excused himself. He tried to contact me a couple of times after that – he said he wanted to see Samuel, meet Lauren. He wanted to talk about the past. I didn't answer. He didn't deserve a relationship with me or Samuel.'

'When was the last time he contacted you?'

'About a month ago.'

'What did he say?'

'He phoned me, said he really wanted to make amends. I told him to go and hang himself. I told him he'd caused so much damage to me I'd never let him do that to my family.'

'How did he take that?'

'He did his usual thing of starting off sounding like a perfectly reasonable person and then suddenly turning into a man who just didn't want to hear anyone else's side of anything. More than that, he didn't understand what made someone a human being. He just saw me as a wet little boy who couldn't face up to life. He hung up on me in the end.' Toby looked away as he wiped his eyes.

'It still affects you, even though you've never been close?'

'No.' He shrugged it off. 'I hated him,' Toby said, as he stood and went to the window to gaze at the apartment blocks on the bank opposite with their bright windows.

Carter watched Toby intently. Toby shook his head, bewildered. 'I thought I might find something to spark a memory at the flat. There was hardly anything personal. I could have been in anybody's place.'

'So you didn't take anything, you didn't empty his drawers?'

'There was a photo on the sideboard in the dining room of my mother holding me as a baby. I took that; then we left.'

'Do you have any contact with your mother?'

'No, not since she left when I was seven. She moved to Argentina, where she still lives. I got in touch with her in my twenties. She told me that she'd tried to see me many times but that my father had prevented it. We were becoming close when she became ill. She didn't come over for the wedding. She has full-blown Alzheimer's now.'

'Why did your parents split up in the first place, do you remember?'

'No. I remember the pain in my mother's eyes and her crying. I remember understanding that my mother was leaving me. I only know what relatives told me after that – they said she had caught my father with someone else. The implication was that he was a womanizer and a lover of swingers' parties. Apparently it was something he expected my mother to enjoy with him. I saw my father with many women when I was young. Looking back, they were probably prostitutes – I remember thinking of them like dolls. Must have been the make-up, I suppose. They didn't seem like real human beings to me.'

Toby moved away from the window. 'I need to lie down, if you don't mind?'

'Okay, Toby.' Toby's energy seemed to completely desert him.

Carter went to talk to Lauren.

'We're going to leave you now for the evening. Try and get some sleep. You don't have to sleep with the phone on – Jeanie will always come and tell you straight away if there's any news of any kind.'

Chapter 10

'Marble must be so easy to look after,' said Carter. 'Where the marble ends the hardwood begins.'

'It's a bit too bling,' said Willis.

'Yes – it's definitely flash ... Cabrina would love it,' Carter replied. 'It's a place made for partying: eight-foot dining table, a well-stocked bar.'

Carter and Willis stood on the wrap-around balcony on the sixteenth floor looking out over night-time London and getting a little buffeted by the arctic wind.

'I'd love to be stood here in summer. If I ever win two and a half million on the lottery, Eb, this is what I'll buy: gym, swimming pool, and valet parking. You even get your own sauna and plunge pool up here. There's even some fake lawn for the dog to shit on, for Christ's sake!'

'He didn't own this place though, did he, guv? You'd need someone to pick up the poop.'

'No, it's rented and, by the sounds of it, it was more than he could afford. But don't spoil it for me now, Eb – I'm enjoying the moment.'

'Guv, ever since I became your partner you've liked every house we've ever visited.'

'No I haven't. Only the ones that cost a million upwards.' He sighed and turned back from the view. 'Yeah, you're right, Eb, shatter my dreams, why don't you? Let's get inside and make it quick. I have to meet the boss after this and I've promised Cabrina I'll make it back before midnight tonight. We're camping at her mum's tonight and I need to go by the flat and salvage what I can, clothes-wise, for me to take tomorrow. Okay – sooner we're in, sooner we're out. If you look at the bedrooms and have a nosy, I'll start with the study.'

'It's tidy,' called Willis from one of the bedrooms, 'but it looks like someone's had a rummage. Drawers are left slightly open. The towel in the en-suite is used.'

'Well, we know the housekeeper came in here to clean while JFW went to stay in the hotel. So someone's messed things up since she was here.'

Willis returned from looking at the bedrooms.

'Nothing worth noting – different-sized condoms in his bedside drawers, that's all.'

'Not averse to experimenting, then. He must have wanted us to see that – he knew he was going to a hotel to top himself. He knew we would come here.'

'Definitely knew Toby would,' Willis said.

'So we have to imagine that he wanted us to find it exactly as it is now.'

'One of the beds looks like it's been made in a hurry, slept in – or on.' Willis looked around at all the white marble and cream leather sofas. 'It's beautiful but much too flash, tasteless. I can't imaging coming home on my own and feeling cosy.'

'No, not even with the dog waiting for you to come through the door.'

Carter sat down at the study desk and pulled out the first of a set of four drawers. He rummaged inside. 'Junk drawer, stapler, spare pens, that kind of thing.' He opened the next two drawers in succession. 'Correspondence, all recent. Mainly bills for caterers. He's clipped the months together. I suppose he got to claim for a fair bit. He must have entertained visiting bigwigs in here. These clips have come undone in this drawer, I think Toby's been looking through these.'

Willis came over to stand by Carter. 'He implied that he just wanted to get the odd souvenir,' she said as she peered into the fourth drawer with him.

'Now, he's made a mess in here. All these papers are just rammed back in.' Carter lifted the bundle of correspondence carefully out and handed it to Willis. 'Let's look at it on the dining table, we can spread out.'

'What are we looking for?'

'Anything with reference to Toby, Samuel, suicide? I don't know. You take half and get started.'

'There's nothing about Toby or the Cornish connection in my lot,' Willis said as she finished looking through it.

'Nor mine.'

'Where else, then? Are there any long-term storage places here in this flat? I mean, he must have had belongings that he'd always kept?'

'They may be in the Cornish house.'

'I get the feeling Toby and Gareth spent some time in here. The ruffled bed?' Willis wandered over to the

CD collection. 'They listened to music, watched the odd DVD? There are some gaps on the shelf here.' Willis tilted her head to look at the titles.

'Jeanie loves music, all kinds. She could sing something from all these albums,' said Willis, who often babysat Jeanie's little girl Chloe on a Saturday night and stayed over to spend Sundays at Jeanie's house –no one made a roast like Jeanie's husband Peter.

'That's for sure,' said Carter. 'Not like Cabrina who has '80s music on all of the time – drives me frigging mad. It's either that or she's watching reruns of *Friends*.'

Willis turned to look at Carter. He went into the kitchen and looked inside the fridge. 'It's as if Jeremy Forbes-Wright had just stepped out.' Carter stuck his head back out of the fridge. 'There's a half-drunk bottle of wine, a loaf of bread.' He opened the wine and smelled it and then he rummaged through the rest of the cupboards before returning to the lounge.

'Looks like they really did make themselves at home here,' he continued. 'They had a bite to eat, opened a bottle of wine. It's all within its sell-by date in there. Considering JFW died a month ago. Interesting what Toby has started revealing about his childhood.'

'Yes, I caught some of it as you were speaking to him. It sounds horrible.'

'You have a lot in common. I'm sure boarding schools are not that different from kids' homes.'

'Both dreading going home, I suppose,' said Willis. 'Maybe we should leave you here and I'll take

Jeanie down to Cornwall?' Carter and Willis locked eyes and he shook his head. 'Maybe not.'

Willis took a call from Robbo. She put him on speaker.

'A cleaner's found some mittens that match Samuel's at a services on the M5 heading south. They were in the car park, no sign of anything else.'

'We need the place shut down, Robbo. Order the dogs sent in; we need a fingertip search of the area. He may have been dumped in the surrounding countryside, so helicopters as well. It's a good lead. It's a relief to feel progress.'

Carter looked across at Willis.

She nodded. 'It narrows down the possible abduction route.'

'I agree. Now we're getting somewhere,' said Carter. 'Let me know the minute they find anything else, Robbo. Meanwhile, we need to trace the Cornish mourners on the way back and see if any stopped at the services.'

'I'm analysing the CCTV footage. I'll make this a priority; I'll work on it overnight. By the way, Malcolm Camber, the child abductor from Greenwich, was out of town when Samuel went missing. He has an alibi that checks out. We've checked out the others of interest and drawn a blank. We'll keep looking,' Robbo said as they finished the call.

'Okay, I've seen enough in here. Let's talk to the concierge on the way out,' Carter said as he prepared to leave.

They locked the flat up and took the lift down to the ground floor, past the waterfall walls and woodland sculptures in the reception area, to a semi-circular bevelled glass station lit from beneath like an Olympic torch.

'Hello, sir.' Carter re-read the name badge. *Tyler Brooks*.

The smart young man stood tall behind his desk.

'Can we just ask you a few questions about Mr Forbes-Wright?'

'Of course, sir.' Tyler already looked slightly nervous but with a bit of cockiness and excitement in the mix.

'How long have you worked here, Tyler?'

'About nine months.'

'And are you always in this apartment block?'

'Yes, sir.'

'Do you work shifts?'

'I work nights from seven thirty each evening until six in the morning.'

'Did you see a lot of Mr Forbes-Wright?'

'Yes, I saw him most evenings. He usually came in late.'

'It looks like he entertained a bit up there?'

'Yes, he did, quite often. I would say most nights he had company.'

'And these would be foreign dignitaries, other politicians, that kind of thing?'

Tyler looked at Willis and back to Carter. He looked embarrassed, amused.

'Sometimes.'

'But not always.'

'Mr Forbes-Wright liked company in the evenings – all sorts, if you know what I mean?'

'What kind are we talking about, Tyler? Don't worry, you can talk freely.'

'Escorts, sometimes more than one; men too.'

'You're sure that they were escorts?'

'Positive.'

'Did you ever talk with them?'

'Yeah, I talked to them. I knew their names because Mr Forbes-Wright had to leave their names at the desk so I could let them in when they got here without him. I still have a business card from one of his regulars.' Tyler took out his wallet and the card. 'I kept it just in case anyone else here ever needed some company.'

He gave it to Carter. It was a smart-looking ivory and gold with *Gentlemen's Services* written in fancy script. On the other side it had *Top Class Escorts*.

'When was the last time you saw Mr Forbes-Wright?'

'Just after Christmas.'

'How did he seem?'

'I don't know, he seemed down. But Christmas is a horrible time for lots of people, isn't it? It's lonely and he didn't seem to have any company.'

'No escorts?'

'No. It was all very quiet.'

'I tell you what, Tyler – you'll go far; can we hang on to this?' Carter held up the escort card. The concierge nodded. 'One more thing, have you let anyone else into the flat since he died?'

'The jacuzzi company needed access for maintenance. The caretaker's been in and out, but he has his own key. I had to let the window cleaner in. Mr

Forbes-Wright's son, Toby, and his friend also came. They didn't know the code for the door. I had to let them in. They had keys for the apartment.'

'They came just the once?'

'Oh no, they've been a few times now in the last two weeks, not always in the evening – I was talking to the day-time concierge and he's seen them here. They always stay for a few hours every time.'

Chapter 11

When they got outside, Carter rang Robbo.

'There have been a few people in the flat since JFW died. Toby and his mate, for starters, add to that the housekeeper, the jacuzzi man, the maintenance guy. Toby's been lying about how many times he went there. It seems like he and Gareth liked to hang out there a fair bit.'

'What did you find in there?'

'Nothing of interest. Surprisingly little, really. Toby had already been through the correspondence, or we presume it was Toby. We need to look at the CCTV to be sure. JFW looks like he couldn't curb his habits – he was partial to an escort or two, or eight. We have the number for one of the escorts that used to visit him – a woman called Louisa from Top Class Escorts.' Carter read out the number. 'The concierge says she was a regular.'

'We're going to get into tricky ground if we start investigating Jeremy Forbes-Wright's dirty secrets.'

'We've got Bowie on board. If there's one thing he hates, it's red tape. He'll want us to get access to anything we need. We need every angle on it we can get.

And, Robbo, it should take us about five and a half hours to get to Cornwall, plus an hour for the stop-over at the services, so we expect to get there at lunchtime tomorrow – we're leaving here at six. Can you dig up everything you have on the retired police sergeant Michael Raymonds for us to read on the way?'

'Do you want me to ring him and tell him you need to talk to him?'

'No, that's okay. We'll surprise him and the others from the funeral.'

'Will do. I've already spoken to a man who knew Raymonds. I'll email you across the transcript of the conversation now. You can see for yourself, he's a character. I'm guessing you saw the lip-reader transcript of the conversation with Toby Forbes-Wright?'

'I saw it and, strangely enough, Toby can't seem to remember anything about it.'

'Maybe he didn't catch it,' said Robbo. 'He looked spaced out to me. Are you headed back to look at your flat now, by the way? We did the best we could with it. Two officers went round and made it secure. We've opened a file on it, taken some prints. You need to make a list for your insurance.'

'Cabrina will do it tomorrow. There's no chance of me having a day off. Any match for fingerprints?'

'No, sorry. Bad timing, huh?'

'Is there ever a good time? I've got a meeting with the boss now.'

'Archway Tavern?'

'How did you guess? What about the mittens found at the services?' asked Carter.

'They're definitely Samuel's,' answered Robbo. 'There's no visible blood. We're running tests on the fibres found on them. It's lucky that it didn't rain on them overnight. They look in good condition.'

Carter finished the call. On the way to drop Willis back at her place, she read out the details Robbo had already sent on Raymonds.

'Nicknamed "the Sheriff". He was well thought of, kept local crime rates down. He was pretty "old school" in his approach by the looks of it. A couple of complaints on record for excessive use of force in restraining suspects. Charges dropped in all cases.'

'Personally speaking,' said Carter, 'that's whetted my appetite for getting up at five to head off to Cornwall in February. I'm looking forward to meeting him.'

He drove up Holloway Road and parked as near as he could get to the pub. He didn't feel enthusiastic. He checked his watch. He wished he'd made Chief Inspector Bowie agree to meet at Fletcher House, but Bowie had been desperate for a drink. True to form, Bowie was necking back a large Scotch when he found him at the bar. Carter ordered a glass of white wine and they moved to a table out of earshot of the few punters.

'Haven't we got anything else? The media are going to get wind of you down in Cornwall pretty quick,' Bowie said, shaking his head.

'No. It's been over twenty-four hours and we haven't found Samuel. We've had a thousand officers searching door to door, bin to bin, searching non-stop. He isn't here. Whoever took him left Greenwich pretty quick. We have the mittens outside Bristol en route.'

'But to Cornwall?'

'There is no way he could be headed for a port – we have them all covered. He didn't get on the Eurostar. This is narrowing it down now for us. He is headed somewhere specific in the UK. If he just wanted to kill or abuse he would have done it and dumped the body,' replied Carter.

'Could still have done that.'

'Yes, but we have sniffer dogs all round the services. We have search teams looking for any more of Samuel's clothing, but so far it's just the mittens.'

'Why those?' asked Bowie.

'I don't know. The idea must have been to disguise his identity. But, why go to that trouble if you mean to kill him quickly? We know they can't leave the UK now,' said Carter.

'Except by private plane or boat,' Bowie cautioned.

'Granted, but we have small airfields alerted to any out of the ordinary activity or requests to use.'

'There are so many loose ends here, Carter. Did Jeremy Forbes-Wright have some sort of relationship with the village of Penhal? Seems unlikely.'

'Yes, I think there was a hint of a threat coming Toby's way at the funeral. It's like this village came up to remind Toby of some commitment he had to them. More a show of strength than sympathy. He seems unable to remember most of the funeral.'

'Even though he doesn't know them, and didn't know his father from Adam?' replied Bowie.

'Yes, even though,' answered Carter. 'And now we hear that Samuel seems to have been taken in that direction.'

'What's the truth about JFW's finances?' asked Bowie.

'We've got access to all his bank statements. Basically, he was broke. All he had was this big house in Cornwall. He spent a fortune living the high life on a politician's wages.'

'What's the house in Cornwall worth?'

'Close to a million.'

'Why didn't he sell the house if he needed the money?' asked Bowie.

'That's the question, isn't it? I'm hoping to find that out,' said Carter. 'Did you hear specifics about him?'

Bowie nodded. 'Back in the day, when I infiltrated the paedophile ring that made money from supplying kids from care homes to prominent politicians – he was on the edge of that inner circle. It was never enough to open a case against him. Helping to bring down one part of the operation felt like a massive achievement at the time, ten years ago,' said Bowie. 'Just a shame that all we did was pick off the scab.' He picked up his drink and swirled the last of the Scotch round the glass. He smiled ruefully. 'Disappointing to have him top himself – he took the coward's way out.'

'Looks like it. DC Willis and I will drive down first thing tomorrow. If it leads nowhere, I'll be back soon as. The fact remains that several people travelled up from Cornwall to come to a funeral of a man that most of them should have despised – second-home owner and probably a posh paedophile,' said Carter.

'I doubt the reason has anything to do with the missing child,' said Bowie, visibly wilting from the whisky. 'More about country folk wanting a day out and maybe hoping the rich guy in the village would leave them something in his will. Willis is a good one to cut through the bullshit.'

'What about Willis? She passed her sergeant's exams over a year ago. Is it going to happen for her?'

'She'd stand a better chance if she went out into the sticks. She's going to have to wait a long time to get a promotion in an MIT team.'

'She has her whole career in the Met mapped out,' said Carter. 'She's already beginning to think she's failed because she hasn't been promoted to sergeant. If the force loses someone like Ebony they lose a precious resource. No one understands life like her. Willis is one of the best.' Carter breathed deeply. He suddenly felt the need to get home; the drink had begun to dull Bowie's senses. He wasn't looking forward to going to the flat, but he wanted to see the mess for himself; then he'd head over to Cabrina's parents' place before it got too late.

Bowie tapped the side of Carter's empty glass and raised an eyebrow with a nod towards the bar.

'No, sorry. I need to get going.'

'You're kidding me – the night is young.'

'Yeah, but I'm feeling old tonight. I've a lot to get right. Tomorrow it's a long drive and a lot waiting for us. I need all my wits.'

Carter realized that Bowie wasn't listening any more – his mind had wandered to a pretty brunette sitting at the bar on her own. Carter smiled to himself.

Time to go.

He reached his flat at ten thirty and let himself in. The inner door was still intact. Whoever had broken in had walked calmly out afterwards. Carter pushed the door open and stood for a few minutes to take it in. There was debris on the stairs. The window halfway on the landing was boarded up. The glass had been pushed into a pile. No way were Cabrina and Archie coming back to this, thought Carter. As he reached the first floor and the kitchen he stopped. The place was ransacked. Pictures were off walls, plants were tipped upside down. He didn't bother to go into the lounge; he could see the mess from where he was. His feet crunched on the stairs as he went up to the bedrooms. He stood in Archie's room and wanted to cry. Somehow, the defacing of his son's room meant so much. His rational side said to take it on the chin; his heart told him he wanted to kill whoever had done it. He went into his own bedroom and the mattress had been turned up and slashed from end to end. The wardrobe doors were open and his and Cabrina's clothes were out, all over the floor.

He picked up a bag and packed what he could see

hadn't been trodden on. He still had to go to Cornwall tomorrow. He had to leave Cabrina to deal with all this. She'd do it, of course, but it didn't make him feel any less like shit.

Chapter 12

Wednesday 5 February

The next morning Carter picked Willis up from outside her house at five forty-five and they drove in silence through London, where the refuse lorries were making their overnight collections and the market traders were getting set up for the day. A few bleary-eyed people were trying to get home after a heavy night out. Willis rested her head on the window and dozed while Carter enjoyed the peace and quiet to think. He didn't often get to drive through the sunrise. The few hours' sleep he'd spent with Cabrina had been enough to make him feel refreshed and looking forward to getting down the motorway. Somehow it felt right to him. He felt renewed with the hope and belief that, against all the odds, this one little boy was still alive.

After just over two hours they pulled into the car park at the Gordano services. Willis opened her eyes as they came to a stop. She wiped her mouth and stretched.

'Wake up, sleeping beauty, you were snoring like a pig,' Carter said as he switched off the engine.

'I wasn't, was I?' she replied, horrified.

'No, of course not – you did dribble, though, I looked over and you had it all down your chin.'

'Shit.' Willis wiped her face with her sleeve.

Carter laughed and she thumped him on the arm.

'Ow, watch it,' Carter muttered under his breath. They could see a member of the local CID waiting for them on the steps by the entrance. He recognized their car and gave a small lift of his hand rather than a wave.

'DC Trevor Burns: sir, ma'am.' He introduced himself as they reached him.

He led them inside the services, into the manager's office.

'Are the search teams still out?' asked Carter.

'Yes, we've got them going up alongside the roads in and out now. So far, they've found nothing else. We've reopened the lorry park.'

'Can we meet the man who found the mittens?' Carter asked.

'Yes, sir, he's waiting in the café area. Can I get you a coffee?' Burns asked.

'We'll get one to go in a minute, thanks.'

Willis followed Carter across the café area. The cleaner was sitting at a table, fiddling with a coffee mug.

'Viktor?' Carter asked as he read the name badge on his uniform.

'Yes, sir.' He stood.

'Can you show us exactly where you found the mittens?'

Viktor led them outside to the car park and then round to the cash machine.

'How often do you check this area?' asked Willis.

'I check it every two hours. I start my shift here at eight o'clock in the morning.'

'What time did you find the mittens?'

'At six in the evening. It was the first time I'd seen the mittens.'

'Do you think you would have noticed the mittens if they'd been there earlier?' asked Carter as Willis walked around the back of the cashpoint. The litter had gathered there and was stacking up in the cracks and crevices. A round plastic lid to a takeaway coffee spun and scuttled along the car park.

He shrugged. 'I don't think so. But it's possible – the wind was blowing so strong.'

'How long have you worked here?' asked Willis.

'Three months, ma'am.' Willis wrote it down.

'Okay, thanks. Detective Burns?' Carter walked away from the cleaner. 'We intend to carry on now towards Cornwall.'

'Yes, sir.'

Carter looked across at Willis as they were left alone. 'What do you think?'

'I think the person who has him is just an ordinary person. I mean, no one professional would have made these kind of mistakes. People who are used to abusing are masters at covering their tracks. This person is making clumsy mistakes. They may have taken money from the cashpoint. There's a camera on it. It was blowing a gale. We can't be sure when these were dropped unless forensics can tie something up for us.'

'Are you ready to go?' She nodded. Her eyes were still searching the car park.

'Okay, then, let's grab a drink. We still have another two and a half hours to go at least.'

They queued up for coffee and then headed back to the car. 'Have you had a look at the info on where we're headed?' Carter asked when they got back in, carefully prising the top off his coffee.

Willis took out her iPad and settled.

'"Penhal is located between the lively resort of Penhaligon and the affluent village of Rockyhead,"' she read as she showed him a photo of sand dunes and sparkling blue seas. 'It's on the Camel Estuary. Famous for golden sands, sailing, seafood and more than a few second homes.'

'I'm not surprised that Jeremy Forbes-Wright had a home there. I would if I could afford it.'

Willis hid a smile as she glanced his way and continued: 'The beach at Penhal is well known for surfing.'

'Anyone famous live there?'

'A couple of authors I've never heard of. But a lot of famous people holiday in the area.'

'How far is the Forbes-Wright house from the beach?'

Willis looked at the map. 'Five-minute walk?'

'Okay, I'm ready. Let's hit the road,' Carter said as he switched on the engine. 'We need to liaise with the local CID first in Penhaligon.'

After half an hour of silence Willis glanced across at Carter. 'You okay, guv?'

'Yeah, just thinking about the burglary.'

'It's not a nice thing to happen.'

'No, but it's life, hey?'

'Do you know what they took?'

'They took pretty much everything that mattered to me material-wise: all the expensive stuff like the music system, cameras, jewellery.' Willis looked at Carter's wrist. He was still sporting the chunky gold bracelet that he always wore. 'Yeah, luckily I didn't lose absolutely all my stuff. It's the personal things like photos and mementoes that you can't replace. They just trashed stuff that wasn't worth anything money-wise. Cabrina was up all night thinking of more things that must have been stolen. When she wasn't making a list, she was crying. They took Archie's christening gifts. That finished her off.'

'I'm sorry, guv, it's a horrible thing to happen.'

'What about you – has anyone ever burgled your house?'

'Ours? No. There'd be nothing to steal. I take my laptop to work every day and I don't have anything else. Tina has a telly in her room, and that's it.'

'They could use her bra as a swag bag. They'd get loads in there.'

'Dan Carter!'

'Just saying, that's all.'

'I don't think I have anything I would mind about losing,' Willis said, as she opened a packet of crisps and offered it to Carter. He declined. 'The things I treasure are all replaceable, like photos on my laptop. They're out in cyberspace – I can easily get them back.'

Willis rested her head and watched the countryside pass by outside.

She sat up at the sound of a message coming through on her iPad. She balanced it on her lap.

'It's Robbo,' she said. 'He's sent us through more information on the funeral-goers. He's broken it down for us into connections and family ties and included a map of where they live.'

'He's good.'

'He's the best.' She began to read from the screen. 'Seven people went up that day from Penhal. There's the Stokes family, they live on a farm about three miles from the beach,' she said as she brought up the map as well. 'There were three of them there: there's Martin, obviously.'

'That's the man who lets Jeremy's house?'

'Yes. Then there were his two children: his son Towan, who's thirty-three, and daughter Mawgan, who's twenty-seven.'

'Excuse me a minute, this is a farming family?'

'Yes, they also own the farm shop in the village.'

'So, what's he doing looking after JFW's house?'

'Not sure. Robbo says he's looked into that and there is no trace of a letting company or any tax files that match.'

'A private arrangement, then.'

'Seems like it.

'Who else?'

'Mary-Jane Trebethin and her son Jago.'

'And they are?'

'Mary-Jane, aged fifty-two, owns the dress shop in Penhal. She's divorced. Lived there for thirty years.

We don't have anything on her son Jago except that he's thirty-one.'

'Okay, so that's five down.'

'Raymonds, of course.'

'Six.'

'The last one is Raymonds' son, Marky.'

'Raymonds has a son, still living in the village?'

'Seems so. He owns the Surfshack – a shop on the beach. He's thirty-one, unmarried.'

'Does it seem strange to you that all these men are in their thirties and they still live near their mum and dad?'

'Not really. You do?'

'Yes, I suppose so, but London is a bit different from a tiny village in Cornwall. How do they make a good enough living?'

'Not everyone needs a lot to be happy.'

'We'll see.'

After an hour and a half on the motorway and another hour on the dual carriageway, they saw the first signs for Penhaligon.

Chapter 13

They followed the signs for Penhaligon town centre.

'I came here on a lads' weekend once,' said Carter. 'I could probably find the exact guesthouse we stayed in.' He leaned forward at the wheel as he scanned the streets. 'There it is.' He pointed out a blue and white house with a stripy awning and a pub bench and chairs outside. 'Atlantic Blue, that's it. What a shit-hole, but a lot of fun.'

'This place looks quite lively.'

'Yes, too lively on a Saturday night. Big problems with antisocial behaviour – drunken louts like me coming down from the city.'

'Second right now, guv.' Willis read out the instructions from her phone.

'I see it.' They pulled into the police station car park. 'This place looks original 1970s,' Carter said as he got out of the car.

'From the Met?' asked the desk sergeant.

'That's right. Major Investigation Team 17; we're expected by DS Pascoe, is he around?'

'Yes. Hello, I'm Pascoe. Nice to meet you.' A muscular-looking man in his late forties with a faint ginger stubble and a bald head that looked like it had taken a few knocks appeared from a door behind the counter, came round and shook both their hands. He had shovel-size hands and a nose that looked like it had been broken a few too many times.

'I've got us an office.' He led them down the corridor and through into a room at the end of the hall. 'Hope this will be okay. You can have whatever you need, just ask. If we've got it, you can have it. I started a helicopter search of the area. I expect you'll bring down more officers if the search intensifies?'

'If we shift the emphasis to here, this place will be crawling.' Carter looked around the office; it had space for ten people at least. 'This is great, thanks. How far is it from Penhal?'

'Can be forty minutes on a busy day.'

'Can we look at other options nearer, if this investigation gets bigger?'

'Of course, I have a place in mind in Penhal itself, just wasn't sure what you'd want. I had a look at the file, what you've got so far, it's a strange case; it's not the father, then?'

'We're not ruling Toby out, but there was something going on that day that was out of his control and that makes me think twice about jumping to conclusions.'

'The funeral, you mean?'

'Yes, and the obvious show of strength from the villagers of Penhal. Plus, one of them is trying to buy up Jeremy Forbes-Wright's holiday home. It looked like there was some pressure put on Toby at the funeral.'

'Did you ever come across Jeremy Forbes-Wright?' asked Willis as she began setting herself up on one of the computers.

'Not personally. I was transferred from Bristol last year,' Pascoe answered.

'Did you hear about an ex-police sergeant who still lives in Penhal?' Carter asked Pascoe as he made himself comfortable in one of the office chairs.

'Raymonds, right?'

'That's it. What can you tell us about him?'

'I can tell you that people consider him a legend around here. In his day he kept a tight hold on things. He looked after his own; villains who he considered worth saving were steered away from prosecution and into a rugby team or a job. He looked after his community and they loved him for it. You almost had to get his blessing before you could buy a house anywhere near the border with Penhal.'

'Do you think it's still like that?'

'I think it is.'

'Did you carry out a search of the property for us?'

'Yes, it was interesting but not interesting enough. No sign of any recent activity in there. I would say it had been a month since anyone had stepped inside there: mail on the mat, spiders' webs in the hallway. We did checks on electricity and gas usage and there was no increase in the last forty-eight hours. There is an alarm system installed there but it isn't working. Here are the keys.' He handed them across to Willis.

'Thanks. Raymonds and another man called Martin Stokes are trying to buy Jeremy

Forbes-Wright's house off the son Toby already; he even approached him at the funeral service,' said Willis.

'Doesn't surprise me. He's single-minded when it comes to Cornwall for the Cornish. I've had a look at the local interest for you. The Stokes family come top of the list. Martin Stokes is a shady character.'

'Why would Raymonds have anything to do with someone like that?'

'He's a cousin of Raymonds on his mother's side. He came to live in Penhal in the 1960s. Ever since then his presence has been growing. He owns a farm. It was a small affair when he bought it, now it's extended to take in the neighbour's land as well.

'Raymonds was questioned over corruption when Stokes was caught with a missing minor on his farm – turned out to be his cleaner's child, who was reported missing from Penhaligon. It was never explained how the boy came to be in a room at Stokes' farm. Charges were dropped and it was all glossed over.'

'So,' said Carter, 'you have to ask the question, why did Raymonds tolerate Jeremy Forbes-Wright all those years if he was such a hater of all second-home owners?'

'He would never do anything unless it was for the benefit of Penhal.'

'Raymonds is going to have to tolerate us and a lot more besides if this investigation ends up down here. He'll have a hard job shrugging us off when the search teams arrive in their hundreds.'

'Well, it's about time the old silverback got tested.' Pascoe grinned.

'If it does we'll need to set up a base in the village itself,' said Carter.

'We can get someone down there to set you up in the old station. It's the tourist office now but would be ideal to use. Ironically it was where Raymonds ruled,' said Pascoe.

'We'd better go and take a look at the residents of Penhal. Thanks for this,' Carter said as he shook Pascoe's hand.

'I'll be up in the helicopter again in a couple of hours,' said Pascoe. 'I'll send you video footage directly to your tablet. Any areas you're particularly interested in, let me know.'

'Is the coastguard alerted?'

'Yes. Fishermen will be helpful. They tend to find the floaters first. I've put all that in place.'

They said goodbye in the corridor and Willis and Carter left.

Willis read out the directions as they made their way to the coast and the road turned into winding lanes.

'When we come to a fork in the road we can choose to go left towards the shops and the beach or right towards the hotel where we're staying.'

'Try the beach, shall we? You said the house is near there?'

'Yes.' Willis opened her window. 'You can smell it. You can hear the sea.' She kept her window down. 'Can't you?' Carter nodded and smiled.

They followed the signs down to where the road levelled out at the entrance to the beach, pulled into a small car park and parked up to watch the waves.

From there they could look across to the parade of shops on the opposite side of the road from the start of the beach. The Stokes farm shop was on the far left, and Mary-Jane Trebethin's dress shop was towards the middle of the six shops. There was a gift shop and newsagent and a small grocer's on the end. On the same side as the car park and the Surfshack, at the other side of the beach entrance, was a café.

'I bet this place is really rammed in summer,' said Carter.

Willis leaned forward and looked out through the windscreen. 'Are those surfers out there?'

'Yes, come hell or high water. I suppose they're making the most of the storms on the other side of the Atlantic. It takes a day or two to reach us.'

'It must be freezing in there. It's February, for God's sake!'

'Yeah – you wouldn't catch me in there. They're a hardy bunch. Surfing takes over their lives. Can you get up Robbo's map on the screen so we can see whereabouts people live in relation to here?'

'Raymonds lives on the cliff side; there's beach side and cliff side in this village. We go back up to the crossroads.'

'It's best to start with him if we don't want to piss him off too much. We'll come back here after. Let's just go up and have a look at the Forbes-Wright house first. We'd better make sure we see Martin Stokes too; I want to know what the deal was with letting the house out, and see if he knows what Forbes-Wright was going to do with it long-term, considering it was his only asset. If we're talking ransom then a kidnapper would know about it.'

They left the car park and drove past the shops. As they passed the café, the road rose steeply and twisted its way between high hedges on both sides as it climbed away from the sea. To the left above the shops was an area of scrubland with yellow gorse and gnarled trees. Halfway up the hill and around a sharp left-hand bend the top of the house came into view and Carter pulled the car over into the gateway.

The house had three storeys and was brick-built Victorian style with Cornish slate roof and granite gateposts. It was half-obscured by pine trees that grew to the right and left of the drive. There was parking space for five or six cars at the front. 'Kellis House' was written on the gate.

'It's a beautiful building but it looks sort of stern – unwelcoming,' said Willis, staring at the austere building.

'Exactly. Where are the welcoming signs? I tell you, if I'd paid two grand for a week's holiday here in July, I'd be disappointed rocking up here at Kellis House.'

'The price goes up another five hundred in August.'

'You're kidding me? We could go to Disneyland for that!' He turned to her. 'How do you know when this house isn't advertised anywhere?'

'I talked to a local letting agent, pretended I was interested in a house that had five bedrooms. That's the going price for something this close to the beach. You could have somewhere like this in February for six hundred a week.'

'I'd rather have one of those bright and breezy

chalet-type things than this – it looks like the Munsters' house.'

'We can carry on up this road and circle back round to the cliff side of Penhal,' said Willis as Carter pulled out of the gateway.

'Okay. Let's go pay the Sheriff a visit.'

Chapter 14

Raymonds lived on a cul-de-sac of smart bungalows. A flag, white cross on a black background,
hung from a flagpole at the corner of the bungalow.
He was coming out of his garage as they parked up
on the street. He stopped to watch them approach
and then turned and locked up behind him. He had
the upright gait of an ex-military man; no pot-belly
for him. He eyed them suspiciously, stood square
on to them.

Carter pushed open the black wrought-iron gate
and headed up the tarmacked drive towards the
watching Raymonds.

Raymonds finished scrutinizing Willis and then
settled on Carter.

'Can we have a word?' Carter asked as they showed
their warrant cards. 'This is Detective Willis. I'm
Detective Carter. Can we come in?'

Raymonds nodded; he waited for them to reach
the front door then he walked in before them. They
stepped into a pristine hallway; a plastic floor runner
covered a beige shagpile carpet. There were small,
tourist-style paintings of Penhal along the walls.

Straight in front of them there was a cuckoo clock on the wall.

'Eileen?' Raymonds called out towards the kitchen. 'There's people here, we're going in the parlour.'

His wife came out of a kitchen at the end of the hall, wiping her hands on a tea towel. She nodded. Her eyes stayed on Willis.

'Coffee? Tea?' asked Raymonds.

Willis shook her head, Carter nodded. 'Love a cup of tea, please, no sugar.' Eileen turned back into the kitchen.

'In here.' Raymonds held a glass-fronted door open. The place had collections of holiday souvenirs. On the wall was the painting of a raven-haired Spanish beauty. She had a flower in her hair, which fell down over her naked shoulder; a promise on her full red lips. There was a glass cabinet with knick-knacks from abroad. Willis ran her eyes over the shelves and saw a miniature *Cutty Sark* in a glass bottle on the third shelf down. When she looked back, Raymonds was staring at her.

'Sit down.' He pointed towards the two-seater salmon-pink sofa. 'Where are you from, Plymouth?' He sat in the armchair opposite them. A small glass coffee table with a driftwood base was between them.

'We're from London.' Carter didn't doubt that he knew they'd come from there.

He nodded, his face stony, waxy. 'The Met, huh?'

'We're part of the Major Investigation Team.'

'Really? What are you doing all the way down here?'

'Jeremy Forbes-Wright?'

'Yes?'

'You went to his funeral?'

'I did.' Raymonds sat stiffly, his hands resting on the arms of the chair, as if he were on a throne.

'You and several others from this area?'

'Yes, that's correct.' He shook his head and smiled. 'What of it?'

Eileen knocked and entered carrying a tray; her hands were shaking. Raymonds got up and took the tray from her. He set it down and she left. He nodded to Carter to help himself. His tea was in the best china.

'You're a long way from home,' he said to Carter, though his eyes settled on Willis. She didn't answer.

'Not really, it took us about five hours. Not a bad run.' Carter decided he really wasn't going to like Raymonds. He noticed Raymonds had beady black eyes, like a small animal waiting to rip your throat out.

'Did you drive up for the funeral or did you go on the train?'

'Oh, I thought about training it, but I decided to drive. We have to drive to a station from here anyway and it's such a tedious journey till you get to Exeter.'

'In your own car?'

'Yes, as it happens, I went in the Honda.' Raymonds' smirk was still there. 'I don't like to push my other car too hard – it's a classic. A Ford Cortina.'

'Nice. How many of you went up?'

'Six in all. There were a few cars.'

'When you left the church where did you go?' asked Carter. Raymonds looked like he had been expecting the question, waiting for it.

'I went into Greenwich. I wanted to see the *Cutty Sark*.' He smiled at Carter and then at Willis. 'I bet you know that, don't you? You have so many cameras up in London, don't you? Always spying on people.'

'Alone?' asked Willis.

'What do you mean, girly?'

'Were you alone in the car?'

'Now, let me see . . . I believe I gave a lift to a few others who wanted to look at the area.'

'Did Mrs Raymonds go with you?' Willis asked.

'God, no. She's never been out of Cornwall. Anyways – she's poorly; you can see by her shakes.'

'Who did you have in your car on the drive back to Cornwall?'

'I was on my own. Everyone else wanted to leave later and, as there was plenty of transport back – I just left.'

'Seems like an awful lot of effort to go to to pay your respects to a man who wasn't even a local MP or resident full-time here,' suggested Carter.

'No, I don't think it was – not really. He owned a house here.'

'Second home,' corrected Carter.

'I think you'll find this was the only house he actually owned.'

'When was the last time Jeremy Forbes-Wright stayed in his house?'

'I saw him at Christmas.'

'Did he come with anyone?'

'I'm not sure.'

'Did you know him well?'

'I knew him well enough to have a chat, to share a

drink when I saw him. He's been to dinner once or twice. But, he was a private man.'

'Private? He was a man who liked to party, wasn't he?'

Raymonds frowned.

Carter continued: 'You mean you didn't know? He brought escorts down here to Kellis House, he was a pretty debauched type by the sound of it. He must have brought some interesting guests with him.'

'I have no idea.'

'Did you never hear rumours about him down here? asked Willis.

'Pardon? I can't understand what you're saying.'

'Did you ever have reason to contact him when he was back in London?'

'Me?' Raymonds shook his head. 'No, of course not.'

'Any reason why someone might want to hurt him or his family?' asked Carter.

'None that I know.'

'When did you first get to know Mr Forbes-Wright?' asked Willis.

'Back in the mists of time.' Raymonds looked at Carter. 'What's your concerns?'

'Answer my question, please,' Willis interrupted. Raymonds glared coldly at her. 'How long had you known Mr Forbes-Wright?' she repeated.

'Well, girly, let me see. It'll be back twenty, actually twenty-five years. When he first bought that house – that was in the early '80s, I think.'

'You were the sergeant here then, weren't you?' Carter asked.

'I was. Over the years I saw him bring his son down.'

'Toby?'

'That's the one; he's hardly changed. He was a skinny little thing then – still is.'

'And what were your impressions of Jeremy?' asked Carter.

'Good bloke, you know, for a Londoner, he was a good sort. So that's why you're here?'

'We are here because, shortly after the funeral, Toby's two-year-old son Samuel was snatched from his buggy.'

'Get on? What the bloody hell is the world coming to? Poor little blighter.'

Carter didn't doubt for one minute that Raymonds knew. He must have seen the news. It was all over the press.

'Did you see the boy at the service?' Willis asked.

'I believe I did. The wife had him.'

'Lauren.' Willis was taking notes.

'I don't know her name.'

'You were seen talking to Toby after the service,' said Willis.

'So what of it? I was showing good manners, good breeding. Paying my respects.'

'We had a lip-reader analyse your words,' she added.

Raymonds' eyes lit with a cold delight at what she said and he burst out laughing.

'Well, what a clever thing. And what did they say I said?'

'Tell us,' said Carter, smiling, but getting increasingly

irritated. 'We'll see if there's a match. Detective Willis has it written in her notebook so we'll see which one of you gets it right.'

'Sorry – I'd love to sit here and play your games but I really don't remember exactly. I probably said sorry for your loss, sadly missed, hope to see you in Penhal in the house. That kind of thing.' He looked at Willis, who looked up from her notebook and stared back but didn't comment.

Raymonds fidgeted in his seat – riled for the first time.

Willis read from her notes: 'You said – "you need to start answering my calls".'

Carter made sure he wasn't the first to blink as he stared Raymonds out.

'What did you want to speak to him about, Mr Raymonds? What did you mean by that?'

'It followed on from an earlier conversation in the church.'

'Which was?'

'I forget now – about some decision on the house. We don't like to leave things empty. I just wanted to know if he wanted us to manage it till they had decided what to do. It may have sounded a little abrupt but it was meant well. The whole of Penhal village wishes the young family well. Of course, it's tragic news that their son has gone missing – tragic.'

'They've had an offer on the house from someone in the village. Any idea who that could be?'

'Yes, it's no secret, the offer is from myself and Martin Stokes.'

'Wow.' Carter feigned surprise. 'I need to get

transferred down here – you must have a hell of a pension?'

'I've been careful, that's all.' Raymonds looked irritated as he repositioned himself in the chair and inhaled deeply.

'But, why would you want it, you and your cousin?'

Raymonds didn't flinch. 'There's not many houses like that in the village. It's unique. Martin Stokes has been managing the property well up to now. No reason not to continue.'

'They haven't accepted your offer, have they?' Willis said as she finished writing in her notebook and looked up.

'They haven't. That's correct. There's still hope.'

'Can you find more cash?' Carter asked.

'Perhaps. Anything else you want to ask me, as I'm finding this line of questioning a bit impolite? My financial affairs are my own.'

Carter smiled and opened his palms in a gesture of apology. 'No offence meant.' He replaced his cup and saucer on the tray and sat forward on the edge of the sofa. 'We found his all-in-one suit in a bin in Greenwich but we found his mittens at a service station outside Bristol, on the M5. We're checking CCTV now.'

'You mean the Gordano services?'

'Yes, that's the one. A cleaner found Samuel's mittens in the car park.'

'They could have gone anywhere, south, east or west, from there then.'

'Yes, but Cornwall seems to be the place where there is a connection.'

Raymonds was watching Willis writing notes. She looked up at him, pen poised. 'What time did you get to the services on the way home from the funeral?'

'Eight-ish. I stopped to use the bathroom and I went in for some kind of a sandwich and a coffee.' Willis wrote it down. The sneer on Raymonds' face returned. 'You're going to ask me what kind of filling was in it in a minute, I expect?'

'No, it's okay.' She looked at him blankly. 'Did you get any money from the cashpoint there?'

'I believe I did. Twenty pounds to pay for my beverages. Maybe it was thirty, I forget.'

'What time was that?'

'It might have been seven thirty – I can't be sure.'

Raymonds sat back in the armchair. He looked at Carter.

'It's a bit far-fetched to pin all this on a few country folk coming up for a funeral in London.' He lost the smile a little; it was beginning to put a strain on the muscles around his mouth. His face was almost line-free: skin taut. His eyes turned cold and almost bored. 'You can think what you like, but this abduction has nothing to do with us. It's a ridiculous idea, made up just to keep you lot busy.'

'Okay, well, we appreciate your help,' Carter said. As he shifted his weight to the front of the sofa ready to stand Willis closed her notebook.

'You won't find any problem here,' Raymonds added.

'Maybe not, but he has to be somewhere. Tell me, if you were to hide a boy here,' Carter asked, 'where would you do it?'

'Dead?' Raymonds shrugged. 'Down a mineshaft, inside a badger sett. That little one would fit snug wherever you put him. You could weight him down and throw him off a boat, the fish would make short work of it. It wouldn't be too big to burn either.'

'What about alive?' asked Willis.

'If he's here you'll never find him. Just about every farm has a million places to hide a little lad, keep him sedated even, and wrap him warm, be right as rain for a while.'

'But not "right as rain" for ever.'

Raymonds looked at Carter with mockery in his eyes. 'He'd die eventually, of course. Look for someone in the family. It's nearly always the father, isn't it?'

They got back into the car in silence.

'What a piece of work.' Carter looked at Raymonds, who was standing on the front step watching them leave. 'We'll drive by the farm shop and see if Stokes is in there; if not, we'll head straight out to his farm to have a word. Thoughts, Willis?'

'On the Neanderthal man?' Willis strained to look up out of the corner of her window at the sound of a helicopter hovering above.

'Yes.'

'I'd say Raymonds is a complete control freak, even now,' answered Willis. 'No way has he retired from anything. What struck me is – even though he's a complete Cornish homeland fanatic – he says he liked the man with the second home from London.'

'Yeah – makes no sense to anyone,' Carter replied.

'I think he must have had some sort of relationship with JFW. Either business, or otherwise. Why didn't he just rejoice in the fact that it was one more second-home owner dead?'

'Because he feels – felt – a bond with either the house or the man,' said Willis. 'Could be the house – he is trying to buy it. If it's the man, we need to find out more. Doesn't make any sense either way. He doesn't care about Samuel at all, does he, guv?'

'He doesn't give a shit if the boy's alive or dead,' said Carter. 'What did he say? "The fish would make short work of it"? Who speaks like that about a missing child?'

'A man who thinks he can say whatever he likes.'

'Exactly. An arrogant git who needs taking down a peg or two. I'm going to make it my business to achieve that before we leave here, Eb.'

'Do you think Samuel is here?'

'You know what, after talking to Raymonds and being subjected to his narrow-minded bigotry, his abject disregard and almost hatred of anything outside his narrow little world, I think I do. Is that Pascoe?'

'Yes, guv.'

Chapter 15

Raymonds looked across the table at Eileen and picked up his spoon. He smashed the crown of his soft-boiled egg with the back of his spoon, picked up his knife, and sliced through the top half of the egg in one clean strike. He looked up at her and smiled watchfully.

'Is something the matter?' she asked, and he could see the mistrust in her eyes.

'Yes. These eggs are underdone. They need to be timed – it's not a haphazard thing, boiling an egg. It's not difficult, for Christ's sake.'

Eileen went to delicately open the top of her egg by carving but it was too soft – she crushed it as she held it. She scraped up the slimy egg that had splattered across the table. Raymonds paused mid-spoonful and watched her with disgust.

'You're putting me off my food.'

'Sorry.'

Raymonds sighed. If there were a way of bullying his wife out of behaving like a victim he would have found it by now. They finished their meal in silence. Raymonds picked up his plate, scraped the remainder in the bin, and stacked it away in the dishwasher.

'I'm going out.' She nodded but didn't answer. She went to look out at the back garden.

He followed her gaze. A pile of logs littering the pathway obstructed the usually neat and tidy pathways. 'I'll tidy that up when I get back,' he said.

'Don't you want me to put the logs into the store?' she asked. 'It might rain.'

'Don't touch anything. I'll be a couple of hours, it can wait till then. Don't let anyone in if those people come back.'

'The coloured girl?'

'Yes. She's a police officer from the Met. I always said no good would ever come of the Met. He's just as bad. They don't know how to conduct themselves properly. If they think they can come down here and lord it over everyone, they're much mistaken.'

'What did they want?'

'They want to find that missing boy, of course. What do you think they want?'

'Are you going to see Marky?'

'Why?'

'Just that he said he'd come and see me yesterday and he didn't. I'm worried that he's not opening the shop like he should. People are talking about it.'

'What, what – spit it out.'

'I don't know, I'm just worried about him, that's all. Can you have a word?'

Raymonds went into the hallway, picked up his keys from the hall table and went outside. He smiled as the cold air hit him, fresh from the Atlantic. He pressed the fob on his key ring and the garage door shuddered and then whirred open. His cars waited shiny, immaculate, sitting neatly in the double garage. At the back of the garage there was a wall of drying logs. He'd spent all morning stacking them neatly on top of one another, like a drystone wall. Each log had its place but now he'd been interrupted it could wait. His mind was on other things.

He heard the helicopter overhead and listened intently. His eyes went skyward and stayed as he clenched his fists, his body going rigid. His face had become so strained that it looked mask-like as his mouth set into a grimace and stayed. He waited until the helicopter had moved on and then he got into the car on the right – a 1970s Ford Cortina 1600 E in metallic grey. He had restored it himself. He called it the Silver Fox. He started the engine, slightly rough and throaty – it was a sports model in its time.

Raymonds sat there for a minute, waiting for the car to warm up, before easing out of the garage and down the driveway, then turning and taking the main road towards the village. He turned in the car park behind the Surfshack and took a look around for the detectives' car but it wasn't there. He parked up and got out, walking round the back of the Surfshack onto the main street, looking into the Surfshack as he passed. It was a large cabin-type shop with broad wooden steps that usually had surfboards strapped to the railings. In the summer, racks of wet suits were wheeled out for people to hire; suntanned girls and boys skipped up and down the sandy steps. Its windows were full of posters of bronzed surfers. Usually it made Raymonds feel good just to be near it, but not today.

He looked inside and saw Marky waxing down a surfboard. Raymonds walked up the steps and shut and locked the door behind him. Marky stopped waxing as he watched his father approach. He was trying to gauge his father's mood, but Raymonds had perfected the expressionless face. As he got close, and without warning, Raymonds raised his hand and whipped his open palm against the side of Marky's head so hard it knocked Marky off his stool and sent the surfboard crashing to the floor. Marky began crawling backwards like an upside-down insect trying to get away.

'I know what you've done.' He caught hold of him as Marky tried to get away. 'The whole village will suffer if you don't get rid of it. Those are police helicopters up in the sky now. The whole of the UK is watching us. You think you're going to come out of this, you and Jago? Think again. This has Jago written all over it and you just went along with it, didn't you? It's a stupid idea, stupidly executed.'

'I don't know what you're talking about.'

Raymonds took another swipe at Marky, who ducked.

'I fucking saw you at the motorway services after the funeral. Now the police are going to look at every angle of every CCTV camera trained on that services and they will see you. Get rid of it. You hear me?' Raymonds tightened his grip on his son's shirt and twisted it tightly around his neck until Marky began to gasp.

'Yes. Okay, get off me.'

'Dump it in the sea, weight it down. You fail me now and I will hand you in myself.'

Raymonds got back to his car and drove up past the shops and on to Kellis House. He stopped for a few minutes and wound his window down to get a better look; to listen to the rooks in the pines. He needed to regain his calm. He'd always loved the house. He loved all things solid and strong. Things that stood their ground, no matter what was thrown at them. This house, grey and mardy-faced, was like him. It would be here long after he was ashes in the wind above Penhal. Long after he was bone fragments floating on the Atlantic, or in the shifting sand that gathered in all the doorways in Penhal. That would be him. Not buried in the earth. He would be in every breath that the people of Penhal took. He would be all around. He'd be damned if a man from beyond the grave or anyone else'd break him now. They would all toe the line in the end and Jeremy Forbes-Wright would not have the last laugh.

He drove up to the brow of the hill and parked where he could look down on the caravans in the field below. There was a line of them at the top of the field. Only one was occupied. He could see the smoke rising from a fire at the back of it. He saw Misty the horse grazing nearby. He murmured to himself then scowled as he watched the occupant of the van, Kensa Cooper, come out and stand in the centre of the field. She was dressed in a dark sack-type dress with her arms wrapped in a shawl. He watched as she started slowly moving her feet and hips; she seemed to contemplate dancing. But instead, she opened out her arms and the blanket blew in the wind. She stood like a crow with wings open – being buffeted but holding strong. Above her, the seagulls were swirling and diving at one another. Misty began galloping around the perimeter of the field. *Christ*, Raymonds muttered to himself. *This whole village has gone mad*. He started the engine again and took the road to Penhaligon. He passed by the sign to Stokes' farm and almost turned but decided the detectives might be already there. Instead, he drove on, taking the narrow lane that led towards the cliffs, then parked above Garra headland and took his walking boots out from the back of the car. He headed towards an old tin mine that he could see above him on the craggy edge of the cliff. Its stack was still strong and tall; the engine house looked like a church, with its steeple sides and arched windows. It was had no roof or glass but stood stoically, facing the Atlantic storms. A reverence and history of men's toil. To his right, he spied the roof of Cam's cottage and saw Cam walking back to his house. Raymonds hadn't looked to see if Cam's café on the beach was closed – he would have to keep an eye on that. The village would fall apart if none of its shop owners could be bothered to open. He would call a meeting of the leaseholders and instil some little home truths into them all. No open shops, no lease. He walked up to the cliff edge and looked down to the mine shaft that was perched so precariously near to the edge of the cliff. Burrowed in the granite.

He stood and breathed in the air – the faintest smell of rotting came from below him to the side of the ruins. He looked about him and saw the remains of a sheep, its wool and bone, blackened flesh freeze-drying in the biting wind. It had fallen on the steep path and died above the entrance to the old mine shaft, where a metal grid was bolted over the hole in the granite. Its leg was caught between the metal and the rock, and twisted shards of bone jutted skywards.

The low sun lit Raymonds' face and set fire to the windows of the ruin. He looked at the waves breaking out in the ocean. The sea was white with spume. Holding tightly to the side of the cliff, he made his way down to the mine below. He passed the sheep and stood looking down through the metal grille covering the mine shaft. Far below, he saw a ripple as the light reflected on the water. He knelt down and examined the bolts. They gave as he twisted them. Pulling on his leather gloves, he knelt over the grille and tightened each of the bolts by hand. As he heard a helicopter returning overhead he walked smartly back up the cliff path and away from the ruins.

Chapter 16

Jeanie had spent the first half of the morning at Fletcher House. She was holding a copy of a tabloid in her hand as she approached the Forbes-Wrights' apartment at Riverview at eleven. The front page was plastered with the story of missing Samuel. The theory that it could have something to do with his grandfather was already making the most attractive headline and probably selling the most papers. Toby was painted as a Stephen Hawking character – brilliant but somehow crippled by his own limitations. Experts on Asperger's had come forward with quotes after someone had mentioned the word autistic. Toby was definitely still in the frame for a murderer, albeit a misunderstood one. Lauren was painted as a cougar who had ensnared one of the UK's brightest but most vulnerable. Outside the building she'd had to get past the press. They were being forced to stay behind a barrier that had been erected at the end of the apartment block. The river police had moved on a press boat that had been taking photos of their apartment with a telephoto lens.

'Bullshit,' Jeanie said aloud before she spoke into the intercom of the door of the Forbes-Wright flat and put the paper into her bag.

'Hello, Lauren – it's Jeanie.'

The door buzzed open and she took the stairs up to the third-floor apartment. As she got near the apartment door Lauren opened it.

'Any news?'

Jeanie shook her head. 'No, but I've just come from a meeting of all the departments involved and we are doing everything.'

Lauren turned to Toby. 'Toby?' He was standing at the far side of the room. The couple had become disconnected. They seemed to have no way of sharing their crisis. There were bags packed at the front door.

Jeanie looked at him.

He nodded and went to stare out of the window. As fidgety as Lauren seemed, Toby was the opposite. He seemed to have gone into shock and was barely breathing.

'Toby and I have agreed that we aren't helping one another. He has decided he can't bear to leave this flat. But I'm going to get out and look for Samuel.'

'I don't recommend it, Lauren. You need to show a united front.'

'I've made up my mind. I can't stay here with Toby. I'm sorry, but I can't cope with the breakdown of my marriage as well as the loss of my son.'

'Lauren, please let's sit down and talk about how we can help,' Jeanie suggested.

'I can't stand it here any more. If Toby won't leave, then I must. I'm going down to Cornwall. If that's where Carter and Willis have gone, then I'm going there too. My bag is packed. I'm going down to see if I can find my son there,' said Lauren.

'It is only one more line of enquiry. They may be back tomorrow,' Jeanie said reassuringly.

'I'd still rather not be here. I feel like I'm dying in this flat.'

'Shall we move you to a hotel near here?'

Lauren shook her head. 'It's up to you, of course,' said Jeanie, still looking at Toby, who didn't move. 'We will need to know where you are staying, though.'

'Yes – I'll stay at Toby's father's house in Penhal. I've made up my mind.' She walked past Jeanie and picked up the cage with the dog in it. Russell crouched low in his basket inside.

'Please, Lauren, wait while I talk to the boss.' Lauren set the dog back down with an irritable sigh and Jeanie stepped outside to phone Carter.

'Lauren wants to come down to Cornwall,' Jeanie said from the landing outside the flat. 'There's such a lot of tension here between her and Toby, she wants to be away from it all. I think they will have to be split up for now – they're not helping one another. If she had a relative nearby, I would suggest she go there, but she hasn't. She wants to go down to Penhal. She wants to stay in the house. Is that possible? She's determined.'

'It's possible,' Carter said. 'It's been searched. I suppose it won't hurt to split them up, especially if they're at one another's throats. We don't have time to nursemaid her. We will need to find a Family Liaison Officer for this area. Or do you want to come down?'

'I'm better off staying with Toby, I think. He knows me now. He's not as tough as Lauren. I'll be able to support him better.'

'Okay, but tell her she has to be escorted down: she can't drive herself. If you don't get anywhere with Toby today, I want him brought in for questioning,' Carter said. 'We can't afford any mistakes. He still isn't painting the whole picture for us. Now we know he's been lying about his trips to his dad's apartment with Gareth too.'

'I'll work on him the minute Lauren is gone, and, if I don't get the information we're looking for, I'll bring him in,' Jeanie promised.

When Jeanie went back into the lounge neither Lauren nor Toby had moved.

'It has been approved, Lauren. You can go to Cornwall in your car but with a police driver. I've phoned and that's being organized right now. He will be with us shortly.'

'I don't want an escort.'

'It's a long drive and you're tired, stressed. You could have an accident. Plus, we are in the middle of this investigation. We need to know where you are all the time. I'm sorry, but that's the way it has to be. Believe me, it's for the best; we need to protect you now.'

Jeanie looked at Toby. He was still staring out of the window. 'Toby, are you all right about Lauren going to Cornwall?' He nodded but he didn't turn.

'It's not up to Toby,' Lauren snapped. 'I can't stay

in this flat a moment longer and do nothing. The press is camped outside. We're prisoners here,' Lauren said as she walked out of the room.

Jeanie looked at Toby. 'Toby?' He nodded. 'I'll stay here with you.'

His hands were raised to the window as if to reach out for someone. He leaned towards the glass, with his forehead touching.

'Toby?' He didn't answer. Jeanie walked towards him. The sky was a swirl of grey cloud. 'Toby?' Jeanie's phone rang. The police driver had arrived to escort Lauren.

Lauren came back into the room. She picked up her keys. 'I saw a police car arrive outside; I presume that's for me? I'll phone you,' she said in Toby's direction.

'Lauren, Ebony will be down there to meet you and stay with you in the house. Okay?'

Lauren looked about to object but then nodded. A detective from the local police station walked up the stairs as Lauren was collecting the last of the things together at the door. He showed his badge.

'Mrs Forbes-Wright? I'll be driving you to Cornwall today.' He picked up the dog cage. 'I'll give you a hand to the car.'

Jeanie went out with Lauren to talk to her.

'Are you sure about this, Lauren?'

'Yes.'

Jeanie hugged her before returning inside. 'She'll be all right, Toby,' Jeanie told him as she came back into the lounge.

He shook his head slowly. 'All this. All this mess. It's all my fault.' He had retreated further into the sofa, doubled over as if in pain; he hugged his legs.

Jeanie sat next to him.

'You're doing all right, Toby. I know it's hard. It's so tough on you all.'

'But, it all comes back to me. My father left all this stuff for me to deal with. Did he hate me so much that he didn't want us to have any happiness from the minute he died?'

'I don't think he hated you, Toby.'

'Then you don't understand anything.'

'Tell me.'

He took a deep breath and stood. 'Do you mind if I go out?'

'No, of course not.'

'I want to walk up to the Observatory.'

'Come on, we'll get some fresh air.'

Toby nodded, his eyes on the floor as he got his coat and waited for Jeanie at the door. They walked down the stairs and through reception. As soon as they came in view of the press twenty feet away, the cameras started flashing. Toby turned his head away. Questions were shouted at him about his father, about Lauren and his relationship. A reporter asked if, given Toby's job, it was possible Samuel had been abducted by aliens. Jeanie glared at them all. They passed a police officer standing outside the entrance to the apartment block who was taking the full brunt of the bitter wind off the river.

'Make sure you step outside if someone approaches the building,' Jeanie said. 'Don't let anyone but residents in – with proof of residency. But get out of the wind, shelter in the foyer.'

'Yes, thank you, ma'am.'

Jeanie stopped to look back at the front door. When they were out of sight of the press and protected by an escort of five officers, Jeanie turned to ask, 'Toby, when you got back here and you saw the empty buggy, where did you think Samuel was? What was the first thought that came into your head?'

'I thought he had undone his belt and run off.'

'Has he ever done that before?'

'No, I don't think so.'

'Can he undo his own belt?'

'I don't know. But, maybe I didn't do it up properly?' He shook his head anxiously.

'Do you think you would have noticed before then that the belt wasn't done up?'

'Yes, I suppose so, but I just didn't understand where he could be. That was the only explanation I could think of.'

'The whole time you were out with him, he never got out of the buggy? You didn't have to take him to the toilet? You didn't have to make him walk a little way?'

'No. He was not himself. He was grizzling a lot and then he fell asleep. I was so relieved that he was not making a fuss any more that I just didn't check on him.'

Toby looked at Jeanie. She nodded, smiled

sympathetically. She knew very well that there wasn't a parent out there that wouldn't have understood.

'Listen, I have a little girl,' she said, 'and I understand the pressures. I know what it's like. I would have felt the same way – thank goodness she's fallen asleep, I can have a little browse in the shops, have a little peace.'

'Yes, I suppose so.'

'You don't have to feel guilty for feeling that, Toby. It's natural. It doesn't mean you're a bad parent.'

Toby looked over at Jeanie and shook his head.

'Lauren does all the parenting with Samuel. I'm still a novice.'

'Just because your dad wasn't a good parent, Toby, doesn't mean that you can't learn to be. Your wife tends to take the reins, I understand, but you love your son just as much as she does, I'm sure. Don't you? We're all human and when our mind's on a million things we take our eye off the ball just for a few seconds. Did you leave him outside a shop, even for a minute?'

'Yes,' Toby blurted, relieved to get it out. 'I left him when I was looking at the saxophone. The pop-up shop that has second-hand instruments.'

Jeanie's mind was working out the CCTV coverage. 'Let's walk, show me the shop.'

They crossed over the busy centre of Greenwich and headed towards the park and then took a side road that ran up and beside it.

'Is this it?' They stopped outside a small temporary shop with writing across the window.

'Yes, I left him here.'

Jeanie looked around. The place was about ten feet from the start of the park. It was a dark side street that would have been known only to those that already knew of its existence. There were no cameras on the street that she could see. They stepped inside.

'Hello.' Jeanie showed her badge. 'Mind if I ask you a few questions?'

The lad with the ginger dreadlocks and the piercings nodded, bemused; he was looking at Toby curiously.

'Go ahead.'

Jeanie turned and pointed to Toby.

'Do you remember seeing this man Monday afternoon?'

Ginger Dreadlocks nodded. 'You were after the sax, right?'

Toby nodded meekly.

'How long do you think he was in here?' asked Jeanie.

'About twenty minutes. We had a good chat about music, didn't we?'

Christ, thought Jeanie. *He completely forgot about Samuel.*

'While this gentlemen was in here, looking at the horn—'

'Sax – a horn is a different instrument,' corrected Ginger Dreadlocks.

'While this customer was in this shop, did you notice the buggy parked outside?'

'No, I can't say I did.'

'Not at all?'

'No. I was more interested in serving this customer; I never imagined he would have a buggy outside.' As he was talking the penny dropped and he realized who Toby was. 'Sorry, man.' He shook his head. 'I didn't realize.'

They left the shop and passed by the search going on around the area where the suit had been found.

'Toby, stay here, please.' Jeanie left him and walked across to the commander in charge of the search operation. She updated him, then rang Robbo.

'We have confirmation from Toby that he left the buggy unattended outside a pop-up music shop on a side street, just off the beginning of the park. It's about a five-minute walk from where the suit was found. I've updated the search parties. The assistant confirms he spent some time in the shop.'

'Okay,' Robbo said. 'I'll get two officers down there to interview the assistant and find out more. We'll get straight onto this and see if we can find any CCTV to back it up.'

Jeanie walked back over to Toby. She squeezed his arm and smiled, trying to ease his worried expression. She indicated that they should keep walking. They took the path up towards the Observatory.

'I have held everything up, haven't I?' Toby asked.

'I won't lie, Toby, we could have done with knowing this straight away.'

'I was just so worried about what Lauren would think of me, what everyone would think. I thought he would be found by now. I'm so sorry.'

'It is done, Toby, and you weren't responsible for

taking Samuel. We need to push forward now and you need to tell us everything you remember about this walk,' Jeanie said firmly.'This must be quite a climb with the buggy,' she said as they headed up the steep last section. Above them the Royal Observatory was still closed to the public. Toby stopped and looked at the 'closed' signs. He'd been quiet since they'd left the shop.

'When will it reopen?' he asked. 'We can't afford the loss of revenue.'

'I expect it will be a few days,' Jeanie answered, trying to hide her surprise at him asking.

'I'm sorry, it's just that I don't want everyone to suffer because of what's happened.'

'You really love this place, don't you?' Jeanie asked, smiling.

'Yes, I suppose I do.'

'Did Samuel like coming up here?'

'I never brought him up here before Monday.'

'Did he like it then?'

'I don't know. He was asleep.'

They passed through the entrance and Jeanie nodded at the police officer on duty. A group of officers were clearing a drain.

'We'll stop here, Toby,' said Jeanie.

'What are they doing?' asked Toby.

'Looking for any clues, anything that might have been dropped. We haven't found Samuel's hat and boots yet.'

Toby stood beneath the bright searchlight as the white-suited forensic team knelt beside the drain.

'Oh God. Do they think he's down there?'

'No, they're looking for something someone might have dropped by accident or on purpose. You mentioned Gareth, is he your friend here?'

Toby's head snapped round to look at Jeanie and then, just as quickly, he returned his stare to the forensic team.

'Gareth works here, that's all. We've become friends.'

'Do you see Gareth outside work?'

'Sometimes, we meet for a beer sometimes.'

'Has Gareth got a partner? Is he the same sort of age as you?'

'I don't think he does have a partner at the moment. He's a bit younger than me, I think.'

'So you're like his mentor.'

'I don't know about that.'

'He looks up to you, I expect?'

'Not really. We just get along.'

'Have a laugh?'

'Yes.'

'What about Lauren?'

'What do you mean?'

'Does she like Gareth?'

'I haven't bothered to introduce them. Lauren has her own social life. She works very hard, long hours. Luckily there is a crèche where she works. She isn't much of a socialite. She goes to the gym in her spare time.'

'But – do you think she'd like Gareth?'

'I can't see why not. I also can't see what this has to do with anything.'

He looked betrayed, as if Jeanie had led him down a path he shouldn't have taken.

'I would be bad at my job if I didn't ask questions, Toby, but I am on your side.' She smiled. Toby smiled guardedly back.

'What do you do together, you and Lauren, on a night out? Cinema? Meals out?'

'Yes, occasionally.'

'You used to play the saxophone, you said?'

'Yes. I love all sorts of music. Lauren listens to the current affairs programmes on the radio. I usually put my earphones in and put on one of my playlists.'

'If you don't mind me asking: you and Lauren seem quite different?'

'Yes, I suppose we are.'

'What made you think – she's the one for me?'

'I'm not sure really.'

'Come on – there must be one thing that comes straight into your mind when you think of when you realized you were in love with Lauren?'

'I suppose I saw security in her.'

'And Samuel?'

'I never wanted kids. I wanted us to have years of travelling, of having fun together. I thought there was so much we had to learn about one another and I was looking forward to shutting ourselves off from the rest of the world and just being us. But then Samuel came along – only now that this has happened do I realize how much I've grown to love him.'

'You will feel like it's your fault—'

'Lauren blames me completely and she's right to.'

Jeanie looked across at Toby. 'But, if someone was

determined to take Samuel, they would have found a way.'

'Not with Lauren, they wouldn't have. Lauren's the one with the balls. She'd kill anyone who tried to touch Samuel.'

Chapter 17

Carter and Willis watched the low circling helicopter above them as they waited to pull out of the layby. It flew away towards the cliffs. Movement in the side mirror caught Willis's eye; she reached across to stop Carter from pulling out. 'Guv, someone just crossed over the road behind us. They went through the gate opposite.'

'Man or woman?'

'I couldn't tell, they were quick.'

'Where does it lead?'

'There's a sign that says it leads to Garra Cove.' Willis looked at her map. 'It leads along the coastal path to the old mine.'

'Let's take a look.'

They left the car parked up behind the hedge in the layby and crossed the road. A narrow path had been cut through trees and shrubs left to grow wild and twisted in the Atlantic gales. After a few minutes the path opened up to scrubby heath and gorse bushes appeared as they neared the cliff edge. The path split in two as it descended towards the cove and carried on over the cliffs above it. They could hear the roar of the waves as the sea smashed into the cliff face below them, where a cavernous split in the rocks allowed water to funnel and rise. They felt spray from the waves. Below them the sea was a foaming cauldron.

'You want to take a look along the cliff top, Eb?' Carter battled against the noise. 'I'll take a look at the cove.'

Willis took off and had disappeared over the top of the grassy slope, strewn with granite boulders. He saw her buffeted by the wind as she hit the rise and disappeared over the other side.

Carter took a few steps towards the cliff edge and the start of the rocky steep descent towards the cove beneath. He looked back along the path and down towards the cliff edge and the rocky ledges below, where resilient shrubs clung to a minute amount of top soil, their bare roots woven into the rocks. As he stood watching, the sea grew and swelled and it roared angry and surged so high that he was knocked backwards with the energy and the spray. Just as he was finding his balance, he felt a huge push in his back. He felt his breath escape in a roar as his back banged against the hard rock and he was pushed over the edge.

Willis turned her head to listen again. She had heard a sound that she knew didn't belong. The wind and the waves were as loud as jets screaming overhead. Over the roar of the ocean she thought she heard someone shout.

Carter felt his stomach lurch as he fell, then he felt the water hit his face and heard the sharp crack of a branch. He didn't dare open his eyes for a few seconds. He stayed still, hardly daring to breathe, waiting to feel the pain hit him, waiting to die.

'Guv, give me your hand.'

Willis lay on her stomach and reached down to him. Carter looked up at her and then back down at his feet as he felt the bush give beneath him. He was sitting half on and half off a straggly shrub, which had taken root in the cliff, on a shelf less than a foot wide. He looked further down towards the churning ocean throwing up fifteen-foot waves to come within a few inches of his feet.

'Guv?'

He looked back up. Willis nodded at him as if to say – it's now or never.

He got onto one foot and knee and then he reached up for her hand.

'Go for it. I can take your weight,' said Willis.

Carter looked at her face. He knew if there was one person who could do it, it was Willis. He knew she would come over the cliff with him rather than let him go. He felt the sea crash into him as the waves grew higher, gathering momentum as the tide rose, and he knew he had no choice.

'You can do it, guv, climb over me.'

Carter looked above him at the cliff face between him and the edge. He looked back at the ocean, each set of waves higher than the last.

He nodded at Willis and she steeled herself. He grabbed hold of her hand and she tightened her fists around his wrists as a massive wave swelled up and covered them as it surged up and crashed over the cliff. He felt his knee give way and the bush crack and crumble beneath him.

He heard Willis yell but he couldn't see her past the spray as he felt her tighten her grip on him. He dug a foot into the cliff face and pushed hard with the foot on the ledge as he reached higher and caught Willis by the back of her jacket – for a few seconds he lost his footing and dangled in the air until a second wave surged and pushed him upwards, and he jammed his toes into the cliff face again and reached blindly up with his left hand and felt it grip as Willis hauled him up and over before the pull of the wave could take him back out to sea.

Carter scrabbled across as they crawled up and away from the cliff edge. He lay on his back and looked at the weight of cloud above him and the few breaks in it where the blue sky showed through.

'I'm getting too old for all this,' he laughed with relief.

Willis hadn't moved either but now she stood and walked back to look over the edge of the cliff where he'd fallen.

'How did it happen, guv?'

'I was pushed. A hundred per cent. Did you see anyone walking further on?' Carter asked, sitting up and brushing himself down.

'No, there was no one on the cliff path.'

'Whoever it was must have seen us in the woods. They could have doubled back.'

Carter took out his radio and called Pascoe.

'Have a look along the coastal path around Garra

for me. There seems to be some interest from the locals in this area.'

'Will do,' came the reply.

Willis was watching Carter closely. 'You didn't mention someone tried to kill you.'

Carter shook his head. 'Let's not confuse things.'

Willis and Carter stood watching the sunset as they saw the blinking of Pascoe's helicopter come into view and then disappear across the farmland.

He came on the radio again: 'I can see a man walking away from the old tin mine. Pretty sure that's Raymonds' car I saw parked at the old Simmons farm. There's one of the jeeps registered to the Stokes farm, that's on the lane near Garra Cove. What's bothering you? There are some deserted barns nearby, we have detected several small heat sources in there. Do you want me to send in a search team?'

'Yes,' said Carter, 'we'll meet them there. Nothing's bothering me, just interested.'

Carter and Willis walked back up to the road and Carter grabbed a towel from his travel bag in the back of the car. 'Have you got the location of this barn, Eb?'

'Got it, guv. It's part of the Stokes farm. We go past the main lane for the farm and take the next turning, along for half a mile then we should see the barns.'

'Okay, I see it.' Carter turned a sharp right and onto a farm track.

The search team had just arrived and they were getting the dogs out of the back of the van.

They pulled over and got out. Pascoe was waiting for them.

'We're stopping the aerial search overnight now,' he said. 'I thought I'd come and join you.'

'Are these barns in use?' asked Carter.

'No, these were from the original farm that belonged to Simmons.'

They opened up the barn doors. Bales of straw were stacked to the roof.

'How long has this been in here?' asked Carter. He waved the dust away from his face as the straw flew around them.

'God knows, years, I don't know. It's been forgotten, by the look of it.'

Willis walked inside and patted her hand against the bales of straw. 'It's still solid.'

'Yeah, it can last fifty years and longer if it's kept dry. They're building houses out of it now, aren't they? This floor is concrete,' Pascoe said as he gave a jump and landed with a solid thump. 'That's the way to keep it fresh. The system they used for stacking the bales at odds to one another gave it strength. It meant, when it was first created, someone could stand on the stack without it collapsing.'

Willis was working her way along the barn, looking at the bales.

The dogs were sniffing furiously at all the bales as they wagged their tails, springer-fashion.

'There's probably a whole host of creatures living in this barn, but no way could a child be hidden in it,' said Pascoe.

'What is it you saw from the helicopter?'

'Pockets of heat. Could be the straw itself, it ferments and gives off enormous heat when it gets mouldy. There's bound to be pockets of heat in this. It's dangerous. We'd better tell Stokes to sort it before it starts a fire. We'll call the dogs off and continue our search in the morning.'

Willis went outside with Carter and the dogs to look around the exterior.

'Will the dogs be able to work with all these farm smells?' Willis asked Pascoe.

'Yes, they're trained. Our only problem is that Samuel's clothes were changed and he's a small child. We don't have a lot of scent to go on.'

'What about the old mine, where you saw Raymonds?'

'That's just near here but there's nothing to see.'

'Can you get access to the mine?'

'We searched it already. All we found was a dead sheep.'

'Can you search it again?' asked Carter.

'No problem. Tomorrow, we won't be able to see now.'

They walked back to their car and Pascoe accompanied them.

'We're expecting Lauren Forbes-Wright down this evening,' said Carter. 'Have you got a Family Liaison Officer we could use?'

'I'll ask for one to come across from Truro. Might take me a day to organize. Is she going to stay at the house?'

'Yes, Detective Willis will stay with her. I'm going to keep to the plan and book into the hotel. If you're around later come and find me.'

'I don't drink – I try and avoid bars. But I'll be up

in the helicopter first thing and I'll be in touch then unless you need me before.'

'We're going to see Martin Stokes now, if you want to come?'

'I need to get the helicopter back and examine the footage tonight, so I'll say no for now. Ask him about the barn.'

'Will do.'

Jeanie phoned. Her voice came over the car radio.

'I had a breakthrough with Toby. Seems he left Samuel unattended for plenty long enough for someone to snatch him. I'm convinced he didn't intend for it to happen. He was just too scared to admit he'd messed up – their marriage is definitely shaky. Anyway, Lauren should be pretty near you now. She left at just after one.'

'Is there any subject I should stay away from?' asked Willis.

'No, just be yourself. Lauren likes you. I'd give her plenty to do. I've written up my report about my time with Toby today. Robbo's working on confirming his story. You can read the rest of it when you log in. Good luck down there, Eb. Dan, is there anything I can do to help Cabrina here?'

'Thanks, Jeanie. I'll give her a ring and see if she's okay. I'll get back to you.'

Jeanie rang off and Carter handed Willis his phone.

'Text Cabrina for me, Eb, and tell her I'll phone her as soon as I can. And tell her she can ring Robbo for anything she needs.'

Chapter 18

Carter and Willis headed back down the road and down the next turning left, signposted for Stokes' farm. After half a mile, past cottages on the left, fields to their right, there was a tin-clad roof over a barn straight ahead as they came to the end of the lane and pulled up onto a concrete standing. Behind that to the right was a farmhouse, Cornish stone, simple and with two storeys. There were outbuildings scattered to the left. Security lights came on. A collie dog came out barking as they got out of the car.

A man appeared, wiping his hands of oil on a cloth that didn't look clean. The smell of manure hit them. The ground was swimming in murky puddles of cows' urine and fresh cowpats. They were difficult to avoid in the semi-dark.

'What can I do you for?'

'Mr Stokes? Martin?'

'Yes.'

They showed their badges.

'Can we have a word? I believe you look after things at Kellis House, Jeremy Forbes-Wright's place?'

'I look after things when he's not there. Or I did – not sure what's happening now he's passed away. Bloody shame.'

'How did you come to be doing that for him?'

'Ah ... I don't know, really – he asked us to, I suppose.'

'Have you got many houses on your books that you look after for the owners?' Carter asked, looking around. 'It's just that you seem to have a lot to do here, plenty, I would have thought?'

'You're right there. I don't have any other houses. It was a favour, really. As you can see – I'm a farmer.'

'You also have the farm shop down in Penhal?' said Willis.

'Yes. Supposed to be run by my son Towan, but that's hit and miss these days.'

'How does it work if people want to stay at Kellis House?' asked Willis.

'Oh, they can't, not the general public, that is. They wouldn't contact me directly unless they've been before; they always used to come through Jeremy. Just his friends, that's all. If they know the place and want to come, they ring me and I clear it with Jeremy. I organize for one of the girls to go in and clean it and whatnot. That was what I was writing to the young couple about – I need to know – there are some long-standing, year-after-year bookings which I want to know if I can accept. 'Tis a bit tricky.'

'You get a fee for doing that?'

'Of course. He was always very grateful.'

'Who do you have booked in at this time of year?' asked Willis, ready with her pen and notebook.

Stokes looked shifty.

'Well, I'd need to go and look up their names and this is feeding time and we're settling the animals down for the night, so I'd appreciate it if you could wait for that answer.'

The sound of squealing and grunting came from beyond the wall to their right.

'Mawgan, Mawgan ... get that ruddy sow out of there when you're seeing to the piglets,' Stokes shouted. He turned back to them. 'Stupid mare, she'll get herself gored to pieces. Never go in there when a sow's got her young. She'll charge at you.'

'So, Mr Forbes-Wright never made any money from letting out the house?'

'Maybe, but I don't see how. He may have charged his friends on the times he was here with them. As I said, he didn't always rent it out.'

A woman came round from the other side of the wall, wiping her face with her sleeve. She stomped along, a tear in the top of her boot that flapped as she walked. She looked at Willis and stared hard at Carter. Stokes shouted at her as she passed: 'You knows you shouldn't go in there.' He shook his head, annoyed. 'Mawgan. Mawgan ... come here.'

She kept on walking towards the stable block at the back of the house.

'Next time she bites me, I'll slit her throat, put her in the freezer,' she said over her shoulder.

'We'd like a word please, Mawgan,' Carter called out.

She nodded as she turned away and kept walking.

'Let me see to my leg.'

'Well, get a move on,' Stokes shouted after her, receiving a glare in return. He laughed it off.

'She's a good girl on the farm. She can do anything a man can do and do it just as well.'

'You have a son too, don't you, Mr Stokes?'

'I have a son, yes, Towan. He mainly works here on this farm with Mawgan or he runs the shop.'

'Is this Mawgan's main job?' asked Willis.

'She does a few jobs. She cleans for folks. She works in the farm shop. She helps out here and there.'

'It's a busy farm, isn't it?' said Carter, looking around.

'We do a bit of everything here, we supply a couple of farm shops with the pork and beef. We have a couple of fields of veg. We have a hundred longhorn cattle – good for eating.'

'We saw some barns that belong to you, further up the road.'

'Those will be the old ones. I keep meaning to get around to emptying them.'

'It's dangerous, apparently, a fire risk?' said Willis.

'Hay, that is, not straw. Hay ferments. Anyway, those bales have been stacked up there for the last twenty years at least. If they were going to cause harm they'd have done so by now.'

Mawgan eyed them up suspiciously as she walked towards them. She had on an oil-skin green jacket, caked in mud. She was a strong-looking woman with a square jaw and piercing blue eyes. She had short red hair.

'Hi, Mawgan.' Carter introduced himself and

Willis to her. 'I expect you've heard that a little boy has gone missing, Jeremy Forbes-Wright's grandson, Samuel.'

'I heard.'

'We'd like to ask you about when you went up to Jeremy Forbes-Wright's funeral.' Stokes was watching her. 'How did you get there?' Willis asked.

'I caught the train up.'

'From here?'

'There's no station here. I went to Bristol on the Sunday and stayed there with friends. I caught the train up Monday morning.'

'Which station in Bristol did you go from?'

'I don't know – Bristol Temple Meads?'

'What time was your train?' Willis had her notebook open and she was writing down the answers to her questions.

'Uh . . . I had to get there by half eleven so it was about nine.'

'You're not sure?'

'No.'

'Where's your ticket?'

'I threw it away.'

'How did you pay for it?'

'Cash at the station.'

'How much was it?'

'I don't remember. About twenty pounds.'

'Did your brother go up by train?' asked Carter.

She glanced at her father, who was watching her closely.

'Towan went with me,' said Stokes, still glaring at Mawgan.

'After the funeral, what did you do?' Willis asked her.

'Went into Greenwich, had a look around. Walked along the Thames looking at places, really. Saw the Shard. Walked across a bridge or two. Don't ask me where – I'm not familiar with any of it.'

'On your own?'

'Yes.'

'What about Towan?'

'Towan took off to see some mate or other: don't ask me what he did. As for Dad here – I don't know where you went.' She looked at her dad with a hint of a smile.

'Oh, I just stayed near the car most of the day. I had a good look at the cemetery, then went for a coffee. I had a meal. I just stayed around the area until people were ready to go home. Towan came back with me and so did Mary-Jane Trebethin.'

'How did you get back, Mawgan?'

'I got a train back.'

'Why didn't you come back with the others?'

'I didn't feel like it.'

'Why did you go up for the funeral?' asked Willis.

She looked at her father and shrugged. 'I was told to, I suppose.'

'Well now, that's not strictly true,' her father interrupted, riled. He hadn't taken his eyes off Mawgan since she started talking. 'You said you wanted to go. You told me.' She didn't answer her father.

'Did you know Jeremy Forbes-Wright very well?' asked Willis.

'I knew him,' Mawgan answered. Her dad sighed and rolled his eyes as if everything she said was a lie.

'Did you like him?'

'Course she did – we all did,' Stokes interrupted again.

Mawgan looked down at her feet and pushed the mud with her toes. 'Not much.'

'Mawgan, for Christ's sake – I don't know why you're talking like this.'

'Why did you go, then?' Willis asked.

'The Sheriff said we all had to. It was a matter of respect, even if we didn't much like him.'

'Don't take any notice of her.' Stokes glared at her. 'It has nothing to do with like or dislike. We owed him respect – that's all.' Mawgan listened to her father but kept her eyes on the ground.

'Is it possible to speak to your son Towan, Mr Stokes?' asked Carter.

'He's here somewhere. Mawgan, go and fetch him.'

'I'm here.' A voice came from behind them.

'Where you been?' Stokes said angrily. 'Me and Mawgan have had to get the herd in to be checked this morning.'

Towan grinned at them as he walked past the detectives' car, looking inside it and nodding approvingly. He was dressed for a night out – clean jeans, clean blue checked shirt. He looked like his father. He was medium build and height with dark blond hair and a swagger in his bow-legged walk.

'Been out and about. I'm here now.' He came up and patted Stokes on the back hard. 'Doubt if you did any of it anyways – you lazy old bugger.' He slapped him again and Stokes laughed, embarrassed.

'Well, that's as may be, but you're needed now.'

'I'm going out.'

'Can we have a word first?' said Carter. 'Where were you an hour ago?'

'These are detectives from London, want to know about Monday, when we went up for the funeral,' Stokes explained to Towan.

'When they buried the great man?' Towan became mock-serious and crossed himself. 'I can't tell you much. I got hammered and had to be looked after by my lovely sis here.' He put his arm around her and kissed her cheek. He held on to her until she elbowed him hard in his ribs.

'Get off.' She looked angry, but her father laughed. Towan caught her again and drew her back to him. She tried to shake him off but he held her tightly, squashed against him, his arm around her.

'I wouldn't have looked after you, I'd have left you in the gutter,' she said.

'Oh well, it was someone anyway. Some maid.'

'Where have you been the last couple of hours?' asked Willis.

Towan looked at her and grinned. 'I've been taking care of a couple of commitments in Penhaligon. One's called Tracy and the other is Shannon.'

'One of the vehicles registered to this farm was seen parked up above Garra Cove an hour or so ago. Was that you?'

'Nope. Couldn't have been.'

'We'll need to contact your friends in Penhaligon. We need addresses, please,' said Willis, getting out her notebook ready.

'No problem.' He grinned again and took out his

phone, then read off the numbers and addresses from his contacts. Willis wrote them down.

'Did you come back with your dad the day of the funeral?' asked Carter.

'I don't know, did I?' He laughed and looked at Stokes as he put his phone back in his pocket.

'Yes, he bloody did. I had to listen to him snoring in the back for six hours.'

Towan turned to Mawgan and pressed his face against her cheek. 'And what about you, sis? Did you listen to my snoring?' He laughed.

Mawgan tipped forward and freed herself. She stepped quickly out of reach and gave Towan a kick in the back of the leg.

'You wait, missy. We're talking to you,' Stokes called after her as she started walking away towards the house.

'They know where I am if they want more,' she shouted back.

Chapter 19

'Is she allowed to just kill a pig?' Willis asked as they drove towards the nearby town of Penhaligon, thirty minutes away up the coast. Willis was checking on the price of rail tickets and times of trains from Bristol to London.

'No, you have to have a licence, be an abattoir or something like that. She was joking.'

'Didn't look like it. She seems pretty pissed off with life.'

'Yes. She looks like she works harder than any of them.'

'Why would she stay there?' asked Willis.

'Maybe she wants the farm when the old man goes? I didn't see a wife, did you?' asked Carter.

'Not unless the pigs have eaten her,' replied Willis.

Carter laughed. 'It was a bit like that there, wasn't it? Not a biscuit-tin photo of a farm.'

'Harsh reality, I suppose. It looks like she's well off with her costs of tickets.' Willis read from her screen, 'The cost would have been about forty pounds, not twenty, and she'd have had to leave well before nine to make it.'

'If we don't find any CCTV of her on the platforms

at that time, or we can't get her story verified, we'll bring her in for questioning,' said Carter. 'I'm not going to be given the run-around here. What did you think of Stokes?'

'Odd: a bully but also very creepy,' replied Willis. 'He had a habit of looking me over – a lot. Not something people usually do when you're there to talk about a case of an abducted child.'

'Fresh blood in the village,' Carter laughed. 'Human sacrifices and all that.' He laughed till a coughing fit stopped him. 'What about Towan?'

'He's like his dad – creepy.'

'I have the feeling Mawgan will be getting it in the neck now from Stokes. He seemed quite surprised to hear her talk like that. Towan's weird with his sister too – too touchy-feely,' agreed Carter.

'I feel sorry for Mawgan,' Willis said as they sat staring ahead at the sky. The sun was setting behind the Penhal headland and its lion's head silhouette was black against the wispy purple streaks of cloud and drifts of deep orange. The sky was ablaze. 'Looks like there's no mother on the scene.'

'She may have lived like this her whole life,' Carter said. 'Do you think you're similar?'

'If I lived like her,' Willis contemplated, 'I'd be tempted to kill more than the sow.'

'I know you would.' Carter grinned. 'So,' he resumed, 'they all had a kind of relationship going with Jeremy Forbes-Wright.'

'Stokes as a letting agent just doesn't work,' added Willis. 'Can you imagine him doing meet and greet with a bunch of foreign dignitaries?'

'It was a personal arrangement with JFW then?'

'Had to be. What's his angle?'

'I think it's the house again, after all, we know he's trying to buy it with Raymonds.'

'That house must have something very special about it.' Willis checked her phone. 'That's Lauren, she's ten minutes away. What do you want her driver to do?'

'Tell him we'll arrange a pick-up from Penhaligon police station and then ring Pascoe for me. The driver can stay the night in Penhaligon. I don't want to swamp the place with Met officers unless we have to. I'll drop you at the house. I'll go and book in at the hotel.'

'Guv, I need to file a report about the incident today. Someone tried to kill you.'

Carter pulled up at the gate and switched off the engine.

He nodded. 'I'll ring Robbo when I leave you.' Willis got her bag out of the boot.

'I've got the times of everything in my notebook.' Willis came round to talk to Carter at his window. 'We can't ignore it.'

'No, but I don't want it to get in the way of things. I don't want it to be a distraction. But you're right; we'll file a report on it. We'll start asking questions.'

Willis lingered at the driver's side. 'I think it's safe to say we're not wanted here.'

Carter shook his head and looked non-committal. 'Could have been a local loony, Eb, who knows?'

'Local loonies tend to hang around and laugh at you,' she smiled.

'Yeah, you're right. Talk to you later, Eb.'

Willis watched Carter drive away and pulled the gate back ready for Lauren. She phoned Pascoe. He told her to send the driver down towards the car park and he'd be picked up from there.

Willis stood on the driveway, waiting for her eyes to adjust to the darkness, listening to the sounds of the countryside. There were no houses visible, no streetlights. She could not see the shops below, or the common that lay behind the house and to the back of the shops. A high wall marked the edge of the property to her left. The evergreen pines all around were an effective screen. Now that the sun had set it was just her and the house that stood eerily quiet. She knew as soon as she saw the house that it reminded her of a children's home she had been in. And the darkness completed her memory of one home in particular – in Wales. There had been isolation there, the countryside all around. This was the same kind of darkness. She breathed in the smell of the sea to centre herself, to remind herself how far she'd come from those days.

She listened to the waves crashing on the beach below. A noise at the left side of the house drew her attention. The sound of something moving there. She strained to see what it was. As she took a few steps towards the sound and shone her phone torch into the area, the bin storage, a badger reared onto its hind legs and Willis took a step backwards. She looked around her for a stick or something to scare it off with, but headlights in the driveway were enough and it was gone.

The police driver pulled in and switched off the engine. Lauren got out of the car and seemed grateful to see Willis. Willis had a chat with the driver. He took out his bag from the car and said his goodbyes as he walked off, closing the gate behind him. Lauren stood looking at the house, her bags and the dog cage on the ground beside her.

'Do you want a hand to bring anything in?' Willis asked, as Lauren seemed hesitant.

No, it's okay, thanks, I can manage.' She looked apprehensive.

'It has already been searched,' Willis said, and instantly regretted the way it sounded.

Lauren nodded her understanding. She stood by her car and looked around her in a daze.

'Not how I imagined it. It's big – very grand, but not very pretty.'

'It's lovely in the day. Well, it's less stern anyway. You brought the dog?' Ebony was pleased to see Russell.

'Yeah, I felt sorry for him. He doesn't know what's going on any more than we do.'

Lauren clipped the lead on the dog's collar and lifted him out onto the driveway; he went for a wee. When he'd finished he started shivering.

'Let's get inside.' Willis picked up her bag and the dog cage and followed Lauren. A security light came on as they approached the house. There was a white veranda over the porch and a statue of Pan was perched just inside. Either side of the porch were two large bay windows with ornate brickwork patterns around the window, their own slate roofs.

Lauren unlocked the door. 'There's no alarm, I take it?' She turned to Willis.

'It's not working any more, according to Stokes.'

She walked on into the hallway. It had dark wooden panels on the walls, a herringbone red and green tile on the floor, and a large carved newel post at the bottom of the stairs.

'Do you want me to set Russell up in the kitchen?' asked Willis.

'Yes, please.'

Willis headed down the hallway to the kitchen, and put Russell's cage on the floor beside the long oak table that had benches either side. The place was a sturdy mix of original features and prettied-up plush interior design. She found his bowls in a bag and gave him some water, then she put the kettle on.

Lauren came into the kitchen. 'The wood-burner is all made up, ready to go. I've never used one, but I guess we can figure it out. It's strange being in this place. It feels like we're intruding. It's a pretty overbearing place.'

'I think we just need to get used to it. Let's have a look around,' said Willis. 'We'll light the wood-burner first.'

'It's in here.'

Lauren led the way into one of the three rooms at the front of the house. It had dark wood flooring and dark red walls with panels of flock wallpaper. Ornate mirrors and heavy brocade curtains made it dark.

'Do you think we're going to sit in here?'

'Probably not, but let's light it anyway.' Lauren

waited while Willis got the fire lit and then closed the wood-burner when it got going.

They walked around the lower floor, which had been given a makeover but still had a Victorian feel.

Willis was imagining what Carter would say once he saw the interior of Kellis House. It wouldn't matter that it wasn't a glass and chrome chalet. It would be added to his list of 'houses I have fallen in love with'. It would keep Cabrina in raptures.

'Shall we check out the bedrooms?' Lauren asked.

Russell followed them as they walked up the first flight of stairs and onto a landing that had a small library space, a sitting area and a desk. The bathroom was to the left – an enormous roll-top bath with gold feet and a walk-in wet room.

'Boy – he seems to have spent a lot of money on this place,' said Lauren as she stepped into the first of the bedrooms. It was all heavy dark wood and red velvet, silk curtains and gold swag. 'Not exactly country chic, is it?'

'He liked his bling – we saw that in the place in Canary Wharf,' answered Willis. 'He liked things to look and be expensive.'

'How strange,' Lauren said as she walked around the room looking at it all, bemused. 'That's just so different to Toby. Toby likes no clutter, no colour. No mess of any kind. This place looks like it would be a nightmare to clean. It has so many nooks and crannies.'

'At least these next two rooms are simply fur-nished,' said Willis as they looked at the other bedrooms on that landing, which were done out in more simple cottons and patchwork bedspreads. There was a pretty pattern of small rosebuds on the curtains and the furniture was white and French.

'This is much more like it,' Lauren said as she followed Willis into the second of the rooms on the landing. They went on up the stairs to what would have been the servants' quarters in the original house and found one massive suite.

'This must be his master's suite.' Lauren shook her head. 'Definitely over-the-top.'

Up the third flight of stairs was a room with a four-poster. It had a chesterfield in the corner. Its heavy brocade curtains were opulent purples and gold.

'Look at this,' Lauren called from the bathroom.

Willis joined her and stood speechless in the middle of a marble-clad wet room with a bath in the centre and a double sink.

'This isn't exactly a family-friendly house, is it? We haven't seen any cots or bunks,' said Lauren.

'No. I haven't seen the telly yet either,' said Willis.

She walked back through to the front of the house and the lounge on her right where the wood-burner was fully alight and throwing out some heat. Willis closed the curtains in the rooms and went to find Lauren.

Lauren was sitting at the kitchen table.

'Can I get you anything?' Willis asked as she put the kettle back on and looked in the cupboards.

'Yes, a glass of wine, please.'

'Okay.' Willis opened the cupboards looking for

any sign of a bottle. She was surprised to see that the cupboards were well stocked.

'There's some already in the fridge. I saw it there,' Lauren said. She was sitting with her head resting on her hands, watching Willis. Russell was doing a smelling tour of the kitchen.

'Are you calling Toby this evening?' asked Willis as she took the wine from the fridge door.

Lauren nodded.

Willis and Carter already knew about Jeanie's day with Toby and what she'd learned. Willis knew that it would be fair to tell Lauren but decided she just wasn't able to. She was hoping Toby would do it for her.

Willis found a corkscrew and made a mess of opening the bottle. After several attempts Lauren got up and took it off her.

'We only have one cold bottle so I better take over.' She smiled. 'You're not much of a wine connoisseur then?'

'No – more of a Coca-Cola expert. What do you want to do this evening?'

Willis found a glass for Lauren.

'I want to go through it all. I want to know what the police are working on. I want to know exactly what you think has happened. I want to be kept informed about everything.'

'Okay, Lauren. I'll do my best to tell you everything I know.'

Willis made herself a cup of tea, still thinking about what she should say and what she shouldn't. She was trying to think what Jeanie would do and decided she'd phone and ask her later. She texted Carter as she set Lauren's wine down and sat across the table from her. Lauren picked up a pad of paper and a pen.

'Where do you want to start?' Willis looked at the blank pad of paper.

'I want to start with Samuel.' She put Samuel's name in block capitals in the middle of the page – from him she drew a line and wrote 'Toby' and then her own name.

She stopped and looked at what she'd written and then up at Willis.

'Do you think he's still alive?' Willis didn't answer straight away.

'Honestly? I do, you know. Carter does and he's the best judge of these things. He has an instinct about people, about what motivates them. He thinks someone has Samuel for a purpose, which we will get to the bottom of. He thinks that they won't harm him, they will keep him until they achieve that purpose.'

'What purpose?'

'Something to do with money and this house; and to do with the man who owned it.'

Lauren breathed in through her nose deeply and sighed as she exhaled. Willis's answer seemed to have exhausted Lauren but the lines on her worried face eased slightly. She seemed calmer.

'I am sure he's out there somewhere,' Lauren said. 'He's calling for me somewhere. My heart is breaking but a part of me feels hope still.'

'What about Toby? Does he feel the same?'

'I don't know what Toby feels,' she answered

dismissively. 'Since it happened he has hardly answered one of my questions. He's shut up shop. Yes, I know he feels like it's his fault and Christ knows so do I. I mean, what kind of father is he? He told me he never wanted Samuel. I always knew that I got pregnant against his wishes. Ultimately it's just as much my fault as his. I forced Toby into a corner and he's tried his best to make himself fit into it but he can't. Somehow I don't care about him any more. I realize I only married him to have Samuel.'

She shook her head. 'No, that's just not true. I loved him, I fancied him. He was so sweet to me. We had a whirlwind romance and then that was it. A few months later I found I was pregnant, no surprise to me, big surprise for him. He tried to be happy but I knew he felt disappointed, more than that really. He felt I'd cheated him in a way. And I had.'

'How has he been recently?'

'What do you mean?'

'The build-up to his dad's funeral and afterwards? He said he didn't get on with his father, but still . . .'

'He's been upset, distracted. He's been nervous about everything but he didn't talk about specifics. I shouldn't have let him take Samuel out – his mind was elsewhere. He couldn't look after him properly. I shouldn't have trusted him. Christ!'

She stood abruptly.

'I can't stay inside a moment longer. Can we go for a look around the area – we might find something to help Samuel. Why aren't the police looking for him down here?'

'We are, I promise you. Both Carter and I have

been searching places today. The helicopter has been up. We are looking, I promise.'

Willis felt her phone buzz in her pocket – she got a text from Carter.

'Excuse me, Lauren.'

How is she?

Tense, she replied, *we're going out for a drive.*

I'll stay here and wait for locals to appear, Carter replied. *Watch yourself – don't go off-piste.*

Chapter 20

Ebony drove slowly on the unlit lanes. Russell settled down in the back of the car. Lauren took out a map she'd printed of the area.

'I wanted to see what's around – I need to get my bearings.'

'I understand.'

They drove down the winding lane towards Penhal and the beach. The shops were all dark, closed up for the night.

Willis drove past the shops and away from the beach, up and out of the village on the other side, past the bed-and-breakfasts and small guesthouses, bungalows perched on the side of the winding lane, until the stone walls and high hedges took over again and the stars were the only light to break up the darkness.

Lauren used the light on her phone to look at the map in her hand.

'It's hard to know where to start,' she said, exasperated.

Willis pulled over into a layby.

'Can I see?'

She handed the map across to Willis.

'We should start on this side tonight and work our way across section by section. Let's look at this part here, since we're this side, and then we can work across bit by bit. I think we should concentrate on places where there are buildings. There are lots of tiny farm tracks that we might have to be careful of. I don't want us to get stuck in the middle of nowhere. But these lanes are going to be easier to negotiate when we can see lights rather than in the day when we could hit a tractor. I think we should look at this section here.' She showed Lauren the map and ringed the area she had in mind. 'We are here. And I suggest we take the next right.'

Lauren nodded her agreement as she took the map back from Willis.

After more than an hour of driving Willis headed for home.

'We've made a good start, Lauren, don't get despondent. We'll continue tomorrow. Dan Carter will be coming over later this evening and the three of us will tackle it together. That is, unless you tell me you're not up to it, and I'd understand if that's so.'

'I'm up for anything that has a chance of finding my son,' she answered indignantly.

'Of course. I'm sorry.'

As they drove back through Penhal they passed the Surfshack. Willis looked at the clock on the dashboard. It was nine. She pulled over and parked outside.

'Stay in the car for me a minute, Lauren, while I take a look.'

It was too dark – she could no longer see the sea although she could still hear it pounding and crashing on the beach: it was a black menace beneath the clouded night sky. She shivered.

From somewhere at the back of the shop, a light was on. The glow from the window in the Surfshack was faint, but definite. Willis walked Russell around to the front of the building and up the steps. Inside the window were posters of bronzed surfers. Willis cupped her hands to see if she could make out movement, but she couldn't. She walked around to the side of the building that had the goods entrance and was elevated up a few steps from the hard-standing car park. As she made her way back around towards the front she saw a light come on in the shop. She doubled back and knocked on the glass. There was movement, then it stopped: froze. She leaned in to look through the glass. She looked towards the car where a man was now leaning in and talking to Lauren.

Willis called out, 'Can I help you, sir?'

He stood up and stepped back as he held his palms up. 'Just asking if this lady was waiting for my shop to open, that's all. No sweat, lady.'

'I'm Detective Constable Willis.' She showed her badge. 'And you are?'

'Marky Raymonds.'

The side door opened and another man stood looking at her in the doorway. He sniffed loudly as he wiped his nose with his sleeve.

'You're working late,' she said, holding her badge up for him to see. 'What's your name?'

'Jago. I'm just inspecting my new surfboard.' He

called over to the man by the car: 'Hey, Marky . . . you all finished in here? Can I lock up?'

'Yeah. Let's get a drink.'

'Jago what?' Willis held out her arm to stop him from going past her. He stopped, grinned and took an exaggerated step backwards.

'Jago Trebethin.' He gave a nod towards the car. 'Is that the woman who lost her son? We heard you were down. You went to the Stokes farm today, didn't you?'

Willis nodded. 'Have you got any information about the missing child?'

'No, I can't tell you anything except how sorry I am for the family.'

'I'll pass that on. Did you know Jeremy Forbes-Wright personally?' asked Willis.

'I met him a few times over the years. He was pretty hard to miss – big character.'

'You went up to the funeral on Monday, didn't you?'

'Yes I did, me and Marky there. We went up to pay our respects. Least we could do, such a great man, meant a lot to the villagers.'

'Right. So I've heard,' she said. 'Where are you working tomorrow in case I need to ask you some more questions?'

'I'll be at home tomorrow unless the surf is good, then you can catch me down here in the water.'

'Where do you live?'

'I'm sharing a place with Marky here, a cottage on the Stokes farm. You must have passed my place on the lane to the farm.'

'Were you there this afternoon?'

'No, I was down here helping my mum; she owns the shop across the road.'

'Were you anywhere near the Garra Cove area?'

He shook his head, looked perplexed. 'I know it; I go there often. It's a pretty beach away from the holidaymakers. Great for collecting mussels and good surfing sometimes. But I didn't go there today, who would? The surf was blown out there. The rocks are dangerous then. Look, we're just on the way across to the other side for a drink in the bar,' he said. 'If you're off duty later you can come and find us.'

'No thanks.'

Willis watched them walk away and disappear around the back of the Surfshack before she got in the car. She drove back to Kellis House and took Russell inside. The fire had gone out.

Willis picked up her bag. 'Which of the rooms do you want?' she asked Lauren.

'Shall we go next to each other in the two front-facing bedrooms?' Lauren replied.

'Yes, that's fine. I don't think either of them have an en-suite.'

'Are you going to bed now?'

'No, don't worry – just taking my bag up, that's all, I'll be straight back.'

'Shall I make us some dinner?' Lauren sounded like she wanted to and Willis was starving.

'Yes, if you don't mind – I'm always hungry. I'll come and chop stuff for you in ten.'

By the time Willis got back down the smell of onion and garlic was all round the house. 'Have I missed my chance?' Willis said as she looked inside the saucepan at the pasta sauce. 'I'm a lousy cook but a good chopper.'

'Just a quick pasta sauce,' Lauren said.

'Great.'

As Lauren stirred the sauce she sighed continually. Her shoulders rose and fell with her exaggerated breathing.

'You want me to do something for you, Lauren?'

'A glass of wine, please.'

Willis went and got the bottle from the fridge and poured Lauren one.

'Are you going to join me?'

'Not tonight, thanks.'

Willis knew what she was in for. She hoped that they would make it to the end of dinner before Lauren broke down.

Chapter 21

Carter sat at the bar with his bottle of beer and watched the bearded barman connect up the new barrel. There was an 'aboard deck' style about the bar that worked in summer but was cold-feeling in winter with albatross carvings and white sail cloth for curtains, ships' portholes along the front of the bar. There was a game of bridge going on. This time of year it could have done with a wood-burner because there was a cold draught from the long thin main part of the bar; at the back and up a few steps were two pool tables and a few gaming machines. The sound of one being played was a constant noise in the background. Carter was thinking how people must be seriously short of somewhere to go to have to come to this place every night. He was going off the idea of owning a second home.

Raymonds had come in at the other entrance to the bar some five minutes ago and was working his way up towards him. He hadn't missed Carter and looked amused by his presence. He walked in with what looked like his son and another man. The son was taller than his dad but had the same stretched skin over fine features. His face was smoothed out.

There was no music in the bar – just the sound of the pool table and the gambling machines. There was a hard-core set of local drinkers present.

'She let you off your leash?' The three men walked up to Carter's end of the bar. Raymonds stopped to talk to him while the other two walked past to have a look at the pool table. Carter did his best to look as if he didn't understand. 'Have you had a good day playing with your gadgets: helicopters, dogs and search teams?'

'It's been interesting. We even saw you out at the old mine.'

'Oh, I expect you'll see me a lot before you're through here. I like to keep a good eye on my flock.' He laughed.

Carter took in the interest in him that Raymonds had generated with his question. Carter smiled, looked back at his beer and took a drink from the bottle.

'You haven't found him yet then?' Raymonds said as he picked up his pint from the barman and moved along the bar next to Carter.

'Not yet.'

'Dead – no doubt about it. He'll be lying in some ditch somewhere. In some dark place that you can't see.'

'Possible, but this case isn't an easy one to call. I could do with a little help from you – ex-officer, you want to share some pearls of wisdom?'

'I'll share one for a start – the father, Toby, did you investigate him like I said?'

Carter gave a small shake of the head. 'We've got

nothing on him.' He ordered another beer and offered Raymonds one. He accepted and downed the half-pint he had in his glass. 'We can't establish a motive at the moment.'

'Some people don't need a motive. Just an opportunity and a bucket-load of malice – bound to come out some day. Busy London streets. A baby could easily go missing from a buggy. Especially if the father was just plain careless with it.'

'As I said, we don't have any idea.'

'Yet, something brings you down here.'

'It's just another line of enquiry.'

'Is his estate tidied up yet?'

Carter shook his head. 'It's a lengthy process, as you know. I'm not the one looking into it – I leave that to the clever ones in London. If it had anything to do with his estate you'd think someone would have waited until it was settled and there was money in the bank.'

'They have plenty of money – I'm sure the wife has a good job. It's a big expense living where they do.'

Carter took a swig of his beer.

'You went sightseeing the day of the funeral – did it include a tour of Toby's apartment?'

'I looked in the estate agents' windows when I walked around Greenwich – colossal amount of money for a tiny place. They've got the house now. They're sitting pretty – it's a million-pound property.' As Raymonds talked, Carter could see the hunger in his eyes.

'Perhaps, but they can't sell it yet. It's part of his estate. Nothing's settled yet. It can take a long time.'

'Yeah. Hey, Marky – come and say hello.' Raymonds pulled his son back as he was walking past. 'Detective Inspector Carter, this is my son Marky who owns the Surfshack down there on the beach, and this is Jago who does very little at the moment, except cause trouble.' He laughed.

Carter shook their hands.

'We met your partner just now down at the beach,' Jago said. He was well spoken with a groomed appearance about him, tailored shirt and jeans. He looked like he shopped in places that charged a hundred pounds for a polo shirt. He also looked like he worked out. He had too much gel in his hair and it was too long on top, it stuck up in the air like a cockerel's comb.

'Are you from here?' asked Carter. He thought Jago's aftershave was nice but there was too much on. Carter wasn't quite sure whom Jago had come to impress. Marky was a surfer type, low-slung jeans, expensive polo shirt and beads around his neck. Marky was watching his father intently.

'He doesn't sound like it, does he?' Raymonds laughed.

'Oh, I can if I chooses,' Jago said in a comical Cornish accent.

'Jago's just come back, isn't that right, Jago?'

'Yes, absolutely. Decided to see what Cornwall could offer me.'

'Lots of people starting up small businesses in the West Country at the moment, I hear,' said Carter.

'Oh, we only want home-grown here, thanks,' Raymonds said with a grin.

'Doesn't it get a bit inbred?' Carter asked.

Marky's laugh came out in a nervous giggle as Jago laughed longer than it was funny.

Raymonds waited for him to simmer down. 'We allow a bit of new blood in the female form now and again, as long as she's Cornish. That's what we need to find for my Marky here – thirty-one years old and not even one wife under his belt.' He slapped Marky on the back and his son smiled uneasily. 'Too busy surfing. Oh well – you lads can scarper now you've said your hellos. You come by and see Mum tomorrow, Marky – she's expecting you. If you go fishing, you make sure you bring back a few scallops.' Marky nodded with a furtive glance towards Carter as he left.

Raymonds waited for Marky and Jago to find their place back at the pool table around the corner and then he looked into his drink. Apart from Raymonds and the two lads, no one had come in or left since Carter arrived; he felt as if he were on a stage, in a play.

Carter glanced at Raymonds' profile as he sipped his beer. Behind Raymonds he saw the eyes flick up and look their way as if people were waiting and watching to see Raymonds' judgement on the newcomer.

'You staying here?' Raymonds asked, as he perched on a barstool.

'Yes, for tonight.'

Raymonds nodded, mock-impressed, as he took in the information. He picked up his pint, and Carter looked at Raymonds' hands – delicate, feminine almost. The half-moon cuticles were white and clean, the nails perfectly filed. Carter could perceive the faintest whiff of what could have been aftershave; but it wasn't pleasant. He hadn't noticed the smell in Raymonds' house when they'd gone there. Carter wondered whether Raymonds had a mistress. He looked around the bar and his eyes met those of Mawgan Stokes, clearing the tables at the far end. She looked away quickly.

Possible, thought Carter. She moved among the tables clearing away the remnants of dinner. Not one of the men at the tables acknowledged her as she leaned across them to clear their glasses.

'This is your local?' Carter leaned one elbow on the bar.

'More or less. It's the only place to come.'

'What about over at Penhaligon?'

Raymonds lifted his chin and smiled in a dismissive gesture.

'Full of kids. The other way gets posher as you go towards Rockyhead. Not to the taste of most locals. Too rich for simple folk.' He smiled and Carter knew he was taking the piss.

'I thought you might have been on the way to Penhaligon when you decided to take a detour this afternoon. You were seen by the helicopter up on the Garra headland. I was at Garra Cove myself this afternoon.'

'Really?' Raymonds eyeballed Carter. 'That's a dangerous place to visit this time of year, when the tides are so high. You can be washed right off the rocks. Gone in a few seconds.'

'Does that happen often?'

'Has been known. We get the young kids coming down, getting drunk and off their heads. Just takes a slip or a little push and that's the last we see of them till their body's washed up.'

'So, this afternoon. What were you doing?'

'I was going to call on Cam up at the cottage but I changed my mind. I spent some time up there just enjoying the view. I never tire of it. You city folks can't comprehend it, I expect.'

'Have you lived here all your life?' asked Carter.

'Yes, and I'm Cornish through and through.'

Carter drank his beer. He watched Raymonds as he smirked into his glass. He was pleased with himself. *Arrogant git,* thought Carter. If it was Raymonds who had pushed him off the cliff he'd have had to run pretty fast to get to where Pascoe had seen him from the helicopter. It was a good mile over the cliffs, but he could have done it. Carter decided to change the subject. He wanted to keep Raymonds on the back foot if he could.

'How do people feel about the lack of a police station here now? The nearest help is, what, twenty miles away?'

He shook his head. 'Disgrace.'

'Pisses you off?'

'Yes, of course it does. You pay peanuts, you get monkeys. I want proper coppers here again, not specials. But . . . there's no money, is there?'

'Not like in the old days.'

'Like in the days when people knew who the troublemakers were, policemen knew their locals; knew where to head at the first sign of mischief.'

'Something you prided yourself on?'

'You're bloody right, I did, and why shouldn't I? I took over as sergeant here and I knew everyone in this place. I knew the good, bad and the fucking ugly. All of them answered to me.'

'Pretty impressive.'

'Bloody right it was, and we never had any trouble here. Never had to call for help then. We sorted things out, kept it contained.'

'Forgive me for saying, but Jeremy Forbes-Wright was a strange choice of friend for you as an outsider, a Londoner, coming down here and throwing his weight around.'

'Ah well. He paid his dues – he knew how to respect the community.'

'How do you mean?'

Mawgan had finished collecting glasses. Raymonds watched her as she walked back towards the kitchen door around the side of the bar by the steps up to the games area. Her eyes flicked up to meet his before she disappeared. 'Yes, everyone had respect in those days. Now we're lucky to see a real copper here at all. It's all unpaid policemen – specials, or whatever you call them now. They're about as useful as a eunuch in a brothel.' He looked back at Carter, a glint in his eyes.

Carter glanced towards the kitchen door now shut and smiled back at Raymonds. 'Looks as if it's still your job, to look after things here?'

Raymonds took a drink and span the beer mat around his fingers as he studied Carter. 'What did you hear about me?'

Carter grinned, shrugged. 'Nothing but praise.'

'Yeah – bullshit. Can smell it a mile off, lad.'

'You must have known what I'd find out – you were a little too quick with your temper at times. You were a bit too physical. Old school.'

Raymonds bowed his head as he pushed back and straightened his arms. He tilted his head and lowered his voice as he forced Carter to lean a little and listen to what he had to say.

'I got things done. I never asked for back-up, or had to be wet-nursed by some girly. People had respect for the police in those days. You won't find one person who's willing to say anything against me.'

There was a challenge in his voice. Carter smiled into his beer as Raymond finished his.

'You know where I am if you need me, but don't waste your time on the wrong people. You won't find the boy here. You want to look closely at the dad; Jeremy Forbes-Wright always hinted that there was something strange about his son. They never got on. We caught him here once, messing about. I had a good mind to lock him up for a few days but his dad persuaded me he'd see the error of his ways. That's what I mean about Jeremy – he respected the way we did things down here, he understood.'

'What was the problem?'

'He got nasty with a girl, a local girl.'

'What do you mean, nasty?'

'He raped her and gave her a beating while he was at it. She was a mess.'

Raymonds glared at Carter.

'What happened? Didn't she press charges?'

'No, they were both young, she was only fourteen, he was a year older. She decided she didn't want to give evidence. But Toby didn't come down here again. Jeremy was very apologetic and he made amends.'

'Did you investigate it? I mean, it's quite something to accuse a fifteen-year-old boy of rape.'

'Well, view it any way you want, but we had enough evidence. If the girl had wanted to, we could have made a strong case against him.'

'Was there forensic evidence?'

'There would have been, but we didn't bother wasting money if she didn't intend to press charges.'

Raymonds pushed himself away from the bar and picked up the car keys he had left on the bar top.

'Take care, sonny.'

Carter watched the locals as they all followed Raymonds out. Jago and Marky were the last to leave.

Jon Weston, the bar landlord and hotel owner, washed up silently as he waited for Carter to finish his drink.

'Excuse me, mate . . .' Carter walked along the bar until he was level with Weston. 'Can I have a word?'

Weston put down his cloth. 'Sir?'

Carter showed his badge for the first time, although he didn't doubt that Weston knew exactly who he was. When he had booked the room he hadn't mentioned it.

'Problem with your room, sir?'

'No. I wanted to ask you about your staff here.'

'Sorry, I can't give out confidential information about my staff.' He turned his back on Carter and began cashing up the till.

'Hello? Yes, you can.' Carter showed his warrant card. 'An official investigation is going on here.'

'Into what?'

'Staff names and addresses, please. If you wouldn't mind? I'll wait.'

Weston shrugged. He had his back to Carter again and Carter drew in a silent but deep breath. He wasn't an angry person, far from it, but he also wasn't someone who would suffer fools. Weston turned round.

'Will the morning be okay?'

'No. It won't take you long, will it? After all, you have nightly lock-ins here in the bar and my presence seems to have been announced and to have cut short any thirst for late-night drinking; so you take as long as you like and I'll wait here with my pint. If you're too long, I will come and find you.'

Weston didn't answer, just gave the till drawer a shove – it crashed noisily shut before he walked off towards the kitchen door.

Carter looked around the bar as he waited. The rain was spraying across the black windows. He checked his phone – Willis hadn't been in touch yet. He texted her to ask her to call him.

After ten minutes Weston came back with the file. He put it on the bar in front of Carter.

'I also wanted to ask you about the public phone here.'

'In the hall on your way up the stairs.'

'Is it used a lot?'

'God, yes. Everyone uses it. The signal down here is crap.'

'Is there any way I can check who's used it and at what time?'

'You're the detective, what you asking me for?'

Carter smiled.

'Is that everything?' Weston asked.

Carter nodded. 'Think so. I'll take it with me if you don't mind.'

Weston hesitated and then gave a resigned nod, but he didn't make eye contact. Carter finished the last of his pint and picked up the file. He walked to the end of the bar and through the door, and headed right up past the hotel reception, which was a booth inside a recess. The light was on and he saw Weston enter and pretend to be busy. Carter took the stairs up towards his room on the second floor. The creak of the stairs and the tick of a large grandfather clock on the landing above was all that he could hear. Then from somewhere below he heard a fire door close with a whoosh and a compressed thud.

He reached his landing, treading quietly on the old carpet. The floorboards creaked and whined beneath his feet. Inside his room he checked his phone for signal and saw just one bar. No reply from Willis. He went towards the window and saw a shadow pass.

He dialled Robbo's number.

'Can you have a look for me for any mention of an attack by Toby on a young fourteen-year-old woman here in Penhal? This would have been when Toby was fifteen, so about 2000. She was raped. There must be some mention of it in police files even if the investigation got dropped.'

'Christ, that's a big accusation.'

'Yes. And made by Raymonds, who is adamant it happened, just not convinced it was worth investigating.'

'What reason does he give?' Robbo asked.

'They were both minors.'

'Okay I'll find out all I can.'

'Thanks.'

Carter checked his phone and tried to ring Cabrina but it went straight to answer machine. He left her a voicemail then he picked up his keys and left.

Chapter 22

Carter walked across the cliff top to the sound of the roar of the crashing waves as they sucked up sand and spewed it back as shingle on the beach. The moonlight touched the line of foam as the wave breached. A few stars had found their way through the rain clouds that had kept the temperature above freezing. The walk across the cliff top was along a narrow path; Carter's eyes got used to the dark. The jagged black outline of the gorse to his right kept at waist height as the path dipped and rose on its descent down towards the village. He turned his head to listen for the sound of someone else. He heard nothing until the wind dropped as he ascended the last twenty yards and the hedges rose around him.

Willis was expecting him. As she met him at the front door she whispered that Lauren had fallen asleep on the sofa, and he took a few steps backwards as she pulled her coat on and closed the door.

'Let's walk,' he said.

'Is she all right?' Carter asked as he waited for Willis to tuck the house keys in her jacket pocket and zip it up. 'What's the inside of that place like?'

'Interesting, like Pascoe said. Not your average holiday let – all heavy curtains and dark walls. Lauren's okay. Before she fell asleep I told her I'd have to go out for a while. She has my number if she wants me.'

'I've learned some things about Toby this evening – Raymonds says there was an allegation of rape against him which was never investigated.'

'Against Toby?'

'Yes, I know that doesn't sound likely but apparently, according to Raymonds, it led to the rift in the father-son relationship,' Carter whispered. He opened the gate for him and Willis to slip through. 'I had a very odd conversation with him this evening.'

'Did it sound like bullshit?'

'Surprisingly not. Maybe because he was calm when he told me. He looked like he'd been hoping not to have to say it.'

'How true do you think that is? Is it possible?'

'I've no idea. Toby's the son of a messed-up man who as far as we know did his best to mess his son up. Anything's possible. Robbo's looking into it.'

They walked down towards the sea. The cloud had cleared and the stars began to assert their presence. Down at the beach there was a light coming from the accommodation above the farm shop; it was barely a glow as the blackout curtains did their job, but a security light was still on above the front door. Someone had either just arrived or left. The light went on in the dress shop a few doors down.

They crossed the road to the Surfshack and walked

round on the sand to its beach side. From there they watched the farm shop. A smartly dressed woman in heels came out. Carter recognized her as the owner of the boutique, Mary-Jane Trebethin. She opened the door with a key.

They waited for thirty-five minutes. She didn't come out.

'Let's go,' Carter said. They headed back up the hill to the house. They were within sight when they saw the glow of the security light shining brightly out from between the branches of the pines. 'There's someone coming out of the gate,' said Carter.

In a second Willis was sprinting up the steep hill and keeping her eyes focused on the person now running not too far ahead. Carter kept pace with Willis as best he could as she gave chase up the hill. He slowed as he struggled for breath. Willis ran on, climbing over a farm gate to her right. She pushed hard up and over the field's rough frozen terrain. She couldn't see her own feet as she lost her footing. She heard someone else to her left, running close to the hedge. Willis looked up and across at the big shadowy body of a horse that was standing still now and taking an interest.

'Stop,' she shouted across. She could hear someone else's hard breathing but no slowing pace. 'Police officer! Stop!' The horse snorted. The top of the field loomed ahead of her. Five caravans stood at the far side of the field. Beyond them and to the right of the field Willis saw a figure run in front of one of the white-sided vans. The light from a torch came bouncing over the hedge. As the horse started to trot over to her, Willis stayed where she was and signalled to Carter, who had caught her up.

'I'm not good with horses . . . someone ran in over there.' Their breaths ballooned, white in the icy night. 'I think they've gone into one of the vans.'

The horse snorted as it came to a standstill in front of them. Its face was white, with large eyes. It had a rug on its back.

Carter reached out to touch its face.

'All right there, lad.'

The horse nuzzled into Carter's hand. It followed them up the field as they walked together towards the first of the vans, which were gleaming in the moonlight. The vans, side-on to them, were spaced unevenly. They walked around and took a van each as they tried to see in, but all the curtains were closed; most of them looked locked up for the winter. On the last van Willis called Carter over. Inside she could see the faint red glow from a fridge light. He nodded. Willis knocked on the door and waited. She knocked again louder. They heard a shuffling noise. Someone shouted from the other side.

'Who is it?' a woman's voice answered. The voice came from somewhere at the back of the caravan. A curtain was pulled aside and the window pushed open.

'What is it?'

'Police officers – could we have a word?'

Carter took a step back from the door as they waited. They heard the turn of a key and the caravan door opened. A woman stood on the other side in an oversized T-shirt that had a Disney logo on the front.

She pulled a blanket around herself as she squinted at them.

'Excuse us for bothering you, but are you alone in this van?' The horse tried to nudge past them.

'Yes. Back, Misty . . . back.'

The woman was trying to hide the fact she was out of breath as she came out and pushed the horse gently backwards with a hand on its chest.

'Lovely horse. Are any of these other vans occupied?' asked Carter.

'Not at present.'

'Can I get your name, please?'

'Kensa Cooper.'

He could smell the poverty coming from the van. The toll life had taken on her was sunken into her hollow cheeks. She had heavy eyeliner, which had smudged and gave her a haunted look as if she was made-up for Halloween. She was probably not even thirty but looked much older. She had a slurring in her voice, madness in her eyes.

'Were you out in the field just now, Kensa?' She didn't answer. 'If you were that was pretty hard going running up that hill and over these fields. No wonder you're still out of breath,' Carter said, smiling kindly. 'Ebony here is a great runner and even she couldn't catch you.'

'I didn't do anything wrong. You shouldn't have chased me.' Kensa pulled the blanket tightly around herself. She went back in and tried to close the door on them but Carter put his foot in the way.

'We can't leave just yet. We need to know a few things then we'll go,' said Carter sternly.

'It's all right, Kensa,' said Willis. 'We're not going to hurt you – we just need to talk to you, that's all, and then we'll leave.'

Kensa looked from one to the other and then nodded.

'What did you want at the Forbes-Wright house?' asked Carter. 'Why did you go there?'

'I was going to see who was there, that's all. I clean there sometimes. Just interested, is all.'

'Did you know Jeremy Forbes-Wright?' Willis asked. Kensa moved her head just enough to indicate that she did.

'You weren't going there to clean at this time of night, though, were you?' asked Carter.

'No. I wanted to see who had come. I saw the woman. I looked in at the kitchen. She was crying. I wanted to tell her something . . . I've seen her boy – I know he's safe. She doesn't need to worry – he's in safe hands.'

'Where, Kensa? Where did you see him?'

'In my dreams.'

'When you went down to the house this evening, is that what you were going to tell her? That you've seen him in your dreams?' asked Willis.

'Yes.'

'Kensa? Is it all right if we take a look inside the van?' asked Carter. She looked behind her and became agitated again. She started to clench and unclench her hands; she made them into fists and knocked her knuckles hard against each other.

'We need to take a quick look, Kensa, and then we'll be gone,' Willis reassured her. 'We won't disturb anything.' Kensa started to shake her head as she looked back inside.

Carter took a step closer.

'Come on, Kensa, it's got to happen – let's get it over with,' he said. 'We won't be here long; we'll leave things as we found them.'

Willis stepped inside and led Kensa to the sofa. 'Stay there, Kensa. Don't worry about anything.'

Carter stepped back outside and closed the van door on them as he had a look around, underneath and at the back of the van with the help of Misty, who was fascinated by the intrusion so late at night. At the back of the van there was a gazebo that was battered but not quite broken. Beneath it were three white plastic chairs and the smell of a bonfire gone cold. There was a spare gas cylinder under the van and a water container.

Willis looked around her. The caravan had the smell of poverty and horse and unwashed bodies. There was no television or laptop, no sound at all besides the creaking of the caravan. Willis found a few bags of weed in the bedroom, hidden on a shelf above the bed.

As Willis came back in the lounge she could see Kensa rocking on her feet.

'Do you have a friend living nearby?'

'No . . .' Kensa shook her head and stared out at nothing as she pulled the blanket around her. She sat down and stared at her hands as they clenched and unclenched.

'You need someone to help you, Kensa. You're not

well. Would you like me to see if I can get help for you?'

Carter was standing at the door – he'd finished his search. He stepped inside and sat down, sliding behind the lounge table. He looked from Willis to Kensa and shook his head. Willis sat down next to Kensa on the sofa.

'Kensa, did you go down to the house tonight to look for someone?' Carter asked.

She nodded.

'Who, Kensa?'

'I thought Toby might have come. I thought he would come now that his son is here.'

'How do you know Toby?'

'We were sweethearts once. A long time ago.'

'How old were you then, Kensa?' asked Willis.

'We were teenagers, but he wasn't very nice to me. I haven't seen him since.'

'Kensa, if you know where Samuel is, you have to tell us. He needs to go home to his mum and dad,' said Willis.

There was a silence.

'Okay, Kensa, we'll go now,' Carter said, looking at Willis to agree. 'Have you got a phone, Kensa?' he asked. She nodded. 'Well, here's my card.'

'Kensa?' Willis laid a hand on Kensa's. 'If you want help, we can get some for you. Just ring that number.'

They walked back towards the house.

'How does she manage to look after a horse? She can't even look after herself,' said Carter, as they walked down the unlit lane. They could hear the roar of the waves below them.

'She probably looks after the horse better than she does herself,' Willis replied.

Carter phoned Robbo again. 'I have a name for you: Kensa Cooper. That's our victim from 2000, I think.'

After Carter left her to go back to the hotel, Willis lay in bed and listened to Lauren crying. It was two in the morning. She heard the dog whimpering too and then she heard the sound of Lauren getting up and going downstairs. Willis stood and went to look out of the window. The moon was bright and the frost was already thick on the roof of Lauren's car.

Willis put the light on and took out her notebook as she sat on her bed in the onesie that Tina had given her for Christmas. She went through everything again and started a new list of questions that she wanted to ask in the morning. Then she got up to put the light off to try and get back to sleep. She heard the sound of Lauren coming up the stairs talking to the dog, so she guessed that they'd be sharing a bed tonight. As she looked up she saw the old security camera in the corner of the room. She looked around for a chair and stood on it to have a look at the camera. She wrote down the name of the manufacturer. Another question to add to her list. Why wasn't the alarm system working?

Unable to sleep, she went downstairs and stood looking over the veranda and out down to the sea.

The moon was bringing light onto the common and the gorse bushes and trees shimmered with frost. There was a mist rising from the ground forming a shroud across the common.

Chapter 23

Thursday 6 February

Willis rang Raymonds' doorbell at ten past ten. Carter was at her side. Raymonds looked almost amused at seeing the officers on his doorstep. He didn't move to allow them to come in.

'We need to ask you about a few things,' Carter said. Raymonds' eyes went back towards Carter.

'Now?'

'Yes, if it's convenient?'

'I was just helping my wife – she has Parkinson's. Some days it gets her worse than others. Today is an "I can't dress myself" day.'

'We will be happy to wait while you see to your wife,' said Willis.

'How kind.' He had a curious look of disdain on his face, as if he were enjoying some joke and just letting it play out. He showed them straight into the front room again and sat in the same chair as last time.

'While I see to my wife should I call my lawyer?' He smiled.

'Not unless you think you need one,' Carter answered.

'Two visits from the Met in as many days – I'm either honoured or I'm in trouble.'

'We just need to ask you about Kensa Cooper.'

'Kensa?'

Eileen called and Raymonds excused himself. Ten minutes later he was back.

'Where were we? Ah yes, you wanted to talk to me about Kensa?'

'We met her last night – she was hanging about Kellis House.'

Raymonds opened his eyes wide, but even allowing for the theatrics Willis could see the heat was coming to his face. A small strand of his immaculately smoothed black hair had fallen over his forehead; he reached a slow hand up to his face and flicked it back.

'She used to do a bit of cleaning for Mr Forbes-Wright. I expect she was just curious. She's harmless.'

'But, this was the woman you talked about being associated with Toby Forbes-Wright?' asked Carter.

'Did Kensa tell you that?'

'No, she just said she and him were sweethearts. I figured it out.'

He grinned at Willis. 'I mean, are we going to talk about things off the record?'

Carter looked across at Willis, who had her notebook perched on her lap. She gave a reluctant nod and closed it.

'She needs some help,' said Willis. 'She really

shouldn't be left to fend for herself in a caravan in a field. Why isn't someone caring for her?'

'Now, now, that's an odd thing to say.' Raymonds looked at Carter as he pretended to try and understand what was meant. 'It's hard for foreigners to understand, but she chooses to live up there in that field. She came from gypsy folk and she always had it in her blood. She has friends in the village – Mawgan Stokes looks out for her. Plus she makes a living from looking after the site.'

'But she has mental health issues,' said Willis.

'She turns them on and off, depends on how much weed she's smoking at the time. Some days you see her and she's perfectly normal; others, she's barking.'

'She says she's seen Samuel in her dreams,' Carter said.

'Hallucinations, those will be. I'm guessing you looked to see if he was hidden in or around the caravan and he wasn't.'

'We looked. I've ordered a bigger search done of all the vans up there.'

'Of course – you get on with whatever it is you think you're doing.'

'Kensa didn't talk about being assaulted by Toby,' said Willis.

'Didn't she?'

'So, Toby was never questioned by you.'

'We had no need to question him when all the evidence spoke for itself, and I didn't want Kensa upset any more than she had been. It was all a storm in a teacup in the end.'

'If she was only fourteen, isn't that something you

would have investigated? The rape of a minor?' asked Carter.

'By another minor?' Raymonds tutted, shook his head. His eyes narrowed in on Carter. Willis stared hard at him. He had learned from the best when it came to staying calm under pressure. She could imagine Raymonds had had a formidable interviewing technique. 'What would have been the point? Things happen at beach parties; no one to blame. This is all getting a little too farcical. You come down here looking for a missing child and end up trying to solve an old rape case that never happened.'

'You said it did. You made it out to be a big deal at the bar last night. Toby was a nasty piece of work, you said. But now you're playing it down.'

'I don't want you to get distracted. There were no charges brought. Forget about it.'

'Yeah – I can understand what you're saying, but it's apparent to me that the truth never came out that night. Is the truth coming out now?' asked Carter.

Willis felt Carter getting angry as she sat beside him.

'The missing boy is nothing to do with us.' Raymonds lifted his chin and stared at Carter, unblinking.

'But Jeremy Forbes-Wright was; and this is his grandson we're talking about. The day Kensa was attacked a deal was done with Jeremy Forbes-Wright and I want to know what that deal was.'

'Nonsense.' Anger flashed over his face and brought a livid colour to it, as it blackened Raymonds' eyes. 'I would watch your tongue, Detective. I can assure you, I acted in Kensa's best interests.'

'Not your own?' Carter returned Raymonds' stare.

Willis felt Carter's heat as he sat next to her. She saw Raymonds was beginning to sweat as he became calmer and eyeballed Carter.

Carter pressed on. 'There were no charges brought even though Kensa had been raped?'

'Rape is one of those grey areas, especially when you're talking about two kids.'

'No, it isn't.'

Chapter 24

Lauren heard the front door close; she held on to her mug of tea and walked out into the summer room at the back of the house to gaze down over the scrubland towards the ocean. She was so tired; she hadn't slept. The day had brought her another day further from her son. It was dark outside when she'd first come downstairs at six o'clock, tired of lying in bed, staring at the ceiling, thinking, willing herself to be beside Samuel wherever he was, be it in the frozen earth, just to be with him. Then she had looked out at the morning – another day when she was alive and her son was waiting to be found.

The smell of the wood-burner was still in the air from the night before. She'd light it again in a minute: get some order to her day; for now she couldn't take her eyes off the sky. Clouds raced across it. The yellow gorse shimmered beneath. The sun lit the edges of the clouds. She looked out across the scrubby heathland before her as it rolled down and then was lost to the dark-blue ocean as far as she could see. There was such a beauty in the landscape that was hard and brutal to her eyes right now. She'd thought that the house would be the perfect weekend retreat – she could even come down and work in the week if she wanted. Or, better still, bring friends from London. But they didn't have any friends, certainly none with children. Now they didn't have a child. Now, as she looked around her, she felt a sense of loathing for it. She felt hostility, mockery.

Toby was right – put it on the market and buy somewhere abroad maybe, or at least rent a few places. Have fun. Maybe they could think about putting a deposit on somewhere and she'd pay the mortgage on her salary. She looked back out at the scrubland and saw a figure move – walk across the common between her and the sea – and she stepped nearer to the window as she watched the woman turn and stare in at her. Lauren saw it was the same woman she'd seen from the window the day Samuel disappeared. As the woman's eyes focused on her, all else slipped away from Lauren's vision. Then the woman turned and walked quickly away and was gone.

Lauren ran back into the kitchen and out of the back door onto the long veranda; she found a way through the low hedge that marked the end of the garden. A path was cut into the common. She stepped over thistles and thorny gorse bushes scraped her as she pushed through to stand where the woman had been and she came to a patch where no gorse grew, where there was soft downy grass and small wild flowers crept along the ground. She heard a sound and saw Russell beside her. He started digging away at the smooth mound beneath her feet. She picked him up and carried him back into the house and closed the veranda door behind her. When she looked again the woman was standing in the lounge, by the door.

'What do you want?'

'My name is Kensa.'

Kensa stared past Lauren and the winter sun reflected in her eyes, it lit her pale skin. She looked like a restless dead spirit, looking for peace. She had deep lines in her face, dark circles around her eyes. She hadn't slept all night.

'Please – can you help me?' said Kensa.

Kensa turned her attention away from the rising sun and back to Lauren. Lauren felt such an urge to run, but Kensa stood in the doorway.

'What do you want me to do?'

Kensa shook her head. Lauren took a step towards her. Kensa stayed where she was and when Lauren held on to her arm she felt paper skin and thin bone that almost melted at her touch. Kensa took a deep breath and stared out at the sea. Her dark-brown eyes reflected the blue of the cold sky.

'I've seen him in my dreams. He is somewhere dark. He is sleeping.'

Kensa's eyes refocused and they turned on Lauren.

'Who is – is it Samuel?'

She nodded. 'He's only sleeping. He's in the safe place.'

'Oh my God, thank God.' Lauren's knees began to buckle. 'Please tell me where he is.'

Kensa moved backwards, away from Lauren's grip. 'I can't tell you any more.' She looked in pain. Kensa's face turned into a child's; she began to cry: '*Mommy . . . Mommy.*'

Chapter 25

'He's a lying bastard,' Carter said as they walked back to the car. They drove to the top of the hill and sat in the layby to run through things. 'We need to find some record of what happened that day. Get in touch with Robbo, bring him up on the screen for me.'

As Willis took out her iPad and waited for it to turn on she looked across at Carter.

'It's a terrible injustice that happened here.'

'Yeah – it is.'

'But it might not lead us to Samuel,' she added.

'No, but we are still not hearing the truth about the day of the funeral either. We need to go and see Mawgan again. If she's a friend of Kensa's we need the truth.'

Carter phoned and put Robbo on Skype. 'What's the latest, Robbo?' he asked.

'I rang the escort Louisa – nice girl. Privately educated.'

'What did she say?'

'That she'd lost one of her best clients in Jeremy Forbes-Wright. She met him when she offered gentlemen's lunches from her flat in Knightsbridge.'

'Did she ever come to Cornwall?'

'No, but she said he invited her several times, but she didn't want to; she's a busy woman. She did, however, recommend others to him and she knows one girl who went a few times.'

'Can we have her number?'

'She's trying to find it – she lost touch with her a while ago. She's being fairly cooperative – I'm hoping we'll get something useful from her.'

'Interesting. So when he came down here it was to party?' asked Carter.

'It would seem so, wouldn't it? Does the house give that impression?'

Carter turned to Willis to answer.

'Yeah – it fits that he didn't rent it to families,' she said. 'The bedrooms are more like plush, short-stay motel rooms. It's all a bit "in your face" – the kind of place that lends itself to swingers' parties. I'll search the place thoroughly when I get back.'

'How is Lauren holding up, Eb?'

'She's one of those "doers" and not "sayers". She doesn't want sympathy, she wants action. She wants a role in finding her son.'

'Jeanie has been talking to Toby again.'

'Did we find out if they took more than just a photo out of the Canary Wharf flat?'

'Toby said he let Gareth take whatever music he wanted; didn't see the harm in it. Jeanie has told him to get it back.'

'How is Toby?' asked Carter.

'Jeanie says he's falling apart, unravelling. He

seems to completely blame himself for Samuel's disappearance.'

'What about surveillance on him?'

'Up and running. It's been confirmed that he's having intimate conversations with Gareth Turnbill but there's been no sign of anything concerning Samuel's whereabouts. There was talk about the father's apartment – it sounded like even Turnbill didn't know what they were looking for. He keeps asking Toby to let him help but it sounds like Toby is beginning to close up shop, waiting for the ground to open up and swallow him.'

'We need to push him hard and find out the truth. I think he's lying about what happened in Cornwall. Apparently, according to the Sheriff, Kensa refused to press charges and Jeremy Forbes-Wright took his son home that day.'

'You'd think they would have been only too happy to prosecute. By what you've said, he hates outsiders.'

'Exactly. But, as people keep stressing to me, he'll do anything for the good of Penhal. We think he brokered some sort of deal,' said Carter.

'We had another session looking at the footage from the funeral. We think that your new friend Kensa was there. Pascoe provided a photo of her for me. She's well known to the shopkeepers in Penhaligon – has a habit of stealing. Have a look at this.'

Willis held it for them both to see.

'On this footage, you can see Mawgan Stokes

comes out of the chapel and is standing with her father and then she gets distracted. Follow her line of vision and there is a woman standing at the far side, out of sight of most of the mourners. She's hanging about there. We haven't got a clear shot yet but we're looking for one. It's definitely someone that Mawgan doesn't think the rest of the funeral-goers will want to see because she waits a while and then she says her goodbyes and slips off, then doubles back around the back of the chapel and we see her here talking to the same woman.

'I've looked at the CCTV footage of the funeral again. I'm getting very familiar with identifying the faces and placing them in their groups.' Robbo shared a cut from the film on the screen. 'Here we see Mawgan leaving the group after the funeral. She is walking away and heading back around the reverse side of the chapel.' Robbo switched to another viewpoint. 'Here is Mawgan heading straight for that person now. We can see her walk between the cars. Look at this.'

He froze the frame. There was a woman wearing an oilskin coat.

'Recognize her?' Robbo asked.

'Yeah – it's Kensa Cooper,' said Willis.

'It's the woman who is supposed to be too mad to look after herself but she can somehow get to London,' added Carter.

'The CCTV from the Gordano services is interesting too,' said Robbo. 'We can trace all of the Cornish cars that stopped here. Raymonds, alone, does what he said, went in for a coffee, came out, used the cashpoint. That's at seven forty-six. But he hangs about a long time, a whole hour. Almost as if he's waiting for someone. We see him twice get out of his car and walk to the far end of the car park.'

'I suppose we were never going to get lucky enough to see him get a kid out of the back,' said Carter.

'No, we can't tell if there's anyone sleeping on the back seat – it's still possible. We don't see him actually in his car at the car park, we just see him when he walks towards the entrance. Martin Stokes was there with Mary-Jane and Towan. This is at ten past nine. Towan does seem to wait until everyone else is inside the services before he gets out and wanders around the car park. We pick him up twice. He needs looking at more closely, I would say. The last surprise I have for you is a car that came during the time Raymonds was hanging about. At eight thirty-one here come two men – Jago and Marky. They don't even use the services – they wait in the car for thirty minutes and then they leave.'

'I'm looking at all the cameras on that exit and along the motorway, seeing where they go. I'll let you know as soon as I have it.'

'Sorry, I have to take this,' Willis interrupted as she looked at her phone and the name on the screen. 'Hello, Lauren? Everything all right?'

'Ebony, can you come back now? I've just seen the woman who was outside our flat in London.'

'On my way.'

'Just one more thing,' said Robbo. 'Before anyone else arrived, a yellow Fiat registered to Mawgan

Stokes came in for petrol at Gordano. That was at seven thirty. The footage shows that while Mawgan goes in to pay for petrol, Kensa is opening the boot. We don't see any more.'

Chapter 26

Jeanie rang the buzzer and waited. Toby Forbes-Wright came to the door. His breath smelled of stale wine, he was a mess. She noticed that he had on the same clothes as the day before. It was nine thirty. When Jeanie followed him into the lounge she knew he'd slept in there. The room was rank and stale. There was a blanket on the sofa.

'You need to make sure you get a good night's sleep, Toby.'

Jeanie followed him into the kitchen and filled up the kettle. She started washing up the dishes and stacked the empty wine bottles in a carrier bag to take out with her when she left. She heard the sound of him crying as she turned off the taps and finished washing the dishes.

She gave him a hug and he held on tightly to her. He didn't want to let go. Jeanie patted his back as if he were a child while he sobbed. When he seemed to be drawing breath she pulled away. She'd seen it before – how sometimes such sorrow was confused with the need for sex. It was comfort.

'I need to talk to you, Toby. We haven't found

Samuel but there have been some developments in Cornwall. I think it might be a good idea if you and I decamp and go down there. Lauren needs you.'

He started shaking his head before she'd even finished saying it.

'No way. I feel safer here.'

'Safer?'

'Yes. Even walking back from Gareth's was too much. I saw people staring at me. I can't leave this flat again. I need you to bring me what I need to stay in here until it's over.'

'Toby, you're under so much stress – I understand. But you need to remember the main thing here is finding Samuel alive.'

'He's dead. I feel it, I know it. He's dead and it's my fault. Lauren has left me and Gareth is making me feel hemmed in. I'll have nothing left to live for soon. My dad will win in the end.'

'Toby, listen to me. I've been doing this job a long time. I've seen all sorts of people react in all sorts of ways when they are in the middle of a crisis. I've lost count of the number of people who've said what you just said to me, and they didn't want to face anything, but they did face it and they did come out of it. You have to help me, help Lauren. You have to help Samuel.' He didn't answer. 'Go and have a shower and get some clean clothes on while I tidy up and make some scrambled egg for you. We'll sit down together and we'll make a plan.'

Toby shuffled off – he came back finished: showered and wearing a fresh T-shirt and clean tracksuit bottoms.

'Better?' Jeanie asked him as she placed some breakfast on the kitchen table for him.

'I can't eat anything. I overdid it last night.'

'That's the very cure for a hangover – scrambled egg, it soaks up the alcohol. Orange juice.'

He sat at the table and she handed him the juice.

He ate in silence while she tidied the kitchen. When she'd finished she suggested they had coffee and she sat down across from him at the table.

'Toby, do you know a man named Raymonds? Do you remember him at all?'

Toby's face had a little more colour than when Jeanie had first arrived that morning but he looked mottled and puffy with the hangover. He was sweating. He blinked nervously as he gave a small nod of the head.

'What do you know of him?'

'It was a long time ago in the house in Cornwall. The last time I ever went there. I was seeing this local girl called Kensa. There was a party on the beach and it got out of hand. A few of us went back to the house; my dad wasn't going to be coming back that night. We thought we'd just chill out, raid the drinks cabinet. I knew it was risky when I said it. I told you, my dad and I didn't have a relationship. I don't know why he even took me to Cornwall that summer. He usually palmed me off on other people while he took his girlfriends.

'I was in love with Kensa. We'd never done more than kiss. I wasn't ready. Kensa was so brittle. She seemed so sad. I don't know what went wrong that evening, I don't know what I did to her but I woke up in the police station. I've tried so hard to remember things but there are large gaps.'

'What had happened on the beach?'

'Five of us hung round together. Me and Kensa, Ella Simmons, who was best friends with Mawgan Stokes, and Cam Simmons, Ella's brother. It was a massive party, it was such a warm evening. Everything was just perfect and then it all seemed to go wrong. Locals came to cause trouble. They started fights. It was Marky Raymonds' eighteenth. He was really aggressive. They'd been taking stuff. They were all off their faces.'

'Who were they?'

'Marky, Jago, Towan, a few more. They were the lads that lorded it over everyone. They were allowed to do what they wanted. They started really bothering Kensa and me. Marky really liked Kensa. It was obvious he didn't appreciate her going with me. They got physical with her and Ella. Ella was a year older than us, she was sixteen; she'd dated Towan for a short while but he was one of the worst among them that night. We decided to leave the beach and go back to mine to get away from them.

'I remember feeling so tired, like my legs were giving way, even on the way back from the beach. It seemed like I just couldn't make it up the hill but I had to help Kensa. She was almost asleep. We weren't drunk, we'd only had a couple of beers.'

'Do you think your drink was spiked?'

'Looking back, I think it must have been.'

'What can you remember about your time when you got back to the house?'

'Kensa was asleep on the sofa. I remember saying to Cam, "I'm sorry, I have to lie down." I heard Ella scream and Mawgan was swearing at her brother. Suddenly there's Towan in the house and dragging Mawgan out. I heard Marky and Jago threatening Cam. There was screaming and someone pushed me and that's all I know. The rest is gone from my memory. I woke up in a police cell with such a banging head and I was so thirsty. I kept asking Sergeant Raymonds about Kensa and the others; he told me I'd attacked Kensa, raped her. That the others had seen me do it. They had proof. There was absolutely no doubt. My father came and got me out. We drove straight back up to London. We hardly spoke on the way up; he said he would handle it all. He never really wanted anything to do with me after that.'

'Did he never discuss it with you?'

'No, I didn't know what happened to Kensa. I never found out about that night. I never went back to Kellis House.'

'She is still living in Penhal.'

'Oh God, poor Lauren, now she has this as well as everything else. She must really hate me. She must think I'm a freak. I am a monster.'

Toby stood and walked into the lounge. He stood by the window as if he wanted to jump off the balcony beyond. The Thames had taken on the colour of the blue sky. It could have been summer by its colour but it was a bitterly cold day in February.

Toby spread out his hands on the cold glass behind him.

'Toby – please – this is all about Samuel. No one is

accusing you of anything. Kensa never pressed charges.'

Toby shook his head. He panted with fear.

'Toby, please . . .' Jeanie held out her hand. 'You're okay. Please come and sit over here.' Jeanie smiled and he took one backward glance before allowing himself to be led over to the sofa. She sat next to him and took his hand.

'This all matters because somehow, some way, this may have something to do with Samuel going missing. Did your father ever say what he saw when he got back that evening?'

'No. I don't think he even realized I was in the house. It was as if I hadn't been. It was all of it like a bad dream from the moment things went wrong on the beach.'

'Listen, Toby, what if Kensa wanted to see you?'

He looked at Jeanie as if she was making a bad joke.

'I can't see her now. I can't take any more. I'd rather stay here. I feel like I'm falling apart.'

'Toby, at some time you're going to have to face it.'

'Believe me, I would never have hurt Kensa. I loved Kensa.'

Chapter 27

'Lauren needs me, guv.'

'Okay, I'll drop you back at the house,' said Carter. 'I'll talk to the shopkeepers down there.'

'What shall we do about this new information and Mawgan Stokes?' Willis asked.

'You go and see her. Go carefully with her, but make sure she knows this is her chance to tell us the truth before she's arrested. I don't want anyone making a rash move where Samuel is concerned.'

Jeanie phoned them as they were driving back.

'I think this rape allegation is remarkable, to say the least,' she said over the speaker phone. 'Toby was fifteen at the time, a virgin, probably more gay than straight, and it's more than likely his drink had been spiked.'

'Yeah, the only versions we have of the story are Raymonds' and Toby's, so we need to ask around.'

'He's listed a few people that were there at the time,' Jeanie said. 'Jago, Marky, Mawgan and a few others. Those were some of the funeral-goers, weren't they? He also mentioned a male called Cam. I don't remember seeing his name on the list of funeral-goers.'

'Raymonds mentioned his name – we'll look into it. Thanks, Jeanie.'

Carter dropped Willis at Kellis House and then he turned back to park at the car park behind the shack.

The shack was open, Marky was putting stock on shelves behind the counter. He turned, saw it was Carter and turned back to continue his task. Carter browsed among the rows of expensive fleeces and tried on a few sunglasses. The Beach Boys were playing in the background. Carter looked around. The cabin had an expensive feel to it, and someone had spent a lot of money on the build.

'Thought you surfers took off to do a bit of snow-boarding this time of year?'

'Been already,' Marky answered him but didn't turn. Carter continued browsing. Marky watched him in the mirror behind the till.

'So you're just waiting for the season now, I suppose?'

'There's a lot to get on with. I spend most of the winter in my workshop mending and making boards, plus the big waves are good this time of year.'

'I get it – so you have the perfect life, no matter what month it is, you're out there having fun?'

'Pretty much.'

'Do you mind if I ask you, is this what you always dreamed of doing?'

'Yep.'

Carter laughed. 'Come on – I'm a London lad – I need to understand what keeps you here – you can really see yourself waxing surfboards when you're sixty?'

'Don't see why not.'

'I can see the appeal, except I'd have thought you might like to set up somewhere else? Isn't it a bit close to home, living here under your parents' noses? I mean, wouldn't you prefer to take the money it took to set this up and go to say Newquay or the North Devon Coast? Croyde, for instance.'

He shrugged. 'I'm thinking about it. What is it you wanted to talk to me about?'

'Oh, mainly chit-chat.' Carter smiled. He took a fleece from the racks and held it up against himself at the mirror.

'Suits you,' Marky said.

'Yeah – I'll have to come back with my kid when it warms up a bit here. I can see the appeal of living here – I honestly can.' He turned on his heels on the wooden floor and nodded, impressed. 'Except, as much as I love my mum and dad, I wouldn't want my father breathing down my neck.'

'Ha . . .' Marky shrugged it off with a smile. 'He's the Sheriff – I expect you heard?'

'The Sheriff, yeah. I bet he's quite the ball-buster when he wants to be?'

Marky sprayed the wooden counter with polish and began dusting. 'He is what he is.'

'You always see eye-to-eye?'

'Not always. But we wouldn't be family if we did.' Marky made eye contact with Carter but couldn't hold it. He began to sniff loudly as he polished.

Carter laughed. 'Yeah, yeah, absolutely – my dad loves to tell me what I should be doing in life, even though he knows nothing about the way things are now. He's sick at the moment but he used to be a London cabbie. He used to love his job – he knew all the places to get a good brew in London. He knew all the other regular drivers on his patch. There's not much he can't tell you about London itself but there's lots he doesn't know that goes on underneath, even under the levels he sees. It's the same in every generation, isn't it?'

'I suppose.'

'But you love it so much here, you love being near your dad so much that nothing would tear you away?' Carter persisted.

'I'm not saying that. I just have a great lifestyle. I get to surf all year round, summers are unbelievable here and good money. Then I go away and snow-board in the winter – what more could I want?'

'What about if there were no restrictions on what business you could have here? If I said to you, you can knock all those shops down across the road and build your dream place, what would it be?'

Marky looked across the street and grinned. 'It would probably have a bar in it.'

'Definitely, nothing nicer than a beach bar,' agreed Carter.

'Live music – there are a good few local bands in Penhaligon.'

'Tick – bands, a bar, tick. What else?' asked Carter.

'A decent restaurant, a new clothes shop, bigger surf shop, I don't know.' Marky turned back to his polishing, daydream over.

'That polish is making you allergic, you haven't stopped sniffing since I walked in here.' Carter winked at Marky and then walked to the back of the shop and peered into the store room. 'These changing rooms?' he asked.

'No, that's the stock room. The changing rooms are to your right.'

'Oh, yes. I can see them. So what other staff do you have?'

'Jago helps me out when he's home.'

'He's home permanently, isn't he?' Carter said.

'Not sure how long he'll stay.'

'What does it depend on?'

'Things, prospects, I suppose, you'll have to talk to him.' Marky became defensive.

'How does he make a living here?' Carter asked.

'You'll have to ask him.'

'Just Jago help you out?' Marky nodded. 'Not Towan?'

He shrugged. 'He's busy.'

Carter picked up the leather wristband collection and tried one on.

'I'm going to get one of these.' He spread them out on top of the cabinet to look at. 'You're a very close-knit society here, aren't you?'

'Have to be. Have to help one another out.'

'Helping one another also means covering for one another's mistakes?'

'I suppose it might do, to a certain extent.'

'What about this missing boy, do you think someone here could be involved?' asked Carter.

'No way, I don't see it.'

'Neither do I, but it's difficult to get past the evidence.'

'What do you mean?' asked Marky.

'So many things point this way. Now we also have the possibility that you lot, you tight-knit lot, are lying to me about the day of the funeral and who came back with who.'

'I came back with Jago.'

'And what time was that?'

'Late – about three in the morning,' answered Marky.

Carter arranged his money on the counter in a neat pile.

'You say you stayed in London till then but we have CCTV footage of you at the Bristol services at half past eight. Why is that?'

Marky's eyes searched the ceiling for the answer, then he grinned awkwardly. 'Yeah – that's right. We did come straight back; well, we went to Exeter to see some mates.'

'I want their names and addresses.'

Marky shuffled and looked around the room; he thrust his hands in his pockets. His face had gone pale.

'What about Kensa?' asked Carter. 'Didn't you see her there at the edge of the cemetery at the funeral?'

He looked uncomfortable, distracted. He'd begun glancing towards the door as if he wanted to leave. 'Yeah, it's possible.'

'You know Kensa, don't you?'

'Of course I do; I've known her all my life.'

'Of course you have. You'd know if she ever had been in trouble, needed help? Like one night at a beach party maybe?'

Marky stared at Carter, speechless.

'Mawgan saw her at the funeral, went to talk with her,' added Carter. 'They even came home together in Mawgan's car.'

'Look, I've got to close up now. I promised to go and visit Mum. Was there anything else?' Marky came out from behind the counter and went to stand by the front door. He waited there for Carter to leave.

'Thanks for the chat and the bracelet,' the detective said as he straightened the column of coins on the counter. Carter slid the leather knotted bracelet up over his hand and adjusted it while Marky waited for him to leave. 'You want to ease up on the coke, your nose is looking pretty lively.'

Carter heard the door shut and lock after he went out and back down the steps. He put a hand up to stop the sand from flying into his face and going into his eyes. He took his sunglasses out of his top pocket and put them on as he crossed the street. Towan was coming out of the farm shop.

'Can I have a word?'

Towan stayed where he was and waited with a petulant look on his face. 'You work here most days?' asked Carter.

'Only when I have to. Look, what is it? I have a date.'

'Not what you wanted to do in life, this?'

'Oh well, it will do, until a better offer comes along,' answered Towan.

'And what would that be?'

'Oh, you know, convert this whole line of rubbish

shops into a casino and have a strip club on the end where the Surfshack is.' He grinned as he watched Marky drive away from across the road.

'Ambitious,' said Carter, pretending to be impressed.

'Yeah – just joking. I intend to leave here pretty soon anyway – I don't really give a shit what happens to it after that. I have to stay here for now – show willing, sell fucking potatoes for a job, keep myself out of trouble.'

'Why, because you've just come out of prison?'

'Yeah, pretty much.'

'Learned your lesson?'

Towan shrugged. 'I learned a lot in prison, that's for sure.'

'But is it a place you'd be keen to go back to?'

'No. I did my time. I'm staying clean now. What do you want? You have nothing to pin on me – you finished?'

'Whoa . . .' Carter rocked back on his heels. 'Calm down, tiger. You're in no position to be rude to me. You may be used to the Sheriff's ways but they're not mine; I assure you, I won't let you off anything. I find you have anything to do with this little boy's disappearance and you'll never surf again except from a belt round your neck in a prison cell.'

'What kid? I don't know anything about a kid,' said Towan, backing off.

'You know what kid I'm talking about. There's not a person in this town who doesn't know. I'm going to find him. I have a lot of resources at my disposal.'

'Hasn't helped you so far, has it? Look, I do what

I'm told to. I can't afford to upset anyone right now. People tell me to jump and I say "How high?".'

'What about if you were told to blame someone for a rape he didn't commit?'

'You've lost me now.'

Chapter 28

Willis found Lauren waiting for her kneeling by the front door.

'There was someone here. A woman called Kensa,' she said, struggling to breathe and talk.

Damn, thought Willis. They should have insisted she stay away from Lauren. 'What did she want?'

'She says she's seen Samuel in her dreams. She was talking, repeating what she'd heard, and it sounded just like him. Even her expression; the face she made – it was just like him. The way she said "Mommy, Mommy" – like Samuel says it.'

Lauren looked up, still on her knees. She closed her eyes as she swayed and hugged herself. Willis got down to help her up.

'Come on, Lauren, we need to talk about this. Come and sit down.'

Willis led her through to the kitchen and sat opposite her at the table. 'Tell me what happened.'

Willis listened and waited for Lauren to finish. Her eyes were so full of hope and her hands were shaking as they held her mug of tea.

'I know who Kensa is – Carter and I met her last evening,' Willis said.

'Who is she?'

'She lives in a caravan in the fields above town. She says she knows Toby, she remembers meeting him years ago when they were teenagers.' Lauren had a confused expression on her face. 'And she would have seen Samuel at the funeral. She was there, at the edge of the cemetery. She didn't come forward but she would have heard Samuel then. We can't be sure that she's not making it up, but we are investigating everything she says. I promise you, we'll take it seriously.'

'Stop a minute . . . how does Toby know her? What do you mean? He hasn't been here since he was a child.'

'Listen, Lauren, I'll tell it to you the way I heard it, the way I understand it – I'm sorry it seems like this is one more problem for you to absorb, but it may help us understand where Samuel is, in its own way. Okay?' Lauren stared back at Willis. 'Something happened here, in this place, that's been covered up for years. It's something that involved Toby.'

Lauren frowned and she shook her head.

'Fourteen years ago, in June 2000, Toby came down here with his father for the summer. He had a holiday romance with Kensa, the woman you met today. Things didn't end well. Toby was accused of attacking her but it never come to court. It wasn't even investigated.'

Lauren looked away as she tried to take in

everything Willis was saying. She picked up her pen
and began writing headings.

'So let me get this straight,' she said. 'Toby is supposed to have attacked the woman who came here
today?'

'Yes.'

'I have to talk to him.' Lauren stood and picked up
her phone.

'Use the landline.'

'No, I need to get some fresh air.'

'Lauren, wait, please sit down. I haven't finished.'

She sat down again.

'The circumstances around the incident are
difficult.'

'What do you mean?'

'The claim is that Toby raped Kensa.'

'Raped? That's not possible. But, even if it were,
what has that got to do with Samuel? Why would
they take my son? Does someone hate Toby that
much?' Willis didn't answer. 'Did he admit to the
rape?' asked Lauren.

'He believes he must have done it.'

'I need to talk to this woman and I have to ring
Toby.'

Lauren stopped to catch her breath as she walked up
the steep and winding road. Willis walked on ahead.
Lauren was clutching her phone in her hand. She
wanted to get to the top of the road to be sure she
had enough signal so they wouldn't get cut off. Willis
stopped and waited at the beginning of the second
field; she stepped into the gateway as Lauren rang

Toby's number; it went straight to answer machine, so she left a message. Willis stood looking out over the green sodden field as it rolled up into the blue sky. She took a few deep breaths as she leaned her arms on the top of the gate and rested her chin. Lauren joined her.

'I can smell wood smoke,' she said. 'I haven't smelled that in years.'

'Lauren, remember to keep as calm as possible with Kensa. She is also a victim in this. If she knows anything about Samuel's whereabouts we need to make her want to tell us. If we upset or scare her she'll be gone.'

'I understand.'

Willis unlatched the gate and pushed it open, avoiding the deep muddy ruts where vehicles had pulled in. Lauren followed Willis as she walked to her left past the thick hedge and up to the line of caravans at the top of the field. As they walked towards them Willis kept her eyes on the last van. She was also looking for the horse but there was no sign. The smoke curled upwards from a fire to the back of the van. She saw movement and Kensa came round to the front and threw out a bucket of water into the grass. She looked their way and stood staring at Lauren for half a minute, watching them push their way up the steep field. Then Kensa turned away and disappeared from sight.

As they reached the van Kensa was sitting on one of the white plastic chairs, poking through the ashes of a fire. She looked up as she raked the ashes; the wood flared red beneath the black of charcoal as it spluttered and spat. Kensa took up a piece of cardboard and began fanning it.

'My horse has gone – someone's taken him. I rode him home, came to see to the fire and now he's gone.'

'Morning, Kensa.' Willis watched as Kensa studied Lauren. 'I've come to ask you some more questions if you don't mind. This is Lauren, you met already at the house?'

'Hello,' Lauren said.

'He's called Misty. I've raised him since he was a foal. He'd never wander.'

Willis pulled out a chair away from the smoke and sat down.

'Kensa, we'll get searching for you when we leave here.' Willis looked up at Lauren. Lauren gave a small nod to reassure Willis that she was okay.

Kensa squinted up at Lauren through the smoke. 'Sorry for scaring you this morning.' She reached over and picked up a few sticks from a pile, snapping them into shorter lengths.

'I've been told about your friendship with Toby,' said Lauren. 'I'm so sorry for anything bad that happened to you.'

'That night was all a big secret until Mr Forbes-Wright took his own life. Funny that.'

Lauren shook her head. 'I never knew him, but he seems to have been important to this place.'

'What happened to me wasn't the worst of it. Has he ever been nasty with you?' Kensa looked up at Lauren as she fed the sticks into the embers.

'Toby?'

'Yes.'

'No. He's a very gentle, sensitive man, very shy.'

Kensa smiled as she reached across for a log for the fire.

'That's him. I thought he was gorgeous.' She looked up at Lauren and smiled. 'He had such a sweet way about him.' She pulled her blanket tightly around herself as she sniffed and wiped her nose with the edge of it.

'It was never proved, never investigated, was it, Kensa?' Willis said.

'Nope. Didn't need to, Sheriff said, facts speak for themselves.' She looked up at them both. Shook her head. A sadness had come over her. It deadened her face. Aged her. 'They said it was an absolute certainty that he had done it to me; they said they had proof, they had witnesses and that was all done and dusted. They said did I want to press charges. Did I want to ruin his life and mine and my dad's – they offered Dad ten thousand pounds and he took it. For the best.'

'Who advised you, Kensa? Who was there that day?' Willis asked.

'Sergeant Raymonds. Raymonds took care of it all. He said it would not make a scrap of difference to the lad, he was one of those lads from public school who looked down on us and he wouldn't give a damn about a girl like me. He said it served me right for going with a lad like that, above my station, and I would have to live with the shame of letting myself be taken advantage of. He said if I agreed not to press charges then no more would ever be said about it, otherwise the whole village would know.

'They said it was your own fault?' Lauren asked, sounding shaky.

'Oh, yes. Should have known better than to trust a stranger. The locals said he brought drugs with him, he planned it all along. Drugged me, raped me, beat me up.'

'I'm sorry you never got justice, Kensa,' Willis said. 'It's not too late.' Willis was staring at the wreck of a woman before her; she could see that all her self-esteem had vanished that night.

'And you never saw Toby again?' asked Lauren.

'No. I try to remember him as the sweet lad I knew. We had two weeks of summer love before it all went wrong. I try and remember him like that.' She smiled sadly.

'Kensa . . .' Lauren leaned into her and spoke. 'When we sell the house and settle his estate, pay the tax, I will make sure you get something.'

Kensa shook her head as she stared into the fire. Then she looked up at Lauren and the embers lit her eyes.

'Don't ever sell the house. The house belongs to the people of the village. It has too many secrets now. You live in it and bear those secrets or you sell it to Raymonds and let things continue as they are. Believe me, you'll never get your boy back.'

Lauren gasped as she rocked on her feet.

'What do you know, Kensa? Who said that?'

'I only know that you cross the town and you pays for it. I've already said too much to you and they will punish me.'

*   *   *

On the way back down the hill Lauren strode forward.

'I'm going to call Toby again now.'

'I'll see you back at the house. There will be another officer with us, a Family Liaison Officer, soon.'

'No, I don't want anyone else in the house,' Lauren said, visibly upset.

'Sorry, Lauren, it's not up to me.'

'But I have you here.'

'I can't stay with you all the time. I need to take an active part in the investigation.'

'Am I a suspect?'

'No.'

'Then I don't need nursemaiding, I need you to get results. I'll tell you if I'm not coping.' She stayed back to try Toby again.

Chapter 29

Raymonds watched the news that morning and the reconstruction on television. It fascinated him as he pulled up his camel-skin pouffe and sat a foot from the TV screen, watching every single move that the pretend Toby took.

Eileen watched him from the doorway.

She stared at the back of his head and thought about the boiled egg and smashing it.

As the reconstruction ended, Raymonds got up to switch the TV off. 'What are you doing?' he asked his wife.

'Waiting.'

'For what?'

'The truth.'

He gave a derisory snort through his nose and snot came out that he hadn't bargained on. He took his cloth handkerchief out of his pocket and wiped his nose.

'What is it you want to know?'

'Marky?'

'Hasn't he been to see you yet?'

'Oh yes, he's been. But he's not himself. He's not well, I know it. He couldn't look at me when he was talking to me. He couldn't stay still. He's talking about Kensa again. He's so worried. I've told him none of it was his fault.'

'Okay. That's interesting. Did you also tell him to stop shoving white snow up his nose? Look ... look ... I had hoped to spare you this but I can't. You think Marky is your blue-eyed boy, who can do no wrong, but the truth is I've been covering his arse since the moment he was born and I'm sick of doing it. He's dragging this town down.'

'Marky is what we've made him and he can't help what he was born.'

'Bullshit, you want to believe that, then you go ahead. He's a weak-minded little shit.'

'It's not him, it's Towan and Jago.'

'Is it? Is it really, Eileen? Okay ...' He raised his palms in the air and shook his head. 'Okay, say you're right and all our son is is a sheep, following the black one in the herd. What then? All we've built up for ourselves is wasted on him?'

'You've kept him too controlled. He doesn't know how to be a man.'

'Blaming me now?'

'Yes, blaming you for not doing what you should have years ago.'

'And what's that?'

'Face the truth.'

'Are you for real? Do you understand what you're saying?'

'Yes.'

'No, no you fucking don't. Get out of my way.'

*   *   *

Raymonds got into his car and drove the long way round to make sure no one saw him. He parked up below Kensa's field where no one would see him.

Kensa was inside the caravan when he got there. She was staring out of the window and watched him approach.

'Kensa?' There was an agonized bewilderment in her expression. 'Kensa?'

Raymonds stood by the open door. Kensa was still looking the opposite way, out of the window. 'Kensa?' She didn't move. 'Turn round.' She breathed in – visibly: her shoulders rose and held on to it, then let it fall; her skinny arms seemed to shiver. She did as she was told. Her thoughts were still elsewhere. He could see it. She was full of panic. She was about to scream and not be able to stop.

'Kensa,' he said in a soft voice, and she responded accordingly. She nodded but she did not see him, her eyes remained focused on some faraway place. 'Are you okay, Kensa?' She didn't answer but she focused on him for a few seconds then turned her head sharply away. He had seen her like this many times. She was on the brink of oblivion. She was crumbling on the inside. She would sit for days like this, staring out at her own thoughts.

'Kensa, snap out of it.' He looked at her cracked lips. So deep were the cracks that her lips had swollen around them. Dark shadows encased her sunken eyes. She wore a scarf on her head. She looked like some refugee hounded from one country to the next, bitten by despair and harshness. 'Where's Mawgan? She needs to get things organized. It's freezing in here. Switch on the fire, Kensa, for Christ's sake.'

As he talked his breath came out white. He stood and switched on the gas heater; its orange glow filled the gloom of the van.

Kensa didn't look at Raymonds. Her eyes remained large and dark, glazed, almost milky, as they stared off into space.

'Misty's gone.'

'He's not gone far. You can fetch him after we have our talk.'

She turned and glared at Raymonds. 'You have no right to take Misty.'

'I have every right. You need to behave yourself, Kensa. People are saying you're not fit to look after a horse like Misty. You've been talking to people you shouldn't.'

'What people? I ain't said nothing.'

'About the boy, about the night in 2000.'

'I said nothing, I promise you. Please, sir, I promise, I'll do anything, just give me my horse back.'

'Okay, if you promise you'll be good.'

'I will.'

'People are sick of seeing you the way you are. You can't sit here all day, Kensa. You're a young woman still. Get washed and dressed and I'll take you out somewhere. Let's get you a hot meal and we'll talk about things. We'll have fun like we used to.'

As he spoke he looked around the shabby van. He was thinking how it had been six months or more since the last time he came up to see Kensa. It had been too long. He needed to make her his priority from now on – he hadn't realized how she wasn't taking care of herself. As he was just thinking of how he was going to sort it in the short term, he saw Mawgan walking up the field towards the van. She didn't know he was there, he could tell. She was walking, head down. Strong powerful legs that were shapely beneath her breeches. It struck him that it was about time he found her a husband to create a new generation in the village. Raymonds stood back a little out of first sight, as she stepped up and opened the door to the van.

'Kensa? I got you some breakfast – a sausage roll from Cam's café. It's still hot. Just like he is . . .' She laughed. 'He sends his love.' Her breath was steaming out, her face glowing with perspiration. She turned and saw Raymonds and registered the strange, malicious, smug expression on his face. She looked back at Kensa.

'Everything all right?'

She didn't answer.

'She's becoming ill again,' said Raymonds. 'She needs you to take better care of her. She's skin and bone and she has almost nothing on.' Raymonds could see beneath her thin layers her scrawny breasts, her ribs, and the loose skin on her stomach. 'In this bitter cold!'

'Kensa?' Kensa turned to look at her friend but she didn't answer. 'It's okay, you can go now,' she said to Raymonds as she pulled Kensa's blanket up around her and started tidying. 'I'll look after her.'

'You better had, otherwise I'll need to call in the doctor and see to Kensa. Get her sectioned again.' Kensa looked up in a panic.

'It's all right; we'll be fine. She can come to the farm with me.'

Raymonds considered his response for a moment and then he nodded, picked up his gloves and keys from the table.

'I'll leave you to it – just walk with me to my car, Mawgan.'

Mawgan agreed reluctantly; she tore open the bag with the sausage roll and placed it in front of Kensa.

'Back in a min.'

As they walked down the hill Raymonds said, 'You make sure that Kensa isn't bothering anyone. When the police officers come and want to talk to her you say she isn't well enough. I'll do my best to keep them away. It's all over town – the upset over that lad. She doesn't help the situation with her dreams and her visions, she should keep those to herself. It's given those detectives a foothold here. None of us wants that. Given them all the ammunition they need to come down here in their thousands and search every house and every field and turn our village upside down.'

He looked Mawgan's way. She didn't look back. He called after her, 'If the boy were to be down here – I'd advise to dispose of him double-quick, no matter who had him – we cannot all suffer for a few. Well, you can hear me well enough, I know. You better listen when I tell you that you're about to bring a ton of trouble down on your stupid head if you don't watch it. You may think you're clever but you're not; you've never been. I'm going to find you a nice hus-band, Mawgan, and you better settle down.'

They paused at the gate where his car was. 'Make Kensa understand she has to behave too, or she won't be welcome here any more. We're sick of her madness. She's a disgrace. I heard she got off her head on booze the other night and was seen giving blow jobs to teenagers in the car park. I'll arrest her next time she makes a spectacle of herself like that.'

'You think Kensa's bad?' retorted Mawgan. 'You should look at your own family before you start picking on her. All your bullshit meetings and procedures and you ignore the things going on right under your nose. We've all had enough.'

'You're talking rubbish.' Raymonds was visibly taken aback by her tone. He'd never heard her say so much. He'd never seen her so angry.

'Really? You want to start asking the right people the right questions. I see what they've been doing – they're laughing at you – you're a joke. The boys are going to turn this place inside out – leave you high and dry. I've heard them plotting in the evenings. They intend to stitch you up, and good luck to them.'

'You be careful what you say, Mawgan, you watch who you accuse of things. There's people in this village who are sick of you and your new-found reckless behaviour. You don't watch it – you and Kensa will be out of here with nothing.'

'This village owes me and Kensa.'

'How do you work that out? I saw to it that she had clothes on her back, food in her mouth. We can't go on spoon-feeding her if she doesn't want to help herself.'

'She should have had justice. We all should have. It wasn't right what happened.'

'Forget all about it. It's better for everyone.'

'I can't. No one can. Don't you realize, as much as you try and cover it up it eats at the heart of Penhal, something rotten, putrid, maggot-ridden, that's what the truth is.'

'That's enough, Mawgan!'

She shook her head. 'You really think it's that simple. You can just flick a switch in your head and all the bad bits are gone? It is what I am now. All this stored-up shit inside me – it is me.'

'Only if you let it be.'

She turned and walked back up the field towards Kensa's van.

He called after her. 'You listen to me, Mawgan Stokes, before it's too late.'

Raymonds left her and drove further up the lane into the Stokes farm. He was angrier than he'd been for a long while at the thought that the town was laughing at him, that the young pretenders were aiming to push him out. It would be a fight to the death. He looked over the hedge and saw Stokes sowing in the field. He watched the seagulls screaming and they swarmed around Stokes. The black crows were already on the red earth. As fast as Stokes was sowing the seed the birds were eating it. They rose and fell in one chequerboard locust. He parked up and walked across the field.

'Get a scarecrow, Martin, for fuck's sake. Those birds are eating your profit. You'll have nothing to sell in the shop.' Stokes switched off his machinery and walked across.

'Get Mawgan to make one for you,' Raymonds shouted above the noisy commotion of the birds. 'Keep her out of mischief, she has too much time on her hands. What's come over her, Martin? You have to do something about her behaviour. Her and Kensa are stirring things up in the village.'

'I can't control her like I used to.'

'You want to show her who's boss.' Stokes shrugged, exasperated. 'Does she listen to her brother?'

'Depends what he's saying. He's not made himself popular since he's been back. He hasn't won many hearts.'

'But at least he's a go-getter. At least he tries things. He's got the balls to stand up for himself. He's a great asset. Mawgan's got to realize we all pull our weight for each other in this place. Towan's done well since he came back. I think he'll make a place for himself here, if he does things right.'

'One day he'll push her too hard. I can see it in her eyes.'

'Is Towan in the house? I need a word with him.'

'What for? We've got no secrets here.'

'I just want to tell him how much I appreciate the work he's doing for us, that's all. Praise is what he needs. Did you find those contact details for the guests at Kellis House yet?'

'No, I can't find them.'

Raymonds eyed him suspiciously. 'Why do I get the feeling you're lying to me?'

'I'm not. I can't think where I put the book with their details in.'

'We won't even be able to buy it unless we put

some pressure on those men in that book. For Christ's sake, Martin, our future is resting on it and you've messed it up as usual.'

'Now just hang on a minute, don't speak to me like that.'

'You're drawing a lot of unwelcome attention to yourself. I heard about your stupid episode in London – what the hell were you thinking, kerb-crawling?'

'I was just thinking maybe . . .'

'What, that you'd draw attention to yourself?'

'There's no need to talk to me like I'm an idiot.' Stokes was fuming.

'Have you asked Towan?'

'Asked him what?'

'To try and find the book for us.'

He shook his head. 'I'm worried about involving Towan in too much.'

'Why? Because he's likely to be better at things than you?'

'No, because he does what he wants in the end. He's always one to spot an opportunity. He's been in trouble for it before. It's every man for himself with him. He's up to something with that Jago and your Marky, I know it.'

'Well, don't tell me we couldn't do with a bit more ambition in this place. We need to push Toby to accept our offer for the house now.'

'What, now, while his son is missing?'

'What better time could there be? They're never going to want to live with the memories down here, added to the fact that their boy is dead, thrown off some cliff somewhere.'

Stokes scrutinized Raymonds for a few seconds than walked back to his tractor. The birds began their flying frenzy again.

Inside the farmhouse Raymonds found Towan looking at porn on his laptop open on the kitchen table. He glanced Raymonds' way as he came in but he didn't stop watching it. Now he viewed the screen with a mocking smile on his lips as he eyed Raymonds out of the corner of his vision, making his way around the kitchen slowly. He was taking it all in, swaggering through; Raymonds leaned slightly backwards as he walked. He came to a standstill beside Towan and snapped the laptop lid down as Towan pulled his fingers out of the way.

'We need to talk. The shop needs opening every day. The shelves need stocking with veg and meat from this farm and you need to get up off your lazy fucking arse, otherwise I'll make sure you go back inside for a good long stretch. You'll be my age by the time you come out.'

'Ha . . . don't think so. After talking to those detectives, I realize that you should be quite grateful to me; after all, you're in deeper than anyone.'

'I want to make a deal with you, Towan. Your father's getting on, he doesn't seem to have the stomach for things any more, and I believe we have the future ahead of us. I'd like you to be my right-hand man here in Penhal. I can see you inheriting all this and more. You just need to prove yourself to me.'

'How?'

'There are people who are out to drag you down.

They just want to stitch you up. I've offered your father a partnership in any new business I set up. That includes buying Kellis House and running it as a highly serviced guest house, but we need to find the clientele. We need the book of contacts that your dad says he can't find. The regular users of Kellis House may want to put money in the pot towards buying it, a timeshare arrangement. And you and your dad can go on providing any extras that will be wanted when they get down here. This is the future for us. That house is ours by right. Forbes-Wright should have kept to his word and it should have been left to us in a will. I haven't invested this much in this town to see it go under and take us all with it. If strangers move in then we've lost the opportunity of a lifetime. At the moment that opportunity is split three ways, but . . . your father has to give over the book.'

Chapter 30

Willis called Jeanie on her police radio.

'I've left Lauren walking back to the house on her own – she's phoning Toby.'

'I don't know where Toby is right now. But I know he's being followed, so I'll find out soon enough. How's Lauren coping? I've asked him, but he's not ready to come to Cornwall.'

'Lauren's coping, as long as she's busy. Toby would have to be prepared to face a lot of hostility here if he comes down,' said Willis.

'From Kensa? I'm not surprised.'

'Actually, not from her; she seems to still have a soft spot for Toby. She doesn't remember it happening. She just remembers people telling her it happened and feeling devastated and bruised. But it wasn't just her and Toby involved that night. Most of the village were at the same party. There's so much going on here, it's hard to focus on the one thing that matters, finding Samuel alive.'

'How's the search going?'

'We have teams looking for him along the cliffs, on the moors and down the mine shafts, which appear around every corner in this county. It's a difficult call. There are so many places he could be. If he's dead, he could have been dumped at sea and may never be found.'

'What are the local people like?'

'Carter's already had an attempt on his life. They don't like interference here. The harder you lean on this village, the tighter people unite against you.'

'A proper close-knit community. In the bad sense. What's the house like?'

Willis moved into the drawing room at the front of the house. 'I'd say it's Victorian, baroque, heavy gold and red curtains, golden statues of pheasants. Every picture on the wall seems to be of naked curvy women feeding some moustached man with his clothes on. There are mirrors and dark panels on the walls. There are pretty risqué statues everywhere. The *Kama Sutra* features big in the artwork here. The bathrooms are my favourite rooms. They are so great – heated floors and wet rooms, massive baths that I can lie right down in. I've never had that before.'

'What are you giving Lauren to do?'

'We've driven around. She has an Ordnance Survey map and makes notes on it, thoughts really. Any updates from your side?'

'We got no new information about Toby except we can be pretty sure he spent the missing time in the music shop. I quizzed the assistant again and it seems they got on so well, time just slipped by.'

'Any sightings of Kensa at the tube stations or at the small Tesco in Greenwich?'

'Not so far, but that Tesco bag could have been from anywhere.'

Lauren came back into the house and Willis came off the phone to Jeanie.

'I'm going to lie down, Ebony.'

'Okay, Lauren, did you get through to Toby?'

'No. I left another message.'

'I'm going out for a while, okay?'

'Yes, I'll phone you if I need you.'

Willis phoned Carter but there was no reply and it went straight to answer machine. She got into the detectives' pool car left for her by Pascoe and drove towards Stokes farm. She wanted to speak to Mawgan about Kensa. She thought she could do it better on her own, woman to woman. As she drove up the farm lane she could see no lights coming from the cottages on the left. The air was heavy and damp as the sea mist covered everything. The sky was full of squawking gulls and she could hear the cows lowing from the barn as she drew into the farm. She parked up and the collie came bounding over to see her. Mawgan emerged from the house. In the light of day Willis could see that even though her jaw was square and her hair short and red, her face had a delicate look about it, smaller than average features, and her eyes were a piercing turquoise. Even though Mawgan was twenty-seven, she had a baby face.

'I need to talk to you.'

'You'll have to follow me, I have chores.'

As they walked past the pig pens, the sow jumped up and rested her front legs upon the wall of her pen.

'Mind she doesn't bite you,' said Mawgan. 'She has young ones in the back.'

Willis walked side-on past the big sow that managed to still come within an inch of her. Past the pens the field opened up and it was dotted with corrugated round shelters for the pigs to live free-range.

'They won't hurt you,' Mawgan shouted back to Willis, who hovered by the gate and waited for Mawgan to finish her feeding chores and check on the pigs inside their huts.

'Are you coming back?'

'Yes.'

'Then I'll wait here for you.' Willis looked around her. The field rose steeply so that she couldn't see over the brow. To her left was a hedge and the glimpse of another field. To the right was the rest of the field and a section that was recovering from the onslaught of pigs foraging in the mud every day. Further down was the sea; she knew it was there but only the smell and the direction of the cold mist as it came across her face in icy draughts gave it away.

'All done?' she asked Mawgan as she came back to Willis at the gate.

'Pigs, yes, not the others.' She marched back, her wellingtons flapping as she strode. There was a mended section on the one the sow had bitten. Megan wore combat trousers for work clothes and a washed-out green fleece beneath her Barbour.

'You're a friend of Kensa's, aren't you?'

Megan nodded. 'Grew up together.'

'Here on this farm?'

'Here and all around. We knew every burrow in every field for a good two miles around.'

'Sounds like an idyllic childhood.'

'Does it?'

'Did Kensa live with you?'

'No, her family had a van on Cam's land, the farm next door. It's owned by us now.'

'Your dad has been very successful with buying up land here.'

'Yeah, he's a canny old sod. He bought at the right time. People wanted to sell, it's not so easy to make money from the land.' They went inside the food store and Mawgan began measuring out cups of food and adding it to buckets.

'I've heard of Cam and his sister Ella – are they still around?'

'Cam is, Ella left. Cam has the café on the beach.'

'Do you keep in touch with Ella?'

'No.' Mawgan paused to look on the wall and check the proportions, make sure she was putting the right things into the right buckets.

'You were very good friends, weren't you?'

'She was like a sister to me.'

'Where did she go?' Mawgan shrugged. 'Do you remember Toby Forbes-Wright, Mawgan?'

'Just about – it was a long time ago when he came down.'

'It was the five of you then, wasn't it, on the Saturday night in June when you all went back to Kellis House?'

'I don't remember that.'

They walked to the field around the outside.

'And you're a good friend of Kensa's?'

'Yes, I try to be.' Mawgan opened the gate and Willis followed into a small penned-off area that had the imprint of hooves in the churned-up soil.

'Kensa was at the funeral, wasn't she?' Mawgan nodded. 'What was she doing there?' She shrugged but didn't reply. 'Why did you feel you had to lie about it before?'

'I didn't think she should be there.'

'How did she get there?'

'She borrowed my car.'

'Where is it now?'

'She says she left it in Penhaligon somewhere but she can't remember where. I need to go and look for it.'

'Has she done that before? Borrowed your car and then left it somewhere?'

'All the time.'

'What did you say to her at the funeral?'

'I told her to wait there and we'd come home together.'

'Did she do that?'

Mawgan nodded.

'So you didn't come back on the train?'

'No.'

'Why did you lie about it?'

'Because I panicked, I suppose.'

'Did she have Samuel with her?'

'No.'

'Is there any way she could have had him in the car?'

'No. I didn't see what happened. She took my car and drove away when we got back here.'

'Why did you lie to us about how you got home? You must have felt that there was a chance Kensa would be involved in Samuel's abduction?'

'I lied because we stick together, I knew she'd be the chief suspect. People would jump to conclusions. I don't think people understand how fragile she is. She told me she only wanted to talk to Toby and she should be allowed to do that. It's Raymonds' fault if anyone's. He didn't listen to her. He knew it meant a lot to her but he chose to ignore it. You should ask him about the missing child. It's his fault all of this happened. He controls everything in this village. He wanted that house for himself. I wouldn't put it past him to try and stitch Kensa up for it. He knew she wanted to talk to Toby so badly she'd risk anything.'

'And, did she talk to him?'

'No. She says not.'

'Why not?'

'She couldn't approach him at the funeral so she gave up and we drove home.'

'So why lie to us?'

She shrugged. 'It's the way it is here.'

'I could do you for perverting the course of justice. Make sure that everything you tell me is the truth now. Tell me how you really got to the funeral. You didn't pay twenty pounds for a ticket.'

'Yes I did. I bought it in advance. I may have left a bit earlier than I said, could have been eight.'

Willis texted Pascoe to put out an alert and find the yellow Fiat. 'When you saw her at the funeral, was she upset?'

'Yes. She wanted to talk to Toby. She drove all the way to speak to him.'

'And you didn't think she should? You didn't want her to?'

'No, it wouldn't have done her any good.'

'She needs more support than she gets, doesn't she?'

'The whole town should do more to help her but they look the other way.'

'Why is that?'

'They're all frightened to go against Raymonds.' She looked at Willis and shook her head. 'And you call my childhood idyllic? You have no idea.'

'Did something happen to you, Mawgan, something you want to tell me about? Maybe I can help?'

Mawgan stopped. Looked round. Martin Stokes was calling her.

'My dad wants me. I'll be back.'

Willis watched her walk over to the gate and then disappear from sight, then she heard the creaking of barn doors and heard bellowing and the thunder of hooves and saw the steam coming off the cattle as they pushed and jostled one another, riding on each other's backs to get through the narrow gap and into the small pen where Willis stood. She looked back towards the gate and realized she was cut off. She started walking – now a hundred were in a pen meant for twenty. She was squashed and jostled as they pushed at her. Willis waved her arms in the air and the bullocks reared, frightened. The noise of their bellowing was deafening, the dust and dirt they churned was creating a cloud around them. Willis tried to climb over the fence but there was nothing to grip on. She tried to get a foothold on one of the posts positioned every eight feet or so. She heaved herself up and tried to kick a space for her feet to stay in the wire, but she fell back down and felt the pushing and the weight of the bullocks.

'Use me to pull yourself over!'

Mawgan was on the other side of the fence. Willis put her right hand on the top of the post and gripped Mawgan's shoulder, holding fast to her coat as she jumped as high as she could, pushing off the top of the post and hauling herself over the fence with Mawgan's help.

'Wanker. Towan let the bullocks out while he cleaned their pen – stupid bastard.'

Willis looked towards the entrance to the covered barn where the bullocks sat out their winter. Towan was laughing to himself.

'Christ – I thought they were going to crush me.' Willis bent over, trying to catch her breath.

'They could have killed you. They wouldn't have meant it – but there's nowhere to go and those horns get in the way. I would offer to have a word, but Dad wouldn't take notice. Towan's stupid. He's just like my dad – always joking about.'

Willis walked around the outside of the pen and called Towan over. He was grinning at his feet as he walked.

'You jumped over that fence like a proper bunny rabbit.' He looked at her and laughed.

'The attempted murder of a police officer will get you twenty years.'

'Harmless mistake. You townies don't have a clue, do you?'

'I am cautioning you, Towan – I don't know whether you think you live by a different set of rules here but you can get a place in prison just as easily as anyone else. One more trick like that and I'll make it my job to put you away.'

Towan laughed as he turned and started walking away. As she went to get back in the car she saw Misty tethered by the house.

'Is that Kensa's horse?' she called to Mawgan.

'Yeah – Towan said he was seen limping. He brought him up. The vet will be coming this afternoon. We have our stallion Brutus that's going to cover one of our mares. We'll get the vet to check him out then.'

'Kensa's worried about him.'

'I know. I'll make sure he's okay.' They walked back to the car.

'Mawgan, I need to understand what's going on in this village, what's under the surface.'

'Everyone has secrets here,' said Mawgan.

'You have to explain.'

'Mawgan!'

Towan came across and glared at Willis as he put his arm around his sister. Mawgan bowed her head as she shrugged him off and muttered that she had to get on.

Willis drove down and parked in the gateway to Kensa's field. She walked across to the line of vans. Kensa was standing at the top of the field clenching her fists as she called Misty's name.

'Kensa?' Kensa didn't move; she waited for Willis to climb the steep field to get to her. 'Kensa, it's okay. Misty is up at the Stokes farm. Mawgan says to tell you the vet is going to look at his leg.'

'There's nothing wrong with his leg. He's just old, that's all. Why did they take him?'

'I'm sorry; I don't know any more than that.'

Kensa pulled her blanket around herself and turned from Willis without another word. She marched back across the top of the hill to the gate into the next field. Willis watched her go, then she returned to her car.

Chapter 31

Mawgan went across to Misty after Willis had left and picked up each hoof in turn to see how Misty stood. She went to get a currycomb to give the animal a brush. Towan walked across to her.

'Misty isn't lame. What's going on?' she asked.

'He was limping in the field,' said Towan. 'Anyway, you tell me what's going on. I saw you sneaking around with that Cam. You and Kensa. You're going to get yourselves in big trouble if you don't watch it.'

'Mind your own business.'

'But it is my business. It'll be everybody's by the time you finish. Cam's always been as weak as water. You want a man in your life, you better choose someone else. He ain't no man.'

Mawgan felt down each of Misty's legs. 'Feels solid. Kensa's going mad looking for her horse. Take him back.'

'I will, I said. But are you listening to me?'

'Yes,' she mumbled.

'Dad wants you in the house.'

'Where is he? What does he want?'

'Down in the cellar. He needs help with the apple

storage – some of the rats have got in there and it all needs separating up and re-boxing.'

Mawgan put down the brush and walked towards the house. The air was damp; the cold clung to her face. She looked back to see Towan staring after her.

'Dad?' she called out as she walked through the kitchen, running her hand along the Aga rail to warm her fingers up as she passed on her way through to the stairs to the cellar.

'Dad, are you down there?' She glanced back up as she heard footsteps in the kitchen.

'Dad, what is it you want me to do?'

There was no reply as she looked down into the darkness of the cellar and the smell of fermenting apples. She flicked on the lights and saw the scurry of a sleek fat rat as it scarpered between the barrels of cider.

She turned to make her way back up the stairs when the cellar door banged shut and was locked from the outside. It went dark.

'Towan, open this door!' She felt her way back up the stairs and banged on the door. 'Dad!' she called, but there was only the sound of the rats moving about.

Towan went back to Misty. Martin Stokes had already undone the horse's rope and was leading him away from the house.

'Better make it quick before the vet gets here,' Stokes said. 'This'll get Brutus going. Come on, Misty, old fella.'

Stokes led Misty into the small paddock while

Towan went to fetch Bluebell the mare. He tethered her just outside the gate. Misty whinnied as he caught a whiff of her scent, but then turned back to eating grass. Brutus was dancing on his strong legs as Towan held him tightly and led him through to the paddock.

Kensa had only flip-flops on her feet as she wrapped the blanket around her and marched up the hill in the direction of Stokes' farm. The sharp cold air grated in her windpipe from the low mist and the cold. She could not see more than ten feet in front of her but she heard the sound of Misty as he whinnied and she felt her heart leap in her chest. She was within half a mile of the farm now, she quickened her pace. She jogged along the main road until she came to the lane that led to the farm. She turned her head to listen to the sounds; above the beating of her heart and the breath that rasped from her throat she heard the snorting of a stallion. She heard the squeals of fear and pain and the stamping of hooves.

Mawgan banged on the door. She kicked at it and felt it give a little but not enough. Her hard boots splintered the wooden door but it didn't break. She raged and smashed the door with her fists until her knuckles cracked on the wood. She heard the squeals of pain. They were coming from her own lungs, her own strangled fear.

Marky was just parking up his jeep next to his cottage when Kensa ran past him. He opened his door and called to her but she didn't stop. She was bare-foot now. The blanket was gone. Her thin nightdress was flapping around her bare legs.

Marky heard the sound of the horses. He ran to catch Kensa up as she pelted into the yard and towards the paddocks beyond. Bluebell stood terri-fied, tied to the gate, as Kensa passed her and ran straight into the paddock to protect Misty. Stokes yelled at her to get back as Brutus reared again and stamped down onto Misty's head as he lay on the ground. Kensa stood over her horse as Brutus reared again. Then the stallion was blasted back as Marky aimed the power washer from the yard at Brutus.

'You fucking psycho!' Marky said to Towan. 'This had to be your idea.' He opened the gate and went to catch Brutus. 'Get the vet.'

'We meant no harm,' Stokes said as Towan slipped away.

Kensa lay across Misty's neck and clung to him as sobs racked from her.

Towan opened the cellar door and Mawgan lunged at him. Her fists were bloody. All she wanted to do was get out of there. Towan stood in her way.

'Move, Towan.' She was shaking violently, but she couldn't look in his eyes.

'Say please.'

'Move or I'll kill you.'

'Yeah – like you could?' he hissed in her face. 'You just do as you're told.'

Towan was dragged backwards from behind before he had a chance to say more. Marky threw him out of the way as Mawgan made a run for it, and Marky landed a few punches into Towan's head that forced them crashing into the kitchen table. Mawgan grabbed the cast-iron kettle from the Aga and swung it in the direction of Towan. It hit his back, bounced and then smashed into the cabinet and sent china crashing to the floor. Martin Stokes bellowed for them to stop as he stood in the doorway.

'Mawgan, go and see to Kensa and take her upstairs. Stay with her till she settles down. Marky, you get back to your cottage and stay there – this has nothing to do with you. Towan, come with me, there's a mess to clear up and a horse to bury.'

Chapter 32

Carter called Pascoe, who was already up in the helicopter. Carter could hear a distant drone.

'I need the old police station available to me. I think it will be good to bring it home here.'

'Okay, I'll send officers over now to get it ready.'

'Anything interesting from the video footage yesterday?'

'We saw Jago and Marky doing a bit of beach-combing at Garra Cove. They saw us, which is the danger when we're so obvious. I'm afraid we're going to spook everyone.'

'Yeah. How long till you've exhausted the search?'

'Tomorrow will do it.'

Carter came off the radio and texted Willis where he was. She replied that she was on her way and then he walked across the street towards the dress shop.

Carter studied Mary-Jane Trebethin as he crossed the street. She was standing just by the entrance, leaning in to adjust a child's outfit in the window display. She stopped fiddling with the display and stared at him through the glass; he thought there was something very quaint about her. She belonged in a dress shop in one of the more prosperous towns. Here she was queen bee with no one to impress. Here in this slightly shabby high street with sand blowing in and with poverty rife in the winter months. He wondered what kept her rooted to the seaside village.

'How can I help?' Mary-Jane said with a pinched expression; she had watched him coming and moved to the safety of the counter. Her bony hands and long, immaculately painted nails rested outstretched on the counter.

Carter gestured towards the Surfshack. 'Gone surfing!'

'Oh yes, I expect Marky has decided to catch some waves instead of working.'

'But it looks like he's done very well, owning the surf shop. It's a big premises, nice-looking.'

'Mmm.' Mary-Jane turned up her nose as she picked at flecks of material that had floated onto her cash desk.

'You don't approve?'

'Oh my goodness, I'm delighted for Marky. All the young people in the village deserve a big helping hand if we want them to stay here and make it their home.'

'Have you lived here long?'

'Since I married my husband, thirty-odd years ago.'

'Is Mr Trebethin available for me to have a chat?' Carter knew the answer but he was taking his time to study her. Her nose was so pinched it didn't look real. She shook her head and frowned.

'Mr Trebethin and I are no longer married. He moved to Australia. Now, how can I help, officer?'

'You attended Jeremy Forbes-Wright's funeral on Monday?'

'That's correct,' she answered smugly.

'Why did you go? Was he a special friend?'

'I went to pay my respects, that's all.' She looked put out.

'Did you hear about his grandson being abducted that afternoon?'

'I did, so distressing. I don't understand why you've come down here looking for him. I hope this village won't become synonymous with a missing child. That's the last thing we want.'

'Let's hope we find him soon then.'

'You'd better go back to London and look.'

'What did you do after the funeral?'

'Uh, a bit of sight-seeing.' The heat had come to her indignant face as she pulled out some cardigans from the shelves to her right and began refolding them.

'Where?'

'Greenwich, I think.'

'Who were you with?'

'Is this really relevant?'

'I wouldn't ask it if it wasn't.'

'Mr Raymonds and I took a look around Greenwich. We went into the *Cutty Sark* museum.'

'But you didn't come back with him?'

'No, he had things to do, something came up. He left early and I went to join Mr Stokes.'

'Whereabouts do you live?'

'I live on the other side of the beach, above the cliffs.'

'Near Mr Raymonds?'

'Well, up the road from him.'

'Your son Jago also went to the funeral, didn't he?'
Her face transformed into a smile.

'Jago wanted to go to the funeral.' The smug smile
had returned but this time it was accompanied by a
slightly nervous tug at the corner.

Carter was half-watching the beach. He saw a VW
van pull in with surfboards on the top. Carter watched
Jago get out.

'It must be great to have your son back home.'

'It is.'

'Are there many prospects for him here, do you
think?'

'He seems to manage very well. He picks up work
here and there. He's finding his feet.'

'How old is your son, if you don't mind me asking?'

'He's thirty-one.' Carter was watching Jago get
into his wet suit and thinking that it probably wasn't
the time of life to just go surfing. Carter was a year
away from forty and he knew how important his
thirties had been, career-wise.

'When you were in London, did you see anything
of Kensa?'

'No. Kensa didn't go to the funeral.'

'Are you certain?'

'Yes.'

'Why wouldn't she have gone, when the rest of the
village went?'

'Well, I don't know, I suppose Kensa didn't have
the same sort of relationship with the Forbes-Wright
family.'

'Tell me, do you know Cam and his sister Ella?'

'Yes. Cam's got the café on the beach. He's doing well.' She looked as if it hurt her to say it.

'And Ella?'

'I have no idea about Ella. She left here a long time ago.'

'Tell me, Mary-Jane, how do you feel about Kellis House being sold? Would it worry you to see strangers living in it?'

'No, I don't think it would. I'm not sure I understand everyone's reluctance to embrace the new. I'd like to see new blood here.'

'Thank you for your help,' he said to Mary-Jane. 'If you get any children's clothes going missing – the size that would fit a small two-year-old – please let me know at once.'

Carter stepped outside, walked back to his car and stood looking out towards the wild waves; they were breaking way out to sea. Their noise was deafening. Willis parked up beside him.

'That sea looks freezing,' Willis said as she got out of her car and rubbed her hands together, blowing on them. Carter gestured for them to get inside his car and talk. 'Lovely to look at,' Willis continued, once inside, 'but frightening to get anywhere near – I'm not used to it, I suppose.'

'It's a bit like a dog,' said Carter wistfully.

'Huh?' Willis frowned at him.

'You know . . . it can sense your fear. If you're not confident it knows. It can kill you just like that.' He snapped his fingers in the air.

'Thanks, very reassuring.'

Carter looked out of his side window. There were a couple of children digging away at the top of the beach.

'This must be a great place to grow up in many ways.'

'Yes, but it's all a bit suffocating here, don't you think? I spoke to Mawgan – she implies her childhood was anything but nice. She says the village is turning against Kensa. She admitted to travelling back with Kensa in the car.'

'I saw you put out an alert for Mawgan's car.'

'Yes, hopefully it won't be long till it's found.'

'Did Mawgan look like she knew where Samuel is?'

'She said she didn't see him in the car; could he have survived in the boot?'

'Yes, wrapped up, sedated,' answered Carter. 'If Kensa did kill Samuel and dump his body in London before she left, she would have known where she was going and how to get there unnoticed. There's no sign of her at the local stations to the cemetery or Greenwich. Is she really capable of planning this? Are we really thinking she could have organized this?'

'She's not really as naive as we think. She manages to get herself dressed now and again. She goes to town by the sounds of it and she drove to the funeral. Maybe somewhere along the line she knows London,' said Willis. 'But also, she went there to talk to Toby and she didn't achieve that at the funeral. She could have followed him back home and to the music shop and then chickened out, or got angry and decided she didn't want to talk to him, she actually wanted to destroy him. His son is outside, left in the cold, and she snatches him. We know she has the car so she doesn't have to carry him far.'

'Robbo still hasn't found any footage of her in Greenwich itself,' added Willis.

'It was a busy day; lots of crowds.' Carter shrugged.

'Revenge?'

Carter looked perplexed. 'Possible, but she's such a loose cannon. If she took him, God knows what she had in mind.'

'She wants to see Toby – we should make him come down. She went all the way to London to speak to him.'

'What about Raymonds? We know he was in Greenwich. He insisted on coming back on his own and he hangs about a service station, waiting for what? Marky and Jago, or someone else? Someone to take the boy off his hands maybe?'

'He's one of the prime suspects – he's up there with about ten others,' Willis sighed, 'because then there's Marky and Jago.'

'Yeah, they called in at the services but didn't even get out of the car. Where did they go then?'

'Robbo's finding that out.'

'But if it's Raymonds, then why?' asked Carter.

'It will be some power game that he's playing,' answered Willis. 'It'll be all about control and him choosing the rules of the game. He must be mad that Jeremy Forbes-Wright died like he did. He must have thought Toby wouldn't dare alter the arrangement; after all, it's haunted Toby all his life as well as Kensa's.'

'But they have no choice with death duties,' said Carter. 'The price offered – five hundred thousand – isn't enough but it surprises me they have it in the kitty. I suppose the house must have been very lucrative, a lot of them must have been paying guests. What do you think, Eb?'

'I think Jeremy Forbes-Wright wanted to make a statement in his death. He wanted to leave them all with a heap of problems. This was his idea of fun and maybe, in his own way, he was trying to make amends for the past.'

'By leaving Toby in all this trouble?'

'By exposing this place.' Willis was looking at the sign beside them:

PLEASE DON'T FEED THE GULLS,
IT MAKES THEM AGGRESSIVE –
THEY SEE HUMANS AS FOOD!!

'Nice!' she said out loud. 'Sums this place up – even the birds will rip you apart given half the chance. Kensa paints quite a picture of this community. Raymonds virtually told her that if she wanted to hold her head up ever again then she should forget about making any charges.'

'Why would he do that when he hates Londoners coming down and spoiling his little world? It would have been a perfect opportunity to stitch up an MP? Now, with JFW gone, he must be trying to think of a way to salvage the situation. He's maybe thinking about a little bit of blackmail if there were escorts involved and VIPs.'

'Profit, lies, secrets – something happened in that house,' answered Willis.

'Absolutely,' replied Carter. 'Raymonds says that the community look after one another and to hell with everyone else. He may be retired from the Force, but he's still the one dishing out the orders. He's built himself quite a dictatorship here.'

'That's a lot to look after, guv.'

'It's a big responsibility, isn't it? How long before someone tries to overthrow you?'

'We know from Toby that there were five of them left the beach to come back to the house. Can we open an investigation into the rape?' asked Willis.

'We can, if we think it will get us something we need towards finding Samuel. But we have enough on our hands. Cam runs the café on the beach. Let's go and talk to him. Jago is one we haven't talked to properly yet, either,' Carter said, straining to see something out at sea. 'I watched him go in surfing earlier when his mother wasn't looking. I reckon that's him in the water – we can go down and see if we can get him out to talk to us.'

'Shall we grab a coffee to go first and establish if that's Cam?' Willis looked over at the café.

'Sure, you okay?' Carter studied her for the first time since she'd got into the car. 'You look a bit washed-out.'

'I'm okay. Towan's idea of a joke was to see if he could trample me in a stampede, but hey – maybe it's a lack of a sense of humour on my part?'

'Shit.'

'I found out I can jump really high.'

'We'll have him arrested for that, the little bastard.'

'No, I'm hoping it won't happen again. But he definitely didn't want me to talk to Mawgan. I think she would have a lot to say to me if she wasn't so scared.'

Carter got out of the car and stretched his back with a groan.

'The bed at the hotel is too soft. Normally it's Archie – he usually ends up in our bed. I wouldn't mind too much but he turns round like the hands of a clock all night.' As he said it, Carter rolled his eyes and shook his head as Willis smiled. She knew he was thinking that he had everything to be thankful for; at least Archie was safe. He took out his phone.

'Two minutes,' he said to Willis as he walked away dialling Cabrina's number.

When he returned to the car ten minutes later he was smiling, upbeat.

'How's she coping?' asked Willis.

'Typical Cabrina fashion. She's rolled up her sleeves and got stuck in. New colour scheme, new curtains. Apparently she's using our holiday in Morocco as an inspiration for the new theme. I hope not, that's when the little blighter was conceived. We don't need any more babies on the scene.'

'You couldn't get a better boy than Archie. Anyway, I bet it will look fab.'

'Yes. Probably.' Carter looked happy, calm. He'd managed to juggle work and home and he had a partner who could survive on her own, which was the main requirement if your other half was a detective.

Chapter 33

They walked across to the café. As they approached they could see a thin-faced man in his thirties looking at them through the glass – he looked like he would rather shut the shop than let them in.

'Hello,' he said, as they opened the door; his eyes didn't smile.

'Hi,' said Carter. 'Are you the owner of this café?'

'Yes. My name's Cam. I heard you were the officers investigating the little boy's disappearance.'

'That's right, do you know the Forbes-Wright family?'

'Well, I know of them. I'd met Jeremy Forbes-Wright a few times. You couldn't really avoid him in this town.'

'I see. Coffees, please, one cappuccino, extra everything, and one black double espresso.' Willis was choosing a cake. 'I gather you weren't that keen on him then?' asked Carter.

Cam got on with the coffees; he glanced back over his shoulder and gave a noncommittal shrug. 'I didn't really have an opinion.'

'And you didn't you go to the funeral in London?'

'I went up that day but I didn't actually go to it.'

'Okay – why was that?'

'I just fancied a day in London. It was going to be so quiet here anyway – I thought, what the hell – I'll cadge a lift and go.'

'Sounds fair enough,' Carter replied. 'Who did you go with?'

'In the end, I decided to catch the train there and back.'

'Are you open every day?'

'Not for the whole day. There's no point when there's no one around. Weekends are busy.'

They picked up their order and walked down the beach towards the water's edge.

Willis had a coffee in one hand and a *pain au chocolat* in the other.

'Okay, well that's another suspect added to the list then. How many more people thought they'd cadge a lift but not actually go to the funeral and then not actually cadge a lift?'

'We need to pull his story apart when we finish with Jago,' answered Carter. 'I want to make sure we don't miss him. I want to ask him about the beach party. Then we'll go back and talk to Cam. Christ, where did that go?' Carter turned round to see her stuffing the last of the pastry into her mouth. He picked at a blueberry muffin and then put it back into the bag. Willis pointed to a group of surfers only now visible as the waves subsided a little.

'They seem to be just sitting out there.'

'Yeah.' Carter stood looking at the surfers lying on their boards. 'That's Jago coming in now, I think.'

'When I met him he was a little too cocky and thought a lot of himself.'

'I saw him the same night at the bar, definitely likes to think he's a cut above the average here.'

They watched him ride a wave and paddle his board towards the shore. He got out shaking the seawater from his ears, holding his board under his arm. He grinned at them.

'Hello, you'll have to take it in turns but you can borrow my board – the wet suit should fit.' He smiled. Carter grinned and shook his head.

'Hardly worth it if it's messy like that, is it?' Willis was impressed – Carter had been swatting up on surf lingo.

'Ah . . . always worth it, just to get in the water.'

'Hello again; you've met my colleague, DC Ebony Willis here?' Carter introduced her.

'Yes, but not properly. Jago. Jago Trebethin.' He shook her hand with a firm, freezing grip, making sure he maintained eye contact as he did so. He was Carter's height – five nine.

'Now, will you excuse me, I need to get out of this wet suit.'

'Of course. Mind if we chat to you while you do it?' asked Carter.

'No, my van is parked up there on the edge of the beach.'

He started walking towards it. When they reached the van he peeled his wet suit down to the waist and slid back the side door of the old VW Camper. He reached in for a towel and dried his blond, sun-bleached shaggy hair. He was lean and muscled.

'I hear you used to live in London?' said Carter, trying to get over his abs-envy. Robbo had got hold of Jago's CV. Carter had read it – Jago hadn't stayed more than two years in a job. He'd been in recruitment in central London with three different companies.

'Yes, till recently. I got done-over work-wise, thought I was embarking on this great career, but it didn't happen – so I decided to head home and have a rethink.'

'You're a local then?' Willis asked. She took the top off her coffee and finished it, looked around for a bin.

'I suppose I am, but I'm not thought of as one. I was sent away to school in Bristol and then I went away to uni and left straight after. I am back now, of course, but most people my age have never left and . . . I don't intend to stay long.'

'And your friends in the water?' Carter turned to look out at the surfers. 'They seem determined to stay out even though it's freezing.'

'Yeah,' he laughed. 'They're hardy locals. Born and bred. Any surf is good surf. Look, I'm really sorry to hear about the little boy,' he said as he pulled a T-shirt over his head. 'It doesn't make any sense why someone should take him.'

'How did you spend your day in London after the funeral?'

'I hung about with Marky for a bit and then I went to do my own thing.'

'Which was?'

'I just went shopping for a few hours and caught

up with the lads before coming home. We didn't stay that long.'

'What did you buy?' asked Willis.

'Nothing, in the end. I wanted some new trainers but I couldn't see any I liked.'

'Where did you look?'

'Oxford Street.'

'Nike Town?'

'No, one of the small sports shoe shops, I forget which.'

'And you met up with them again?'

'We went to a few pubs around town.'

'Which pubs?'

He shook his head.

'Sorry – wish I could remember.'

'Have you talked to Marky today?'

'No,' he said, puzzled. He looked very practised at hiding what he was thinking, thought Ebony.

'Oh, it's just that I had a very illuminating conversation with him about the fact that you actually left London at five on the day of the funeral,' said Carter.

'Did we?' Jago laughed. 'Oh well, apologies if my memory isn't good. I'm obviously a much worse drinker than I realized. Marky would know what time for sure. I remember now – we decided we'd rather see our mates in Exeter instead.'

'You can see them any time, it's just up the road, isn't it?'

'Well, you're probably right, but it was just one of those snap decisions, I expect – a few beers and we decided to hit the road.'

'Funny – I even thought it might be to wind Raymonds up?'

'What? No way. He's so regimented about things; but sometimes it just doesn't work out the way he plans it.'

'Funny thing was, he was at the motorway services at the same time as you and you didn't seem to talk to one another.'

'Really? Bizarre.'

'You didn't even get out of the car; what was the point in going into the services?'

'Um, I think we needed petrol.'

'So you sat outside the refreshments section.'

'Well, I have no answer for you, I'm sorry. We pulled over for Marky to have a rest, I expect. He probably had a little snooze in the car. It's a long way.'

'We've been hearing all about an incident with Kensa and Toby Forbes-Wright that happened after a party on this beach,' Willis said. 'What do you know about it?'

Jago stopped drying and stood gawking, shaking his head.

'On this beach?'

'We were told you saw what happened?' Willis continued. 'You were there.'

'You mean back when I was a teenager?'

'Yes, June 2000.'

'I don't remember much – I guess you mean the beach party? That's mostly what I remember – it was the largest beach party I've ever seen here. I just happened to be here that night. I don't know any more than anyone else. Whoever told you that I saw anything is wrong.'

'So, why did you say you didn't know what I was talking about?' asked Willis.

'I don't know – it's such a long time ago. It was just a beach party that got a bit messy.'

'What do you remember about it?' Carter asked.

Jago shook his head, splattering water from his hair, and frowned with a hint of 'What's your point?'

'I told you – I know about as much as anyone else.'

'What do you remember?'

'I remember it was packed with kids off their faces, they were partying, drinking. They'd lit a couple of fires. There were people swimming, dancing. A bit of stuff going on that shouldn't have been.'

'Like?'

'Sex on the beach. Drugs, skinny dipping – so many of them were wrecked already.'

'What time was that?'

'Eleven?'

'You said they were wrecked. Where did they get the drugs?'

'Brought them with them, I suppose. Who knows?'

'There was no local supplier at the time?'

'Here in Penhal? I don't think so. I wasn't home enough to know things like that. It wasn't my type of thing – I've always been heavily into sport. The two don't mix.'

'Someone should have told Lance Armstrong that,' said Carter.

'I really don't remember much about that night, sorry – I was the same age as the kids, more or less.'

'Four years older than Kensa, three years older than Toby – it's a lot of difference in your teens,' argued Willis. 'You must remember going back to Kellis House, where it all kicked off?'

'No.' Jago's face dropped.

'Cam and Ella Simmons were there, Mawgan too. You decided to disrupt their little get-together at the house?'

Jago shook his head and stared at Willis.

'No idea, sorry.'

'Okay, well, we'll be staying here for a few days – if you think of something, get in touch.'

'Will do.'

'Don't forget the surf,' he called after them, and waved Carter back to him. 'Anything you need to borrow you can ring me. Wait a tick.' He left his wet suit under the tap at the edge of the Surfshack and went back to his van, went round to the driver's seat and leaned in. He emerged with a piece of paper and scribbled his number down before handing it to Carter.

Carter pushed it in his pocket.

'Thanks.'

'And you too, of course.' He looked across and grinned at Willis as he picked up his wet suit and held it up to drip. 'We'll get you fitted up with a board and a wet suit no problem. You won't believe how great it is out there. A real adrenalin rush.'

'Don't think so,' she muttered under her breath. 'They've already tried to kill me once.'

Jago finished rinsing his wet suit. He hung it on the top of his van to drip off the side and then he got into the VW and pulled the door shut; he sat there sweating. After five minutes he climbed over into the front and started it up. He drove up to the Penhal Hotel, parked up on the street in front and ran up the steps. He went straight to the public phone.

'Marky?' Marky answered it from home. 'Trouble. I've just had a couple of visitors. We have to move the merchandise. Get rid of it.'

'Where? Where can we move it to? We can't shift it now. It's better where it is.'

'No, it isn't. Believe me,' he hissed into the phone.

'I'm not moving it. We have to sell it to give them their money. It's not some fucking game to those guys. We have to come out of this. Just stay calm, stay chilled.'

'Listen to me. They're going to have a thousand officers in this place any day. They will find it. Get rid of it. I'm not going to spend ten years in jail just because of a stupid mistake. We messed up. We'll just have to lie low for a while. Move away, sell up the business and go to Scotland, anywhere, for a year or so. Those guys will be gone by then. An anonymous tip-off to the law and we'll help put them inside. Man up. We'll be okay. It was a mistake. Learn from it.'

'Oh, I've learned a lot. I've learned that you just worm your way out of any trouble. I'll never go into business with you again. I'm moving it today and I'm going to stick to the plan and sell it.'

'It's all yours, bro.'

Chapter 34

As they went past Cam's café it had closed. They drove to Kellis House, and Willis asked Carter to pull his car in by the gateway.

'Do you want me to come in as well?' Carter asked as she got out of the car.

'No, it's okay, I'll be as quick as I can. I just need to check on Lauren. She was having a rest when I left.'

Inside the cottage Willis could hear Lauren tapping on her keyboard. The sound came from the lounge.

'Lauren? You okay? Sorry I've been so long; we need to try and get around to take a statement from all those people at Jeremy's funeral. What are you doing, working?'

'I'm doing what you suggested – I'm researching the land all around here and looking for possible places where Samuel could be. I don't understand why the search parties are not looking for him down here in the village.'

'We have helicopters out and searches in the remote areas around the cliff. We are searching, I promise. We need to handle this community with kid gloves, Lauren. The harder we squeeze them, the more tightly knitted they become. But we are making cracks in their armour. They are beginning to turn on one another. We will get the truth.'

'What about Kensa, what about what she said? She seemed so certain that she'd seen Samuel.'

'We're looking into it all. Kensa has been sectioned a few times.'

'I suspect she never even got counselling for what she went through. Since I found that out about Kensa it explains a lot about Toby. I can see how frightened he is now of being accused of anything. He'll say anything to get himself out of trouble. He says he blocked it out, that he never remembered it at all. But it makes me feel that I don't know him at all. If he did that to another human being, could he harm Samuel?'

'Did you know about his close friendship with his workmate, Gareth?'

She shook her head. 'I feel like he couldn't confide anything in me.'

'Lauren, why don't you get your coat? You can bring your phone and continue researching. You can get out and have a bit of a walk while we're talking to people? Bring Russell.'

Outside in the car, Carter was on the phone. He looked at Willis as she came out with Lauren.

'Lauren's coming along for the ride.'

'Okay, no problem. As long as you don't mind waiting around a bit?'

'No, that's all I'm doing at the house anyway.'

They drove past the field where Kensa's caravan was and up over the brow of the hill. The farmland stretched down towards the sea to the left and to the right the road wound round, fenced in by high hedges as thick as the lanes they bordered. Occasionally gateways opened up and then the countryside spread out in hills.

'There's a sign for Stokes' farm on the left,' Willis said as they passed a small crossroads where the road turned right into the nearby market town of Wadebridge or on to a fishing village along the coast. 'We go down this way – I want to go back to the farm.'

They took the track and Willis looked back at Lauren to see her with a map spread out on her lap.

'This is the cottage where Marky and Jago live.'

They pulled up outside a white-painted workman's cottage. To the right of it was a dumping ground for cars and farm vehicles.

Lauren got out of the car. 'Is it okay if I have a wander?' She held the folded map in one hand and Russell's lead in the other.

Willis turned to Lauren. 'Fine, see you back here in about thirty minutes? If we're out early I'll phone you.'

Lauren nodded as she set off up the lane.

The door to the cottage opened and Marky stood stripped to his waist.

'Sorry, were you showering?' said Carter. 'Can we have a word?' Marky stepped back from the door.

Carter looked at the machines waiting for repair beside the house. 'So, which one do you drive? You starting a collection of old farm machinery?'

'I drive the Suzuki jeep,' Marky replied. He didn't look happy. 'The rest I look after for the farm.'

'Which one has this space?' Willis asked as they

stood in front of a car-sized gap and different tyre prints.

'That's Mawgan's car, she parks it here sometimes.'

'Where is it now?'

'I really don't know.'

'Has she asked you to look for it?' asked Willis.

'No.'

'Mind if we come in?' Carter asked as they followed Marky back into the house. Inside the cottage it was dark and smelled of unwashed boys mixed with the ripe smell of farm.

'Are you going to open the shop again today?' asked Carter.

He shook his head. 'This time of year – most of my time is spent making and mending surfboards.'

Carter looked at Marky as he began searching through the washing pile. He saw a rolled note coming out of a pair of trousers. Marky hastily covered it up.

'You must get on well with the Stokes family to rent a cottage and a workshop space from them?'

'I help mend the farm machinery in exchange for renting the workshop. Jago's just moved in with me.'

'You're a mechanic then as well – very impressive.'

'Look, we already spoke this morning? I need to get on.'

'Yes, and then we spoke with Jago. Perhaps you have too? Did he just phone?'

'Yes.'

'I bet. You want to get your stories right, I expect.'

'We don't have any stories.'

'What about the fact that you sat in a service station

for half an hour. The same service station where an item of Samuel Forbes-Wright's clothes was found.'

'I was having a nap.'

'Yes, Jago came up with that one, didn't he? You seem a little edgy, you okay?' Marky was shaking.

Lauren walked along the lane towards the farm. She looked at her map and cut left as she saw a path following the hedge around the field. Russell scampered alongside. The earth was ploughed and churned up ready to plant in the spring. The wind had died down but still the ferocious gulls screamed in the skies above her. They swirled over her head and attacked one another as they flew in circles above the field. She watched them and smiled to herself – much good the scarecrow was doing in the middle of the field!

As she felt the earth crumble beneath her feet she picked her way carefully and wished she'd worn her walking boots. She looked back at the gate that she'd come in by and almost turned back but then she felt the impulse to walk further. She looked at her map again. This was a short cut to the farm, then she could double-back and meet the cottage again along the lane. It wasn't exactly 'out of her way'. It wasn't exactly 'in the middle of nowhere' either but her heart began to race. The screaming gulls made an eerie sound as they fought each other in midair. Russell came close to Lauren's side.

'You went to the funeral – why?' asked Carter. 'The Sheriff wanted to create a united front? Why was that, do you think?'

Marky shrugged and looked around for a shirt to put on; he smelled it and then decided it would do.

'It's no secret that my dad is fiercely loyal to Cornwall. He saw Jeremy Forbes-Wright as one of our community.'

'Yeah, right. You're all scared about something.'

Marky shook his head. He looked away.

'I don't think so.'

'Do you know Kensa well?'

'Of course,' he said. 'I've known her all her life.'

'Were you ever a couple?'

'No.'

'But you would have liked to be?"

'No. Years ago when we were young, then people thought we might have been together but it never happened. I love Kensa as a friend.'

'Why didn't it happen?'

'How do I know? Things do or don't happen,' he said, exasperated.

'It had nothing to do with the rape, the brutal attack?'

'What attack?'

'The one that was hushed up, the one on Saturday June the 17th, fourteen years ago? You were on the beach that night.'

'No one ever said it was rape.'

'Didn't they?'

'Seems to be common knowledge.'

'It was covered up. Why, because it involved the police sergeant's son? You were there that night. You forced your way into Kellis House when it was just

Toby and four of his little friends. You were all off your skulls on drugs that you sold to people, you sourced. It started off as a laugh, then it all went hideously wrong, didn't it? At what point did you call your dad in to help? Which one of you *men* raped your friend?'

'I don't remember any of it, and anyway, what's this got to do with the little boy going missing?'

'Because Kensa was up there on the day of the funeral: the same day the boy was snatched. The funeral of the man who paid Kensa off so that she wouldn't press rape charges against his son. That's why? But we don't believe it was Toby who did it, you know why? Because his drink had been spiked and so had Kensa's. He wouldn't have been capable in a month of Sundays. Whereas you lot? You were off your faces on God knows what – the one thing you didn't feel was tired.'

'This is all crap. You're talking to the wrong person.' Marky shook his head. He looked as if he wanted to leave. 'I was barely sober myself that night. I have no idea what went on. I mean – it was my eighteenth birthday.'

Lauren kept her eye on the scarecrow as she walked at the edge of the ploughed field. She wasn't a lover of them. It had always scared her when she watched *The Wizard of Oz* as a child. The time when he was set on fire had made her scream. Still she couldn't see the farm, but there was the top of a barn coming into view at the middle top edge of the field and she could see a gap in the hedge. She looked back at the gate

again – it was further now to go back than it was to
go on. All this trauma, tiredness, unbearable anxiety
in her life right now had affected even the way she
coped with quite ordinary events like a scarecrow in
the middle of a field and screaming big orange-beaked
gulls that seemed to have drops of blood on their
beaks.

She stumbled over the clods of earth and fell on her
knees. Russell jumped up on her. The earth was hard
in peaks and she felt a sharp dig into her kneecap as
she landed hard and awkward. As she went to push
herself back up she felt the whoosh of feathers near
her face and the scream of a gull as it flew so close to
her that she could see its beady eyes glaring angrily at
her.

Shit . . .

She stood and dusted herself off and looked
towards the scarecrow, whose head seemed to move
as the gulls came down and nestled over its face and
bit chunks from its feet, hands and face. Lauren kept
staring at it.

'You wanted to beat the crap out of Toby and teach
him a lesson for getting with Kensa? She's a local girl,
you said yourself you loved her in your own way –
must have stung a bit? She chose some posh kid who
was a piece of piss compared to you tough farm
boys,' said Carter.

'It wasn't like that,' replied Marky. 'We just wanted
a bit of fun. Towan got nasty with her and Ella had
been a girlfriend of his. He hadn't got over it. I don't
remember what happened. I was too drunk.'

'No you weren't, Marky. You were all looking for a fight that evening – fuck or fight, wasn't it? Wasn't it?'

'No, I didn't touch them. I wouldn't. I don't remember anything.'

'But you were happy for Toby to be blamed for this attack on Kensa?'

'It wasn't up to me. I was told that it was down to him and I accepted it.'

'Of course you did, it got you and the others off the hook. And afterwards no one spoke of it?'

'No.'

'Kensa just forgot about it?'

'No ... she changed. She got into drugs, sex with just about anyone and everyone. She didn't seem to care about anything any more.'

'Do you think she is capable of snatching Samuel?'

'I guess so – what does it take? I don't know. She's probably angry enough.'

'If she took him, where would she hide him?'

'Kensa knows all the stone huts and the deserted second homes. At some time she's been in a lot of them. That's where he'd be, in someone's second home.'

'And, if not Kensa, is there anyone else here that you think could have had a personal reason to want to take Samuel?'

'No, why would they?'

'As some kind of retribution? Some form of black-mail? Revenge? Some people in this community are very aggrieved that Toby has inherited the house.'

'I don't know why you're saying this to me. I'm not

responsible for any of it. I don't know where the boy is.'

Lauren stood where she was and then took one careful step after another towards the scarecrow. She didn't know why, but she knew she couldn't bear to walk any further into the field. She could turn and run but something held her there. Something in the way the gulls opened their beaks and screeched at her both mesmerized her and repulsed her. Something in the way they watched her. She tucked Russell under her jacket as they swooped down to attack him.

The scarecrow had a farmer's hat but it was tilted to one side where the seagulls' wings had flapped so hard and dislodged it. The scarecrow's head hung down. He seemed to be focused on the space ten feet ahead of him. His arms were not outstretched, they were caught behind him, tied to the pole. He had on a blue checked shirt with patterns of red. As she walked further forward the seagulls became more aggressive. They stared at her with their beady eyes and now she saw the crows, black and shiny, their long thick beaks stabbing at the scarecrow's feet. They hopped about the red churned soil and lunged at the angry seagulls. They turned to glare at Lauren.

She was within twenty feet of the scarecrow now and she couldn't keep her eyes from it. Its head drooped forward and down. The seagulls jabbed their beaks at its head. Pulling at the straw. But there was no straw. This was a Guy Fawkes type of scarecrow, it was meant to represent a man. She tried to see what they had used for a face. Its head was too obscured by warring gulls and opportunist crows to see properly. The scarecrow wore baggy old trousers under his shirt. He had a watch on his wrist.

Lauren took one more step and a seagull pecked furiously at the head of the scarecrow and the hat came off and the head was jerked and jolted between the gulls as they fought over it. White and grey feathers so bright in the gloom of the day; so sharp-edged and brightly contrasted against the black crows.

Mommy . . . Mommy . . . She gasped.

She could hear it in the screams of the gulls.

I'm here. I'm here . . . Mommy . . . Mommy.

Their voices so angry, and they flew at her to ward her off. They scratched her face with their sharp, blood-specked beaks and when she touched her face there was blood on her fingers. Russell tried to wriggle free and run. He was squealing in fear.

Now she was within ten feet of the scarecrow and the more she looked at its hands and feet the more she saw blood. She tried to look away but the screaming gulls seemed to both repel her and compel her to come closer.

Here, here, here . . .

She could hardly breathe. So caught in the middle of the swirling gulls and the black crows that at first she didn't see the scarecrow's head tip backwards and she saw he had no features, just blood and white gristle and loose-hanging shards of flesh.

* * *

As Willis and Carter walked along the lane towards the farm they heard the deafening cacophony of gulls and crows – and in among the sound was a woman screaming.

Chapter 35

Carter called Pascoe aside to talk in private. Pascoe excused himself from the doctor who had come from Penhaligon to certify the death. Stokes' body was still attached to the post.

'SOCOs are on their way, sir, they are coming from Truro,' he said as he got near to Carter.

'Okay, I need them to start working on the scene, but I've asked for my colleague from the MIT team to come down and he'll be taking over when he arrives first thing in the morning.'

Pascoe looked at him curiously. 'We have a specialist team, they can handle it.'

'I know and I appreciate that, but I have my reasons. This farm is of interest to us in the abduction case. I don't want anything overlooked while we're investigating two separate cases.'

'It's up to you, sir.' Pascoe looked slightly put out.

Carter went to find the Stokes family and Marky in the farmhouse kitchen.

'My sympathies,' he said, standing in the doorway.

'Are you going to cut Martin down?' asked Marky. 'You can't just leave him tied to the post. It's not right.'

Carter looked around at the broken crockery on the floor. Mawgan was sweeping it up. Towan was sitting at the table, holding a mug of coffee. He was staring at the table top. His hands were scraped with grazes and blood. His shirt was dirty with blood and mud.

'I appreciate how upsetting it must be to you all but Martin Stokes needs to stay where he is until the forensics team have arrived. He will be covered with a tent as soon as they get here – I suggest you wait in here for the next hour until that's done. I will need all your clothes,' said Carter. Towan didn't move. He didn't look at Carter. 'And, no one leaves this farm until they've been seen by the forensics officers.'

Marky nodded. He was standing resting against the Aga, his arms crossed over his chest. His face was set in a stony mask of anger and grief.

'Where's the woman who found him?' asked Towan.

'Lauren's gone.'

'She could have done it,' Towan muttered into his mug.

'Not likely though, is it, Towan?' Carter said. 'The doctor said he'd been dead an hour at the most. When did you see him last? Mawgan?'

'When he left to bury Misty. Towan went with him. That was the last time I saw him alive.'

Towan laughed. 'Yeah . . . and you think I didn't see that coming, you stupid bitch? If you think you and Marky are going to stitch me up over this one – think again.'

'Well?' Carter looked at Marky.

'It's true Mr Stokes ordered Towan to go and bury the horse. The last I saw was them going out to do it. I left here and went down to my cottage for a shower. You came after that.'

Towan pushed his mug away and sat back in his chair so that he could see everyone properly. 'And me and Dad got outside and I decided I had better things to do. I went to see if Marky had finished my surf-board. I went to his workshop. I went to check in the farm store next door. I'm supposed to be in charge of ordering when stocks get low.'

'Who else was here today?'

Towan reeled off the list.

'And Raymonds?' Carter looked surprised.

'He left a while ago; he picked up some things from the farm and drove up over the field, left that way,' said Towan.

'He didn't come up the lane, we would have passed him,' Carter pointed out.

'He came over the back too. There's a lane we use for getting the cows into the far fields.'

'Mawgan, are you okay?' Carter was staring at the bandages around her knuckles. One had slipped down as she bent her hands around the broom handle and he could already see the blackening and swelling around her knuckle. 'Looks pretty nasty that.' She shook her head but kept sweeping. 'What happened here? Does someone want to tell me?'

'Nothing happened,' said Towan. 'Just a bit of high spirits among siblings. Mawgan went off like a wild cat.' He smiled.

'Was Kensa here?'

'She still is,' answered Marky.

'Where is she?'

'Upstairs in my room,' answered Mawgan. 'I was going to take her home but she's in no fit state. Not since her horse was stamped to death.'

Towan tittered to himself.

'What happened there?' Carter asked.

Marky and Mawgan looked at Towan to answer. When he didn't, Marky did instead.

'Bluebell's in season. Towan thought it would be funny to have a stallion fight, except Brutus is two and Misty's eighteen – not ever meant to be a fair fight. Thankfully it was over quickly.'

Towan looked up and around the room. He turned his chair to look at Carter.

'Disappointing, really.'

Carter shook his head and stepped back out into the yard. He called an officer over to stand where he had been.

'Start writing down your statements. I'll send a Scene of Crimes Officer up here to take DNA swabs, and so on.'

Carter walked back down the lane to see Willis talking to the forensic teams who had arrived and were getting set up.

'This is Phil Leonard, the Crime Scene Manager from Penhaligon.' Willis did the introductions. 'DI Dan Carter, my colleague from MIT 17.'

'Pleased to meet you. I understand you have your own team arriving tomorrow?'

'Correct. But we need you to make a start.'

Leonard was nodding thoughtfully as Carter spoke. His eyes were on the field where Stokes' body, covered in a net, was being temporarily protected from further attacks by the birds.

'We'll carry on as we would normally here, and leave the rest of the farm to your guy.'

'Good, appreciate it.'

'Can we keep these birds off?' Leonard asked, as the herring gulls continued trying to attack both the body and the forensic officer approaching to work around it.

'Here.' An officer appeared with a packet in his hand and gave it to Willis as she stood watching from the gate. 'If you hang this over a tree and light it, it will get rid of the birds.'

She took it from him and read the instructions, then borrowed a lighter and walked back up the lane to the adjoining field. She hooked the string of bangers over a sturdy part of the hedge between the two fields and lit the rope. As she walked back down the lane she shouted over to Carter that he was about to hear a noise. When it came it boomed over the fields and scattered the birds as they flew squawking up and away.

'Shit!' Carter laughed and Leonard shook his head, smiling.

'Willis – bit of an understatement.'

Leonard called back to the officer managing the forensic equipment. 'We'll need to take him down and get a tent up.'

They unloaded the tent from the trailer and brought it into the field. An officer was taking soil samples from around the base of the post.

Willis came back to stand at the gate.

'It looks likely he was lured away from burying the horse,' Leonard explained as he walked across to the corner of the field where a tractor stood sideways on to a pile of earth. 'He hasn't filled it in yet. Something got him down off his tractor, then there's evidence of a scuffle and he was dragged from there to here. If the birds hadn't opened up the wounds on his hands we might have been able to get someone else's DNA on them. We might still get something from the postmortem. It was quite a big fight. We have shoe marks here, leather sole, but we can try for a match. The fact that someone killed him with an impromptu murder weapon speaks more of manslaughter.'

'Yeah – they might have come up here just to talk to him and it turned into an argument.'

Carter looked at Stokes' body.

'Was he dead by the time he got to here?'

'Probably.'

'They did a good job tying him onto it,' said Carter. 'It may have been manslaughter but they didn't run away straight after – they had time to gloat.'

Leonard was making a sketch of the body. 'He's secured with wire and there's a spike driven into the base of his spine,' he said as he drew the proportions of the stake in the ground. 'Which I presume was meant to hold a real scarecrow in place. It had to be driven pretty hard into the base of his back to make sure he didn't move.'

'It's not subtle, is it?' Carter said as he moved to get a better view of the body without overstepping into Leonard's zone. 'Someone has really thought this through. Sort of a triumphant gesture, isn't it? Bit like putting his head on a spike, but in a farming community way.'

'Heads on spikes were a warning to transgressors – a deterrent,' Leonard said as he wrote up his notes in the crime scene log.

'Yeah – well, puts me off thinking of getting an allotment. Someone hates him – really hates him. Would it have to be a man to do it? Would he be too heavy for a woman to lift onto that spike, do you think? The killer has to ram it home.'

'Someone used to lifting could do it, a man or a strong woman. I reckon he weighs about thirteen stone.'

Leonard was called back to oversee the erection of the tent.

Carter walked across to Willis: 'Any luck?'

'Robbo says he's getting somewhere – he's found one of the women who used to come to Cornwall. He's talking to her today. She's not happy to come to the police station but she'll speak on the phone.'

'While Kensa's here at the farm recovering – use the time now to get down to that van of hers and have a really good look at the others too. Take Pascoe and five officers with you. You go into Kensa's van on your own.' He lowered his voice. 'I don't want it trampled over. Have you got your forensics case?'

'It's in the car.'

'Take it and keep in touch. I can't see me leaving here for a few hours.'

'Yes, guv.' Willis went across to talk to Pascoe and organize the search team.

Leonard walked back over to them. 'Looks like we can cut the body down now. It can go to the mortuary ready for the post-mortem. We'll wait for your man from the MET to tell us what he wants done about that but we'll get all the paperwork in order.'

'Thanks. I'm going to talk to the family again,' Carter said, as he took off back up towards the house. He stopped in at the cottage to see Marky, who'd been allowed back to get some more clothes.

'You want to tell me what happened at the house?' Carter asked, as he closed the door behind him. 'The place looks like after one of the Arsenal and Tottenham games. There's debris everywhere and a lot of people nursing their wounds.'

'A few broken plates,' Marky said, 'that's all. I didn't see anything else.'

'Sure, okay,' Carter sighed, exasperated. 'Tell me ... what is it with this place? Supposed to be a great place to live – everyone knows everyone else and you all look after one another – what kind of bullshit is that? You'd think you'd want to help me discover who killed one of your friends, but instead you're trying to be as difficult as you can with me. You're trying to give me the run-around.'

'I'd like to help, but I just don't know what you're talking about. I don't know what you want me to say.'

Carter sighed heavily again. 'I see it. I can see what your problem is. There's so much going on that's secret in this village, isn't there? So many things that no one wants to speak about.'

'Probably.' Marky rummaged through his pile of clothes. 'And it's never been any different. After you leave it will be the same,' he said, as he rooted out two odd socks. He flashed Carter a look of defiance.

'Ah . . . that's where you're wrong.' Carter smiled. 'By the time I leave here I will know what happened to Samuel, and I will know who killed Martin Stokes. I'll go home after doing my job, same as I always do. After all, it's just a job, right? My life will go back to normal. But yours? Your life will never be the same again, because this village is a boiling cyst that's ready to burst. It's not a bubble you have here – it's a bubbling, angry, pus-filled boil, and we aim to tease it with a squeeze, enough to make it pop all by itself. When it does, it's going to erupt good and proper, and cover you and all those people who think that the outside world can't touch them here in Penhal. You think what occurs here in Penhal stays in Penhal? Sorry, mate, but you're so wrong.

'Soon you're going to have every camera crew in the world focused in on this village and waiting for you to explode. BOOM.' Carter mimed an explosion in the air. 'The truth will come out whether you want it to or not, and I hope, for your sake, as well as mine, it comes out ASAP, so I can go home to people who know what it's like to care about one another.'

Marky was watching Leonard and the SOCO team out of his front window.

'So, tell me, surprise me with the truth, how did Mawgan get injured?'

'I can't interfere with family stuff. Ask her yourself.'

'I will, and I will take her in for questioning and keep her there if I find matching injuries on her father's body. But I've noticed that Mawgan is a woman of few words, and I've noticed that Towan is a pig, so I'm asking you first.'

'You need to look on the back of the cellar door if you want to see how she got injured.' Marky held Carter's gaze.

'What was she doing in there?'

'She was locked in by Towan. His idea of a joke – mainly to stop her interfering with the horse fight, I expect.'

'And the mess in the kitchen?'

'When I found her, he got there first. He wasn't going to let her out.'

'Fights are common in this family, are they?'

Marky shrugged. 'Not unless Towan is around.'

'Him and the old man were close, weren't they?'

'Yeah, it wouldn't stop him though. He should have gone far away when he came out of the nick. He only came back to try and get money out of his dad.'

Carter went outside and watched as Stokes' body was bagged up. Marky followed and stood in the rain, watching them remove it. Towan stood in his cottage doorway.

The white forensic tent stood flapping as it took the brunt of the wind. The pigs were squealing to be fed, the horses whinnying. The noise of the cattle moving inside the barn, clashing their horns against the metal stalls, added to the din.

Mawgan appeared in the lane and she glared at her father's body as it passed.

Robbo rang. Carter walked back down the lane to get privacy. He was still watching Mawgan as she passed. She touched Marky's hand as he reached out to comfort her as she went by. She shook her head and walked on.

Willis waited while the caravans were jimmied open by Pascoe. They were empty – all except one which contained outside furniture for all of them stacked up inside. She left Pascoe to search them thoroughly inside and out, while she went back to Kensa's. When he'd finished, he came to tell her he was going down to make sure things were fully operational for them at the old police station.

Kensa's van was unlocked. Outside, the fire was still smouldering from the night before and the smell of horse hit her as she opened the door. The rain began pelting on the caravan roof and the wind came out of nowhere to buffet it, as if it was made of cardboard.

Willis took a step inside the van and took her time to look in every corner as she carefully lifted and replaced all of Kensa's belongings. The shelves were full of things that didn't seem to have a purpose. There were corks and bar mats and even dead flowers. Willis examined everything, hearing the officers getting on and searching the other vans. She took down a small photo album from the shelf above the seating in the lounge. It had been hidden beneath a few pictures of Misty and some horseshoes. She opened it up; it was affected by damp and some photos had begun to disintegrate and stick to the plastic. Turning the pages carefully, Willis saw it was a cross between a scrapbook and a photo album. There were stuck-in sweet wrappers and a love-heart drawn. There were photos of Kensa as a young teenager with her arms around a boy, who looked like Cam, and with Mawgan modelling hot pants, pouting at the camera. Another girl was in the shot, long blonde hair and Lolita looks. There were so many photos of the girls messing around. They were standing by a Kylie poster. Willis put the photo album aside to show Carter.

She went into the bedroom, and looked in the place she'd found weed before, but found nothing this time. As she felt along inside the cupboard, she felt a soft carrier bag and pulled it down to have a look. Inside were babies' clothes. They were little boy's outfits; Willis smelled them, noticing they had a damp odour. She was sure she hadn't missed them out on her search last time. They looked like they'd never been worn, except among them was a newborn baby's nightdress, which was covered in blood.

'It's mine.' Willis turned to see Kensa standing in the bedroom doorway. 'You shouldn't touch it. You shouldn't be in here.'

'I'm sorry, Kensa – I thought you'd be resting up at the farm. We needed to take another look in here. Are you feeling okay?'

'I've come back to get my things.'

'Whose is this?' Willis asked, holding up the bloodied garment.

'It's my baby's.'

Mawgan stepped into the van as well and stood beside her friend; she put her arm around her.

'What happened to your baby?' Willis asked, as Kensa held out her hand for the infant's nightdress. 'Shall we sit down and talk, Kensa?'

Kensa looked at Mawgan, who nodded. Mawgan led the way into the lounge. The sickly yellow hue of the one remaining bulb over the cooker lit up the cold lounge.

Kensa unfolded the bloodstained nightdress.

'You've nothing to be afraid of, Kensa,' Mawgan said, as she closed the caravan door and turned on the gas fire. 'I have to go back to the farm now. You text me when you're ready to leave and I'll walk down and meet you.'

Willis nodded to Mawgan that she, at least, had understood, and Mawgan left.

'This was my baby's. Yes, this is my baby Caden's. He was born in my old caravan and Raymonds took him from me – told me he was a stillborn but I could swear I heard him crying outside. Raymonds said it was just wishful thinking and the sound of the wind as it whistles round the old mine. He never took one breath.'

'Why didn't you go to hospital?' asked Willis.

'I don't know. My da left me to it by that time. He scarpered along with the gypsy folk he used to know – gone back to where he came from. They wouldn't take me; they were ashamed for me to be pregnant with a gadjo. But I didn't belong with them anyway. My mum was from here. She was a local girl. She'd set her heart on a traveller and he'd done his best to stay put but after she died, his heart told him to go.'

'So you were on your own in here?'

'They, the authorities, the schools, didn't know it,' Kensa said, 'but yes, I was.'

'Raymonds knew it?'

'Yes, him and Eileen looked after me, brought me food and gave me money if I needed it.'

'What did Raymonds say about the pregnancy?'

'He said no one was to know; I was to stay in my van. I lived further out then. It was in the woods near the old mine. Raymonds or Cam brought me what I needed.'

'Cam Simmons?'

'Yes, he was a friend then. Still is. He's more than a friend. We've been in love since we were kids but I never realized it till he came back. We've shared so many times together. There's a bond between us that no one can break.'

Willis took out the photo album and opened it up.

'I believe it. These look like happy times, Kensa? Is that boy Cam?'

'Yes. We were just friends then, but great ones. We understood each other.'

She smiled as she wiped her eyes, then took the book from Willis, touching the photos through their plastic sleeves. She sang: 'I'm spinning around, get out of my way – you wanna move it – move it like this . . . la la la.'

Kensa hummed to herself as she turned the pages and laughed out loud as she looked at the photos.

'Mawgan was a good friend to you?'

'Yes. But there was no one there when I went into labour early. Mawgan was at school. Cam said he'd come after, as soon as he could. I waited all day until Raymonds came later in the evening. He told Cam to wait outside. He kept banging on the door. I could hear Cam saying, "Sergeant, shall I go for help?" He told him *no*.

'Raymonds looked at me and I remember thinking – he's not afraid. This is going to be okay. He said, "Lift your legs and rest them on my shoulders and you push when you feel the need." I pushed because I had no choice. My body just pushed even though I felt it would split me in two. Raymonds didn't say anything. Sometimes I asked him what was happening. And he would just say, "Not much longer. Keep pushing."

'I only knew that the baby was born because the pain stopped on the last massive contraction. "One more push to get the rest out," he said. I remember asking, "Is it born?" Raymonds said yes; but there was no cry. "Is it a girl?" I asked. "No, it's a boy," Raymonds replied.

'"Then, his name is Caden," I said, and I gave him the outfit to put on. He didn't say any more to me; I felt the cold wind as the door opened.'

'Kensa, where is Samuel, do you know?'

She shook her head. 'Not any more.'

'What do you know about him?'

'I know that he sneezes a lot. He cries a lot. He shakes his head when you give him a drink, but he's just a dream. Isn't he?'

Willis walked across the field away from Kensa's

van and out of earshot, then called Carter and told him what she'd found.

'I think she knows enough for us to take her in. We can't ignore her.'

'Do you think we'll get any sense out of her?' asked Carter.

'No, probably not. But we have to reach her somehow.'

'You're the one with knowledge in this field,' Carter said. 'You tell me. If we have her arrested and she cracks on us and ends up sectioned, that tiny window of finding Samuel alive disappears for ever, agreed?'

'Yes.'

Carter sighed. 'Bring her back up to the farm and leave her here with them and we'll see what breaks in the morning.'

Willis went back to Lauren and dismissed the officer who was there looking after her. They said little as both were exhausted. Lauren cooked them some pasta. Then Willis switched on the television as Lauren opened a bottle of wine and they sat together in the snug room at the end of the hall.

Lauren flicked through the channels as Willis went over the day in her head, trying to capture every detail and record it in her notebook in case it was lost for ever. She needed to write up her report before she went to sleep.

Carter looked at his phone – it was a message from Sandford, the Crime Scene Manager from MIT 17. He was still packing up. He would grab a few hours' sleep and be down by ten the next morning. He had the address and he would meet Carter at the farm. Carter signed off and stepped outside the hotel bar. In the hotel stairwell he rang Cabrina.

'Sorry it's late, babe.' He looked at his watch; it was ten past ten.

She sighed in her sleepy state and he could hear the rustle of bed clothes as she sat up.

'You exhausted, honey?'

'Absolutely,' replied Cabrina. 'Sorry, I've been hard at it with the flat and Archie. He misses you, even though you're hardly ever here.' She sighed as she smiled, he could hear it.

'I'll leave you to get some rest,' Carter said, as he looked back into the bar and saw Raymonds ordering a drink.

'Okay, honey, speak tomorrow. Love you.' Cabrina signed off.

Carter took a few seconds to reflect and decided it was no longer the time or place to have a drink with Raymonds. Things had gone too far now in the investigation. He called Willis. She was in her room.

'Is Lauren all right?'

'I think so. She's watching television,' replied Willis.

'I'm calling a meeting tomorrow morning at eight. Pascoe told me that the old police station is ready for us to use now, so I'll see you there. Have you rung Robbo this evening?'

'Not yet. I'm just about to start writing up my report from today. I'll ring Jeanie now and tell her how things stand with Kensa.'

'Where is Kensa this evening?' asked Carter.

'She's staying at the farm with Mawgan. She seems

to think a lot of Cam Simmons. She even talks about them getting married.'

'I wonder if he agrees.'

'Did you want me to come over, guv? Are there things you need us to go through together?'

'Why, what's on your mind?'

'I don't know, but it feels a bit "us and them" with the local police. What are they going to feel like when we tell them we're investigating Raymonds, one of the all-time heroes round here?'

'We'll keep that to ourselves until we're ready to spring it,' Carter said.

'Okay, I'll ring Jeanie and update her.' Willis hung up.

Carter phoned Robbo. Robbo was on his own in the office. Hector was out of the room looking through CCTV footage of around Greenwich. Pam had gone home for the night, and Robbo had brewed himself a new pot of strong coffee.

'Carter, how is it going down there? Sandford is setting off in a few hours.'

'Yeah, I spoke to him. It will be good to have him here. I want to keep the focus on Samuel.'

'Is it getting too much for you to manage?' Robbo asked.

'No, we can do it,' Carter said. 'I'm leaving the murder of Stokes to the local police. I'm just pulling rank when it comes to prioritizing resources. Samuel still has it and I want nothing to get in the way.'

'Do you know how Stokes was killed?'

'Oh yes,' Carter replied.'He was hit with a spade till his skull was smashed then he was impaled on a spike which pierced his liver. The post-mortem is due in two days, but we found the murder weapon beside him. They are waiting for Sandford to take a look at the body when he gets down here, then I've told them they can go ahead and do the autopsy.'

'We have increased the number of people looking at video footage of Greenwich and of the services,' Robbo let him know.

'I was thinking, it would be worth sending an officer over with photos of all the Cornish folk who were in London that day and showing them around Greenwich. The lad who works on the front desk in the *Cutty Sark* museum had a keen ear for an accent.'

'I'll organize that for the morning,' replied Robbo. 'I'm about to call one of the escorts who used to visit Jeremy Forbes-Wright, if you'd like to listen in?'

'Go ahead. I need you to ask whether she met any of the locals. What has Bowie found out about Jeremy – anything?'

'He's being hampered with red tape, but we're making some progress. The phone records have helped. We have full access to his bank statements now.'

'Any hint of paying blackmail?'

'None. But he was on the brink of bankruptcy. That might have led him to slit his wrists. Once people started to find out he had defaulted on credit cards and loan repayments, he would have had no chance of making people vote for him. You can get away with having a love child, but not a bad debt. Okay it's time – I'll call.'

'Is that Josie?'

'Yes, it is.'

'My name's Derek Robinson,' Robbo said. 'I'm part of the Met's Major Investigation Team. I was told that I could contact you about Jeremy Forbes-Wright?'

'Josie, I want to thank you for agreeing to talk to me.'

'It's completely private, right? Anonymous?'

'Yes, absolutely. Nothing will involve you speaking in court. You knew Jeremy Forbes-Wright?'

'Yes, I did. I knew him for two years. Stopped seeing him about eighteen months ago.'

'And you used to see him regularly?' Robbo asked.

'Yes, he used to call me over about once a fortnight to his place in Canary Wharf. We had hot-tub parties, that kind of thing.'

'Just you and Jeremy?'

'No, not always.'

'I'm interested in the times he took you to stay in Cornwall.'

'Oh yes, I went there about ten times?'

'When was that?'

'All in the space of the two years. I think the last time I saw him was in late summer of 2013. I went to Cornwall a few times that summer.'

'Where did you usually stay?'

'We always stayed in Kellis House, his place there in Penhal. A great place. Just a walk down to the beach.'

'Was it usually just the two of you?'

'It was once or twice. Sometimes he invited other guests, men like himself. Sometimes I went down there to meet with them without Jeremy being there at all – he would set it up. Privacy, that was his thing, sworn to secrecy. Once he knew he could trust you it was okay. But he was so old school, even in that; I don't think he had any idea how easy it would be to find out what he was doing.'

'These were friends of his?' Robbo clarified.

'That's right. It was a regular-type arrangement he had with some people. Often they brought their own company with them, if not then he would ask me if I wanted to go. Sometimes I took a friend with me, depends on what Jeremy was after.'

'But you were always happy to go down there?'

'I was, well, until I'd had enough. He got bored very easily. He was hard work. It was like running the marathon going down to Penhal with him. I mean, I don't mind sharing the odd line of coke with a client but it was one thing after the other with him. When he wanted it, nothing would stop him. I've seen him do more stuff in a night than I could manage in a year. I used to see him on the telly and laugh to myself – if only they knew the real Jeremy like I do.'

'What kind of men were his other guests?'

'They were dignitaries, sometimes foreign. Politicians. All sorts.'

'When you were down there, did you meet any of the locals?'

'Oh yeah – there would be the posh woman in the dress shop, Rosie in the gift shop. I always said I was his niece, of course, but they must have all known. Martin Stokes was the man who organized it and was there with the key sometimes, if I had to get there before guests arrived.'

'What about a local man called Raymonds?'

'I heard about him. I met him once or twice.'

'Do you think he knew who you were?'

'They all knew. I think the house was notorious for its goings-on.'

Robbo came off the phone.

'What do you think?' he asked Carter.

'It's going to make for interesting evidence if we end up investigating Jeremy Forbes-Wright's life. It seems like the whole village formed a pact with him.'

'But, things could have turned sour for him,' said Robbo. 'Maybe it's not a coincidence that he killed himself after his last visit to Penhal?'

'Yes, and he wasn't his usual self when he came back to London, according to the concierge at his place. No escorts, no company. Something was bothering him. I'm going to start pulling in the locals for interviews from tomorrow, Robbo. I'm looking forward to hearing them deny all knowledge of what went on at Kellis House. We'll Skype you during the meeting tomorrow morning.'

The next morning, the newly emerged sun streaked the sky with a peach glow that made it look angry rather than warm. The rain had stopped but the waves rolled in on the Atlantic swell, bigger than ever.

'Bad weather to come. Shepherd's warning and all that.' Lauren came to stand behind Willis, a cup of coffee in her hands. They stood looking down over the common to the sea. 'I wonder what today will bring?' said Lauren.

'Will you be all right here on your own?' asked Willis. 'I can organize someone to come and be here with you?'

'No. I'm okay. I will get out for a walk with Russell.'

'We're going to be just down the road now in the old police station if you need anything.'

'Okay, thanks.'

Willis turned to leave and she looked at Lauren's face. It was grey and her eyes looked sore. 'Try and get some rest, Lauren. It's important to keep strong.' Lauren nodded, she was hugging herself. Her eyes focused on the distance beyond the common. She was rocking as if nursing a baby.

'Lauren?'

'I'm okay, really. Will you come and get me if something happens?'

'I promise.'

Willis walked down the road to the beach and past the newsagent's. The sea had come right in over the road during the night. It had brought and dumped odd bits of debris with it: tins and bits of wood, plastic bottles and shards of glass jutted out from sandy mounds everywhere. She looked across at Cam's café and wondered what time he opened. There was no sign of activity at nearly eight o'clock.

'Morning, Eb.'

Carter was waiting for her outside the old station. He was beginning to get a slightly dishevelled look about him as the lack of home comforts took their toll. Willis always travelled light and washed her things out overnight. She didn't need more than two sets of everything to function perfectly well. She had a toothbrush and some Simple face wash and Nivea cream for when her face felt dry. Willis didn't collect things, whereas Carter loved his gadgets and his designer garments. She knew he would have struggled to get a shirt ironed, the way he liked it, at the hotel. And all his hair products had not managed to stop his hair from looking a little flat in the sea air.

Willis cupped her hands against the glass as she looked through the window.

'Such a tiny place.'

'Yeah, but this was Raymonds' mission control. From here, his eye could reach into the four corners of his kingdom.'

Willis giggled. 'The shire folk, you mean.'

'Yes, Master.'

'Morning.' Pascoe appeared from around the corner of the building, hiding a smile.

'I hope this will do. We've got internet, landlines. We've moved over as many desktop computers as we could fit.'

'I'm sure it will be fine.'

'I picked up some coffees for us in town before I came,' Pascoe said. 'I wasn't sure if the café would be open.'

'Cam's place?' Willis asked as she took the coffees with thanks.

'Yes. It doesn't seem to open a lot. He opens for maybe three hours and then shuts up shop for the rest of the day. I suppose it must be like that here.'

'You wonder how he manages to support himself,' said Willis.

'Oh, he's got money,' said Pascoe. 'The land he inherited from his father and sold to Stokes.'

'How do you know he's still got it?' asked Carter.

'Because he had to prove he had the funds when he made an application to extend his café up a floor and create a restaurant. Shall we go inside?'

Carter turned to raise an eyebrow at Willis as they followed Pascoe into the station.

'So, here is the main reception area which I thought we'd use as our office. Through there is the old interview room; it now has a window but it's got bevelled glass in it, so may do. This place was used as a tourist office for a while. There is another room to your right and that was the sergeant's office in the old days. I thought we could use that as a second interview room?' asked Pascoe. 'I can recommend a couple of detectives from Penhaligon who are highly qualified at interviewing.'

'Thanks, that's worth bearing in mind,' answered Carter. 'Okay, let's get this on the road. I'd like to conference call my colleague in London.'

Willis had been fiddling with the set-up of the computers and gave Carter the thumbs-up as the screen came to life and the Met insignia appeared. Robbo's face materialized. Willis introduced him to Pascoe.

'Nice to put a face to the voice,' said Robbo.

'Shall we start with an update on the search from you, Pascoe?' Carter asked.

Pascoe got out his notes.

'Did you search the mine on Garra Headland?' asked Willis.

'Yes, I just finished the report. Here it is.'

He handed Willis and Carter a copy then emailed the file over to Robbo, before putting his laptop down on the table with his notes.

'It's coming your way, Robbo.'

'Many thanks.'

'You have a lot of mine shafts around your area,' said Robbo. 'How do you manage to search them?'

'With some difficulty,' answered Pascoe, as he looked at his notes. 'So far, I've only ordered the cameras to go down the one at Garra: it's the nearest and the deepest.'

They studied the video footage.

'It's L-shaped underground?' Carter asked, as they looked.

'Yes. It was quite a simple process. What people did is chisel straight down through the granite and if they hit a seam they followed it along the horizontal. Those days the water was pumped out. These days the mines are full of water.'

'How difficult are they to access?' asked Willis.

'Easy. They are all covered but the cover is only bolted on. We've had a few bodies thrown down over the years but it's not a clever choice for disposal. The cold water keeps bodies from decaying fast and there is no vermin down there. We've been unable to access the exit to this mine. It comes out in a cave below the water level and the seas won't allow us to get anywhere near it right now.'

Pascoe brought up a map of the area on his screen and Willis shared her laptop with Carter and Leonard as they listened to Pascoe's details of the search areas and the findings of the helicopter.

'We concentrated on the cliff sections that were accessible on foot. These storms would make it an impossible task to find him in the water. The tidal surge is so high that it would be impossible to predict where he'd wash up. If he was even here.' Pascoe looked at Carter.

'For now, this is the best we have. The only leads we have end here. So now we make a plan for phase two. House to house, calling in people for interviews, DNA testing every adult in this village.'

'Local people will want to focus on Martin Stokes' murder. I thought Leonard was going to be here at this meeting?' asked Pascoe.

'No, I decided we needed to stay on track. While it's understandable that people are wanting us to concentrate on his murder, Stokes and Raymonds have had a chokehold on this village for too long. I'm not that flippin' interested who killed Stokes unless it gets me one step closer to finding Samuel,' answered Carter.

Pascoe faltered for a few seconds and then continued:

'We've had a confirmation of clothes bought that would be the right size for Samuel, bought by Kensa Cooper last week from a shop in Penhaligon. The woman remembers that Kensa had been in her shop a few times in the past. She thought she'd bought baby clothes before. This was the first time she'd seen her buy for a toddler.'

'Did she know anything about Kensa?'

'She always recognizes her because she seems off her

head most of the time. I have some more background on the locals for you. Cam Simmons' father used to own the farm alongside the Stokes place. Mrs Simmons died in 1989 of cancer. Les Simmons was a quiet character, there was talk of brutality against his wife and kids. He died in a farming accident, fell into the container of chicken shit when Cam was in his late teens. There was just him and his father by that time and it was briefly investigated as the body showed signs of bruising on the skull and back, but farming accidents are very hard to disprove. Cam's sister Ella went missing in summer 2000 when she was sixteen. Presumed runaway; she's never been located.'

'Cam went on to inherit it all?'

'Yes, his father must have felt pretty sure Ella wasn't coming back. He named him sole heir. Martin Stokes bought up most of the land from Cam, who kept just an acre and the cottage out by the mine in Garra. Cam went away. He's only been back a little while. He applied for a licence to extend the café upwards.'

'I'm surprised he got it.'

'It seems Raymonds recommended it be granted. I guess he's honoured if Raymonds likes him.'

'Raymonds doesn't like anyone. Did you find Mawgan's car yet?'

'Not a sign. Can I just say something?' Pascoe asked.

'Shoot.'

'People are going to want immediate action when it comes to Martin Stokes. For all his faults he was well liked here. He was seen as an important person. I know you have your priorities but... '

Carter held up his hand to speak.

'Stokes means nothing. He was a corrupt, nasty paedophile who, when this is all over, everyone will rush to forget. They won't want to fucking know. Raymonds is not looking too clean either. There's been some serious police corruption going on here, and I don't know how far it extends. I don't know who to trust, but I'm hoping I can trust you. Since we came down to this quaint little picturesque village in idyllic Cornwall, all I've seen is the ugly side of human nature. These people honestly believe they're above the law. If Raymonds says it's okay, then it's beyond prosecution, it's morally sound. Well, I want these people to wake up and smell the fucking manure! I find that boy dead, I'm going to do my damnedest to hold each one of them responsible, and I expect full cooperation from you.'

There was a silence in the room as Robbo's face remained motionless on the screen. Willis stared at Carter's profile, gauging how angry he was from one to ten. This was a nine. Pascoe, still standing, opened his eyes wide, and looked about to do a haka dance in Carter's face, but instead he gave a sharp nod and grunted.

'Understood. You have my full support.'

'Robbo? Continue.' Carter breathed again and tried to calm down.

'There were several calls to JFW from the Stokes farm number in the days before he died,' said Robbo, 'also a lot of missed calls from the Penhal Hotel – that's where you're staying, isn't it Carter?'

'Yeah, it's the heart of this village. It's the only

place to drink in the evening, and there's a public phone there. Signal in a lot of Cornwall is really bad. I'll talk to the manager about it when I get back. What time were the calls?'

'Between twelve noon and twelve midnight.'

'How is it going with Toby?' asked Willis. 'Jeanie seems to be more nurse than liaison officer.'

'Yes, he's falling apart, apparently,' answered Robbo. 'Not sure he can tell us any more of any use.'

'He has to come down to Cornwall,' Carter said, 'he might trigger a reaction down here. He might force someone's hand.'

'Okay, I'll pass the message on, but I think that's the last place he wants to be. A public appeal is going out in Cornwall,' said Robbo. 'Bowie asks if you're sure it's the right move.'

'I'm sure. I'll work with these hundred officers for this next twenty-four, and make tactical searches of areas of interest before we swamp the place with officers. Everything has to be in place.'

'Pascoe, you head the Stokes murder enquiry, call in witnesses and then I want the emphasis in the questioning to be shifted to Samuel's disappearance and don't allow lawyers present. Don't keep anyone in custody and make the interviews all informal,' Carter instructed. 'Any problem with that?'

'None.'

'I'm going up to see if Sandford has arrived at the farm. Meanwhile, if you and Willis can work out who you're going to bring in first. Eb? I'll be back in an hour and then I want us to go and have a chat with Cam Simmons.'

Chapter 36

After the meeting, Carter went out to Stokes' farm to meet Sandford who'd arrived. Willis stayed behind to work with Pascoe.

'Sandford, thanks for coming,' Carter said as he approached. 'I appreciate it.'

Sandford had come down from Archway at Carter's request. His tall white-suited frame looked reassuringly familiar, even in such an alien environment.

'Yeah, it took a while with the trailer. Couldn't you have got someone more local?'

'I could, but then why break up a winning team?' Carter grinned and slapped Sandford on the back. 'Plus, this isn't just about the obvious. This could be linked to Samuel's disappearance and I need people who understand that. I need to keep it tight.'

'So what are we looking for here? Seems to be a busy farm? I saw all the machinery parked up back there.'

'It gets mended here.'

Sandford was taking his equipment out of his car. He was directing proceedings. He'd brought a team of three others with him and a trailer full of equipment.

'Yeah, it's a problem,' said Carter. 'Basically anyone can get access to this farm and not come in by the front door. Tyre tracks are not easy to pin down. It's a narrow lane where tractors go and everyone drives on the same track. We have already found the murder weapon, a spade, probably taken from the the pit over there. It was left in clear view.'

'Get suited up and you can come in with me so far. I need to know some background here,' Sandford said to Carter.

Carter took out a suit from the back of Sandford's car and joined him in the field.

'Well?' asked Sandford. 'You're supposed to be solving a crime here, not creating a new one. Why did you want me down? Has this murder anything to do with Samuel's abduction?'

'If Samuel is here, then yes it does. I think this shows a breakdown in society here. A deal of some sort has been broken. Jeremy Forbes-Wright had an odd relationship with the people of this village. I expect Robbo's told you that Toby was accused of an attack on a local girl, Kensa Cooper in 2000? Yet it was never investigated. Jeremy lived the life of Riley here. He came down with his VIP friends and basically did whatever he liked. I think it's all about the money. Now, he's dead, and the money is going to dry up and someone is trying to squeeze Jeremy's son.'

'Robbo filled me in with the story. But they can't hope to gain anything, money-wise? They cannot get the house, Toby is the only heir.'

'They definitely want it though,' Carter said. 'The

man that died here, Martin Stokes, he provided escorts for Jeremy Forbes-Wright. It's possible some were under age. I need you to look through Stokes' private papers and find anything that might help us regarding the house and goings on. Stokes is a cousin to Raymonds, the ex-police sergeant here. If he didn't make money directly from it, Raymonds certainly knew all about it and didn't stop it. Plus, he didn't investigate the attack on Kensa and he concealed the death of her infant.'

'Why haven't you got him locked up?'

'Because I'm waiting.'

'Whose was the horse?' asked Sandford. 'What happened to it?'

'Belonged to Kensa. She's a sad character. She lives in a caravan on the edge of Penhal. Stokes and his son Towan put her horse in a ring with a prize stallion just for the hell of it. They baited the stallion with a mare in season. That old horse was the only good thing in her life. She's suffered rape and humiliation and hasn't had any justice in her entire life. Now they've killed her best friend *for fun.*'

'Bastards.'

'Yeah. I want you to use this excuse to search through this farm. I have a horrible feeling that Samuel won't be alive for much longer if I'm right about the internal politics of this place,' Carter said.

'Where do you want me to start in the house?' asked Sandford. 'It's a big property.'

'I say we start in the main living areas and work our way out.'

'Where have you set up shop?' asked Sandford.

'We're setting up a temporary police station in the old tourist office – going back to what it was originally. Three rooms and one cell. The body has gone to Penhaligon,' said Carter, 'there's a well-equipped mortuary there. They were waiting till you got here to start the post-mortem. I don't want them to realize I'm not interested in investigating Stokes' death. Now you're here, we'll say you've seen it.

Are you booked into the hotel?' asked Carter.

'Yes. The Penhal?'

'You'll like it, it's all nautical themes, badger's-bum beer and not a flat-screen TV in sight.' Carter grinned.

'What makes you so sure Samuel was brought here to Penhal?'

'Because we've exhausted every lead in Greenwich and we have the kind of set-up in this place that could make it happen. This is the village that Raymonds built and now it's pissed off with him – the worm is turning.'

'You have such an original turn of phrase, Carter.'

'Thanks.' Carter knew Sandford was being sarcastic but he decided he'd take it as a compliment.

'Cam's opened the café,' said Willis, as Carter came back inside the police station.

'Where's Pascoe now?'

'Gone back to Penhaligon to brief the detectives helping with Stokes' murder.'

'That should be an interesting conversation.'

'He'll manage,' Willis said. 'Robbo came back to me about sightings of people in Greenwich. The lad at the *Cutty Sark* museum was shown photos of everyone. He picked out Raymonds, Mary-Jane Trebethin, Kensa and Mawgan and Cam Simmons.'

'Cam?'

'Yes, he was also caught on camera talking with Mawgan. I got Robbo to double check the entrance to the train station and there's no sign of Cam. Robbo's checking all the service stations on all possible routes to and from London to see if we can find Kensa.'

'Kensa thinks Cam is sweet on her. I wonder if he's meant to give her that impression,' said Carter.

Willis and Carter crossed the street and opened the door to Cam's café.

'Hello, Cam. Can we get a couple of coffees, please.'

'Same as last time?'

They waited while he prepared the drinks and then took them from the counter.

'We'd like to have a chat.'

'Yes . . .' He looked around at the empty café. 'Rushed off my feet today, as you can see.' He laughed nervously.

Willis pointed to a corner table away from the window.

'Here okay?'

Cam nodded. He poured himself a glass of water and came to sit opposite them in the booth. Willis got out her notebook.

'Mr Simmons, Cam,' Carter began. 'We're just trying to get a little background on everyone. Could you tell us how long you've had this café?'

'About a year now. I've been back here eighteen months.'

'Where were you before?'

'I was in Bristol.'

'But you were from here originally?' Carter kept a smile on his face, but it was strained.

'Yes. I was brought up here.'

'Something pulled you back to the old mother ship?'

He smiled. 'Yes, I suppose so.'

'Did you come back here with a partner?'

'I'm divorced. I have two children who I see every other weekend. They come and stay with me.'

'Great place for kids here. You don't live in the village, do you?'

'No, just outside. Near the old mine workings on the way to Penhaligon, past Garra Cove.'

Willis looked at him with pen poised. 'What's the address?' Willis asked.

'Wheal Cottage, Garra.'

'It's your own place?'

'Yes, it was part of my family's farm. I inherited it.'

'And then sold it off?'

'Most of it. I wasn't much of a farmer.'

'Your father was, wasn't he? He died in a farming accident, we were told. I guess that's enough to put you off?' Cam nodded, smiled, looked from one detective to the other. 'What about your sister?'

'My sister?'

'Yes, Ella, isn't it?'

'My sister's been missing for a long time. She was presumed dead.'

'I'm sorry, it's tough, you seem to have had more than your fair share of family tragedy.'

'That's the way it goes in the farming community. People die in accidents all the time.'

'But your sister went missing, you said?' Carter asked the questions while Willis wrote in her notebook.

'Yes. She disappeared, ran away.'

'Sixteen, I remember hearing?'

'Yes.'

'Martin Stokes is dead, did you hear?'

'Yes. It's very worrying.'

'Yes, it is,' Carter replied. 'We are treating his death as murder. Were you up at the farm yesterday? We're asking everyone their whereabouts. Nothing to worry about.'

'Briefly, first thing.'

'Why was that, if you don't mind me asking?'

'I wanted to speak to Mawgan,' Cam said.

'About?'

'Just some personal stuff.'

'Did you see anyone else at that time?'

'When I was leaving I saw Mr Raymonds.'

'What time was that?' asked Carter.

'Abut ten.'

'Did you intend to open the café?'

'I changed my mind.'

'When you left the farm, did you come back down the lane to the main road to Penhaligon?'

'No,' Cam said. 'I think I went over the back way.'

'Why was that?'

'Just force of habit, no reason.'

'You and Mawgan are good friends?' asked Carter.

'We've known one another all our lives.'

'More than good friends?'

'Not especially. Nothing that we want to share with anyone else.'

'Especially Kensa?'

'I'm very fond of Kensa, but I don't feel any more than that,' replied Cam.

'But she thinks you do, did you know that?' asked Carter. 'She thinks you're getting married.'

'I've never given her hope of that. She lives in a fantasy world. I've always been honest with her.'

'In your opinion, is Mawgan an honest person?'

'Yes, I would say so.'

'It's just that she hasn't been completely honest with us about the day of the funeral, the day Samuel was abducted in Greenwich,' Carter said. 'At first Mawgan said she went up and back by train and then she changed it to going up by train and coming back with Kensa. You also say you went up by train, is that still correct? You want to think if there's anything here you need to amend? Because while we are spending valuable resources on scouring all the CCTV footage of passengers coming and going at stations, a little boy is dying somewhere.' Willis passed Carter a photo from her bag and Carter slid it across the table.

'Is this a photo of you and Mawgan in Greenwich on the Monday of the funeral?'

Cam stared at the photo for a few minutes and then he nodded. He took a drink of water. 'Okay, I'm sorry. Mawgan phoned me in a panic. I wasn't going to go that day and then Mawgan said Kensa had her car and intended to go and talk to Toby. I drove her up there. We went up in my car. We went to make sure Kensa was okay.' He shook his head. 'That's all it was. Trouble is it coincided with the little boy being abducted. I didn't want us to get blamed, or mixed up; I don't know what I was thinking. I'm sorry, really sorry.'

'Why did you think you'd be blamed?'

'I thought Kensa would. I didn't want to admit seeing her there or going near Greenwich.'

'So you made all of this up as soon as you heard about Samuel's abduction?' asked Carter.

'Yes, I heard it that evening on the way home, on the news.'

'Why didn't Mawgan come back with you?'

'Because Kensa was in a state and very unstable,' Cam said. 'Mawgan had no choice.'

'Did Mawgan ask you to lie for her?'

'No.'

'Did you see any of the other people from Penhal while you were in Greenwich?'

'I saw Raymonds.'

'Did he see you?'

'I'm not sure.'

'Mawgan is someone you love, I think you'd lie for her.'

'Not in this. Not to help her or Kensa or anyone else abduct a little boy.'

'Mawgan's had a tough life, hasn't she?' asked Carter.

'Yes, farm life is hard round here.' The sweat had

gathered on Cam's upper lip. He wiped it with the back of his hand.

'You grew up on a farm next to Stokes' place?'

'Yes, we were neighbours.'

'And Kensa?'

'We were great friends when we were kids.'

Willis looked at Cam's face – there was a hint of something in his eyes. There was a touch of dread and sadness at the line of questioning.

'Did you get on with your father?'

'Not too well.'

'And Stokes?'

'No. I didn't like Martin Stokes.'

'Why was that?'

'He abused children.'

'You?'

'Yes, me and the girls.' Cam took another drink of water.

'What are we saying here, Cam?'

He closed his eyes and took a deep breath. 'Martin Stokes abused his kids and me and my sister on a regular basis. My father allowed it and participated in it. We lived in constant fear for our lives. What else is there for me to say?' He blurted it out and then sat back in his chair and tapped his palms on the table as he looked towards the door.

'I'm sorry, Cam.' Willis studied Cam for signs of lying; there were none. He looked straight ahead and said it matter-of-factly but at the same time he sounded like he was trying to swallow something stuck in his throat.

'Have you ever talked about this before?' Willis

asked. He shook his head. 'Was there anyone else involved in this abuse apart from the two men?'

'No.'

'Did Raymonds know about it?'

'I think so.'

'Kensa told us she gave birth in the caravan. Must have been a tough thing, seeing your friend go through that?' asked Carter.

'I'm . . . sorry.' Cam took another drink of water and a moment to gather his senses. 'I'm truly sorry about that day. I have agonized over it and tried to make sense of it time and time again. Replayed it in my head. But, I was a minor. I was not in any position to question Sergeant Raymonds' actions. I was so totally out of my depth. I have spent years regretting not helping her more.'

'What could you have done?' asked Willis.

'I could have stayed with her that morning. I used to go and see her every day on my way to school. That day she was uncomfortable. She was restless. She kept moving around the van. I should have known something was wrong, but I didn't, she wasn't due for a month.'

'What happened to her baby son?' Willis asked.

Cam shook his head. 'I have no idea. Raymonds brought the baby outside and went to fetch his wife, who was a nurse. I stayed with Kensa.'

'Has she ever spoken to you about that time?'

'Occasionally I see her on the cliff top near the old mine by my house. That's where her caravan was then, just down the hill from my cottage. I see her and my heart breaks for her. She thinks she can hear him crying but it's the wind in the old mine stack – it makes a horrible sound when it's blowing in the wrong direction.'

'I can see you are upset about what happened that day,' Carter said as he watched Cam becoming more agitated.

'It was something I never got over. After everything she'd been through, she deserved this one piece of happiness, but she didn't get it.'

'Do you know if the baby was born alive?'

'Raymonds said it never drew breath. That's all I know. I stayed with Kensa until Eileen came.'

'What did Raymonds do with the baby's body?' asked Willis.

'I have no idea.'

'You didn't ask him?' Willis asked.

'I didn't really want to know. I was traumatized enough by it all. All I cared about was Kensa. I blamed myself for leaving her that morning – what if I'd gone to get help then? What if she'd gone to hospital then?'

'What happened after that?'

'Sergeant Raymonds and Eileen took over and I went back to my life. I didn't see Kensa for a month after that. Every time I tried to see her they said she didn't want to. When I did see her, I could see her falling apart; no one else knew about the baby except me and anyone Kensa told, like Mawgan. Kensa went to live in the caravan she has now and she became more isolated. She started to spend more time in Penhaligon. Social services took her in a couple of times but she always came back. I tried to reach her.

I really tried. But I was just a kid myself and no one seemed to want to help her. Everyone thought it was someone else's problem. In the end I had to leave. My own home situation wasn't great and I went to live in Bristol.'

'Why did you come back?'

'I told you, my marriage ended and I came home. Like you do sometimes when you feel completely lost.'

'You came home to this, that's lucky?' Carter sat back and took a sweeping gaze around the café. 'That was a smart move, and now you have plans to expand up another level?'

'That's right. They've just been approved now. I'm hoping to put a restaurant on the top.'

'Well, good luck with that. How do you feel about Raymonds now? You said it was a hard thing to get over, what happened to Kensa and the way it was dealt with?'

'I suppose a lot of time has passed.' He shook his head.

'So, you didn't come back here hoping to get justice for Kensa?'

Simmons reddened and shook his head.

'She knows she can always come in here and get a meal. I'll always come if she needs me, but the past belongs there. I can't change it. Raymonds did what he believed was right, no doubt. I have to live with my life and move on. I've learned to do that; I don't want to be like Kensa or even Mawgan. I don't want my past to ruin my future. I'm glad I went away and went through what I did. It almost destroyed me, it ruined my marriage, and I'm sad about that, but I have learned to exist with my past.'

'Cam, what did your sister say happened that night at the house?'

He shook his head. He looked exhausted.

'I never saw her again, she never came home that night. That was the night she left town.'

Chapter 37

Lauren stood on the doorstep waiting for Russell to finish his business. She couldn't trust him to go out on the common because he didn't come back for hours. She leaned against the front door frame and watched as the sun came out and sent everything shimmering in the breeze. She took a deep breath and heard the scurry of canine feet on the tile floor. Russell came scampering past her and straight onto the driveway but stopped as he caught a scent and disappeared inside the undergrowth. She waited for him to reappear and then called him back into the house. She stopped by the carved newel post at the foot of the stairs and rested her hand there, feeling the carved faces of the animals that decorated it.

She wondered if Toby had touched the same post as he had stood where she did nearly fourteen years ago. He must have. She walked up the stairs and reached the landing. Lauren turned into the space there and stood and imagined what Toby would have seen. *Which room was his?* she wondered, and then realized it was probably the one she slept in. It could have been the one Ebony was in – doubtful that it would have been the other one because it was too near the bathroom. That would have been the guest room, guests came first. She turned the handle of her bedroom door and let the door push open while she stayed looking around, opening her eyes to see things Toby must have seen. This was probably never a place for children, it struck her. She remembered what Toby had told her – that his father never spent time with him if he could help it, that he paid for him to holiday with other people. That he only ever brought him down here that once after his mother left.

Why did he bring him that one time? Lauren wondered. He couldn't have known it would end so badly?

She stepped into her bedroom and walked around opening the wardrobes again, even though she'd done it when she arrived – she did it again, this time imagining Toby as he put his things away. The fifteen-year-old, excited about coming away with his father at long last. So happy that his exams were over and so in love with a local girl.

It made her heart ache. In her mind she saw Kensa and Toby together and it didn't seem so strange. They must have both been skinny little things, holding hands, kissing. It must have seemed like the beginning of something wonderful. Lauren went to stand in front of the mirror on the chimneybreast. Snowdrops and garden flower tiles decorated the hearth and grate surround. She looked into her own eyes and she imagined Toby standing behind her, his arms encircling her the way he did when they fell asleep after sex, and she always felt so loved at that moment, so content, sometimes she'd say to herself – if it all ends now this is the way I'd like to go. She felt the sting on the bridge of her nose that told her she was going to cry, but she had exhausted her crying capabilities on her son. Samuel got all her tears.

Then she knew she'd been wrong to push Toby away just when he needed her most. It wasn't Toby's fault. It was the person's who took Samuel from them. When she thought about Toby and Kensa, she understood that what they had felt was real too. The first love – the first cut – deep pain and sweetness that stays for ever. Kensa still had love in her eyes. Kensa didn't know what happened that night. Kensa and Lauren were the two women who knew what Toby was really like. Lauren smiled into the mirror as Toby's image smiled back at her. She felt a surge of strength. She phoned him.

'Toby?'

'Lauren.'

'Are you okay, Toby?'

'Lauren, I'm so sorry I haven't been honest with you.' He took a deep breath. 'There is someone else – I can't live here without you and Samuel, but I also need Gareth in my life. He's the man I work with. He's become more than a good friend. I didn't plan it. I didn't want it. I always thought we'd be together for ever, you and I, and I've tried. I just can't pretend any more.'

Lauren sighed deeply as she closed her eyes and hung on to the phone. 'Toby, I am sorry. So sorry for all of us. I understand what you're saying. I had hoped that we could turn our marriage round. We were so happy once. I thought we could be again but, I accept it if you say you love someone else. Do this last thing for me, Toby. Do it for your son. For yourself. Come down, Toby, and we can face this together.'

'No, I can't. I can't face it. What good can I be?'

'We still think Samuel is alive, Toby. It looks likely Kensa may have taken him, but she is mentally unhinged. She still holds a lot of affection for you. You could talk to her. It may be the only chance we have of getting Samuel back alive.'

Toby came off the phone and walked back into the lounge where Jeanie was waiting for him. She was sitting on the sofa and working on her laptop. She closed it as he approached. He sat thinking for a few minutes and then he looked up as she waited for him.

'I've told Lauren that our marriage is over. I've told her I love Gareth. He makes me feel like I can be me. No more pretence, no more trying too hard. I want to be happy. I want Lauren to be happy.'

Jeanie nodded. 'I understand. Was she okay?'

'Lauren gets on with life. She's not someone to buckle. She'll pick herself up and carry on, no matter what. But, she has told me some home truths and said that I need to do more, everything I can, to try and find my son.'

'What does she want you to do?'

'She wants me to go down to Cornwall and face things. She thinks Kensa will talk to me.' Toby was sweating at the thought of it.

Chapter 38

Carter and Willis left Cam's café, crossed the road and headed towards the car park.

'Cam's story was something, wasn't it? What do you make of it?' asked Carter.

'Some parts of his story are so sad, they have to be true,'

'But?'

'Cam Simmons definitely has something he's not mentioning. He has a bit of a love triangle thing going on with the women.'

Carter walked up the steps to the Surfshack and cupped his hands as he looked through the glass. He knocked on the door. As he waited he heard a car start up and watched Raymonds appear from the car park and pull alongside. Carter held up his hand to him and Raymonds opened his window. He smiled.

'Raymonds?'

'I hear you've been asking about Kensa.'

'Really? Who told you that?'

'Well, let's just say, if you want to know anything then come and ask me.'

'Okay, well, where's the report on the assault on her in 2000? Where are the photos of the injuries?'

'Destroyed. We didn't keep any of it – no charges were brought. What was the point?'

'Tell me, then, who were the suspects?'

'What suspects?' He started to drive off. Carter stepped closer.

'Local lads, men, at the time. Men who were at the party where sixteen-year-olds and under were getting off their faces. Men who spiked drinks and then followed their victims to a house where girls were raped. Those fucking men, Raymonds. Where are they?'

'They don't exist. It's all been made up – it's all lies.'

'Oh really? How come I have their names then? How come one of them is your son? This is the beginning of the end of it all, Raymonds. There isn't one sordid thing that's happened in this village that you're not at the heart of. Where were you when Martin Stokes was murdered earlier on today?'

'I'll be available with my lawyer any time you choose – I'm not going anywhere – I have nothing to hide. Come and find me when you're ready, sonny.'

'Be in the old police station ready to be interviewed at nine tomorrow morning.'

Raymonds drove off. Carter was shaking with anger.

'We need to go up and make sure Lauren is okay, guv?' Willis walked back towards the car. Carter didn't speak as he got in, started it up and sent dust flying as he spun it around in the sand-covered car park. He took the steep hill up from the shops in first gear and kept the engine screaming. He hadn't realized.

'Bastard . . . sorry.' He pushed the gear stick into second then third. 'I won't leave this village until we see that man destroyed.'

'Raymonds must have had some noble intentions at one time, guv.'

'Noble, my arse.' He shook his head, took a deep breath. 'Okay. I know one thing, Eb, cracks are beginning to appear beneath Raymonds' feet. He's losing control of his empire.'

Sandford phoned as they drove to Stokes' farm. They parked up and saw him in the field where Stokes was killed. He waved and smiled when he saw Willis. He walked across to the gate, on a path of stepping pads.

Willis shook his hand over the top of the gate. It felt ages to her since she'd seen him, a different world. In reality it was just three weeks ago and in north London.

'Leonards has just been,' said Sandford. 'He's a nice bloke. We have come to a compromise. They've done what they can outside, for now. They're prepared to wait twenty-four hours for me to finish my search and then they'll move in.'

'Generous.'

'Yeah, not sure I would be that kind, if I was them, but I've told Leonard I'll alert him of anything I find. They're leaving the tents in place.' Sandford turned and pointed towards the back of the field.

'They've covered the area around the tractor, and where the fight took place, with a second tent so the

horse has to stay unburied for now. It's vital to pre-
serve as much as we can from this bloody rain. One
minute it's bright sunshine, the next it's two inches in
an hour.'

'How's your search going?' asked Willis.

'No sign of anything that might indicate Samuel
has been here. But I've sent samples back to see if we
can find a match to anything on the suit or the mittens. We've cordoned off Martin Stokes' bedroom
from the rest of the house and searched everyone's
rooms and found nothing of interest. I've been going
through Stokes' paperwork. He wasn't a computer
man so he has a lot of ledgers here that are about the
farm. He has all his stock accounted for. He has clear
spread sheets to do with the sales in the farm shop
but nothing to do with Kellis House.'

'Why was he so adamant in his letters to Lauren
and Toby that there were pre-existing arrangements
that he wanted to honour if they weren't written
down?'

'Someone had definitely been looking through his
room before I got here. We're in the process of taking
DNA samples from everyone who's been to the farm
in the last week or so. We need to get one from
Raymonds. I'm looking forward to getting a sample
from him.'

'Who have you seen here?' asked Willis.

'Mawgan mainly. I introduced myself when I
turned round to see her in the field behind me. She
seems to be the one doing all the work with the animals. She spends a good deal of her day in with the
pigs or the cows. The farm covers a lot of acres. You

see her going off on her tractor. She stares a lot, but then she's got a lot on her mind. No time to grieve when you have a farm to run.'

'What about Kensa? Either of the men who live in the cottage? Jago and Marky?'

'No, not yet,' Sandford said. 'I met Towan briefly. He was in his dad's room when I cordoned it off.'

'Did he have anything in his hands?'

'Not as far as I could see. I can't be sure that no one will go into Stokes' room while I'm gone – not unless we're going to insist that they all leave the farm, and that's pretty impossible with the work load and the animals.'

'No, I'd prefer to have them where I can see them. We'll catch up with you again later.'

They left Sandford and drove back towards Penhal. Willis phoned Robbo and put him on speaker phone. 'Robbo, can you investigate the disappearance of Ella Simmons in the year 2000?' she asked.

'I'll get Hector on it now. But local information's got to be the best. What are people saying about it?'

'Yeah, I'll start asking but I won't get anywhere,' replied Willis. 'You haven't met the locals. Did Marky and Jago's stories about where they went in Exeter pan out?' she asked.

'I've been looking at some interesting footage of them,' answered Robbo, 'and I'm waiting to see what comes of it. They were seen talking to some people who we know have trafficked kids in the past. Gordano services has been used as the switch point.'

'Send us everything you have on this story, Robbo. I wouldn't put anything past those two.'

'Okay, will do. Who's your number-one suspect for Samuel's abduction at this point?' asked Robbo.

'It's got to be Kensa Cooper,' said Willis with a glance towards Carter, who nodded his agreement.

'Have you brought her in for questioning?' Robbo asked.

Carter answered, he was instantly irritated.

'If we hound Kensa she will freak and we'll never find him, and if we take her into custody, and she is Samuel's carer, he will die. Simple as.'

'That's a big dilemma, isn't it?'

'Yes, Robbo,' answered Carter. There was a pause as both sides of the telephone line understood that what was said next had to be said.

'The public, and Bowie, are getting impatient, Dan, they want him found. They don't want all these other things to distract you. There've been murmurings of possible disciplinary action over your handling of this Stokes murder. Raymonds has friends in high places.'

'Yeah, we have a pretty good idea how he got those. His cousin, the pimp, made sure it was party central for VIPs down here.'

'Bowie has been told to warn you off any investigation into the goings on in Kellis House.'

'Even though it may have a direct link to Samuel's abduction?'

'Yes.'

Carter took a deep breath. He knew what would be happening there in MIT 17. Bowie would be going ballistic on a daily basis. Carter was not filing his reports on time; thank God Willis was getting hers in.

The pressure on Bowie to answer questions he didn't have a clue about would be unbearable and the rest of the team would be getting it in the neck.

'No problem, Robbo. He remains my number-one priority. I'll make sure DS Pascoe has all the help he needs with the Stokes murder and I'll stay well clear of any historical stuff at Kellis House.'

Robbo signed off. Carter looked across at Willis. He smirked.

'We have ruffled some influential feathers, Eb. But it's all right. Don't look so worried.'

'What do you want to do?'

'I want Sandford into Kellis House and I want it taken apart. We don't know what kind of search was done before we got here. We don't know whose orders Pascoe and the team are following. The only people we can rely on are ourselves, right?'

Willis didn't answer. She was staring out into space as she ran things through in her head. Carter was used to waiting. She nodded.

'I think we should bring Towan in for our first interview.'

'Yes,' answered Carter. 'We'll leave Raymonds to stew a little. I don't want him to think he's first in the queue for anything.

Chapter 39

Robbo finished the call to Carter and looked across at Pam, who was peering intently at her monitor. Her face was lit with the reflection from the screen; as it changed and she typed, her eyes read from left to right and it was reflected in her glasses.

'I've contacted his last employer, the recruitment agency in Marylebone. It seems he was a rising star for a while but then partied too hard. There was mention of a drug dependency and he used up his three warnings. The manager I talked to said it was a sad outcome. They had him earmarked for a share in the company but he messed up. He ended up being a bad influence on the newer members in his team.'

'So, do we have the connections in place in Gordano services?' He looked across at Hector. 'All set?'

Hector was watching his screen intently.

'Just waiting for confirmation from the contact. They're getting nervous. They don't want to blow their own investigation: it's been going for nearly a year. They don't want any information leaked.'

'Understandable. Tell them, these two will be taken out of the frame – they're just a couple of amateurs.' Pam stopped typing.

Hector continued his online conversation and then sat waiting, tapping his pencil tip on a notebook. Watching the screen.

'Yes! And thank you kindly, sir.' Hector tapped his reply as he talked. 'We can watch the transaction on here. It's about to start.'

Robbo and Pam dashed across to watch the footage.

'This is shot from a haulage lorry,' said Hector.

The filming started as the lorry was coming into the Gordano services and heading for the signs towards the lorry park. The date and time was running in the corner of the screen.

3/2/2014 time 21:31

'Look, there's Marky's car. They must have moved from one car park to the other.'

From the camera angle they could make out the back end of Marky's car tucked in between two lorries. There was a break as the film jumped; the lorry came to a standstill.

'Here we go,' said Robbo as they watched first Marky then Jago get out of the car and be approached by a man dressed in a cleaner's uniform from the services. When he spoke his voice had been wiped so that they couldn't hear the names being used.

'He must be the undercover officer they have working at the station,' said Robbo. Two men got out of their lorry and joined them. The undercover officer shook their hands.

'Do we know anything about who these men are?' asked Pam.

'We just know they are a large Ukrainian outfit who smuggle just about anything.'

The men were dressed in dark jackets and wore peaked caps on their heads.

'These two are brothers apparently.'

One of the brothers walked out of shot and came back with three bags. He handed them across to Marky and Jago and they placed them in the boot. There was five minutes of leaning into the boot as the goods were examined.

'Now, where's the exchange?' muttered Robbo as they all held their breath and watched the screen.

'Here we go,' said Hector as Marky reached in the back seat of the car, pulled out a holdall and handed it over to one of the two men.

'Freeze that, Hector,' Robbo said as they examined it in close-up.

'Is that Samuel in the bag? Samuel weighs twenty-four pounds. Pam, you got that ready?'

'Yes.' Pam went to her desk and pulled out a carrier bag with groceries in it. 'This is exactly that, I made sure.'

Robbo took it off her and stood in front of the screen looking at the angle of Marky's arm, the flex of his bicep. He handed it to each of the others in turn. 'Are we agreed?'

'One hundred per cent.' They ran the rest of the film footage. 'Even the way he's passing it over,' said

Pam. 'There's nothing weighty in that bag, there's certainly not a child. He'd have handed it over with a little more care.'

Hector ran the film on. One of the brothers put the bag onto the floor and opened it; he checked inside.

Deal done, Marky and Jago got back in the car.

Chapter 40

As Carter and Willis parked outside Kellis House, Robbo phoned them to give them the news about Marky and Jago. They got out of the car and rang the doorbell. Russell started barking at the sound. Lauren opened the door and looked expectantly at them both, but Willis shook her head.

'He's settled in, hasn't he?' Carter bent down to pat Russell.

'A bit too much. He's not going to want to go back to a balcony in Greenwich.' Lauren walked back through to the kitchen.

'How are you feeling now after the shock yesterday? Sorry you had to be the one to find him.'

'I'm trying not to think about it. It still doesn't seem real. I guess because I'm so tired it seems like some part of an ongoing nightmare. Do you know who killed him?'

'Not yet,' Carter said. 'But his murder will not be a priority for us. We're leaving our Cornish colleagues to get to grips with that. We're concentrating on any relevance it has to Samuel. How are you managing for supplies, got enough to eat? Drink? I can pick up some food for us to eat here this evening from the hotel, if you'd like?'

'Is it any good?'

'I'd like to say it's not bad, but breakfast was pretty ropy.'

'Then I'll stick to making pasta. Ebony is an easy person to cook for, aren't you, Eb?'

Carter laughed. 'That's for sure. It's quantity rather than quality she likes – no offence meant about your cooking, mind.'

'None taken.'

Carter sat at the table and Willis perched by the sink.

'Well, how do you like this house, Lauren?' asked Carter.

'I don't, really.'

'No, neither do I. It's the first time I've seen it,' said Carter. 'It's very dark and Gothic-looking.'

'I guess those were his tastes,' answered Lauren.

'Just walking through the hall there – are there any paintings that have women with clothes on?'

'Nope – all bare-breasted.'

'Must have been a strange place for Toby to come when he was young. He must have spent his teenage years staring at the walls.'

Lauren smiled. 'There was a long gap between when he came here with his mum and when he came here again after she left,' she said. 'Literally years. I think the décor would have been very different in the beginning, when they first bought the place.'

'Are there any photos around from that time?' asked Carter. 'Be good to see what's been done up.'

'None that I've seen.' 'We haven't really had a good look on the top floor yet,' said Lauren. 'That was obviously his master bedroom. There's a four-poster and swathes of red velvet and chintzy materials. It spans the whole of the top floor.'

'You'd hate it, guv – a spiders' heaven,' said Willis. 'And the thing is, you can't see them either until you've nearly stepped on one because the floor is dark.'

Carter shivered. 'Spiders and snakes . . . hate them. What do you feel about this house then, will you be happy to sell it?'

'It's not my decision. It will be Toby's. But I would want to get rid of it. Although I don't want to leave Penhal. I don't know how Toby can stand it in the flat in Greenwich. I feel so much nearer to Samuel here. I feel like there is still hope here and, when we find him, I want mine to be the arms he runs into.' She turned away to stop herself from crying. 'I wish Toby would see that we have a fight on our hands and put on his boxing gloves and get down here. People think he's a coward, along with everything else.'

'Lauren, we'd like to order a proper search of this house,' said Carter. 'I've ordered our Crime Scene Manager in here this evening – that means you two will have to sleep in the guest house up the road. We've commandeered nearly all the holiday lets in the area for our police teams. I've made sure you two get the places with heating. You going to show me round, Eb?'

'Sure.' They walked into the room to their right with the veranda.

'Okay. Nice room.'

Willis moved swiftly on into the front rooms.

'So here is where Toby and the others were when they came off the beach?' Carter lowered his voice. They could hear Lauren washing dishes in the kitchen.

'Most of this stuff is bought within the last ten years. He seems to have enjoyed adding bits all the time. The floor is original, the wallpaper hasn't been changed in twenty years. There've been numerous paint jobs but no major work except to the bathrooms and his room at the top.'

Carter followed her up the stairs and had a quick look into the four bedrooms on the first floor.

'I can tell why you didn't sleep in either of those,' Carter said, coming out of the ornate rooms and into Willis's and Lauren's.

Willis pushed open the door to the bathroom.

'Wow.' Carter stepped inside and squatted down. He touched the tiled floor with his hand. 'Heated.'

'Yes, a lot of money spent here, and it's all been spent since 2000. It has a date on the instructions for the extractor and the shower; they were installed July 2000.'

'Funny time to do major work inside your holiday house, right in the peak season?'

'That's what I thought.'

'This bathroom comes out, then, tile by tile.'

'And let me show you upstairs.' Willis led Carter up a separate set of stairs that took them to the top floor.

Carter stood in the doorway of the suite. The sun had come out and was streaming in via the long window that had replaced the original attic one and now afforded a breathtaking view of the coastline.

Carter stood looking out to sea.

'Do we have enough to bring Marky and Jago in and charge them with the drugs?'

'I think we need to wait, guv, till we find Samuel.'

'Yes, okay, but Raymonds has to start really feeling the squeeze. I want him to understand we are closing in on him.'

Carter and Willis left Lauren and drove down to the police station. They pulled up and saw Pascoe's car outside.

Pascoe looked up from his desk as they walked in.

'All okay?' asked Carter, putting his bag down on a desk.

'Yes, I've made a good start. I've told the team in Penhaligon that I'll be running the murder enquiry from here, but it will run alongside the abduction investigation. It will not take priority.'

'Was there any problem with that?' asked Carter.

'Everyone understands that we need to keep it contained. We can't end up with more officers than residents here. We solve one crime at a time. Plus, it's unlikely to be an outsider. It wasn't a random act.'

'We'll interview everyone who was at the farm,' said Carter. 'We'll start today, but I don't want them interviewed under caution for now. I want to keep people moving around here. I want us where we can still watch them. Okay, Willis will take the notes for us and make sure we all understand where we are. We've just had a development that at least discounts two of our possible suspects for the abduction of Samuel.'

Willis brought up the edited footage of Marky and Jago at Gordano services and turned it round for Pascoe to see.

'Here we have Marky and Jago handing over a lot of cash in exchange for a lot of drugs.'

'Jesus, that will destroy so many lives if that goes on the street down here,' said Pascoe, almost choking on his coffee. 'We have a big drug problem here as it is.'

'We estimate, by the size and look of it, that these lads, Marky and Jago, have managed to buy themselves fifty grand's-worth of what we think is probably a mix of cocaine, methamphetamine and heroin. That's apparently what the brothers from Ukraine like to deal. But, what they also like to do is cut it with rat poison and horse tranquillizer.'

'Shit. We have to find that stuff.'

'You've seen them beachcombing, we can definitely pull Penhal apart to find it. Sandford's up at the farm at the moment; I'll tell him to test for these substances as well.'

'We searched down the mine again, as you requested,' said Pascoe. 'If we want to drain it we could have a better look in there but you're talking about an unsafe environment and it's going to take a lot of time and resources.'

'We'll consider it,' said Carter. 'Where did Marky and Jago get the money to buy this stuff? Jago has no money and no real job and Marky is in the middle of the low season in his business.'

'Does he own that Surfshack? Could he raise funds on it?' asked Willis.

'I'll find out,' Pascoe said.

'Meanwhile we need house-to-house searches starting with all the people who were at the funeral or in London that day,' said Carter. 'We have to find Mawgan's car.'

'Pascoe, we need to know what investigation was made into the disappearance of Ella Simmons in 2000.'

'Yes, I brought the file on it.' He stood and went to the corner of the room where he'd put his belongings brought over from Penhaligon police station. 'I've made you both a copy.' He handed them out. 'Raymonds was in charge, of course. That means we cannot be sure of any real investigation. It looks thorough, on the surface; they had a possible sighting of her hitching up on the dual carriageway.'

After five minutes' reading Carter sat back in his seat and shook his head in disbelief. Willis glanced up at him and spread out the pages from the file. She picked up the photo of Ella.

'I don't think she ever left here,' said Willis.

Carter looked at her and felt a chill reach down his spine.

'Right, that house gets pulled apart,' he said. 'We need to know which parts of it have been redone and at what time. We'll rip up floorboards to get samples.'

'Will this find Samuel?' asked Pascoe.

Carter sat back in his chair to think.

'If we think Kensa took Samuel then we give her what she wants to get him back.'

'Which is?' asked Pascoe.

Willis answered: 'Justice.'

Chapter 41

Raymonds drove into Penhaligon to see the bank about the life insurance he'd taken out on Martin Stokes and then he phoned Towan.

In the background Raymonds could hear a squeal of a piglet and the grunt of a large sow. He heard Towan's breathing as he walked outside to talk in private.

'How far have the forensics got?' Raymonds asked.

'They've been through the house, cordoned off Dad's room with tape.'

'How are you holding up?'

'Just waiting to go down to the village for the police interview this evening.'

'The best thing is for you to say nothing.'

'I'm relying on you to bail me out if they should try and pin Dad's death on me.'

'They have no evidence. Besides, there was everybody coming through there at that time and the rain has begun to flood the lower lane. Soon any scrap of evidence they did have will be washed away.'

'What do you think they'll ask me?'

'They'll ask you about your relationship with the

old man. Everyone knows that was pretty testing at times. It's no good lying and saying it was good.'

'There's more people than me with good reason to kill him.'

'Yes, that's the main thing to keep in your head.'

'Except they've not been inside with GBH before, and I have.'

'While you're up at the house you need to keep searching for your dad's ledger. The old man was tight with money. Every penny was traceable from the farm. Somewhere there's a list of men who stayed at Kellis House and what they paid your dad for, what service they got. It won't take much to work it out, then we can make a few phone calls and get some more money in. We buy the house and the empire continues. It's a real shame Martin won't be here to reap the benefit. He must have really pissed someone off to make them do that to him. You need to have a word with Mawgan. I think she could have stolen the contacts book.'

'I'll get it off her if she has.'

On his way back Raymonds drove round to the village and as he passed the shops he slowed right down so that he could check on who was where. The Surfshack was closed again. People would think Marky was taking the piss. This was his chance to make something of himself. *Useless piece of shit.*

He parked up behind it. There were four police cars in the car park. He watched them knock at the farm shop, which was closed.

Raymonds crossed over and asked the officers if

they would like him to open up for them, as he had keys to all the shops in the street. As he talked to them in the middle of the road he glanced across to Mary-Jane sipping tea behind her desk. He smiled. She averted her eyes from him and he smiled to himself. Those nails of hers ... he watched them tap against one another on the desk – *sharp as claws digging into his back*. He finished talking to the police officers and walked along to Mary-Jane's shop. She was decorating the window. She turned her back on him and he stood there looking at it for a few minutes. Her slim frame would break beneath him. Her sharp tongue would slice into his flesh, if he let it. She waited. She knew he was watching. He coughed, moved on. He walked down to Cam's café.

'Espresso, and make it a double.' Raymonds watched Cam prepare his coffee. 'Did you hear about Martin Stokes?' he said almost under his breath.

'Yes. The police came in earlier.'

'Thought they must have.' Raymonds held eye contact for a few seconds and then sniffed loudly as he picked up his coffee and took it across to the window seat. 'When I allowed you back here, Cam, it was because I respected you. There was something I admired in the way you coped with everything when you were young. You moved away and that took guts too. Okay, it didn't work out so well for you, but you're not a quitter and you came back and set up this. What a great place you have here, Cam.'

Cam nodded but he didn't smile.

'You're getting stronger here by the day. How's it been going?'

'Okay,' he answered as he cleaned up the counter. 'It's busy now with the police arriving.'

'Any problems?'

'No, I don't think so, Mr Raymonds.'

'No, quite right too. Remember, every day you draw a line under the last and you start as if it were all new.' Cam nodded. 'You have a great future ahead of you. Have they been in here to ask about other things apart from Stokes?'

'Yes. They came in and asked some stuff.'

'Don't tell them anything that happened in the past. Talk about the trip to London, okay, but don't trouble going back into the mists of fucking time. They're just nosy – prying. They don't need to know any of it.'

'Any of what?'

'I'm saying to you – tell them the truth. Tell them something they can confirm and then that's enough. Do you understand?'

'Yes. I'm very grateful for everything you've done for me.'

Raymonds looked around as if to make sure no one had snuck in while they'd been talking. 'What I'm saying is – loose tongues cost lives and all that – you want all this to continue?' He opened his arms out in a theatrical gesture as he turned on his heels.

'Yes, of course.'

'Well, believe me, laddie, it needs some clever foot-work from you. I know these detective types – all smiles and sweetness but they just want to trick you into relaxing and spilling out your guts. And . . . let me tell you now . . . your guts will be all over this café floor.' He smiled. 'Hypothetically, of course. Did they talk to you about the beach party in 2000?'

'Yes.'

'You told them nothing happened at the house? It was just a bit of tomfoolery. Kensa never got in trouble from one of our lads. It was all that Toby's doing. Is that what you said?'

'More or less.'

'Oh . . . did they ask about Ella?'

'Yes. I said she ran away.'

'Yes, she did. She was seen hitchhiking up the road the next day.'

'It's odd she's never contacted,' Cam said.

Raymonds eyed him suspiciously as if, just for a second, he thought he might be toying with him. 'Oh well, some things in life you have to learn to accept. You have to try and view them positively. You inherited your old man's money. He was a nasty piece of work, I know, and I also know what happened to him; we both do. I was glad I could help at the time.' Cam nodded. 'Don't think I didn't try and help you when you were young 'uns, all of you, because I did. But it was hard to prove.'

'Stokes was just as bad. Mawgan suffered the most.'

'Yes, and even though Martin was my cousin I would have done him for abuse if I had thought there was a chance. I want you to believe that.'

Cam was staring into Raymonds' eyes for the first time in his life. It made Raymonds uncomfortable.

'Well, that's all I want to say for now. You . . .' He smiled as he poked Cam in the chest. Cam stayed where he was, unflinching. 'Do as you're fucking told and keep your mouth shut.' Cam didn't answer, he stood where he was, watching as Raymonds left the café and walked back across the street. Cam smiled to himself.

Raymonds walked back past the dress shop and stooped in the doorway. He filled it with his arms resting against the doorframe.

'Mary-Jane?'

'Yes? Did you want to talk to me?'

'I want to ask you what's going on with Jago.'

'What do you mean?'

'Jago has a hell of an opportunity in this place but he seems hell-bent on destroying this village. He's dragging my Marky down again, just like in the old days. I tell you, it has to stop, otherwise I'll have to be strict and say Jago will have to leave, for good this time.'

'No, he hasn't done anything wrong.'

'Where do you think he gets his money from? Haven't you heard him sniffing all the time? He's sticking stuff up that stuck-up nose of his. He's making my gullible Marky into a bigger fool than he already is. Marky was doing well before Jago came back. I even signed over the Surfshack to him. He was full of plans for the future but now all he does is go surfing.'

'Don't be ridiculous, that's not Jago's fault.'

'He's always been the smart one, your Jago. He's always had the upper hand when it comes to intellectual capabilities, but my Marky is a trier. Eileen is breaking her heart with worry over him.'

'He's just not used to the way things are here any more.'

'No, that's for sure. You better remind him how we all depend on one another. We're a game of dominoes – one falls, we all fall.'

'Tell that to Kensa – she's getting madder every day. She's out of control. She needs reining in. I don't know why you haven't done more to stop her from behaving like an animal, having sex in the car park, wearing provocative clothes.'

He scratched his eyebrow. There was a small scar that ran through it, split it almost. It was the only imperfection on his smooth, stretched skin like crispy roast chicken: always evenly golden-browned. The scar had never healed completely and when the heat came to his face it made it itch. He took a step back to look out of the window and then he started to walk towards the back of the shop.

'We need to make sure you're not missing any clothes, any children's outfits.'

'Now?'

'Yes. No one but the police will be coming in here today. Don't bother to put the closed sign up, just come with me, we won't be long.'

She followed him down into the stock room at the back. Boxes were packed on shelves and on the floor. There was a toilet, and a kettle on a tray on a draining board.

'Christ, it's freezing out here,' Raymonds complained. He switched the overhead electric fan heater on.

'Well, I don't have to keep the clothes above a

certain temperature, they are perfectly okay as they are.' Mary-Jane kept an eye on the shop as she hovered. 'I haven't seen you since London.' She turned back to him.

'All this commotion going on – I'm finding it hard to take five minutes, plus Eileen is becoming more demanding by the day.'

'Eileen, Eileen, that's all I ever hear. I've wasted a good part of my prime waiting for you.'

'Not wasted.' Raymonds looped his arm around her waist and drew her to him. She was melting a little; he saw it in her eyes. 'I could hug you so hard that you wouldn't be able to breathe and you'd pass out in my arms – carry you off to bed, or take you here between the boxes.'

She laughed, breathless as Raymonds lifted her skirt. He stopped and looked across at three bags on the floor.

'What are you doing with Marky's stock over here? Those bags are from his shop.'

'Jago brought them over, asked me to keep them for Marky. I don't mind. I don't know what's in them, they've put a padlock on them. Special stock to bring out at the beginning of the season, apparently.'

Raymonds walked across, picked up one of the bags and weighed it in his hand, and then he rested it on a box.

'Give me a knife.'

'You can't cut it open, for goodness' sake, that's a perfectly good bag. It's none of our business.'

'Pass me that knife, now.'

She passed him one from the draining board. He

slit the stitching next to the zip and pulled the bag open, snapping the stitches. He reached in and pulled out a bag of white powder.

'I will fucking kill them.'

Chapter 42

'Mrs Raymonds, is your husband about?' asked Willis.

'No, he's gone out.'

Carter took a step back from the doorstep and looked towards the garage.

'Has he driven?'

'Yes, I expect so.'

'Any idea where he went?' Eileen Raymonds had the shakes, badly.

'Are you all right, Mrs Raymonds, can we assist you?' asked Willis.

'The door has come off the cupboard – it's so heavy, I can't lift it. It fell on me.'

'We can help,' said Willis. 'Can you find me a screwdriver?'

Eileen looked nervous but then nodded and stood back to let them in. She went off to find a screwdriver kit and came back and handed it to Carter. He handed it straight over to Willis.

'Ebony's my apprentice.' He winked at Eileen.

'Yeah ... taught me all he knows,' Willis joked, 'then I had to start from scratch with someone who actually knew something about DIY.'

Eileen smiled.

'Please, Mrs Raymonds, sit down.' Carter eased her into the kitchen chair while Willis propped a small stool under the drooping door. Carter sat down opposite Eileen while Willis set about mending the cupboard.

'We were told that you were a nurse at one time in your life?'

'Yes. A long time ago now.'

'Was there ever a hospital here in Penhal?'

'No, I was a district nurse mainly but before that I worked in Penhaligon.'

'This house keeps you busy and I suppose now that Mr Raymonds has retired – there's probably plenty to do here?' Eileen didn't answer. Willis glanced over at Carter and was wondering if he was going to give any examples of things to do – she was amused to hear what they'd be. Once when they were working on a job Ebony had tried to engage Carter in a game of Scrabble but he was hopeless and even lost when he cheated; she'd found four vowels under the seat after he left.

'I'm staying at the Penhal,' he said, 'and Ebony here is staying at Kellis House.'

'The Penhal Hotel is nice.'

'I haven't seen you in the bar yet,' Carter joked.

'Oh my word, no, that's more for the men here. I've got better things to do than drink all evening.'

Again, Willis was all ears, wondering what she was going to say.

'Ebony, how is it over at Kellis House?' he asked.

Eileen seemed to perk up and be interested to hear

the answer. She turned in her chair and watched Willis tightening the screws on the hinge.

'It's not my cup of tea.'

'It wouldn't be mine either,' Eileen said, suddenly quite keen to talk. 'I only went in there the once but I thought it very dour.'

'It is; it's dark and heavy and the opposite of what you'd want on holiday I'd have thought – and yet it was always booked up, apparently.'

'Jeremy Forbes-Wright loved staying there,' said Eileen.

'Did you know him well?' asked Carter.

'I knew him a long time . . . but I don't think I ever knew him well,' answered Eileen.

'It must be quite lonely here for you in the evenings,' suggested Carter.

She shrugged. 'I don't think of it like that.'

'Mr Raymonds is just as busy now as when he was a serving police officer, by the look of it.'

'He's been having affairs for years. That keeps him busy.'

'Oh?' Carter was stunned.

Willis stopped her work. *Oh shit*, she thought, *now he's going to ask her how she feels about that.*

'And how do you feel about that?'

The door opened and some keys slammed down on the side table in the hallway.

'Carter?' Raymonds stood in the kitchen doorway. Carter stayed where he was. Raymonds looked around. He took the screwdriver set from Willis. 'You've no right to come into my house when I'm not here.'

'They helped me with the cupboard.'

'I told you I'd fix it when I got home.'

'It fell off onto my leg. It was dangerous.'

Raymonds held up his hand for his wife to stop talking. He was breathing heavily with anger but kept a fixed smile on his face. Carter stood, slowly pushing the chair back.

'We won't keep you long. We need DNA samples,' said Carter.

'DNA? What for?'

'Because everyone has to and you're no exception.'

'This is intolerable that you come into my home distressing my wife when you can see she's ill.'

Willis opened her forensic kit and got out her DNA tester.

'Ready?' she asked. He nodded but he was fuming.

'Mrs Raymonds, you'll need to give a sample too.'

'Why does my wife need to?'

'Because there are only so many people living in this village and everyone gets a turn at the DNA.'

'No, my wife is ill. This is ridiculous.'

'You find this a bit much, do you, Mr Raymonds?' Carter asked as Willis finished taking the tests. 'Yet, you have the stomach for helping a fifteen-year-old give birth without medical help in a caravan in February?'

'She was cared for – I looked after her,' said Eileen. 'I promise you I got to her as soon as I knew.' Eileen looked from one detective to the other. 'The baby was too small, so premature, it could never have survived. We didn't have time to get her an ambulance.'

'Oh, I see, Cam's had his little say, the ungrateful bugger.' Raymonds raised his eyes and shook his head slowly. 'Now, unless you have proof on that I'd watch what you're saying.'

'I think you're a big fat liar, Raymonds. And I'm only beginning to touch the surface here. I think you're missing the end of the rape story. You're covering for someone. That person would have to mean a lot to you. What was Marky doing that night?'

'Marky?' Eileen said, shocked. 'My Marky involved in that night? It can't be. That Jago is more like it – Marky's so sensitive inside, he wouldn't hurt anyone. He may have had trouble with drugs in the past, but that's all behind him.'

'Be quiet, Eileen, you've said enough. They have nothing on Marky, because there is nothing.'

'We are beginning to find out lots of things about you, Raymonds. You had quite some business arrangement going with the late Jeremy Forbes-Wright. Who was the main pimp, you or Stokes? Stokes abused his own kids and you never stopped him. Plus there's the case of the missing teenage girl Ella Simmons, the case that you investigated and, surprisingly, it was never resolved. I'm going to make it my personal business to find Ella.'

Raymonds did not take his eyes off Carter. The two men squared up to one another and Willis kept her eye on Raymonds. She was wondering if she would be able to take him down if he made a lunge for Carter.

Eileen pushed back her chair and stood awkwardly. Raymonds went to assist her but she pushed him off.

'Why am I not surprised at all of this? You smell like *that* woman. I can smell her perfume a mile off.' He tried to help her again. 'Don't. Don't . . . I've had enough. I want to make a statement about the night you delivered Kensa Cooper's baby and other things.'

'Don't do this now, Eileen, it's not just me involved in this, is it?'

'No. I'm done with talking. I want to be free of it. That girl deserves help.'

'Mrs Raymonds, would you like me to take you down to the station to make a statement?' asked Willis.

'Yes, I would.' She stepped out towards the hall and went to reach a coat down from the peg.

'Think what you're doing, Eileen. Marky needs our support. Don't betray him.'

She glanced back at Raymonds and then turned to Willis and shook her head.

'No . . . I'm sorry, I can't.'

'Would you prefer me to take your statement here?' asked Willis.

She shook her head. 'No. I have nothing to say. I've changed my mind.'

Chapter 43

Sandford stood and stretched his aching back. He wasn't built for the work, he told himself. He stopped to listen to the weather outside the window. The clatter of rain pellets on the tin roof meant that he knew the score; he was waiting for the weather to clear and he would be going back outside. Meanwhile he was having a nose through the farm-shop store next to Marky's workshop, where all the produce for sale in the farm shop was kept. It was all neatly packed on three-feet-deep shelves. Sandford had shelf envy. He wished the shelves in the evidence room back at Fletcher House were this well constructed. He could never find a thing on them. He went back to searching through Marky's workshop. So far all Sandford had found was Marky's prints. He wanted to get this finished this evening to start afresh on Kellis House first thing in the morning.

The relentless rain filled the pit where Misty lay. The horse's limbs were twisted under him where Stokes had tipped him from the digger.

Then rain soaked his mane and collected in the bite

wounds on his neck. The crows hopped around over his body as his intestines began to fill with gas. As the soil slipped and moved around him, the side of the pit collapsed and rolled down to lie across his neck and head so only his muzzle and his bared teeth were visible above his shoulder.

The soil swept down and mud began to cover him. He began to bury himself.

The skeleton of a baby boy was curled on its side, turned towards the open jaw of Misty's last squeal of pain and crush of Brutus's hooves.

As one was buried so one arose.

Sandford paused, listened: *Good – no noise on the roof; he needed to get outside, the smell of the fibreglass was making him light-headed.* He looked down towards the farmhouse and saw the lights on in the lower half of the house. His team were working their way outwards now. The last time Sandford had looked he'd seen Mawgan out feeding the animals, putting the rugs on the horses for the night. Marky was in his cottage with Jago and Towan was in the village at the police station. Sandford watched Mawgan as she took an hour to see to the animals and settle them for the night. From the doorway of Marky's workshop he could see the stables, and Bluebell had come to watch Mawgan as she passed by. Mawgan took her time to rest her head on the horse's neck and talk tenderly to her. He waited until she was back inside the house before walking down the lane and into the field where the crime scene tents stood so white and alien on the dark soil.

He walked across to the tractor and the pit where the horse was lying and stooped to enter the tent. He switched on the battery-powered light, moved onto the stepping plates and walked around to the far side of the pit to continue his search of the area. He wouldn't do a lot more tonight. He just wanted to make sure he had protected things as well as he could from the elements to continue tomorrow. It was then he noticed that the mud was slowly collapsing in on Misty.

Damn ... need to get a move on, he thought to himself. The elements were against him. As he was about to flick the switch on the light he nudged it with his leg and the beam of light bounced and rocked to illuminate the horse's wide-open jaw and broken teeth, and Sandford stepped forward onto the furthest plate and squatted beside the pit. It was then he saw the skeletal hand of a baby reaching out from the dirt.

By the time Carter and Willis reached the farm Sandford had begun the excavation of the body. He'd placed more lights inside the tent and was gently scraping the soil and collecting it for analysis.

'How old do you reckon?' asked Carter.

'This baby boy is newborn,' answered Sandford. 'The medical examiner can't come out tonight but we'll excavate the body in case we get badgers or foxes getting too interested in the night. I can't tell you how it died.'

'The horse seems to have sunk into the ground,' said Willis.

'Yes, it's quite a weight and the ground is slowly giving way to it. But the pit is basically collapsing, that's what it is.'

Willis nodded her head. She stared at the infant.

'We may have found Kensa's baby, then?'

'We need a DNA match done as fast as we can now,' said Carter.

'Okay, I'll start that off,' said Sandford.

'If I were Kensa I would feel glad that at least he could be given a proper burial now,' said Willis.

'Yes, but someone, probably Raymonds, committed an illegal act burying it here on the farm.'

'Why here, I wonder?'

'Things can resurface from the sea, I suppose.'

'But Stokes couldn't have known it was here, otherwise he wouldn't have decided to bury the horse here.'

'Could have just forgotten, I guess, forgotten where the baby was buried – whoever it was – it's been here a long time. It's thirteen years since Kensa lost her baby.'

'What are you going to do with him tonight?'

'I'll finish excavating him then I'll bag him and take him with me.'

'What, into your hotel room?'

'It's either that or leave him in the car, and what if it gets broken into? Plus, it seems disrespectful.'

'We can take it back to the police station; it's all sorted in there. We still have to interview Towan tonight.'

'Do any of the family know about this find yet?' asked Carter.

Sandford stood and lifted the baby's body bag.

'No, no one yet. Mawgan and Kensa are in the house, plus a male friend – Cam Simmons? Jago and Marky were here but I heard a jeep taking off about an hour ago and there's no lights on in the cottage now.'

'I'll go and have a word with Mawgan,' said Willis, walking off towards the farmhouse. She knocked at the inner door and pushed it open. The kitchen was dark. There was a television on in a room off to her left. She knocked at that door and walked in. Mawgan was sitting on her own.

'Hello. I just wanted to see how you and Kensa were doing. Where is she?'

'Upstairs. Cam's up there talking to her.'

Willis moved further into the room. 'Are you okay, Mawgan? There's a lot to cope with. Has Cam come to help?'

She nodded. She had the television on but she wasn't really focused on it. 'Is Towan coming back later?' she asked. 'After you take him in, that's all.'

'It's just for an informal interview; we'll be talking to all of you in the next day or so.'

'So you're not charging him then?'

'No, we haven't got far enough in the investigation.'

'You should.'

'Are you scared to be here with him, Mawgan?'

'No, I'm a better shot than him.' She turned back to the television and flicked the channels. 'Cam will stay with us, anyway.'

'Do you know why your dad was murdered, Mawgan?'

She shrugged. 'Because he deserved it? He'd done so many wrong things to so many folk and, in the end, he got what he deserved. Wait . . .' She got up and handed something to Willis.

'What is this?'

'It's a contact book that my dad kept on the people who stayed at Kellis House and the deals he did.'

Willis opened the book, which was a simple ledger, but inside were the names of guests. Besides the dates that they stayed, there were dots and numbers.

'What does all this mean?'

'It means these were the times he had to provide escorts for these people. Their names are written in the back.'

'Why are you giving this to me?'

'Because Raymonds and Towan are going into business. They intend to contact these people from the book and make demands. Maybe, if they get the house, then nothing will change here. It will all continue as it did when Dad was alive and I can't bear that. Things happen at that house and people go unpunished. Towan will take over where my dad left off. He'll be twice as bad. That's why he's always going off into Penhaligon; he picks up young girls in there, schoolgirls, he grooms them, brings them back, they end up in Kellis House, out of their skulls on stuff. The private parties and the VIPs that come down and abuse them, they think they're untouchable. That's not right.'

'No, it's not. I can help you, Mawgan. Tell me what's gone on in the house, make a statement. I can get help for Kensa, too.'

'No one can help erase the past. No one can give us back our childhood. I don't want your help. I don't want it to continue, that's all. I don't want other people to suffer.'

'And what about Samuel? He shouldn't have to suffer for other people's mistakes, should he?' Mawgan didn't answer. 'Where is he, do you know?'

She looked at Willis and said nothing. 'Mawgan?'

Cam Simmons appeared at the doorway to the stairs.

'Cam?' Willis looked behind him to see if he was alone. 'Is Kensa all right?'

'Not really.'

'Has she said anything about Samuel?'

He shook his head. 'But she's talking about seeing Toby.'

'I think he's coming down tomorrow.'

'She may talk to him.'

'If she took Samuel she couldn't have done it alone.' Willis looked at Mawgan, who was back staring at the screen.

'Neither of us know anything about it. Do we, Mawgan?'

She shook her head.

Willis went back to talk to Carter. She showed him the ledger.

'Kensa's inside, upstairs. I think we should have her sectioned.'

'If we do, we lose any chance of finding Samuel alive. By the time they finish medicating her, he'll be dead.'

'They all need help here, guv.'

'And we'll make sure they get it – when this is over.' He looked at the book in her hands.

'VIPs who regularly use Kellis House,' she said. 'This book is going to be a who's who of the upper-class degenerate.'

'That's a bit harsh, isn't it?' Sandford overheard her as he prepared to load up his car for the night.

'Not according to Mawgan. I wouldn't be surprised if she hasn't suffered abuse all her life in that place. She says that Towan does a sideline in conning vulnerable kids and plying them with drink and drugs and then they end up being abused in Kellis House. Stokes got paid for it, now it looks like Towan wants to carry it on.'

Carter took the book from Willis to have a look.

'There are the ages of these kids, some as young as twelve.'

'Who are these kids?' asked Sandford.

'Towan's waiting for us in the police station – let's go and find out.'

Mawgan went outside to make sure that the animals were settled. She stayed a while resting her head on Bluebell's neck as the horse stood patiently at her stable door. Mawgan stroked her as she thought about what she should do. Then she locked up, went back inside and unlocked the gun cupboard. She loaded the shotgun and took it upstairs. Cam was lying on the bed next to Kensa, who was sleeping. Mawgan lay down next to Cam and placed the shotgun beside the bed as she lay there listening in the dark to the sound of Kensa's breathing. Cam slipped his arm around her and she sighed as she relaxed heavily in his arms. In the darkness, Kensa opened her eyes and lay listening to their whispers. She felt the heat from their bodies and everything that had seemed clear was now muddied. All her hopes vanished as she lay there listening.

Jeanie had allowed Toby to go and see Gareth. Now, they were listening to music in his shed. They hadn't spoken for half an hour as Toby lay back on the cushions, staring at the ceiling. A paper model of the solar system hung down. Toby was looking at the Milky Way that he had helped Gareth stick up there in 'glow-in-the-dark' stars. He felt the tears tickle and slide down to wet the cushion under his head.

Gareth was making a new playlist. Occasionally he looked across at Toby. He switched the volume right down on the music and waited for Toby to look his way.

'Did you find what you were looking for in the stars?' asked Gareth. He began rolling a cigarette.

Toby looked back up at the Milky Way and sighed heavily as he shook his head. Then he turned again to look at Gareth.

'I was hoping to see an alien craft heading our way ready to whisk us up and take us to another galaxy.'

'What would I tell my mum?' Gareth grinned.

Toby half laughed, half sobbed. 'That's right, exactly,' he said. 'What would I tell Samuel? Can't keep running. Can't live in a world without conse-quences.' Gareth offered him his cigarette and Toby took it from him. He took a few drags and then handed it back.

'Can I come and live with you in this shed?'

Gareth stared across, trying to gauge if Toby meant it. He was frightened to agree to something if it wasn't real.

Toby smiled at him. 'I mean it. I don't know if we have a future, but I know that right now I'd rather be with you than with Lauren.'

'Is it just a reaction from Samuel going missing?' Gareth returned the smile, but he looked worried.

'No. I've felt this for a long time. I want to be with you, if you'll have me?' Toby reached out and took Gareth's hand.

Gareth nodded happily. Toby sat up and crossed his legs and reached out for Gareth's tobacco to roll a cigarette.

'I need to face everything now.'

'What are you going to do?'

'I'm going to find my son.'

Chapter 44

Towan looked around anxiously. 'I requested a lawyer to be here.'

'That isn't possible – lawyers are thin on the ground here and we have a lot of people to interview – anyway, you're not formally being charged. This is just a chat – you're free to go, but I expect you'll be keen to help find out who killed your father?'

'It wasn't me.'

'Can we talk about your relationship with your father? When you came out of prison he welcomed you home, didn't he?'

'Yes.'

'Did you get on well?'

'Well enough.'

'Even though you had an almighty fight with him the day he was killed?'

'I had a fight with my sister and Marky Raymonds, not him.'

Willis looked at her notes.

'You stated that you were asked to accompany your father to bury the horse but instead you went to Marky's workshop to look at your surfboard. But Marky wasn't there, was he?'

'No, he wasn't.'

'So we can't verify that,' said Willis.

'It's more likely to be any of the others than me. I had no reason to do the old man in. We had plans together.'

'What plans?'

'We were going to open a guest house.'

Willis took out the ledger Mawgan had given her. 'We found this. It has the names and contacts of a lot of important people who stayed at Kellis House. Were you going to contact all of them and invite them to stay?' Towan's eyes widened at the sight of the ledger, at the same time as he began to sweat. Willis continued, 'Were you going to use these contacts and continue at Kellis House, as if nothing had happened?'

Carter smiled at Towan. 'That's why your dad and Raymonds wanted to buy Kellis House, they have a good system going there. After all, most of the people in this book didn't come down to spend time with Jeremy Forbes-Wright, did they? They came to have a good time. And your dad bent over backwards to give them what they wanted.'

'I had a lot of respect for my dad.'

'I hate to speak ill of the dead, Towan,' said Carter, 'but your father had a record for certain unsavoury acts in the past and not-so-past. So you were going to call these people and say "Nothing's changed, come on down"?' Carter said.

'Not me, this was Dad and Raymonds' business.'

'But you brought new blood into it, didn't you? You were making yourself into an important business partner for them?' said Carter.

'I was going to be part of it from now on, yes. We were talking about opening another guest house if we couldn't buy Kellis House.'

Willis opened the ledger out at the back pages and turned them round for Towan to see the lists of names.

'Recognize any of these names?'

He peered forwards and shook his head.

'You see, next to the names are ages and "F" for female, "M" for male, you get the picture?'

'I don't have any idea who they are but, I told you, I'm new to the business.'

'Your dad gave them a number and he marked them with a code of dots. Helpfully for us, he wasn't much of a spy and he slips up now and again and, well, to be honest, it's pretty easy to work out it refers to sexual services these children delivered,' Willis said, bluffing. But it was clear Towan had never got his hands on the ledger before – he didn't know what system his father had applied.

Towan had taken to staring from beneath his fringe at Willis. His eyes flickered incessantly as his brain was churning, trying to concoct something believable.

'A couple of these names are crossed out. Why is that?' asked Willis.

'I have no idea. I told you, these names have nothing to do with me.'

'You're a liar, Towan. We are in the process of contacting all of these kids, all of the people on this list,' Willis said.

'Your father worked as a pimp for Jeremy

Forbes-Wright and now you're taking over the job?' suggested Carter.

'A pimp? Don't make me laugh. It's a private arrangement. Yes, he was asked to find girls some-times. He just passed it over to an escort agency in Penhaligon. Talk to them, not me. My dad was a simple farmer – he did what he was asked to.'

'Don't sell him short – he wasn't simple. He knew how to work the system. He knew how to provide a good service for a refined man of taste like Jeremy Forbes-Wright and his friends.'

Towan looked away in irritation; he rubbed at the side of his neck and then pulled his shirt collar to cover a scratch there.

'Who do you think murdered your father?' asked Carter.

'It could have been any one of a number of people.'

'What about Mawgan?'

'What about her?'

'People in London have this idea about country folk, you know, Towan. We think that all sisters are introduced to the world of sexual relationships either by their fathers or by their brothers. How did that work out for you?'

Towan jumped across the desk just as Carter knew he would, and he and Willis restrained him, turned his head to the side and pressed his face into the desk.

'Sore point, huh?' Carter said. Willis waited for Towan to calm down then she put him back in his seat.

'You're an angry person, aren't you, Towan? It's in your nature,' said Carter. 'I can see why you're angry

– it must be really hard living in a place like Penhal that seems to have so much injustice going on.' Towan was still fuming. 'I'd be angry if I lived here. I'd be mad,' said Carter. 'There seem to be a fair few of you that are a bit of both. But why do you stay here, Towan?'

'There's not a lot of opportunity out there for an ex-con.'

'But there is here?'

'Yeah, there's the farm.'

'You can see yourself as a farmer, can you?'

'Well, it's not too bad. There are other opportunities here.'

'Like what?'

'Things can come along, like I told you, the guest house, opportunities can open up. They look after their own here.'

'No, not unless you're one of Raymonds' golden boys they don't. Is that what you are?'

'Me and Raymonds get on all right.'

'What, the ex-con and the Sheriff? You have to be kidding me, Towan – surely you're not that stupid? You really think Raymonds is going to want someone like you on his team? He's using you the way he uses everyone, like he used your father.'

Towan didn't answer. He was thinking things through, he was rocking on the chair, tapping his finger on the desk.

'You know Raymonds is keeping all of you hanging on for some prize or other. Marky, Jago, even Cam Simmons, all waiting with bated breath to hear what the Sheriff has in store for them. You all need to man up, you know, Towan – get some balls. It's never going to happen for you.' Towan looked away. He crossed his arms in front of his chest. 'You know what I think? Raymonds is working towards stitching you up for things here in Penhal,' said Carter. 'After all, you're an obvious candidate.' Towan tried to look as if Carter didn't know what he was talking about. 'Take the night Kensa got raped in Kellis House. You do know that everyone is saying it was you?'

'It wasn't.'

'They say you came up to the house; you followed the kids after you spiked their drinks. You followed them with the express purpose of teaching Ella and Kensa a lesson.'

'Ella was all right when I left. I had nothing to do with Kensa.'

'Okay, then. You're going to have no problem making a formal statement, are you?' Carter asked, as Willis pushed across paper and pen.

Carter and Willis left the room and went to sit in the office while they considered what to do. They put Bowie and Robbo on conference call on Skype and brought them up to date.

'It's your call,' said Bowie, but Carter could see that he wished it wasn't. 'You're in charge of this investigation, Carter, but I think you're getting bogged down there. You're going off on tangents. It's four days in and we're still no nearer to finding Samuel. And we're collecting a host more problems along the way.'

'I don't agree, sir. Penhal is our strongest lead so far.'

Bowie turned away as he considered what Carter was saying. Then he turned back with a resigned expression. 'If we had just one lead here in Greenwich I would do my best to persuade you, but we don't, do we, Robbo?'

Robbo shook his head. 'Every one's a dead end. I believe we're doing the right thing by moving the investigation to Penhal. I think the fact that these other crimes are occurring or being uncovered is proof that this is a community capable of Samuel's abduction. And that it has a direct link to JFW.'

'Except that now we hear that, after the night of the rape in June 2000, JFW and Raymonds decided how they'd handle the situation and this information came from an ex-con who is responsible for providing underage children for abuse at Kellis House.' Bowie was doing his best to stay calm. 'Have any of the names on the list been traced yet?'

'DS Pascoe's already coming up against a wall of silence with the names on the list, sir,' said Willis. 'A lot of the kids are from problem families. It's going to take a lot of coordination with social services down here to uncover what's been going on in Kellis House.'

'We don't have time for that,' Bowie replied from his office, frustration showing through.

'The ledger is going to be invaluable to Operation Elmtree,' added Robbo.

'Yes, but we are not looking into abuse rings, are we? And it doesn't help us find Samuel. If he dies while we're helping track down abused kids from the nearby town, we'll all be roasted.' Bowie shook his head and took a deep breath as he fought to stay calm.

'What date was the last visit by JFW?' he asked.

'He came at Christmas, sir,' Willis answered.

'Is that in the ledger? Was there anyone visiting with him then?' asked Robbo.

Willis turned the pages.

'He came alone but he had someone visit him who's numbered at the back of the book: Bethany Smith, seventeen years old. DS Pascoe got hold of her – said she had a private arrangement with JFW – it was consensual.'

'In my opinion, you should hand the ledger over to the locals and let them deal with it,' Bowie said as he waited for Carter to enter into the conversation; he'd been a little too quiet as he mulled things over.

'Carter, convince me you're on the right track,' said Bowie, 'and then maybe I can convince my bosses.' Bowie had been chewing the cuticle on his thumbnail. He sucked the blood as it came. 'I've been asked to give another press conference to update.'

'What about basing it on the reconstruction?' said Carter.

'We achieved very little with that. There is nothing new we really want to share with the press. The longer we can keep them away from Penhal, the better. What about ex-Sergeant Raymonds? Can we charge him with perverting the course of justice where the rape is concerned?'

'If we charge him we take him away from the community he controls. The people will close ranks rather

than give him up. He's running around like a blue-
arsed fly at the moment, trying to cover his tracks.
He's losing control of this community and that's what
we're waiting for. We need to give this village enough
rope to hang itself,' said Carter.

Chapter 45

Towan got out of the police station with a feeling of immense relief. He really hadn't expected it. He didn't usually get off so lightly. He dodged the spray from the sea crashing into the side of Cam's café. It was a once-a-year phenomenon: high spring tides and Atlantic storms. There were thirty-foot waves expected the next day and a high tide that threatened to close Penhall off and flood the shops. He had left his Land-Rover in the car park behind the Surfshack. It was already a foot under seawater with the waves breaking over the defence. He took no notice of the shouts from excited teenagers who were pouring out of their homes to watch the waves crash in.

He jumped into his car and sped back up the hill and across to the other side. He pulled up outside Raymonds' house and saw that his garage was open and the Silver Fox was missing, so he decided that at some time or other Raymonds would be driving it down to the bar, like he always did. Towan would wait for him down there. There were some things he wanted to have out with him. Too much of what the detectives had said rang true. What if Raymonds had no intention of allowing Towan to take over the farm or his dad's share of Kellis House? What if he was just mugging him off? He parked up on the road outside the Penhal Hotel and had to hold on to his door as the wind came blasting off the sea and over the cliffs. Towan walked up the steps to the bar and looked around the usual local crowd. No one smiled his way. The whole bar thought he'd killed his father.

'I'll have a pint of the usual.' Towan made some space at the bar. He didn't mind the hostility too much. But it irked him that he'd spent all these months convincing people that he'd put his past behind him and now they were so quick to see him as a murderer.

Raymonds turned up when Towan was on his third pint and scowling into his glass. Raymonds stopped to hold court along the way and Towan watched him, half-amused but wholly angry, as Raymonds accepted all the sympathy over the death of his cousin, Stokes. There were nervous glances Towan's way as people expressed their horror at his father's killing. Raymonds spent his time reassuring them that they were safe – that the killer was almost caught, for sure. The killer was on borrowed time.

Towan's eyes had become a little glazed from the beer and his face was a little red, his lips wet from the constant licking in anxiety. Raymonds had spotted him and was wondering how to manage the situation. As he got near to Towan, Towan called him over to have a pint. Everyone in the bar watched. Raymonds came near and slapped him on the shoulder.

'You all right, Towan, bearing up? Let me buy you

a beer on this sad night.' He whispered in his ear, 'What the fuck are you doing here?'

'Why shouldn't I be?'

'Because your dad has just been murdered and any grieving son who hasn't been inside for GBH would be at home getting pissed on his own, not in a bar with his enemies. Now drink up and be gone. I can tell everyone how upset you are.'

'I don't need you to talk for me.'

'Course you don't – but you're going to be my next business partner and I want people to have respect for you.'

'Yeah – about that – I want some proof. I want something in writing.' People began to look at Raymonds and Towan. Raymonds was beginning to sweat through the smile.

'Did you find the ledger?'

'No – the police have it.'

'Shit.' Raymonds scowled and then smiled, tight-lipped. 'I'll think of something. Leave it to me. You have the numbers and names somewhere of your contacts in Penhaligon?'

'Some, yeah – lots I just gave to Dad to deal with after they'd been here once.'

'Okay, well, that's your job, you get straight on that again and start remembering.'

'That's all my job is, is it?'

'For now, and I left a few Surfshack bags for you out on the path to Garra Cove. I need you to take them down and throw them weighted into the water for me. I can't risk being seen. You're quicker on your feet than me.'

'What's in the bags?'

'You're better off not knowing.'

'Is it the boy?'

'Would it matter if it was?'

'No, I'm just asking, that's all.'

'It's some papers I don't want them finding if they search my house.'

'If you are aiming to set me up, Raymonds, I'll feed you to my pigs, I swear.'

'Keep your voice down.'

Towan muttered a few choice expletives at Raymonds then he left half of his drink and slammed the door on his way out of the bar. He walked back down the steps and the air was filled with the roar of the waves breaking onto the cliffs below. He passed Raymonds' car. The Silver Fox was sleek and fine; Towan took out his key and was about to scrape all along the side when he changed his mind and tried the door.

Chapter 46

Sandford's idea of starting at Kellis House in the morning hadn't panned out. He'd decided he had too much on his plate to delay and if he could give his team something to get working on then he could hop between the sites.

He let himself into Kellis House and flicked the switch in the hall. It reminded him of a nutty stately home he'd been in once where it turned out the architect was out of his skull on opium. It was dark and so wood-panelled it was like being inside a coffin. He changed into his forensic suit and had a look at Carter's request. The bathroom was a definite for ripping out, so was the downstairs front room that overlooked the driveway at the front. Sandford opened his forensic kit and mixed the bottle of Luminol, a fluorescent chemical, with the same amount of distilled water, then decanted it into a spray with a fine nozzle. He walked into the front room, rolled up the rug and used a crowbar to lever up three planks in equidistance on the floor. He sprayed the Luminol and shone an ultraviolet torch into the area. It was so sensitive that it could detect blood present in such small amounts – one part per million, even on walls that had been painted over and on floors that had been thoroughly cleaned. He found nothing. He walked down towards the back room with the veranda and into the kitchen area. The kitchen had the usual amount of blood you'd expect from an area that saw animal blood spilled in food preparation. He walked up the stairs slowly as he sprayed the chemical and shone his torch into the crevices of the stairs. He took a brief look into the bedrooms and then went into the bathroom marked on Carter's plan. He'd had his team drop off some tools before they left for the evening. They were staying in Penhaligon. There were too many of them to lodge at the hotel.

He was about to get started with seeing the best way to lift the floor when there was a ring on the doorbell. Carter stood there with a couple of beers in his hand.

'I figured you'd start work this evening, and I'd be grateful if you'd let me help. I know there's going to be a fair amount of pure wrecking-ball stuff and I'm your man.'

'Come in.'

Sandford didn't want to seem too grateful for the help. He knew it was Carter's way of saying he was sorry for the enormous amount of work he had lumped on Sandford's shoulders. Offering to break up a few tiles and coming armed with beer didn't really make up for it, but then Carter produced a nice bottle of cold Chablis that had cost him thirty pounds from the sour-faced barman, and Sandford warmed to him.

'Okay, where shall we start?' Carter said as he donned a forensic suit and booties and stood on the other side of the bathroom door waiting for orders. He handed Sandford a glass of cold white wine and it was accepted. He took one good-sized glug then set it aside as he made up a fresh solution of Luminol and sprayed liberally around the bathroom floor and walls. They turned the lights down and Carter watched while Sandford shone his light around.

'There's a small amount on the walls, a spray, could have come from the toilet area.' Sandford knelt down to examine the feet of the bath. 'There's definitely blood between the detail on these feet and the nearer you get to the floor the stronger the smell of bleach.'

'It's not normal to clean tiles with bleach.'

Sandford picked at the grouting between the tiles and shone his torch into the scraped-out groove. 'We're going to have to get these tiles up after all.'

Carter grabbed a pickaxe.

'Not with that. We chisel in between the grouting on the floor tiles and we do it systematically. We start at the furthest corner and work our way backwards. You're on the left, I'm right.'

It took them two hours until they'd finished getting all the floor tiles up and neatly stacked on the landing outside the bathroom.

'Okay, here we go.' Sandford shone his torch into the plastic layer that housed the heated-floor system. They stood in the semi-darkness and watched the light trace the outline of a rectangular area, the outsides of which allowed blood to seep through, and it pooled onto the plastic.

'You want to record this for posterity?' Sandford handed Carter the video camera for low light and Carter scanned slowly around the room as Sandford continued to spray and uncover new areas of blood saturation.

'My thoughts,' said Sandford, 'are that someone started to try and cut up a body in the bath but couldn't do it, so they dragged it into the middle of this floor and began the dissection. Here we can see the major bleed-out. There are those minor blood splatters around the walls, which might indicate a small power tool was used. The section where the body lay would indicate this was a person of about five feet tall. This blood has been here for about six weeks.'

Raymonds got into the black Honda Jazz at five in the morning and drove along the road to the layby opposite the path down to Garra Cove. He unlatched the gate and walked a few strides in before pulling out the bags from where he'd hidden them in the hedge that met the road. He was seething with anger. The thought of Towan driving his car had kept him awake most of the night. Towan had gone too far. He'd made a fatal error in not doing as he was commanded. Now Raymonds had to take matters into his own hands. He crossed the road and put the Surfshack bags into his boot, then he drove towards Stokes' farm.

Marky couldn't sleep. He tried so hard, but the last few days he'd increased his cocaine up to a gram a day. The less he slept, the more he took, until he was beyond exhausted. His body felt as weak as a baby's, but his mind was racing at a million miles an hour and he couldn't close his eyes for more than a few seconds. He decided to get up and go in his workshop.

Raymonds caught Marky as he was coming out of the cottage. Marky froze in the doorway when he saw his father. It was too dark to make out Raymonds' expression but he was rigid with anger.

'We'll walk and talk,' he said to Marky as they moved along the lane. 'Who's in the house?'

'Mawgan, Kensa and Cam are in there. The forensic guys have gone.'

'We'll stay away from the house, then. I don't want them to hear what I've got to say to you. Did they look in your workshop?' Raymonds opened the gate to the paddock on his right.

'What for?' They climbed over the gate towards the pig field. 'They won't find anything in there.' He looked across to gauge his father's meaning. 'I told Jago to get rid of it, like you said,' he lied.

'You told Jago? So you're the boss of this little drug-peddling outfit, are you? You're the one dishing out the orders?'

'No. I didn't say that.'

'Jago can run rings around you, boy. Jago looks on you as thick as one of these pigs here. Thick as shit.' Marky didn't answer. 'Well, I've found your stash and I've got it in my car and I intend to dump it in the sea.'

'We can't do that, Dad.'

'We can't?'

'Please. We owe a lot of money. I made a big mistake, I admit it. I got the drugs on account. If I don't sell the drugs, I'm screwed. I'm as good as dead. Don't do this to me, Dad. I promise you, I'll straighten out. This is the last mess, I promise. Dad, I will make it up to you, please help me.'

'See, the thing is, son, I've realized you are everything I despise. You're weak-willed, easily led and you're a sneaky bully under all of it.'

'I am what you made me.'

'Now we get to the truth behind it all. Let's blame someone else for the way I am, huh? You're a sad excuse for a human being and I won't carry you any further down this road. You're on your own and I'm washing my hands of you. I've changed my mind about those bags of drugs. I'm taking them to the police station now and I'm telling them the truth. That's all the evidence they've been waiting for. They'll lock you away with all the other losers and throw away the key. I won't even let your mother come and see you. It would kill her anyway. But, you don't care about anyone but yourself.'

'That's not true. I've always tried to please you, to be like you.'

'Don't you fucking insult me, boy. You're nothing like me. You hear me?' Raymonds pushed Marky ahead of him. 'Get over there with the pigs where you belong. Go on.'

'Don't, Dad, I'm not taking this from you any more.'

'Not taking what? You'll do as you're told, you always have.'

Marky raised his fist and stood, sweating and shaking, in the middle of the field.

'Come on, then, if you think you're hard enough,' Raymonds laughed.

At seven that morning, the search teams were parked in the driveway of Kellis House. The sun hadn't long been up and there was a cold sharpness to the frosted landscape.

Willis was in the bathroom when Carter came to find her. She was wearing her forensic suit.

'How was your night at the cottage?' asked Carter.

'Cosy. Russell liked it.'

'How's Lauren?'

'She talked about Toby coming down today; she seems relieved by the idea.'

She turned to look at Carter from her kneeling position by the bathroom entrance. 'I see you were busy – I would have come and helped.'

'I know, but you have a big enough job as our stand-in FLO. We uncovered more complications than we needed here. I don't know why, but I was hoping to uncover something historical. I thought Ella Simmons?'

'I know, but this might explain the suicide, if he had something like this to cover up?'

'Yeah, Bowie's not going to like it, though – another tangent.'

'We don't know whether there's another layer to this yet, guv. What's under the heated floor?'

'Sandford's already done the tests, there's nothing.'

'We should have Sandford look upstairs in the

master bedroom. If JFW killed someone here, they probably started off there, there might be blood or semen traces.'

'You go and see him, he's up there now.'

Willis climbed the stairs and stood waiting for Sandford to turn round. He was dusting the window for prints.

'There's not a lot of blood down there,' Willis said.

'Morning, Ebony. They laid the victim out on a plastic sheet; there's the faint shred of black plastic caught on the heating mat.' Sandford looked at her with a wry smile. 'Do "banging", "head" and "brick wall" come to mind? You have everything but the boy?'

'Absolutely. Any semen?'

'What, me?'

'No.' She smiled, embarrassed. She knew Sandford loved winding her up. There weren't many people he liked enough to bother, so she felt honoured. 'The bed, the floor, the en-suite?'

'Haven't got there yet.' He looked down at the common. 'That wouldn't be my ideal choice for a place to bury a body, but at least it's never going to get sold for development. It's probably protected by the council.'

'Difficult soil to dig?' asked Willis as she came nearer and they stood together looking down at the common below. The sea was frothing and grey in the distance. Overhead, the bulky blankets of grey cloud sat wedged on one another. Each looked so full of rain and thunder it was almost biblical.

'Sandy soil; you'd want to go deep but it's not impossible,' said Sandford.

'Yes, and plenty of water to start the decomposition process off,' added Willis.

'The dogs have been let loose now, are you going outside?' asked Sandford.

'I'll wait. There's just as much of interest in here,' replied Willis.

'Thanks, but you know I'm married.'

Willis rolled her eyes and turned to leave. 'If I can help, please just tell me.'

'Ebony, you should retrain as a forensics expert. You love it and you're good at it: you have a degree in it, for Christ's sake. You've been a DC for how long now?'

'Ten years.'

'Do you think there is some reason why you're not getting promoted?'

'I want to stay in the MIT team.'

'But what about your plans for the future: a house, a family some day? You're thirty?'

'Twenty-nine.'

'Yeah, well, you'd better think about it, Eb. You should think about doing Robbo's job or mine. Not literally, of course, you'd have to work for another MIT team.'

'I'll think about what you've said; thanks.'

She went to find Carter. 'What shall we do about the baby's body from the farm?'

'Pascoe's taking it to the lab in Penhaligon.'

'We should tell Kensa,' said Willis.

'We will, but we're still waiting for confirmation on the DNA. It'll take a couple more hours. If it turns out to be Kensa's we will have a service and a proper burial.'

'That's good. We have Jago and Marky coming in this morning at the same time as Raymonds, guv. Which do you want to interview first?'

'Definitely keep Raymonds waiting while we talk to Jago, then Marky. Are you all right, Eb? You seem a little tense.'

'I'm fine. Just thinking.'

Carter stepped back as someone shouted for him from the door. 'Dogs are on to something.'

Willis and Carter went via the veranda and walked across the garden through the gap in the shrub bushes and onto the common. The shroud of mist had dissipated so that it was wispy between the gorse bushes. Dogs' tails could be seen wagging frantically as the cadaver springers hunted, nose to the ground. They congregated on a six-foot-long patch, which had neither gorse nor tree and only the creeping wild flower across the ground. Carter and Willis walked towards the spot.

Carter looked at the search team and gave his okay to start the digging.

As the sun rose higher in the sky and the wind and cloud gathered momentum the dig began. The sandy soil was still loose around the boards that had been laid to shore up the grave. As they reached down to lift the planks that went across width-ways, they uncovered the dismembered remains of a young adult. The white limbs were laid out in the bottom of the grave, the head had rolled from the blackened torso and it was resting against the sides of the grave.

'We need to collect a selection of the worms,' said Willis as she eased herself down inside the grave and gently rolled back the head by its black hair. The eye-less head was alive with insects.

'It's a white teenage male. I estimate he's been in here less than eight weeks,' Willis continued. 'Decomposition has been fairly fast because of the amount of water in this ground but the cold air will have helped to slow it a little. The grave is approximately four feet deep and has been supported with planks inside as well as above the body to stop the grave collapsing as the body rotted.'

Sandford picked up one of the lengths of wood and set it to one side to take with him, then he reached inside and handed Willis the camera.

Chapter 47

After they left the common, Willis and Carter drove down to the beach side and the police station.

Pascoe came in and handed Willis a note just as Jago Trebethin made himself comfortable and looked around the interview room as if he felt completely at home and it was all very normal for him.

'Martin Stokes was a nice old man – it's a terrible shame,' he said, shaking his head.

'You were at the farm that morning?' asked Willis.

'No, you know I wasn't, I was surfing. I saw you.'

'What about before you went in the water, or when you left us?'

Jago smiled at Willis: she was staring at him. She was trying to work out if he was the sort of man who could stick a man through the base of the spine with a spike. She thought Jago would be a lot more discreet than that. Perhaps drowning might be more his style, or poison. Nothing too messy, she decided. The expensive shirt would be ruined.

'Talk to others about it, Raymonds for a start.'

'We will talk to Raymonds. I thought you'd feel quite close to him,' Carter continued.

'What do you mean by that?'

'Your mother and Raymonds? It's a long-standing affair, I hear?'

A real flash of anger crossed over Jago's face and then disappeared just as quickly. 'Gossip, that's all. This is a small town and tongues wag.'

He smiled and tapped the heel of his boot on the floor as if ready to leave.

'We got it from a reliable source. Him and your mum go way back. In fact, it's commonly understood that all your school fees, your uni fees, all paid by Raymonds,' said Carter. 'No wonder your dad left.'

'My dad left because he found someone else. The affair didn't start till after. What does it matter, anyway? I never asked him to do these things. I didn't ask to be sent away to school.'

'Better to get you out of the way, I suppose.'

'Whatever – I had a good education out of it. For that, I'm grateful.'

'I expect you came back here hoping to be one of Raymonds' favourites but Cam seems to have worked his way in the back door. It looks like he's set to build an empire for himself with his new restaurant on the beach while you struggle to get a licence for an ice-cream van, I think.'

He shrugged. His hands were clasped between his knees as he sat forward in the chair, occasionally pushing back his fringe with the heel of his hand.

'Who knows? Dreams can come true,' he said in a cheesy way.

'Did Martin Stokes stand in your way?'

'God, I wouldn't waste my time killing an old farmer; he was always going to find a way to get that done without my help.'

'He had a history of paedophilia, did you know?'

'I knew, everyone knew.'

'Why, because Kensa and Mawgan told you?'

'No, I didn't know it involved them. Kensa's always had trouble keeping her legs together.'

'Kensa was raped,' said Willis. 'You knew that.'

'I knew the accusation had been flying about. But Kensa says lots of things. She's a psycho.'

Willis opened her notebook and read from Towan's statement: '"After we got into the house, Jago raped Ella."' Jago choked on the saliva in his throat and coughed uncontrollably for a minute. Carter pushed the water across to him.

'Are you mad? Why would I need to?'

'You wanted to teach her a lesson, maybe?'

'I was drunk, hardly able to rape anyone.'

'You weren't drunk, though, were you? You were off your head, you'd taken a concoction of things. After all, it was Marky's birthday and you and him were used to mixing it up. You were the local lads, weren't you? You got away with things because Marky's dad was the Sheriff. You got away with it until it went too far. You liked Kensa. Did you think you had the right?'

'I didn't touch her. Toby Forbes-Wright was the one responsible.'

'What, a little fifteen-year-old virgin asleep on Rohypnol? I'll tell you what may interest you, we found a baby's skeleton and we're running DNA tests on it at the moment. Those tests will show us not only if that's Kensa's baby, but who the baby's father was.'

Jago shrugged.

'Ella Simmons was there that night too,' Willis said, taking out a photo of Ella and sliding it across. 'She was sixteen at the time, a beautiful-looking girl.' Jago nodded as he looked at the photo. He could not take his eyes off it. 'After you kicked Mawgan and Cam out, and Towan left, you carried Toby up to his bed, then it was just you and Kensa and Ella Simmons, wasn't it?'

'Marky was there,' he said, staring at the floor.

'What went on that night?'

'I didn't rape anyone. Towan spent a lot of time arguing with Ella. I was with Marky and Kensa until he took her upstairs. I heard a lot of weird stuff going on. I didn't know whether Ella had gone in there and was causing a fuss because of Marky doing her friend. I was thinking I better go when Marky came downstairs in a state and he said Toby had come round, seen them having sex, and gone berserk. He had beaten Kensa really badly. He'd raped her.'

'Did you believe him?'

'He was really upset. I didn't know what to think. I don't suppose I had any reason not to believe him.'

'Did you see her?'

He nodded. 'I thought she was dead. She wasn't conscious. Marky kept asking what should we do. I asked him where Ella was and he said she was gone. He said he'd knocked Toby out and he was on his bed. I went in and Toby looked pretty beaten up.'

'What happened then?'

'Marky called his dad. He kept saying to me that he didn't want to get blamed for it.'

'What was Raymonds' reaction when he came?'

'Raymonds told us to go home, he said he would sort it.'

'Did you see Ella again that day?'

'I didn't see Ella again at all.'

Willis unfolded the piece of paper Pascoe had given her at the start. She re-read it and then handed it to Carter to read.

'Do you want the good news or the bad news?' asked Carter. Carter looked out of the window and saw Raymonds' black Honda Jazz park up outside.

Jago shook his head, still stunned.

'Good news, you weren't the father. Bad news, we saw you buy that shipment of Class A drugs from the Ukrainians.'

Willis took out a still from the film footage at Gordano services and slid it towards Jago as Carter cautioned him.

She looked at her phone as a text came through from Jeanie.

We are ten minutes away.

'I'm having Jago taken straight over to Penhaligon now,' said Carter. 'He can be formally charged there. I think it's better we stay out of it. You ready to interview Raymonds?' Carter asked Willis as they got back to their desks. She was engrossed in something on the screen.

'What is it?' asked Carter.

'I'm just looking at the samples from the farm that

Sandford's taken. We have a match to the mittens at Gordano. There are fibres that contain fibreglass residue, they match the ones found in Marky's workshop – plus we have a small amount of dust particles that are a dry pig food. It's the one used at Stokes' farm. It's confirmation that Mawgan's got to be involved in some way. Nothing goes on in that farm without her knowing.'

'What about Marky? Where is he? He's supposed to be in here by now.'

Chapter 48

'Is it all right to bring my dog inside?' Lauren stuck her head around the door to Cam's café as Russell tried hard to pull her the opposite way.

Cam looked shocked to see her. He nodded.

'Americano, please,' she said after she came in and stood waiting for Cam to ask her what she wanted and it didn't happen.

'I'm sorry about your son. I hope they find him soon.'

'Thank you.'

She watched him prepare her coffee.

'Where are you from?' he asked as he turned and smiled awkwardly.

'Originally?' she asked as she undid her coat, took off her bobble hat.

'Yes.'

'New York.'

She looked back at the door – the sand was swirling, the spray from the waves was showering down on the glass conservatory. Outside the window the furniture was being upturned.

'Milk?'

'Yes, please.'

Cam picked up her coffee cup and walked around the counter.

'Where would you like to sit?'

'Oh, over there is great, thanks.' Lauren nodded in the direction of a table at the edge of the aisle near the door. 'Aren't you worried about the high tide? The sea looks pretty fierce.' She smiled nervously. 'Are we safe?'

Cam went back to stand by the counter. The place was empty except for Lauren. She looked outside, she was beginning to think she'd better cut the café visit short and head home while she could do so safely.

'Don't worry – we'll be able to see if the sea starts coming over the road and then you can make a break for it, you'll be fine walking up the hill,' said Cam.

Lauren took a sip of her coffee and avoided looking at Cam. She told herself not to be silly.

'Is it your first time in Cornwall?' Cam asked. He came to stand by her table.

'Yes. It's a beautiful place.'

'Yes, we like it, most of the time, except when we're invaded.'

'Invaded?'

'Holidaymakers.'

'Oh, I see.'

'Yes, we have a love–hate relationship with the grockles, we call them. We love their money but we hate them.' He smiled. 'Sorry – I'm only joking.' She smiled back. But the tension in both of them showed.

Lauren tried to see the man beneath. She thought how he would have been an overly pretty boy. Now his face was thin but his eyes were bright blue, his hair curly and sandy-coloured.

'Do you live in the village?' Lauren decided to turn the tables and ask the questions.

'I live on the outskirts.'

'Did you know my father-in-law, Jeremy Forbes-Wright?'

'Yes. We all knew him.'

'We were very grateful to the people of the village for coming to the funeral.'

He shook his head. 'I didn't go.'

Lauren wished she could add some personal thought regarding Jeremy's death, his life even, but she had nothing to say on the matter.

'Have you lived here all your life?' she asked Cam.

'No, I moved away for a big part of it but I've come back to stay. This is my home.' The day was becoming dark with heavy rain clouds outside as the sea began creeping up the beach. With every wave, it pushed a little further and ribbons of foam plumed up into the air as it hit the car park wall.

'Oh dear, we'd better go,' Lauren said nervously. 'The sea is coming right up over the road.'

'Yes,' Cam answered, but at the same time he was distracted, watching a yellow Fiat pull up outside. A look of panic crossed his face; Lauren followed his gaze and saw Kensa getting out of the car.

'We better get going,' she said looking urgently for Russell's lead. Cam didn't answer; he was staring at Kensa. She had opened the door and was standing in the doorway, pointing a gun at Lauren.

Chapter 49

Sandford left for the farm. It was just him working at there today. He drove up the lane and stopped in the gateway to the crime scene. The tents were still there. He sat for a few minutes and listened to the silence, just the sweet song of a blackbird. Then he drove on and parked on the hard standing in the yard. The collie came out, excited to see him. Sandford stood by the car and looked around. Something was missing from the day. He realized that there was no one around. He called out, but didn't get an answer, so he picked out the plank of wood he'd taken from the grave site, now wrapped in two paper bags to protect it, and he carried it up to the farm-shop store next to Marky's workshop. He had something on his mind that needed checking. He cleared an area of shelving and opened up the crime scene bag for him to compare the planks. He took photos to show Carter and then walked back out and down towards the house again.

Brutus the stallion shoved his chest against his stable door and snorted. Bluebell shook her mane and whinnied at him. Sandford walked into the farmhouse kitchen and called out a hello. No one answered. He felt the kettle on the Aga; it was cold. Back out into the yard, he went in search of Mawgan.

The cattle started mooing from the shed as they heard his footsteps approach. He looked at his watch – he was sure they should have been let out by now. He'd come from farming country originally. He knew what had to happen on farms. Brutus stamped his foot and banged his knee against his door continually. Sandford came over and looked inside his stall – he had no hay and very little water.

He was headed for the field. There, free-range pigs lived in corrugated huts. He could hear the sound of pigs chomping. *Pigs happy as . . .* he thought. He walked round the corner to the farrowing pens; a sow jumped up on her hind legs as he passed along the narrow walkway. The pens on either side were empty. As he glanced inside one of them, he saw something flapping. He opened the pen and went inside to take a look. A toddler's night-time nappy had been left dirty and screwed up, thrown in the corner of the sty. It was flapping in the wind.

He walked out and up to the field. The noise of the pigs was deafening as he got to the gate. They were fighting over food in one of the huts, squealing as they bit one another to get their share.

He walked around the side of the largest of the huts and he saw legs, shattered remains of chewed shin bones.

Lauren looked towards Cam – he stood motionless behind the counter.

She looked back at the table in front of her, where Kensa had put an open photo album.

'Look at them,' she screeched.

'Kensa, calm down,' Cam said.

'No, you betrayed me, Cam. You and Mawgan lied to me all this time.'

'No, we wouldn't do that. We love you, Kensa.'

'Toby was the only one for me, still is.'

Lauren looked at Kensa. Her face was blotchy and mottled. She was wheezing as she ranted.

'Yes. He was my first love.'

'And you were his.'

'Is that what he says?' She looked at Lauren with joy.

'Yes.'

'Kensa…' Cam started to speak. She stopped him as she aimed the gun at him.

'I'll shoot us all, Cam, I don't have nothing left to live for now. Every dream I had is shattered. Even Misty is taken from me. My life is over. No one wants me here any more. You and Mawgan have been lying to me. You don't care about me. You never helped me that night when I was raped. Raymonds told me you left me.'

'That's not true. They threw us out. Towan, Marky and Jago, they picked us up and threw us out and locked the door. We were only young. We tried everything to take you with us but you and Toby were already unconscious. We were in such a state, all of us. Marky, Jago and Towan: it was all their doing and Raymonds did nothing to stop it. I came back here to help us start again, Kensa. My life has been in ruins just like yours, just like Mawgan's. This is our chance to start afresh. We have so much to look forward to.'

'Not any more.' She looked at Lauren. 'I took your son.'

Lauren looked at Kensa to see if it could be true and not the dreams.

'Why did you have to take him?'

'I couldn't help myself. I wanted a baby so bad. I've never carried another child since I lost mine and Toby's. All this time I've been waiting for him to come back to me but he never came. I wanted something of my own. Toby owed me that. I got his address from Towan and I followed him from his house to the Observatory and then I waited in the park for him to come out. I changed my mind. I decided I would just talk to him. It didn't feel right taking the boy. But then he left Samuel outside the music shop. I watched him through the window. He was talking to the man behind the counter. He was laughing and smiling with him and I thought how much he'd changed. I stood by the buggy looking in at the window for ages. If he had looked at me, maybe come out to talk to me, I wouldn't have taken Samuel but, I kept looking down at the little boy, he was sleeping. I waited twenty minutes at least, just stood there by the buggy and Toby didn't care. He didn't even come out to check on him. I undid the boy's belt and I carried him into the park and he never woke up. I gave him a few drops of Misty's sedative. I changed him there and I put his suit in a carrier bag and threw it in the bin. People couldn't see what I was carrying. I hid him under my coat. He was sleeping all the way till I laid him in the boot of the car and made him cosy and then I called Mawgan and I drove to the top of the park to pick her up.'

'Where's my son, Kensa?' Lauren pleaded. 'Please tell me. Please.'

She was shaking so much her knees gave way.

'Your son is in the safe place and no one can ever find him.' Kensa looked at Cam as she said it.

Lauren held her face in her hands, crippled with anguish.

Outside a scream went up as a large wave crashed across the road, and under the door a small gurgle of seawater forced its way beneath the door and inside the café. Kensa looked towards the Fiat, which had water surging up to its wheel arches.

'Here's a photo of Toby again. See!'

Lauren nodded, as she was trying to think of every way of coming out of the situation alive. All she could think of was that Samuel was alive and needed her.

'He met me every day after school. He was broken up for the summer but I still had a month to go. We couldn't help ourselves, getting hot and bothered in the dunes. We kissed for hours.' She laughed and Lauren stared at her. 'I didn't need to worry, I thought, because I hadn't started my periods. They didn't start till a few months after I had my baby.' She sighed. 'I never saw him. I never held my baby. I would give anything to see a photo of him.'

'It was very wrong of them not to allow you to hold your baby, Kensa,' said Lauren. She swallowed hard. Russell started barking.

'I don't even know what Raymonds did with him. I don't know where he's buried, or was he left to the animals? Was he thrown in the sea like a piece of rubbish? Sometimes I go back up there to look for him and I swear I can hear him crying.'

'Kensa?' Cam said. 'You need help. You have to give the boy back now.'

Kensa turned to Lauren. 'Do you want to see him?'

'Yes. Where is he?'

'If you want to see him you have to come with me now. No phones, no nothing. Just come.'

'Where is Mawgan?' asked Cam.

Kensa looked sheepish. ' I wasn't going to hurt her. I was angry. I'm sorry. She didn't need to run away from me.' Kensa lifted the gun and aimed it at Cam.

'You're not going to shoot me, Kensa. I'll come with you, but put the gun down.'

'I need it. I'm not leaving it.'

Back in the house, Sandford searched the rooms as he phoned Carter.

'There's a man's body, I think it's Marky, he's been murdered. His body is in with the pigs. I've found evidence that a toddler-sized child was being kept here on the farm. I would say he was here, right up to a few hours ago.'

'Are Mawgan or Towan in the house?' asked Carter.

'No,' replied Sandford. 'There's no sign of anyone here. But it looks like someone's taken some items out of the gun safe – it's been left open.'

'Can you see what's missing?' asked Carter.

'A shotgun, for sure.'

'Eb,' Carter said as he hung up. 'Get hold of Pascoe and tell him he needs to get Leonard and the forensic team over to Stokes' farm. Tell him what's happened. And, get him to put out an alert for Mawgan and Kensa. Tell him we are keeping Raymonds in custody.'

After calling Pascoe, Willis phoned Lauren; there was no reply, and she left a message: 'Lauren, Kensa's gone missing. She may be headed your way. Lock all doors and stay inside.'

Another call came from Pascoe.

'We're following the sighting of a yellow Fiat. It's been seen heading towards Penhal. We think it was hidden in a barn with farm machinery on the out-skirts of Penhaligon.'

Carter grabbed his keys as Willis got to her feet.

'Let's go. We want to be ready.'

'What about Raymonds?'

'He can wait. Lock the door.'

Mawgan stood outside Cam's cottage watching the yellow Fiat coming over the cliff road towards her. She thought about running, but then she saw Cam at the wheel. Kensa got out brandishing the shotgun and called to Mawgan to come over. Mawgan walked towards them. All the time she kept her eye on Kensa. When she had left her that morning she was sure there wasn't a sane thought left in Kensa's head. She'd threatened to skin Mawgan alive as she chased her round the house. Now, when she looked at Kensa, she saw she was beyond help or hope, but Mawgan had to try.

'Walk towards the mine,' Kensa said as she waved the shotgun at them.

'Is my son there?' asked Lauren, shouting so her voice could be heard above the sea pounding the cliff face below.

Kensa didn't answer as she marched them down towards the mine. They stood on the side of the derelict building and the wind died right down as they sheltered outside the old ruins.

'Kensa, stop all this now, before it's too late.'

Kensa shook her head as she turned to look out to sea; the sun's rays were creeping through the storm clouds. She put up a hand to shelter her eyes from the glare.

'You've lied to me.'

'No, Kensa. I'd never lie to you. We've shared so much, you and me.'

'Did you know she had my son?' Lauren asked. Mawgan nodded.

Cam shook his head and groaned, 'Why would you do such a thing?'

'I didn't know until we were home. Then she gave him to me to help look after and I panicked. I didn't know what to do with him. I moved him around the place. I promise I looked after him, kept him warm. I kept thinking I would tell the police that day but I didn't know what would happen to us. Then my dad found him and threatened to tell Raymonds. He said he would say that Cam was involved, and that would mean the end of Cam getting his restaurant. It would mean the end of all our dreams. I couldn't let him do that. I hit him over the head with the spade till he was dead and I stuck him on the spike. I didn't care at that moment. I hated him so much for all the things he did to us. I went to get the boy, to give him back, but Kensa had already taken him. I'm so sorry.' Cam was staring at Mawgan with a look of disbelief and devastation. 'Oh my God, my poor little boy.' Lauren looked at Kensa. 'How could you do that to a little boy? Why did you take him?' said Lauren. 'You had no right.'

'You want to talk about rights?' Kensa snapped. 'Where are mine? I want what I've lost. I never had a childhood. They took it from me. The only good thing that ever happened to me was Toby. I wanted that baby so badly, but they wouldn't even let me have that. Where are my rights?' She shook her head and said remorsefully, 'I'm sorry. I've been feeding him. I've been finding clothes for him to wear. But now Misty's gone . . . I can't do it. I don't want to see him any more. I didn't want to hurt him, but he's crying all the time. I'm sorry.' She started to cry. 'I'm so sorry.'

'Please don't say you hurt my son?'

The police helicopter hovered above them.

'We have a sighting by the old mine at Garra. I can see Kensa, she has a gun, possibly a shotgun. She appears to be holding Lauren, Cam Simmons and Mawgan Stokes. Armed response teams are on their way.' Pascoe radioed back to Carter and Willis. 'It's too windy for us to set down close. We'll drop behind the headland and meet you up there.'

Willis and Carter drove through the seawater that

had completely covered the road and had reached the door of the police station. As they turned at the end of the shops, ready to take the cliff road, they met Jeanie and Toby coming the other way.

'Follow us,' Willis mouthed to Jeanie. They led the way towards Garra.

Chapter 50

Raymonds sat bolt upright in the chair as he waited. He looked around the room – it had been many years since he'd sat in the police station that he'd known as a second home for the most part of his life. This was the only real interview room they had. This was the room without the window, cold in winter, hot in summer. He strained to hear the comings and goings in the rest of the building. He couldn't. There was a terrible stillness in the room and he began to feel that panic build in him that he'd felt the night he'd waited in the services car park. It was the panic he felt now when he had to admit that some things were beyond his control. He no longer had the might of the law behind him, the unquestionable authority.

He was dreading going home to Eileen. He would have to tell her that her only son was dead. She would look at him with that expression that he loathed so much and all the pain in the world would be reflected in her eyes and she would ask him how.

Kensa seemed to cling to the old mine wall as if she were hanging on to the earth as it turned.

'Where's my son, Kensa? You said you'd take me to him.' Lauren spoke as calmly as she could.

'I come up here to think, be close to people,' Kensa said, as she stared out to sea.

She picked up the gun and aimed it at Lauren. 'Come with me.'

'No, Kensa, what are you doing?' Cam called. Mawgan stepped towards her.

'Kensa, don't do it.'

'There they are,' Willis said, as they came in sight of the mine. They pulled up and Jeanie parked beside them. Carter got out and went around to talk with Toby.

'Make sure you stay in the car until it's safe. Stay with him, Jeanie, and make sure he has a vest on if he comes out.'

Carter and Willis walked towards the mine.

Kensa called out: 'I want to speak with Toby,' as she saw them coming.

'You'll have to put the gun down,' replied Carter. 'We can't let Toby or anyone else be at risk. You need to tell us where Samuel is.' Above them, the seagulls screamed as they circled on the wind. 'He needs to be found now. He's an innocent little boy, it isn't right, you know that. Mawgan, do you know where he is?'

'What's right or wrong?' Kensa walked backwards towards the cliff edge. 'Old man Simmons pushed Ella off this edge after he'd brought her back from Plymouth. I saw him but I was too frightened to tell anyone. I can still hear her scream as she fell. Was that right?'

Cam started to cry. Mawgan held him as he staggered back and slumped against the mine wall.

'I was abused all my life, we all were,' said Kensa. 'We were hunted down like animals when we were children. Was that right?'

'No,' replied Carter. 'It wasn't, and we will find the people responsible.'

'They're dead now. Martin Stokes, Old Man Simmons. They're dead and never made to speak the truth about it.'

'But we can take Raymonds to court. He knew what was going on.'

'Oh yes, he knew. But the Sheriff is untouchable.'

'Kensa?' Willis stood forward. 'Listen to me; no one can make it up to you. It's a dreadful thing that happened to you and no one can make the bad memories disappear. But there are so many people that can help you cope, help you build a great life for yourself. You've been brave all your life. You've been a fighter. Don't give up now. Samuel is a small child like you were. Don't let these horrible things happen to him too. You have the power to make him happy again. Just tell us where he is.'

'Toby?' Kensa shouted up to the car. 'I need to talk to you. Then I'll tell.'

Toby looked petrified as he sat watching the cliff top through the windscreen. He reached for the handle of the door. Then he turned to Jeanie.

'I have to go to her, I have to get out of the car,' he said to Jeanie.

'Okay, I'm coming with you,' said Jeanie. The door was almost whipped out of her hands as she opened it. She went around to the boot and fitted him with a bullet-proof vest.

Kensa allowed the gun to grow heavy and low in her hand as she watched Toby walk towards her and she seemed to teeter towards the edge of the cliff as the wind returned in gusts, but she kept Lauren near her.

Carter watched the officers take up their positions on the perimeter of his vision. He trusted Pascoe to know what he had to do. No one would want to be the officer to pull the trigger on Kensa, but they would, if they had to.

'Kensa, Toby cannot come any closer while you're holding the gun,' Carter said, but it was more to try and halt Toby than influence Kensa.

'Hello, Kensa,' said Toby as he kept his eyes on her trying to see the girl he had loved, all those years ago.

'Toby, stay back,' ordered Willis, but Toby only slowed down his pace.

Kensa was breathless, she was smiling, and at the same time her eyes were swimming with tears as she looked at him.

'Toby? I've been waiting for you, for so long.'

'Please, I'm begging you, let Samuel go. Tell us where he is.'

'He is in the safe place. I never loved anyone but you, you know? I know you would never have hurt me, it was all lies.'

'I wasn't capable of harming you, I loved you.'

Kensa gasped as if someone had kicked her in the chest.

'You don't love me any more?'

'I will always love you, but I've realized I cannot control who I love. Lauren understands too. I'm sorry.'

Kensa pulled Lauren towards her and Carter could feel the tension as twenty officers got ready to fire. Kensa moved closer to the edge of the cliff, taking Lauren with her.

'Don't do it, Kensa, don't do it,' pleaded Mawgan, 'otherwise no one will ever believe our stories. No one will ever care what we have to say; they will just remember us as those "mad ones" on the cliff top. They'll never know what we did to stay alive, what we suffered. Kensa, don't do this to me, don't do it to us. Step away from the edge. Let Lauren go.'

Lauren took a step away as Mawgan stepped forward.

'We deserve better. All the pacts we made as kids. We knew we had to stay alive at all costs, didn't we? I'll go to court and tell them about my dad, what he did to us. I'll make sure the town knows what happened to us. Things will be different now.'

Kensa turned and looked out to sea. The Atlantic raged and churned.

Mawgan held out her arms and reached for Kensa.

'Come on, we'll face this together, like we've always done.'

Kensa smiled as she cried. But her eyes still burned. She was distracted by Toby. He had begun walking away.

'Kensa, please,' Mawgan said as she saw Kensa getting anxious again. She held the gun tight.

'Toby, stop where you are,' Carter shouted.

'Give me the gun, Kensa,' Mawgan said, and walked forwards, reaching for it.

Kensa fired, and the bullet hit Mawgan full on. She was blown backwards. Carter held up his hand to stop the officers from firing.

Cam knelt and held Mawgan on the ground as he looked around blindly for help.

'I came back for you, Mawgan. I came back to be with you. I would have done anything to make us happy.'

Her eyes were losing their focus as she smiled. 'It's not our time, is it? Run to the safe place, Cam, that's where the boy will be.' Mawgan looked at Cam to see if he understood – he nodded. Then she passed away. Cam bowed his head and sobbed.

Kensa turned and opened her arms like a bird. Then she dropped off the edge of the cliff.

Raymonds looked around the room and thought how they had done a rather shoddy job in putting the place back as it was. There were still tourist posters on the walls advertising the Poldark Mine and the Traditional Cornish Village where time had stood still. He stood and went to the door and listened: no noise, no sound at all. He tried the door, it was locked. He stood in the middle of the room and for a moment he closed his eyes and he felt as if he were falling.

Outside in the street, Towan revved up Raymonds' Silver Fox till it was smoking. Then he spun the Ford Cortina in the sand as he roared past the police station, spinning the car round in the entrance to the beach outside Cam's café and then racing back along the road. He turned into the car park behind Marky's Surfshack and lined up the Silver Fox with the bottle banks at the edge of the car park, beneath the sign saying not to feed the seagulls. He revved, and then he let her fly, and the Silver Fox smashed into the bottle bank.

Raymonds stood tall, breathing deep; he could still smell the old police station. Those were good times. He had no regrets. He'd made a few bad judgement calls, it was true. But he hoped that people would remember him for the good things he'd done. He'd always had the good of the community in mind. It was never about him.

He looked up at the ceiling. The strip lights of the original room had been replaced with a pendant light. He shook his head.

'Shoddy.'

Chapter 51

'What did she mean by the safe place?' asked Willis.

'It was a place where we hid where no one would find us,' answered Cam. He stood watching them zip up the body bag with Mawgan inside.

'Will you show us where that is?' Willis asked.

Cam nodded as he turned away from the cliff top.

Pascoe left instructions for his officers while he took one of the police vans and, led by Cam, they headed away in convoy.

They drove back towards the Stokes farm but went off on a track before they got there and pulled up at the old barn that Willis and Carter had been to before, with Pascoe. It was still stacked with straw bales up to the ceiling. Carter went round to talk to Cam when he got out of the car and they opened the barn doors. The dust from the straw flew around them.

'Are you sure this is the place?' Carter asked incredulously.

Cam got out of the car and stood looking at the barn, pale-faced and shell-shocked as he tried to cope with what had happened. Carter put his hand on his shoulder. He nodded.

'Thank you, Cam, we appreciate how hard this is for you.'

It was eerily quiet inside the barn, until a dove flew out from the roof cavity. It sent a shower of dust and then the barn settled again into silence.

Cam stood for a few minutes looking at the bales. They had been stacked so that their load was balanced. He ran his hands along the lowest row, counting until he stopped by a section that had two bales, end on. He knelt and slid his hands either side of one of the bales, wriggling it out like a piece out of a Jenga puzzle.

Lauren was watching, quietly terrified, from the entrance.

'Do you want to wait in the car, Lauren?' asked Jeanie, looking back at her. She shook her head.

Toby came to stand next to her.

'When we were young we had a farmhand called Billy who was really kind to us kids,' said Cam as Willis knelt beside him and helped him gently dislodge the bale.

'He could see what was going on and so, when he stacked these bales in here, he created a tunnel for us as he went.' They finished sliding out the bale.

'We'd try and make it to here and then we'd scramble in and pull the bale to, and we'd hide in here, all night sometimes.'

'Could Samuel really be in there now?' asked Carter as he joined Willis on her knees by the tunnel. 'Is there any air?'

'There's enough,' answered Cam, 'the stack is still standing, I presume the tunnel is still there.'

Willis lay down on her side and peered into the gap between the bales. Does it widen out?'

'Yes, to the width of the two bales after about ten feet, just briefly. There's a section in the middle where we used to stay overnight if we could get here. There is an exit over here,' Cam said as he walked along the front of the bales and stopped at the far left, feeling along until he found the bale on the second level. He carefully slid it out. Carter and Willis followed him over to take a look.

'This drops down into the stack then?' asked Willis, as she reached her arm inside to try and gauge what was beyond where she could see with her torch.

'Yes.'

Carter cupped his hands to his mouth and called Samuel. There was no reply.

'We need a camera probe like they put in drains. Have we got one?' Carter looked across at Pascoe for an answer.

'I can get one within the hour.'

'Then we will wait.' Carter was just getting to his feet when he paused and looked at Willis's face. She held her finger to her lips and listened hard at the tunnel exit. 'You heard a noise?' She nodded. Carter called across to Lauren and Toby. 'Come over here and try calling him.'

They hurried across and knelt together and Lauren called into the darkness.

'Samuel? Hello, Samuel. Talk to Mommy. Can you hear me? Samuel?'

Carter and Willis strained to listen as the faintest reply came from deep inside the stacks.

'Mommy?'

'Samuel, baby. We're coming. You be a good boy now and stay still, stay there. We're coming to get you.' She couldn't speak as she looked at Toby. She swallowed and breathed and wiped her eyes.

'What can we do?' she asked.

A bale shifted at the top of the stack and toppled down onto the floor in a shower of dust.

'He's going to die in there, get him out. You have to get him out.'

'No, Lauren. It's unstable. We'll have to wait,' replied Jeanie. 'We have no choice.'

'The specialist rescue team will be here within the hour,' Pascoe said, but his eyes went up to the large crack that was starting to appear in the top centre of the stack. The stack was beginning to give way. Willis saw it too.

'I'll go in now, guv. We can't wait.'

'No, Eb, you can't risk it,' Jeanie said.

'I think I can get through.' She looked at Cam. He shook his head in response.

'I have no idea what it's like in there any more. It was always a small space, even when we were kids.'

'No, Eb. You can't, it's too dangerous,' said Jeanie.

'But Kensa has been in there,' answered Willis. 'I'm bigger, but I reckon I can squeeze in. We know Samuel is in there. We have to try and get him out. We can't wait an hour and then another hour trying to get in there. Let me give it a go.' Jeanie looked at Carter to try and stop Willis. He was staring up at the stack. He looked at Willis and nodded.

Pascoe went to his van and came back with a length of rope and a safety helmet.

'This is all I can find.'

Willis took it and switched on the torch on top of the helmet. She strapped it on tightly and tied the rope around her waist.

'We have to go for it now,' she said as she gave Jeanie her jacket but kept her radio, making a last-minute check it was working before giving Jeanie the end of the rope.

'If it collapses, you'll be able to locate me?' she asked, as she looked across at Carter. It was a rhetorical question but Carter couldn't answer anyway. He was struck with some sort of fear he'd never felt before. It was all right sending himself into danger, but not someone he cared so deeply for.

'Guv?'

He nodded.

Willis lay down on her side and began to wriggle between the bales and work her way through.

The barn fell silent as the others listened to the sounds of her exertion until she disappeared from sight. Carter knelt on the ground and called through the darkness, 'Okay, Eb?'

'Still moving forward, guv,' she replied, though she was barely audible. 'The space is pretty small.'

Inside the stack, Willis shone her hand-held torch forward in the darkness and saw the edges of the straw walls widening in front of her.

'Samuel?' she called.

'Mommy?' came a reply in the dark, muffled heat and dust. Willis paused as she listened to a rumble around her and stayed absolutely still as a dust cloud enveloped her.

'Eb?' Carter called into the tunnel but he could see it had collapsed inside.

'Guv?' Willis waited for the rumbling sound to stop and then she called back down the tunnel. There was no reply. 'Guv?' she called again, and her voice went flat and nowhere. There didn't seem to be any air left. She felt each breath burn her lungs with dust and heat. She waited in the dark for a minute and then pulled herself onwards into a space two bales wide. It was wide enough for her to turn onto her stomach and pull herself up onto her elbows before her head touched straw.

'Samuel? Good boy.' She found him. He was strapped into a car seat. There was a bottle of water next to him. She picked it up and gave him a drink as she shone the torch over his face to see how he was. He was covered in dust and snorting as he drank.

'Hello, Samuel, your mummy's waiting for you but you're going to have to be a very good boy for me, okay?'

'Eb, can you hear me?' Carter spoke into his radio. 'Eb, are you okay?'

'We're here, guv. Samuel is in good condition. Tell Lauren and Toby he's all right. He's strapped into a car seat so I think he'll have a good chance if this collapses.'

'You can't come out the way you went in, now.'

'Okay.' She shone her torch around the space. 'I can see where the tunnel continues,' she radioed back. 'Are we sure that's the way out?'

'Wait. I'll move to the exit and you listen for me calling.'

He called out her name.

'I can hear you – just,' said Willis over her radio.

'Can you follow the noise?'

'I don't know. It seems to be coming from further inside the barn, I'm not sure if I want to risk it.'

'Cam?' Carter turned to ask him, 'Does the tunnel come straight out?'

'No, it goes around in a semicircle then it rises to the next level before it comes out here.'

'Is there any other exit at the back maybe?'

'No.'

'There's no choice, Eb. That's the only way out. It bends and then it rises and then you're out. It's fifteen feet, at the most.' Carter looked at Cam for confirmation. He shook his head. He wasn't sure. 'We think,' Carter added.

'Okay, I understand.' Willis inched towards the gap, sliding her body as she pushed the car seat and Samuel forward inch by inch. She felt the walls around her start to groan and slide. She stopped.

'Not sure whether I can make it through that gap, guv, I risk bringing the place down if I try and force the car seat through.'

'You have to, Eb. This way is the only way out for you both. It's still clear, for now. You have to move fast.' Carter turned to Pascoe. 'Have the paramedics stand by. Get the fire brigade out here, anyone who will be able to help shift these bales if this thing collapses.'

Jeanie held on to Ebony's rope.

'I can try and push Samuel through if you can coax him through your end,' said Willis into her radio. 'But I'll have to take him out of the seat. He's very scared, but if Lauren calls him and I push him from this end I think he can make it.'

Carter looked at Lauren; she nodded.

Willis was so cramped now that she couldn't raise her head, only lie on her side as she unstrapped Samuel.

'Samuel? You want to see Mommy? Mommy and Daddy? Do you think you can squeeze through like a clever little wiggly worm?'

'Little worm?' His voice was cracked and sore with the dust.

'Yes, listen, Samuel, who is that?'

Lauren's voice came through calling him. 'Mommy's here, my darling. I'm waiting for you. Come to me.'

'Mommy?'

'Yes, she's waiting for you, Samuel.'

Willis managed to ease him out of his chair and push it to one side as she pushed him forward.

'Keep calling,' she said into the radio.

Toby and Lauren took it in turns to call, and Willis watched Samuel as he crawled forward and through the gap. She moved with him and shone her torch for him to see. When she could go no further into the gap, which was the size of a cereal packet, she continued talking to Samuel, encouraging him to keep moving. She spoke into her radio.

'He's coming to the raised bit now, I think. I can't move any further forward. He won't be able to get up there on his own. Can you try and reach in and get him out your end?'

Carter reached his arm into the tunnel and felt nothing. He looked at everyone. Finally, he assessed Toby's chances.

'Toby, you're the thinnest, the tallest. Get in there as far as you can and try and get him.'

Toby moved inside and was lodged waist-deep into the tunnel when they heard the bales groan as he pushed harder to reach Samuel. He let out a muffled yell and Carter and Pascoe dragged him out. He was holding Samuel in his arms.

'We got him, Eb, well done,' Carter radioed.

'That's great, guv.' Willis rolled onto her side to try and breathe freely. She wiped the sweat and dust from her stinging eyes.

'Your turn now, Eb, don't hang about.'

There was the sound of the bales shifting above her, the squeak of straw sliding on straw.

'I'm too big to make it through this last section, guv.'

'The bales are shifting. There might be a chance then. Get ready.'

Willis looked behind her. Her exit was completely cut off now. There was nowhere to go. She grabbed the car seat and pulled it against her chest.

Carter looked around as the rope round Ebony's waist was yanked out of Jeanie's hands and sucked into the tunnel as bales began to tumble inside and the cracks in the structure began to widen.

'Come on, Eb, it's collapsing. You have to try now.'

Willis saw her chance as she crawled forward on her stomach and squeezed through. But then the gap was gone. She opened her mouth to scream as pain hit her and bales began crushing her from above, but her lungs had no space to expand. Her vision became a view of the starriest night she'd ever seen, and then there was only blackness.

Chapter 52

Carter waited for the air ambulance to take off, watching its lights disappear into the dark sky. He walked back across the field and stood in the lane outside the barn, leaning against the cold metal roof of his car as he stretched his shoulders; he'd pulled a muscle trying to get Ebony out. He'd never felt so done-in, in all his life. The exertion of pulling off the bales and dragging her from underneath, the exhilaration and relief to find her still breathing, alive, was utterly exhausting. She was unconscious when they'd stretchered her off with Samuel. Lauren and Toby went with them.

Jeanie came up behind Carter and touched his arm to make him turn round. She held out her arms and hugged him.

'She will be all right, Dan.'

'I bloody hope so.'

Jeanie stood back to look at him.

'Are you okay?'

She held his face in her hands. He closed his eyes and had such an urge to kiss her out of: relief, adrenalin, gratitude, he didn't know which. He was grateful when Pascoe came out to speak to him.

'What shall we do with Cam Simmons?'

'It's late and he's been through enough today,' replied Carter. 'We'll give him a lift home.'

'Are you headed back to interview Raymonds?'

'Yes, he's been in there for hours. He's going to be madder than a wasp in a jar,' replied Carter. 'I'm looking forward to enlightening him on a whole host of local issues.' He looked at Jeanie.

'I need to drive to the hospital in Truro and see that Lauren and Toby are okay,' she said. 'I'll keep you informed about Eb. They might let me see her.'

'Give her my love. Will you stay over there?'

'I doubt it. There's room for me at one of the B&Bs here. I'll text you later.'

Carter got a call from Sandford.

'I'm back at the hotel. How's Eb?'

'Just taken off in the chopper. We don't know anything yet. I'll see you back there. I need a stiff drink after the day I've had. What's happening at the farm?'

'Leonard has taken over there now. There was a large quantity of the white stuff in some surfing bags near the body.'

'Yeah, a little project Marky and Jago were working on. Any dealer who killed him would have taken the drugs. This was a personal matter then.'

'There's plenty for Leonard to look over here,' said Sandford. 'There was quite a fight and there are shoe prints leading to and from the field. It doesn't seem like any attempt was made to cover it up.'

Pascoe got a lift with Carter as he handed back the police van to his colleague.

The cliff top area was still cordoned off. They had to drive the long way round to get to Cam's cottage.

'Thanks for your help, Cam,' said Carter. 'We will need a statement from you tomorrow. Will you be all right here on your own tonight?'

Pascoe interrupted.

'I'll come back and see you in an hour or two if that's okay? I pass this way on my way home.'

Cam thanked him and hesitated as he was getting out of the car.

'I want to make a full statement about the abuse I suffered as a child. I want people in this village to know that Raymonds never once intervened. He knew it went on and he allowed it to. I came back here to expose him. I came back here to try and make a life for me and Mawgan and to help Kensa. I can at least achieve part of that.'

After they left Cam, they drove down towards the beach. As they came level with the car park, Pascoe told Carter to pull over. Raymonds' Ford Cortina was in the car park. It was crushed front and back. Towan was standing beside it smoking a cigarette.

Carter flicked the lights on in the police station as they led Towan in. He smelt of booze.

'I'll put him straight in the interview room,' said Pascoe.

'I'll check on Raymonds,' Carter replied.

'Tell him I remodelled the old Silver Fox,' Towan shouted out as he was led away by Pascoe.

Carter unlocked the door and switched on the light.

Raymonds was hanging. His face was pressed against the light bulb. His bulging eyes were half closed as they stared at the door. His legs dangled in mid-air. His neck was broken.

'You bastard,' Carter muttered under his breath.

He walked across to the desk. Raymonds had taken off his shoes and placed them neatly on the floor. Carter picked them up; their soles were caked in mud.

Towan stared down at the table in front of him.

'Would you like a glass of water?' Carter asked. Towan nodded.

Pascoe stood to go and get him one. They heard the sound of officers talking as they carried Raymonds' body away. Pascoe looked at Carter expectantly.

'You go, if you feel you should,' Carter said as Pascoe brought Towan's water, and then left the room.

Towan grinned at Carter.

'I saw the body bag. Don't tell me Raymonds has topped himself right here in this station? Now, that's got to be the best thing I've heard in a long time. Why did he do it? Didn't think he was the type,' said Towan. 'He's always been such a hard-nosed, self-righteous bastard. Never had him down as a quitter.'

Carter sat back in his chair and looked across at Towan.

'He couldn't bear to lose control of his empire. He

was scared of the consequences. Prison wouldn't have been fun either, would it? You know what that's like, don't you?'

'Yeah, he would have been beaten to a pulp in a week. He had a good run for his money. It was fun while it lasted, like.'

'I thought you got on with Raymonds. Why did you trash his car?'

'Just pissed me off.'

'So you and Raymonds fell out, why was that?'

Towan shrugged. 'He made some promises to me that he didn't intend to keep.'

'Like?'

'Future plans. Getting a stake in the village. He promised me a lot, if I worked with him, we'd be partners.'

'For what? What did he get in return?'

'I have the contacts in Penhaligon. I have a younger, fresher eye for things.'

'He said jump and you asked how high. Wasn't that it?'

Towan turned away and tapped his foot irritably on the floor.

'We discovered a baby's body that we know was Kensa's. We also now know that the father was Marky. Does it surprise you to know it was probably Marky who raped her?'

'Makes sense. Raymonds wouldn't have felt the need to protect anyone else. I told you it wasn't me. When I left that house Ella was okay; she was talking about leaving but that was it. I was angry with her, yes. I left and went home.'

Who was there when you left?'

'Jago and Marky.'

'No one else?'

'Toby was unconscious, asleep upstairs. There was no one else until Raymonds and Jeremy Forbes-Wright turned up.'

'How do you know they came?'

'Because I didn't make it home. I fell asleep on the common and I woke up with the noise of someone opening the doors and coming out on the veranda. When I looked, it was Raymonds and Jeremy Forbes-Wright. I scarpered. Afterwards, Raymonds told me never to speak about that night. That Toby had as good as admitted he'd attacked Kensa. I knew he was being set up. I thought it was just so Raymonds could profit from Forbes-Wright. Raymonds always needed a hold over everyone.'

'So, you're a survivor against the odds here, Towan. You inherit the farm. How does that feel?'

Towan sat back in the chair and grinned.

'Feels fucking marvellous. I've got some great ideas for it. I was thinking a stud farm if I didn't make it into a hotel. Look, Inspector, if you ever think of relocating, we could have a good thing going here. Let me buy you a drink when we leave here. I'll see you up at the hotel bar.'

Carter stared at Towan. He felt faintly amused that Towan seriously thought he was looking at walking out of there this time. Pascoe came back in and sat down. Carter read Towan his rights. Pascoe switched on the tape machine.

'If this is about Raymonds' car, I'll pay for it. It's

no use to him no more. I should have a lawyer here if you're charging me.'

'We tried, we couldn't get one for you. No one wants to come out.'

'What is this about? You know I had nothing to do with Dad's death. You can't do me for anything, other than Raymonds' car.'

'We dug up a body on the common in the back of Kellis House,' said Carter.

'A boy from Penhaligon,' said Pascoe, looking at his notes. 'Peter Adams, dark hair, white-skinned, five foot. Thirteen years of age.'

'Don't know what you're talking about,' said Towan. 'I don't know anyone like that.'

'Except the planks you used to line Peter's grave match the ones you used to build the shelves in your farm store at Stokes' farm.'

'Really? Sounds like flimsy evidence to me.'

'Well, there's also the fact that he was a boy on your list of contacts for pimping. The famous ledger that you and Raymonds were going to use to build yourself a depraved empire with. Or rather, Raymonds was going to reap the benefits and you were going to do all the dirty work.'

'That was Dad's book, not mine.'

Pascoe pushed a photo across to Towan.

'This is you and the murdered boy, we got it from his bedroom. It was on his wall.'

Towan stared open-mouthed at the photo.

'Nothing to say, Towan?' asked Carter.

'We went round to his house,' said Pascoe. 'His mother is beside herself, she said he was a lovely lad.

He was a bit of a loner, not many friends. Bit way-ward, bit impressionable.'

'He would have looked up to you, then?' added Carter.

'I didn't kill him. I was called out on fucking Christmas Eve and the old guy, Jeremy, had had a bit of trouble with this lad. Christ, I should never have got involved. It was none of my business.' Towan threw the photo back across the desk.

'But then you'd have had nothing to blackmail him with, would you? All the phone calls from the farm, from the hotel. Is that what they were all about? You will never change, Towan.'

'All I did was help Jeremy. He called me out when he couldn't resuscitate the boy.'

'Why didn't you call for an ambulance when you got there, or call the police?'

He shrugged. 'The boy was dead, what was the point?'

'What did Jeremy say happened?'

'The way he described it was that this lad didn't fully understand what he was letting himself in for. I don't really know. I thought it was all agreed between them. I got there and the lad had choked on some-thing too big to swallow, you get what I'm saying? He was dead a while. There was nothing I could do. I helped Jeremy cut him up and we buried him out on the common.'

'Why blackmail him now?'

'Covering my options. I took a few photos at the time; I kept the boy's shorts as insurance, just in case I needed it. I didn't think he'd top himself.'

Carter shook his head, suddenly exhausted by it all.

'Interview terminated at ten twenty p.m. on Saturday 8 February 2014. Detective Sergeant Pascoe will now transport the prisoner to the police station in Penhaligon for further questioning. Towan Stokes, you are being charged with the illegal disposal of a dead body. For a start.' Carter stood and left the room.

Ten minutes later, Pascoe brought Towan out in cuffs. An officer was waiting to escort him away.

Carter ignored Towan's ranting as he kicked his way out of the station.

He sat at his desk and rang Jeanie.

'How is Eb?'

'She will lose a kidney. They say she was lucky, the car seat and the helmet saved her,' said Jeanie. 'I'm going to spend the night here.'

'Okay, ring me if there's any developments.'

'Will do.'

Carter locked up the station and Pascoe went up to see how Cam Simmons was doing before driving back to Penhaligon.

At half eleven Jeanie was sitting in the waiting area outside the intensive care ward, when she heard the whoosh of the door and the clip of expensive shoes on linoleum. She looked up to see Carter walking towards her.

He handed her a deli bag from the supermarket.

'Muffin, but you're limited for choice round here, so just look grateful, okay?'

She took the bag from him with a smile.

'So, where am I sleeping?' asked Carter. 'I gave up having a drink with Sandford to be here.'

Jeanie pointed to the row of seats opposite.

Epilogue

A week later

'Where are Lauren and Toby Forbes-Wright now?' asked Chief Inspector Bowie.

Carter and Jeanie were standing in his office in Fletcher House. It was Saturday morning.

'They are back here now, sir: Samuel was discharged from hospital after twenty-four hours,' answered Jeanie.

'He's a very lucky lad, and so are we,' Bowie said. 'The local police can take over now. Sorry to hear about Raymonds.'

'Yeah, we had enough to charge him several times over. He would never have seen the light of day. I'm pretty sure he killed his own son, in the end. He'd lost control over everything.'

'It would have been one hell of a case,' said Bowie. 'Imagine heading that?'

'I'd have loved to do it,' said Carter.

'You were robbed.' Bowie smiled.

'What about the historical cases against Jeremy Forbes-Wright, sir?' asked Jeanie.

'Out of our hands now. That's a vast investigation of its own and they will take it on under Operation Elmtree. Anyway, I think we should have a celebration. Archway Tavern tonight?' said Bowie.

'I'm heading back to Cornwall this morning, sir,' said Jeanie. 'I thought I could see Eb and make a weekend of it.'

'My plan too,' said Carter. 'We're bringing the kids and we're renting a house down there. Cabrina needs a break after the burglary.'

'Are you all staying in the one place?' asked Bowie, unable to hide his amusement.

'No, we are next door, though. Should be fine. First time for everything.' Carter smiled, embarrassed.

'Have a great time and please give Eb my regards. How's she doing?'

'Very good, sir,' answered Jeanie. 'She's starting to get fidgety. She wants to get out of there.'

'How much longer?'

'Two weeks at least,' answered Jeanie. 'Then we better persuade her to take a bit of leave – she's owed a lot anyway.'

'Good luck with that,' said Bowie. 'Give her this from me.' He handed Jeanie an envelope.

'Thanks, sir.'

'Christ yeah,' said Carter, 'we better get a card and take some food in for Eb.'

Outside Bowie's office, Carter put his hand on Jeanie's arm.

'See you down there then, pal.'

'Check-in is at two,' said Jeanie.

'Shall we book somewhere for dinner?'

'Nope, let's not get too keen on the group thing, Dan. Let's give Pete and Cabrina time to say what they want.'

'Good plan.'

At seven that evening Carter and Jeanie were standing by Ebony's bedside.

'Did you bring me any food?' she asked.

'We wouldn't dare turn up here without it.' Carter began unloading junk food onto the cabinet next to her bed.

Jeanie came round and started moving it.

'They won't be able to see the machines for all that. You'll have to ask them when you want something, Eb.'

'No, don't worry, I've worked out a system of getting in and out of bed without coming unplugged.'

'Oh, for goodness' sake!' Jeanie frowned.

Carter laughed. 'That's the spirit, Eb, don't let the bastards grind you down.'

Carter took out three bottles of Babycham from his bag.

'Here's something extra for us to celebrate with.'

'Dan, what the hell is that?' Jeanie asked in a whisper.

'We're celebrating the fact that Willis still has a kidney. Where's that card from the boss, Jeanie?'

'Here.' Jeanie handed the envelope across to Willis.

Carter took the tops off the Babychams and handed them round.

Willis looked at him.

'How did you know?' She grinned.

'What?' Jeanie asked.

Willis held up her bottle of Babycham.

'I'm being promoted.'

'Detective Sergeant Ebony Willis. Cheers.' Carter took a drink from his bottle. 'It has a great ring to it, Eb.'

Acknowledgements

I dedicated this book to Darley Anderson, who I owe so much to. He is so much more to me than my friend and agent. But there isn't just Darley, there is a team of women behind the scenes who he relies on. I feel very close to them and respect them greatly. They are: Mary, Camila, Emma, Rosanna, Sophie, Andrea and Sheila – thank-you.

This book was a challenge, in many ways, and the help came from many places. So much gratitude and thanks to Dave Willis; his years as a Detective Inspector on the "Dark Side", continue to prove invaluable to me. Many thanks go to the Devon Rape Crisis Service for helping me research both historical rape cases and modern procedure. Thanks to Alison from Friends of Brockly Cemetery and to Paul Read, who was a great help. Also thanks to the Cornish Tourist Office for an insight into the mining industry. Big thanks to Becky from Visage, Della from True Colours, Norma and Noreen, my children Ginny and Robert and my sisters Clare and Sue; and to all my family and friends who provide an invaluable sounding-board for my ideas. Lastly, my heartfelt thanks to my editor, Jo Dickinson, and the dedicated team at Simon and Schuster. They continue to press me for the best work I can produce, and I am confident that I have the best team behind me to achieve it.